winter flower

winter flower

Charles Sheehan-Miles

sheehanmiles.com

Published by Cincinnatus Press
South Hadley, Massachusetts
United States of America

Copyright © 2019 Charles Miles.

Edited by Lori Sabin

ISBN: 978-1-63202-171-7

v05262019

Dedication

~~~~~~

In Memory of

Patricia Chase McJunkins

Acknowledgements

I want to start by thanking my amazing beta readers group.

Dimitra Fleissner, Kirsten Papi, Michelle Kannan, Laura Wilson and Michelle Pace and Jackie Yeadon read through the first draft and gave me tremendous insight, suggestions and criticism.

Tanya Hall, Robin Wagner, Brett Lewis, Kirsty Lander, Kelly Moorhouse, Beth Suit and Sally Bouley read the second round, helping me tighten it up and filling the gaps.

I'm grateful to each of you for your criticism, suggestions and encouragement.

Barbara Elsner: you know why. Thank you.

Lori Sabin: Thank you so much for being an amazing editor and friend.

Andrea: you've been my biggest supporter, cheerleader and writing partner. It's hard for me to imagine or remember what life was like before you, and I am so incredible grateful.

Prologue

Sam: September 13

The day before my sister Brenna disappeared I felt a hint of chill in the air as I stepped out of James Madison High School. Brenna stayed late for the drama club, because *of course* she was in drama, and I stayed late for extra help in chemistry. I glanced to the end of the sheltered walkway, slung my backpack over my shoulder, and walked toward the parking lot where Brenna and I were meeting up with Mom.

I didn't even see Jake Fennel and his sidekick Matt until Jake slapped me in the face. With broad shoulders and powerful forearms, Jake had a military-style crew cut and red, fleshy cheeks that looked out of place on someone so spiteful. Jerking me around had been his favorite activity since elementary school, when he'd punched me at Cynthia's ninth birthday party.

"Hey, little bitch!" Jake said.

I tried to pull away, but Jake shoved me against the wall again, grabbing the front of my shirt. With half-lowered eyelids squeezed into narrow, hateful slits, he whispered, "You told Mrs. Reed I was bothering you? Do you have a fucking death wish?"

Matt, his sidekick, spit at my feet. "Bitch."

"I ought to kick your ass." Jake's face flushed as he worked himself up.

Tears bubbled way too close to the surface. I wanted to run or sink into the ground and disappear. I'd tried to be invisible in the three weeks since high school had started. No such luck. I'd hoped it would be better than middle school. Maybe the jerks and bullies who had made middle school miserable for me would find someone else to bother, or they'd mature, or the lessons of a hundred seminars on bullying would stick and they'd embrace brotherhood with people different from themselves.

1

Failing that, maybe I'd be invisible.

Brenna refused to be invisible. Bursting out of the doors of the gym, she saw me thrown up against the wall and marched toward us, face tight with anger.

She slapped Jake on the back of his head. "Let go, little jerk."

Fear flashed across Jake's face, reinforced most likely by the biker chain Brenna had hanging from her belt, the combat boots, and the crazy purple spiked hair. A deep, blue-green jewel, the same color as her eyes, pierced her right nostril.

Leaning forward to look eye-to-eye at Jake, she whispered, "I'm gonna jam my boot right up your ass if you don't run away right now."

Jake shoved me against the wall one last time. Backing off, he said, "You won't always be around to protect the little freak, you crazy bitch."

Jake Fennel was right. Brenna wouldn't always be around to protect me. Not anymore. But I didn't know that then, and when she turned to me after Jake and Matt's retreat, I hugged her. "Thank you," I said.

She didn't reply at first, nor return the hug. "What are you going to do when I'm gone? Don't you think it's time you learned to stand up for yourself?"

"Gone?" I asked. "What are you talking about?"

Eyes averted. "Never mind. Let's go."

I didn't like her answer. But what was I going to do about it? Walking out to the parking lot, we saw Mom behind the wheel of the Mercedes Dad bought her Valentine's year before last.

"Hey, guys." Closing her book and putting it in her purse behind the center console, she started the van. Seniority ruled, so Brenna sat in the front seat, me in the middle. "How was your day?"

"Okay," Brenna said.

"Fine," I echoed.

Mom shook her head and gave a wry smile. "I should know better than to ask teenagers anything."

Erin: September 15

At ten o'clock, after my husband Cole and Brenna left for her driver's license test, it was time for me to get into gear. Only a few Department of Motor Vehicles offices were open on Saturday, so they would be gone a couple of hours. I had to put up the decorations, unlock the garage door, stage the car, lay out food, dishes, and fifteen other things, all before they got back. I texted my younger sister Lori: They're leaving now. Come on over.

Brenna babbled with excitement, talking about all the things she wanted to do once she was legal to drive. Cole's eyes locked on mine over her head, and the grin on his face gave me a shiver. After eighteen years of marriage—which had a lot of ups and some spectacular downs—Cole still had the power to make me weak in the knees.

"Sam!" I called up the stairs as I headed into the kitchen.

Lori would arrive any minute. In the meantime, I pulled supplies from the pantry. Sodas. Chips. Pizza would be here at noon, along with Marion, Brenna's best friend since elementary school. Though when I thought about it, I rarely saw them together these days.

The doorbell rang, and Sam called out, "I'll get it!"

A few moments later, Lori came in the room, trailed by Sam. Lori had changed her hair since I'd seen her last, dyed a deep black and shaved around the ear on one side of her head. On a sixteen-year-old it might not have looked out of place, but Lori was thirty-five. Mom and Dad once despaired of her ever having a productive job, but her art had paid off—her latest masterpiece hung in the North Carolina Museum of Art.

"Oh, I missed you," she crooned, slipping her arms around me.

The past few years had been tough on our relationship. Raleigh was a solid five-hour drive, so she didn't make it up here often, nor did I frequently visit her. Something was always going on with the kids—sports or concerts or other activities—and when I wasn't busy, she had gallery showings and other events taking up her time. The last couple of years, she'd been traveling throughout the South showing her work.

Having her here brought tears to my eyes.

She tilted her head. "Crying?"

I shrugged and laughed. "Just a little."

Sam ignored everything, slipping into the den, undoubtedly to get back to a video game.

"Do we have time for a cup of coffee?"

"I'm sure we do; they'll be a couple hours. What would you like? Decaf? Regular? Chai? I think I've got some others too."

"Leaded, please. Is Brenna excited? Do you think she'll ever speak to me again?"

"Yes, she's excited about getting her license. She doesn't know about the car yet. And ... I don't know."

Lori nodded. She'd always been a confidante for Brenna, someone safe to talk to. It was a relationship I approved of—teenagers need an adult they can trust. But when Brenna started dating a twenty-year-old, concern for her safety

3

overrode that trust. Lori had told me, and that precipitated a crisis. Now we had to wait, wondering if their relationship would recover.

"Did I do the right thing?"

"If you knew she was dating Chase and didn't tell me, I'd have never forgiven you. So … yeah, you did the right thing."

She nodded, her expression glum.

"The bad news?" I said. "She's still seeing him."

"What?"

"Yeah. Cole is pissed. But he's never around anyway, so a lot of help he is. I had to pick my battles … she's committed to him. I'm not willing to lose my daughter in this battle."

Lori sighed. "I don't know what to say."

"How about, *thank God I don't have teenagers?*"

She snickered. "And Cole? How are things with him?"

I shrugged. "We've been in therapy, and he's been making a real effort." One corner of her mouth curled down. "I don't want to talk about it right now." *Because you'll just repeat what you always say: leave him. And I'm not leaving my husband.*

"Okay."

After the coffee, we got busy decorating the cavernous living room. Brenna thought she was too old for a birthday party, unless it was a bunch of *too-cool* teenagers standing around pretending to be cynical. But she'd be okay with this party, if only because of her gift.

Marion had arrived, and we finished setting up long before they got home— Cole sitting in the passenger seat, and Brenna driving, a huge grin on her face. She pulled the car to a stop and parked behind Lori. They got out and Brenna gestured to Lori's car. Cole shrugged and followed her as she skipped toward the house.

The front door opened. Lori, Sam, and Marion shouted, "Happy birthday!"

Brenna's eyes widened, the blue highlighted by her purple hair. "Marion!" She grabbed her best friend in a huge hug.

Brenna didn't even say hi to Lori, whose smile faltered. Sometimes Brenna could be such a *bitch.*

I tried to remind myself that selfishness was typical behavior for sixteen-year-olds.

But Brenna surprised me. She turned away from Marion and said, "Aunt Lori." She reached for Lori, and Lori slipped her arms around my daughter. Brenna's eyes were squeezed shut as she whispered, "I missed you."

"You forgive me?" Lori asked.

4

"Yeah," Brenna said.

"So, what's first?" Cole asked. "Food? Or presents?"

"Presents," Brenna said. "Are you kidding?"

He chuckled and our eyes met. I didn't look away, instead giving him a half smile.

Cole swallowed and his mouth twitched into a smile. Maybe we had hope.

"All right," he said. "Presents! Sam, can you help me with it?"

Sam stood and nodded. They walked out of the room.

Marion spoke in a shy voice and held out a hand gripping an envelope. "Here."

Brenna smiled. "Can I open it?"

"Well, *yeah*," Marion replied.

Brenna tore it open and whooped. "Fifty dollars!" She waved an iTunes gift card in the air.

"Nice," Lori said.

"Thank you, bestie!" Brenna said as Sam and Cole came back in the room carrying a huge package wrapped in orange and blue paper. *What?* Had Cole gotten her something else? We'd agreed the car was enough … *more* than enough.

I sighed.

"Oh my," Brenna said. Her eyes darted between the huge box and the more modest-sized gift Lori had brought.

"Open mine first," Lori said quietly. "Otherwise, you'll forget it when you see what your mom and dad got you."

Brenna smiled and tore open the gift. A huge smile spread on her face. "Oh my God, it's beautiful!" she breathed. The box contained a stainless-steel bracelet, the chain embedded with stones that looked like jade.

"This looks handmade," Brenna said.

Lori nodded. "I got it at the Ren Fair."

"I love it," Brenna said. She put it on her left wrist. It hung a little loose.

"You can have it adjusted," Lori said. "The guy who made it is local."

Brenna smiled and hugged Lori.

She eyed the huge box, one eyebrow raised. "I can't even imagine what this is," she said.

"Open it and find out," Cole suggested.

She ripped the paper. Underneath was a brown cardboard box. I gave Cole a puzzled look.

He *winked* at me.

Brenna got the box open, then muttered, "Are you kidding me?"

Inside was another box. Sam smiled. "This part was my idea."

5

Ahhhh. Now it made sense. Brenna tore open the second box, only to find a third one inside. And an even smaller one in that. I completely believed that it was Sam's idea to torture Brenna.

Brenna tore the smallest one open, growling, and her eyes widened. It *was* a small jewelry box, sized for a bracelet. She opened it, then looked up, eyes swiveling from me to Cole and back. Inside lay a set of keys with a "VW" logo on them.

"Um…" she said.

"Go look in the garage," Cole said.

Brenna's mouth gaped. She jumped to her feet and stumbled down the hall.

I stood and leaned close to him as we all followed her. "It's been nice having you back," I whispered to him.

"I still love you," he said.

Shivers down my spine.

From the garage, Brenna's voice echoed, "Oh my God! Oh my God! Oh my God!"

Cole chuckled. "She found it."

"I guess so," I said. We strolled down the hall to the three-car garage. Brenna sat in a brand new white VW Beetle with bright pink polka dots. Tears ran down her face.

"Can I take it for a drive?" she asked. "Can I? Can I?"

"Go!" Cole waved at her. "Go!"

She ran across the garage and threw her arms around me and Cole at the same time. "I love you, Daddy. I love you, Mom."

Cole: September 15

I took a sip of my coffee and looked out the back bay window, a huge expanse of glass overlooking the garden and backyard, which sloped away from the house for the length of a football field. It was a lovely morning. *Exquisite.* I ought to feel good. Erin and I had slept in the same bed—for the first time in months. Brenna was growing up to be a delightful young woman, and Sam was getting good grades even with several Advanced Placement classes.

To make Erin happy, I could tolerate Lori's presence in the house for a few days. Thank God the place was big enough she could sleep at the other end of the house. Erin's sister had never liked me, but over the past few years her level of tolerance had slipped. I was sure her only goal these days was to convince Erin to leave me.

I looked at my watch. Nine a.m. A conference call about the merger was scheduled for ten. I'd take that in my office while Erin was at church with the kids. I'd never been much of a churchgoer, but all the same, I hated the idea of a Sunday morning conference call. But I was under a lot of pressure with this merger. After the call, I'd have free time to prep my surprise for Erin and the kids. The day the kids got out of school for Christmas, we were flying to Europe. Two days in Paris (for Brenna, who idolized the French, God only knew why), two in Ireland (for Erin, who had distant Irish ancestry) and two more in London (for me and Sam). The tickets were in my desk—I was planning to present them over lunch after Erin and the kids returned.

"Cole?" Erin stepped into the kitchen. "Have you seen Brenna?"

"No," I said. "Not since bedtime. Isn't she in her room?"

Erin shook her head. "No. And her bed's still made."

"I ... *she made her bed?*" I couldn't keep the disbelief out of my tone.

"No. Sofia made it *yesterday.*" Sofia was our cleaning lady.

I stood up, setting my iPad on the table. I walked to the garage and opened it.

The Beetle wasn't there.

"She must have gone over to a friend's," I said, unsure of myself.

Erin ignored me. She had her cell phone to her ear. Her eyes rolled and her left hand jerked spasmodically. "It's going straight to voicemail. I *told her* to keep her phone charged. She's so *irresponsible.*"

I thought back to the night before. Brenna had been home for hours before we went to bed, and I hadn't heard a car running or leaving the house. No doors opening or closing. But we'd been ... occupied. I wouldn't have noticed if a herd of cattle came racing through last night. Afterward, both of us fell into a deep sleep. "Call her friends?"

She shrugged. "I guess. I was going to take her shopping after church. Where *is* she?"

"Careless," I said. "Maybe she shouldn't have the car after all."

"I don't know, Cole. I'm so frustrated with her!"

"Let's give it a little while and try her again. I'm sure she's at a friend's sleeping in," I said.

I sat back to finish my coffee and read the paper, but concentration eluded me.

What I didn't know was my daughter was already gone: out of the house, out of town, out of our lives.

7

Part One

Two Years Later

One

~~~~~~~~~~~~~~~~~~~~~~~~~~~~~~~~~~~~~~~

Cole

Two years later and a thousand miles away, I sat in an insignificant office, looking out through the one-way mirror. My paperwork was complete, and I'd been stalling for over fifteen minutes. I wasn't ready to go home yet.

I rose and double-checked the padlocks on the safe and switched out the light. My office was two feet wide and four feet deep and had sufficient room for one person at a time. I closed the steel door with a crash and padlocked it.

I glanced around the back room. Prep sinks were clean, everything tidy. Storage room locked. I put a plastic loop through the bolt of the back door and secured it. The staff couldn't open it without splitting the loop.

Out front, customers occupied three booths and several seats at the high counter. The restaurant would be slow all night. My eyes scanned the room. For a thirty-year-old restaurant that never closed, the place was clean.

I never imagined I'd end up doing this for a living, but landing a job as an IT executive with no college degree and a felony conviction can be … a challenge.

When I'd given up hope, my oldest friend, Jeremiah Walker, hooked me up with Waffle House—a job I'd sneered at when he took it long ago. During the years I'd worked for a flashy technology company, he'd been working his way up. While I ran up hundreds of thousands of dollars of debt, he'd paced himself, paid off his house and student loans, and became wealthy. And then he reached out and rescued me.

And here I stood, inspecting the dining room with a critical eye. I *hated* it when the restaurant was dirty.

Linda Poole, the cook, stood at the grill humming to herself as she prepared an omelet. She had a strong accent from somewhere far up North, and I couldn't tell if that helped or hurt in her dealings with the folks around here—some customers thought her accent was charming. Others were hostile to anybody originating north of the Confederacy.

Dakota said, "You getting out of here, boss? It's late." At seventeen, she ought to have been in school, but she had a one-year-old daughter to feed.

I nodded. "Yeah, I think so. I'll see you guys in the morning."

Linda replied, "Is that a threat?"

I chuckled. "Yeah, Linda. Do me a favor, make sure we've got at least five pots of grits for the morning? Going to be busy tomorrow."

"Will do." She flipped the omelet a foot in the air above the pan and caught it neatly. She went to lift two slices of toast out of the toaster with her bare hands, and I raised my eyebrows. "Gloves, Linda. Gloves. Please."

She flushed. "Sorry, Cole. Trying to remember. And ... Cole? Can I ask you a question?"

I stopped and raised an eyebrow. "What is it?"

She looked down at the floor, then said, "I'm sorry I didn't say anything earlier, I'd misplaced my appointment slip. My daughter's got a doctor's appointment in the morning. Do you mind if I take off an hour early?"

I sighed. Linda leaving an hour early meant I had to come back in an hour early, which meant losing an hour of already short sleep.

Still. "Yeah, that's fine. Just let me know a little further in advance next time, okay?"

She brightened. "Thanks, Cole."

Mary Anne, the other waitress, yelled in an order and Linda started cooking. I walked out into the customer area, took one last look around, then said, "All right, I'll see you guys in the morning."

Outside the restaurant, the sweltering air draped over me. Sticky heat washed up from the asphalt, the smell of tar thick in my nose. I heard traffic and the buzzing of insects. I stooped to pick up cigarette butts from near the front door, then carried them around the side of the building to the dumpster. In back, I sat in my tiny 2003 Hyundai Accent, distinguished only by the fact that it was the cheapest car on the lot after I took in my almost-new BMW 535i and returned it to the dealership. BMW was still chasing me for payments on a car I no longer owned, but Erin's Mercedes minivan was paid for, so we'd managed to hold on to that. It still hurt to be driving a vehicle that cost less than my laptop.

I didn't start the car right away, instead breathing, trying to calm the tightness in my chest. I always felt a tight pinch of anxiety when getting ready to go home. Sam would be doing God knows what, locked in his room on his computer, and Erin ... I had no idea what she would be doing. I never knew anymore.

No point in sitting here feeling sorry for myself. I started the car, backed out of the parking space, and turned out of the parking lot. I didn't, however, turn left out of the parking lot to go home. Instead, I turned on the radio and drove north, into Anniston.

I drove without destination, eyes scanning the traffic, music turned up loud enough to make it difficult to think. My route took me past Fort McClellan; a wide circle that brought me back toward Oxford after thirty minutes. As I approached Oxford, I pulled over.

I rested my forehead on the steering wheel and pictured my daughter. In my vision, her braided hair hung down over the blue sundress my mother had sewn for her. Her eighth birthday, and the smile on her face as she ran with a mob of little girls was innocent and heartbreaking. Erin had organized a party for her at the neighborhood pool, a full production with games, gift bags for the twenty kids who attended, a clown and other entertainment. She was a popular kid, full of smiles, and always ready with a kind word for other children.

Why did we have to lose her?

Time to go home. I had to be back at the restaurant at six in the morning and wasn't getting any sleep sitting here.

I put the car back in gear and drove into the dark.

Sam: Now

I stood at the bus stop on the first day of school, arms crossed over my chest, looking at the ground. I was trying my best not to shake, not to freak out or do anything to draw attention to myself. Three other teenagers waited for the bus, a boy and two girls, and I stood a bit behind them. They knew each other, obvious because of the easy banter between them, and the fact that we were in rural Alabama and they'd all known each other since first grade. I wore jeans and a too-big sweatshirt, and even though it was close to ninety degrees, I kept the hood of my sweatshirt up.

For the past few months we'd lived on this small street. Beyond the houses were fields. Cows grazed in the closest field, and throughout the summer, whenever the wind blew in the right direction, I could smell the stink from the field. In the distance, rolling, tree-covered hills towered over the fields like chaperones at an elementary school dance.

Mom pushed me all summer to get outside. *Go meet people. Make friends.* Like that was a possibility. I'd never been much in the making friends department, especially after Brenna vanished. But now? Here? Friends? Seriously? The

13

fear was so palpable I wanted to hurl. The bullies and assholes would see right through me and make me their target. Again.

In the distance, the straining, high-pitched sound of the school bus approached on the road across the fields to the south. The others at the bus stop stirred, and one of the girls looked over her shoulder at me, with a look that carried a mix of curiosity and contempt. Our eyes met for the barest of seconds, and I looked away and swallowed.

It would be nice to have a friend.

The bus showed up, almost full. I began to shake. I kept my arms crossed over my chest and inched my way toward the bus, following the two girls and the boy onto the bus.

The other three headed for the first open row, but the bus driver stopped me. "Stop. You new?"

I nodded, trying to get a grip on my shaking.

"What's yer name?"

"Sam," I whispered.

"Speak up."

"Sam." A little louder.

"All right, Sam. You won't know none-a-this cause you're new, but you fill in the next open seat as you get on the bus, startin' from front to back. No fighting, no yelling, no bullying. Ya hear?"

I nodded.

"Where'd you learn your manners?"

I coughed, and said, "Yes."

Without turning away from me, he said in a loud, but conversational tone, "Children, how do you respond to your elders?"

In a loud shout, most of the kids in the first four rows shouted, "Yes, sir!"

I froze, unable to breathe, my stomach twisting so hard I needed to run for the bathroom, or home, or anywhere but here. I wanted to be invisible. Instead, the bus driver had called me out in front of everyone on the bus. Shaking so hard I could feel the fear all the way to my toes, I said, "Yes, sir."

"Go take yer seat, Sam."

I nodded, trying to stop myself from hyperventilating. Then, as his face shifted to irritation, I said, "Yes, sir."

After I spoke, he looked away and put the bus in gear.

The *yes, sir* routine reminded me of Grandpa. Not Mom's dad, but Dad's. He was a Marine, a stocky, red-faced man who kept his white hair cropped short and always looked ready to strap on combat gear and wade into battle. Brenna loved Grandpa and used to be really close to him. I loved him too, of course,

14

but we've never been close, and I hadn't even seen Grandpa since the Christmas Dad was in jail.

I made my way between the rows of seats. The first open seat was about fifteen rows back. I made it past the first three before I heard someone mutter, "*Freak.*"

Hair hanging in my face, I watched my feet to make sure no one tried to trip me and slid into the seat next to the boy from the bus stop.

"Don't mind Mr. Elliot. He's kind of a dick." The statement came from the boy sitting next to me. The two girls from our stop sat across the aisle.

"Thanks," I muttered.

"I'm Billy," he said.

"Sam," I replied.

"Y'all just moved on Hubbard Lane, right? Few months ago?"

"That's right," I said.

"How come I ain't never seen you?"

"I don't get outside much."

"You got any brothers or sisters?"

The question froze me. Everyone at Fairfax High knew Brenna had disappeared. It had given me a few months of reprieve from bullying, a legacy I'm sure Brenna hadn't calculated on. Somehow, in the two years she'd been gone, no one had asked me this question. Now, alone in a strange place, I didn't know how to answer. If I said yes, it would lead to questions. Where was my sister? Was she going to school? If I answered, that would lead to even more questions, more visibility, more everything.

"No," I said.

"How come y'all moved to Oxford?"

"My, uh, Dad, he's managing the Waffle House."

"Oh yeah? You get any free coupons or anything?"

"I guess. I never asked."

The bus stopped at a crowded corner. As the new kids filed on to get in the seats behind me, one of them said, "Hey Billy, who's the freak?"

Two rows up from me, several of the girls, all of them dressed more or less alike, burst into laughter. One, a raven-haired girl who wore a blue halter, caught my eye. She wore too much makeup ... the foundation and blush caked on, lashes clumped together. Without the makeup, she'd have been beautiful: the kind of beauty I wanted to touch.

I tried to look away and couldn't.

Then she called out, "What are you looking at, freak? Cody!"

Next to me, Billy said, "Jesus, Sam, what are you doing?"

15

I blinked and looked away from the girl. "Sorry."

But I was too late. A hulking kid, six feet tall, stood and moved down the aisle.

"You bothering my girlfriend? You some kinda perv?"

"Sorry!"

Fear twisted in my stomach. Jake Fennel all over again, but twice as big. He stared at me with undisguised disgust, and said, "You ever look at my girlfriend again, you'll die."

I swallowed and squeaked out, "I didn't mean anything by it. I didn't."

"Faggot." He turned around and started to swagger back up the aisle. I breathed a sigh of relief, but I was premature, because the moment I relaxed he spun around again, swinging a fist. I didn't have time to raise my arms, or react, or do anything before his fist hit my left ear. The hit was sudden, a shock, and set my ear ringing. My eyes watered, and I wanted to curl up and die. He hadn't hit hard enough to hurt … just to humiliate. He gave a short contemptuous laugh then walked back up the aisle away from me.

The bus driver didn't say a word.

"Helpful hint," Billy said. "Don't mess with the populars. They'll make your life miserable."

Like it wasn't already. "I wish they'd just leave me alone," I said.

Billy gave a sound of disgust and shook his head. "That's Cody Hendricks. And he'll leave you alone as soon as he finds someone else to mess with."

I filed away the name for future reference. Cody Hendricks. Would Cody be my reason to want to die?

I've never been popular. I had two friends in middle school, but as high school started they drifted away, and for the first few weeks of high school, Brenna was the only protection I had. And then she was gone. I was out of school the first couple days after she went missing, but when I went back on Wednesday, a bubble of empathy surrounded me. Her picture had been in the news and everyone at school knew she'd disappeared.

The bubble disappeared just like she had. By sophomore year I became a target for the bullies again. It didn't help that by that time, Dad had been in jail and lost his job. Everything in our life had changed. Everything.

My parents were so numb they didn't even notice the day I came home bloody and bruised from a run-in with Jake Fennel. I kept a low profile through the rest of sophomore year. We didn't have the money for me to participate in any clubs or other activities in school, so I kept my head down, rode the bus to and from school, and hoped for the best.

Then Dad found a job. In *Alabama*. My parents had long since stopped making mortgage payments, and we got thrown out of the old house, so they rented the dump we're living in now. All summer long, I'd been dreading the day school started. Terror in the pit of my stomach, nightmares, shaking fits. Because I wasn't like other kids.

When the bus arrived at the school, I watched in numb silence as the crowds of teenagers headed toward the entrance. They were all there, masses of them, jocks and cheerleaders and druggies and geeks and no one like me.

I made it off the bus with no further mishaps and edged my way through the crowd of laughing and yelling. I kept my arms wrapped around me, my backpack on my back, hair in my face. At the entrance I scanned my schedule. Homeroom, then gym.

A fresh wave of anxiety hit me. I'd managed to get out of taking gym when we lived in Virginia. I didn't think I'd get away with that here.

The school was huge, mazelike. I was supposed to go to room 204, but it wasn't at the end of the 200 hall. "Do you know where 204 is?" I asked a boy who walked by me like I wasn't there.

"Get to homeroom, young man," a teacher called out. Her voice echoed in the now empty hall.

"204?" I asked, waving my schedule. She pointed down the hall. I ran.

When I walked into homeroom ten minutes late, everyone looked up. Too stupid to make it to class on time.

I tried to just slink into the class without anyone noticing, but that was impossible. I was halfway to the back when the teacher, a gaunt old woman with skin almost as grey as her hair, called out, "You there. What's your name?"

I turned around, and quietly said, "Sam Roberts."

"Speak up, I can't hear you. Come here."

I said my name, louder this time, and approached the desk. The woman peered at me over the top of thick bifocal glasses. I would have pegged her age at approaching seventy.

"I couldn't hear you back there. Are you sure this is the right homeroom? What was your name again?"

Someone had written the room number on the whiteboard underneath the name Mrs. Givens. I double-checked it against my schedule and gave her my name for the third time.

She frowned. "Oh, there you are. Sam Roberts. Well, you don't look like a junior."

Behind me, muffled laughter. Heat rose on my neck, my face. I didn't want to turn around, to see them looking at me, pointing, wondering who I was and

17

why I was new around here. I didn't want them noticing the gaping hole where my sister used to be. I didn't want them to notice the gaping hole where I used to be.

When Mrs. Givens let me go, I kept my eyes on the floor as I turned and walked to a seat in the back row. I wanted to cry. To be alone. To go home.

I'd been afraid before. But not like this. The dread that filled my body was worse than anything I'd ever experienced before. My cheeks were numb and my lips were rubber, and I struggled to hold my breath together, to keep from crying.

Mrs. Givens talked for several minutes in front of the class. Joining clubs. The Bible Club met on Monday, the Conservative Club on Tuesday, the Intelligent Design Club on Wednesday, Sons of Confederate Veterans on Thursday, and Football on Friday. Okay. Maybe I exaggerated. But the Bible Club did meet on Monday. This was a very different world than suburban Washington, DC.

Noise erupted from the room when the bell rang. Laughter, joking, horsing around. I kept my distance, kept my eyes to the floor, and got out of there as quickly as I could.

The gym was at the opposite end of the building, near the front office. I made my way to the back stairwell and waited until the traffic died down. No teachers in sight. I sat down, slipped a paperback out of my bag, and started to read.

The book was a good one, about a girl in high school in San Francisco who fell in love with the captain of the baseball team. They were friends, but he didn't see her that way. I read up to the part where she was going to tell him how she felt when I heard the loud clicking of heels coming up the stairs.

I panicked. It had to be a teacher, or one of the vice principals. As the heels echoed off the steps, I put my bag over my shoulder, forgetting to zip it up. When I stood, the bag opened and dumped out, scattering my notebooks all over the steps. Stupid!

Heart hammering, I scrambled to gather my things and get out of there. But I was too late.

"Excuse me, young lady, why aren't you in class?"

I jerked up, my eyes widening.

It was a black woman in her thirties. She wore a conservative brown suit with a string of pearls around her neck and a beautiful ring with a large stone decorated her left ring finger. Her hair was straight, long and shiny. Her eyes opened wide when I faced her.

"I'm sorry. Young *man*. Why aren't you in class?"

I opened my mouth and tried to speak, but nothing came out.

She blinked and said, "What's your name?"

"Sam," I said. "Sam Roberts."

"Well, Sam, what class are you supposed to be in right now?"

"Gym," I whispered.

"And ... why aren't you there?"

I tried to answer. I did. But I didn't have an answer, not one I could explain to anyone. Going to gym meant undressing in front of other people. It meant being in a locker room and maybe showers with a bunch of guys. I couldn't go there. I just couldn't. And when I tried to explain it, to say something, anything, I just started to shake again.

Her eyebrows pulled inward, mouth turning down in a sad expression. "Why don't you come with me. I'm Mrs. Mullins with the counseling department. What grade are you in, Sam?"

"Eleventh," I said.

She looked surprised and said, "Well, that's perfect. I'm the eleventh grade counselor. Let's go talk."

Two: August

~~~~~~

Erin.

When my eyes drifted open in the morning, Cole and Sam were gone. Only the ticking of the grandfather clock broke the silence. My clothes from the day before, which I hadn't changed, felt sticky and rumpled. A headache that began at the base of my neck and ran all the way to my forehead clouded my brain.

I slowly sat up and surveyed the living room. I'd slept on the couch again, and the heat had awakened me. The morning sun glared through the front picture window, silhouetting the duct-taped crack in the bottom-left corner. The house would soon be an oven. Our financial situation had been so dire, for so long, that I didn't run the air-conditioning until the afternoon, just before Sam got home from school.

I stood and stripped down to my underclothes. The heat pummeled me, enough that sweat slicked my skin and I smelled. I needed a cool shower. To clean the house. To check Sam's computer. I needed to get a handle on my life. On our lives.

Instead, I padded into the kitchen and put on a pot of coffee. The clock on the microwave read 11:05. No wonder my head was filled with fog. I filled a tall glass of water from the sink, drinking back the chemical-tasting tap water.

Days like this, I felt paralyzed. I was bored and needed something productive to do, but I couldn't bring myself to do the things I needed to do. Sam and Cole had added their coffee cups and Sam's cereal bowl to the pile of dishes in the sink. I stared at the dishes and wanted to scream. But I didn't have enough motivation or energy to do it. This was my life. Dishes. Laundry. Iron Cole's uniforms. Go to sleep. Do it over again.

At least when the children were small, they brought meaning to being a stay-at-home mom. But they weren't little anymore. They weren't mine anymore. Brenna was gone. Every time I thought of her it was like a mini-seizure. And Sam had shut me out. I knew nothing about my youngest child. Sam spent too much time locked behind his bedroom door on the computer.

I shook my head a little, trying to shake loose from the oppressive thoughts. The coffee had been ready several minutes, and I'd just been standing here. I poured myself a cup, stirred in a packet of Splenda. I opened the kitchen window, and despite the heat outside, well over a hundred degrees, the slight breeze cooled my skin a little. The heat, laden with moisture, brought an intense flash of memory. Summer in Georgia, twenty years ago. I still remembered when he touched my skin. When we desired each other. When the heat burned so close to the surface, it took nothing more than a word, a whisper, a breeze, for it to flare up and pull us into each other's arms.

It had been a long time since I'd experienced that. Instead, most of the time a blanket muffled my emotions, dulling the pain, true ... but also dulling joy and love and desire, leaving me with nothing but bare existence. Maybe because it had been two years, or because Sam was back in school and I was alone at home for the first time in months, or it was nothing at all, but I squeezed my eyes shut as fresh grief washed over me.

Brenna would be eighteen soon.

If she was alive.

I finally made my way into the shower. I thrust the past out of my mind, trying to concentrate on nothing more than the water beating against my skin.

Head finally clear, I stepped out of the shower and dried off, then dressed in jeans and a T-shirt. I wouldn't be going out today. Honestly, I hadn't worked that hard to find a job. Because every day, after Cole and Sam left, I worked on the computer. Searching. Today I would push that off a little, because I planned to get a look at Sam's computer. I was no technophile, but I'd learned enough about computers to check his history and cookies.

I didn't find anything. No cookies on the computer. No history in the web browser. Which meant that Sam had cleared everything before leaving for school.

Not a good sign. If I had found random websites in there, I guess that would be fine. But nothing? That meant he was hiding something. I sighed, shut the computer down, and walked out into the living room. Still broiling in there. I sat down on the couch and opened my aging laptop. The battery no longer functioned, so I had to keep it plugged in all the time, and one of the keys had broken off, but it still worked. We weren't likely to be able to afford another one for a long time. Once it booted up, I started my daily search.

I started with public arrest records. After two years, the only way I could stay alive was to have hope *she* was still alive.

But I'd learned so much, so many horrible things about what happened to sixteen-year-old girls who ran away or were abducted. If she still lived, one day she might turn up in these records. Arrested for jaywalking or theft or worse. A thin hope, but it was hope. Not long after she disappeared, I'd learned of the teeming markets that existed online for women. Dozens of sites where you could pick a city, any city, and shop for a woman or a girl. Men who called themselves "mongers" or "hobbyists" even operated review websites and discussion boards where they would discuss how a particular woman behaved or what she was willing to do.

Today I found nothing. No new records, nothing with her name on it. Earlier this year, I'd had a terrifying moment, when an arrest record for prostitution turned up in Detroit with her name on it. I'd contacted the National Crime Information Center and the Detroit Police Department. It turned out to be another girl, a different girl.

Someone else's *child*. Someone else who was lost.

From there, I moved on. This was the difficult part. Every day I picked a different city, mostly focusing on the larger ones, because that's where the market for young teenage girls existed. Craigslist once, and Backpage, and worse. I read the headlines and looked at the pictures.

Toe Curling * Highly Skilled * $60 Incall * 18 years old.
Busty tantalizing blonde * Outcalls * 20
Brunette College Girl * Let me be your fantasy * 180/hour

Scanning through the pictures, I saw hundreds of girls and women. Some of them were undoubtedly still children, though all of them claimed to be at least eighteen. I looked into their faces and their eyes, and whenever I came across one close to my daughter's age and build I'd peer into their faces if they weren't blurred out. This one? Was it her? I tried to picture her at eighteen and match her features up to the pictures.

I'd learned the patterns. In the big cities, like Atlanta and New York and Washington, the girls were younger, dressed more provocatively, and charged less. The Asian girls worked in massage parlors mostly, and the young white girls worked hotels and outcalls, and sometimes the street. I'd spent two years researching the fates of missing girls, and I still couldn't look at it, think about it, envision it, without horror catching my throat.

The statistics were harsh, horrifying. Impersonal, until you realized each one was a person. Twenty-three hundred Americans reported missing every day, and all but a small fraction were children. Half of those were family abductions; many more were runaways. Only a tiny fraction were "stranger" abductions.

But the stranger abductions had a pattern. A few hundred each year. Nearly all were young women, ages twelve to seventeen, just like Brenna. Most were abducted by men. Virtually all of them sexually assaulted. I knew the numbers. Far too many of these girls ended up abused or dead. And so, I kept looking. I kept peering into those faces, those bodies, wondering if one day I'd open up this computer and see her face staring out at me.

I'd know my daughter anywhere, at any age. Today I didn't find her amongst these women. But, as always, my rage stoked, a slow-burning coal in my gut that threatened to boil over at any moment. As always, I found myself sick to my stomach. The first time I did this search, I vomited. Because those girls on those pages had mothers somewhere. Because I'd learned hard facts in my search.

Nothing today. I checked my email to see if any Google alerts had come, mentions of her name on the Internet. Nothing. I closed my laptop and leaned my head back against the couch, the images of those contorted, barely dressed women running through my mind.

For a few moments I toyed with the idea of getting a glass of wine or four. I felt exhausted. That was nothing new—I was always tired these days.

My phone rang while I was still considering the possibilities. Despite the expense we couldn't afford, we'd kept our cell phones, and added a new one, which we transferred our old home number to. We'd kept the same email addresses, kept as many lines of communication open as possible. Any way for Brenna to reach us. The one exception was the house, and we'd stayed *there* until the bank, followed by the Sheriff's department, threw us out, and the only option for employment was to come to this shithole of a town in the middle of nowhere.

The caller was my sister. I sighed. Lori would be full of concern, wanting to know how I was. But if I didn't answer, she'd keep calling, and eventually she'd break down and call Cole. That had happened twice in the months since he'd gotten out of prison, and neither time went well. Lori hated Cole and the feeling was mutual.

I didn't need that kind of hassle. I answered the phone.

"Erin? I wanted to check in and see how you're doing."

"I'm all right." We both knew I was lying.

"I haven't heard from you in a couple weeks."

The silence grew uncomfortable when I didn't respond.

"I'm worried about you," she said.

"Please don't, Lori. I'm doing the best I can."

"Listen ... I was thinking ... maybe you can come visit again."

"Lori. Stop. We just moved here a few months ago. Sam started school today. I can't go anywhere."

"I could come visit you," she replied.

My eyes grazed across the house. The dirty walls and ragged carpet. The cracked front window. Neither Cole or I had put family pictures on the walls. No art. Nothing that represented us. Most of our things remained in boxes in the shed out back, at least what we hadn't discarded when we left Virginia.

"I don't think that's a good idea," I replied. "I'm really okay, Lori. We're just getting settled in. I've been busy."

She stayed silent for a few seconds, then said, "Erin ... it's okay to grieve. You have to. But it's been almost two years."

My lips turned up in scorn. "What do you want, Lori? To just let it go? Forget about my daughter and move on? Is that what you want?" As I said the words, my voice rose.

She sighed at the other end. "I ... I want my sister back."

My eyes watered. "Well, we can't get what we want, can we? I want my daughter back."

My words hit her. She sobbed, then said, "I'm sorry, Erin. Please let me help."

I pulled my legs up and leaned my forehead on my knees. "There's nothing you can do, Lori. Nothing."

I disconnected the phone.

Sam.

I took the seat Mrs. Mullins indicated, across the desk from her.

Chaos spilled across her desk, which was piled high with papers and folders and a huge bowl full of candy. She sat down across from me, and rested her hands in her lap.

"So, Sam. Talk to me. Why did you skip gym?"

I opened my mouth. I tried to say something, but I didn't know what. There was nothing I could say. So I looked at the desk, avoiding her eyes.

She frowned. "Not ready to talk? I'm patient."

"Please don't make me go," I whispered.

"I'll have a very difficult time going to the principal and asking him to let you out if I don't have a reason."

I looked down at the floor.

"Did something happen to you in gym last year?"

I shook my head.

"Is there something you're afraid of?"

I looked down at the floor again. Of course there was. I was afraid of everything. Of them seeing me. Of having to change in front of the boys in the locker room. I was afraid of the possibility of dealing with bullies, of the certainty of being terrorized.

Her eyes bore into me, like she was studying me, like she could see me. I slid my hands into the pockets of my hoodie and hunched over.

"Well, then. Let's look at your schedule."

She turned to her computer and began typing. A moment later, she said, "You just transferred here?"

"From Fairfax County, Virginia."

She nodded. "I see you're taking AP classes. That's good. You don't have any phys ed credits at all, though."

I swallowed and said, "At my old school you were exempt if you were in music theater."

"I see. Well, it's a graduation requirement here. We require two semesters. You could put it off this year, but you'll end up with no choice for next year."

I closed my eyes.

"Sam ... talk to me. Is something going on at home?"

I shrugged.

"Do you have any brothers and sisters?"

I looked away. "I had a sister."

"Had?"

I swallowed hard. "She disappeared almost two years ago."

Mrs. Mullins' face froze in place, impassive, lips in a thin line. "Disappeared?"

"They never found her. I don't know if she's alive or not."

"Were you and your sister close?"

Were we close? She was my hero. My protector. She was the only person who knew my secret. She was the only person in the world who called me by my name. The only person who accepted me and loved me for who I am, not for ... whatever it was they thought they saw. Brenna dominated my memories; she was all that mattered to me. Her disappearance left a gaping wound. I didn't have words to answer her question, so I answered with a simple, "Yes."

25

She sighed, and said, "Sam ... I'm so sorry. Can you tell me what happened?"

I shrugged. "No one knows. She ... she snuck out after bedtime. It was her sixteenth birthday. And she ... never came home. They found her car fifty miles away."

Mrs. Mullins closed her eyes and took a deep breath. "It must have been a nightmare."

I nodded. "It was," I whispered. "It still is."

"Can I ask you a question?"

I nodded.

"Are you in any kind of therapy?"

I shook my head. "No. I know my parents talked about it. But there's no money. My dad lost his job not long after she disappeared."

A frown briefly appeared on her face. "What was your sister's name?"

"Brenna."

She sucked in a breath. "Brenna Roberts. I remember seeing her in the news."

Yeah. Everyone in the country saw her in the news.

For a few moments she seemed to study me, putting a pen in her mouth and chewing on it unconsciously. Then, abruptly, she said, "Stay here."

She walked out of the office, closing the door behind her. I stared up at the ceiling. All day long I'd been fighting tears. I wasn't prepared to deal with kindness. I almost wanted Mrs. Mullins to come back and tell me to tough it out, that I had to go deal with gym, that I needed to stop acting like a scared little girl. Because her empathetic eyes, her kindness, it made me feel like ... it made me feel vulnerable.

But I waited.

Her questions brought back to mind those first terrible weeks after Brenna vanished. I stared off into space, trying not to think of it, but always stuck at that moment when my Mom said, "*Sam, have you seen Brenna?*"

I jerked in my chair when Mrs. Mullins returned to her office. She gave me a warm look that mystified me and returned to her seat, then turned and began typing on her computer without a word. I sat up straight, watching her.

A moment later, her printer began warming up, and spat out a sheet of paper.

She lifted it off the printer and said, "I spoke with Principal Higgins about your situation. And, though I'm not qualified as a physical education teacher, she agrees that for this semester, at least, you don't need to be assigned in the regular gym class. You'll report to me for first period."

She handed me the paper. The schedule was the same as before, except for the first period line, which read: Physical Education, Mullins, Patricia.

I couldn't stop myself. My hand raised to my mouth, stifling a sob, and my eyes watered uncontrollably. I shook, hard, staggering back into my seat. "You didn't have to do this," I whispered.

She gave me a warm smile. "I did, actually."

I sniffed back snot that was threatening to run down my nose, and asked, "Why?"

Her eyes stayed on me, and she said, "Sam … you seem a little lost. If I can help, I will. So for now, relax, read a book or something until second period. Tomorrow you and I will go for a run, so bring gym shorts. I've been needing to get more exercise anyway."

"Thank you," I whispered. I didn't know how to react. Mrs. Mullins had punched a hole right through the protective distance I normally maintained, and it shook me up. A few minutes later the bell rang. I shot out the door as if I'd been launched and made my way to my second period, AP Biology.

It was on the third floor, which was stifling hot, despite the overworked air-conditioning. Made worse by the fact that I was wearing baggy clothes and a sweatshirt. The other kids in the hall, mostly juniors and seniors, gave me odd looks as I approached the classroom. They mostly wore shorts and T-shirts.

I made it to class in time, and the teacher waved me in. According to my schedule, his name was Mr. Bernard. A short, balding man, the teacher looked almost bizarre in khaki shorts and a Hawaiian shirt.

"Everyone take your seats," he called out as the bell rang.

I scanned the room. All of the tables were occupied by two students, except for one at the very back of the room. A gangly red-headed girl sat alone. I froze for just a second, and then Mr. Bernard said, "Go on, take a seat. I'm pretty sure she won't bite."

I felt my skin flush, but I didn't need any more attention called to me today. I went to the back of the room and slumped into the chair next to the girl without saying anything.

Mr. Bernard took a position at the head of the class and began speaking. I studied the red-headed girl out of the corner of my eye. She was pretty. Extremely pale skin scattered with freckles, blue eyes. Her hair was a tangle, tied in the back in a ponytail which ended just below her shoulders. She wore a sleeveless and threadbare baby blue shirt, which accentuated how washed out she was and how tiny her bony arms were.

Bruises marked her left arm just above the wrist.

"I'm Hayley," she whispered.

"Sam," I replied. I tried my best to sound natural. But what's natural? What's normal? Was it being a jerk like Jake Fennel, or Cody Hendricks? If it was, I

27

didn't want to be that. I never wanted to be that. Ever since middle school, it was like they just sought me ought, a magnetic attraction, but I attracted cruelty instead of love, brutality rather than care, scorn instead of respect. And I didn't know why.

But Hayley glanced over at me, swallowing, and I realized she was nervous. She licked her lips, then whispered, "You from around here?"

"No. I'm new."

"Me too." She stopped speaking as Mr. Bernard approached us, handing out papers. When he got to our table, he gave each of us a two-page syllabus. I scanned it. By the time I was finished reading, he was back at the front of the room talking.

I wanted to say, *Maybe since we're both new, we should stick together.* But my throat closed up, chest tight, and I could feel my pulse at my temples. I hadn't had a friend, someone I could trust, since Brenna disappeared. The one or two times I'd tried hadn't gone well. Everyone had their own little group, their own ways of doing things.

"Can I see your schedule?" she whispered.

It was crumpled up in my pocket. I took it out, smoothing the paper. She studied the paper for a second. "We've got three classes together. And lunch. Want to hang out?"

Was she kidding? I studied her for a second for signs of cruelty, signs that she was going to turn around and use dumping on me as a way to get in with the popular kids. But it didn't seem likely. Her clothes were cheap, and one of her shoes looked extremely worn, the threads coming out at the seam. The popular kids wouldn't have anything to do with her.

I tried to squash the brief hope I felt. I tried not to sound too eager. I tried not to sound like I cared. "Sure."

I almost held my breath. But she didn't laugh. She didn't do anything horrible at all. But as class broke, we headed to third period together. As we walked down the hall I caught a glimpse of Cody Hendricks. He was hard to miss, because he stood a full head taller than most of the other students crowding the hallway. I kept my head down.

"Where did you go to school before?" Hayley asked.

"Fairfax County, Virginia. You?"

"Birmingham. I moved here to live with my dad."

My eyes darted to her bruised forearm before I could stop them, but I didn't think she caught it. "My dad lost his job and had to move here for a new one."

She looked at the numbers above the doors then back to her schedule. "This is it."

So we sat through US History together then split up for fourth period. I'd only known her two hours, but I didn't want to leave her behind to go to my precalculus class. Not that I had a choice.

We waved, and I walked downstairs and finally found the precalculus class. I kept my eyes to the floor as I made my way to the back of the classroom and slid into a seat, so it wasn't until I was seated and opening a notebook at my desk that I saw the girl from the bus. The black-haired girl with too much makeup, the girl who had called her boyfriend out like a guard dog.

I pretended to not look at her, even as I examined her. She wore what appeared to be a Prada skirt, which probably wasn't, with a sleeveless white T-shirt. She hunched over in her seat, leaning to the right, whispering to another girl with long blonde hair, perfect in this heat and humidity.

The two girls giggled, and I wondered if they were laughing at me. Then I realized they were looking at a phone in the dark-haired girl's hands. The blonde giggled again. Something on Snapchat or Facebook or Instagram I imagined; something embarrassing about someone else. I'd seen their type before.

All the same, I couldn't help but sneak glances at the girl. I wanted to know her name. I wanted to know more about her.

Why? So I could humiliate myself again? So I could be rejected again? I'd made a friend already today, and that was more than I had expected or even dreamed of. Don't push it, Sam.

The teacher entered the classroom. She was a doughy woman with rough, mottled skin and a dress that appeared to be sewn from a floral tablecloth. Her hair was grey and curled into one-inch ringlets. She wore a cheap-looking necklace and large garish rings on several fingers. This was our precalculus teacher, Mrs. Watson.

She stomped around the room for the next twenty minutes describing the rules of her classroom. No whispering, no talking, no laughing. No trips to the bathroom. Cell phones, if seen, would be confiscated. The dark-haired girl looked away from the teacher and rolled her eyes.

The dark-haired girl didn't put her phone away. Instead, she held it in her lap, barely hidden by the desk. Mrs. Watson would have to be a complete idiot to miss it, but she said nothing. Either she didn't enforce her own rules, or she enforced them for some kids. I'd encountered that before and I wouldn't make any assumptions about how things operated here until I saw it with my own eyes.

Mrs. Watson took the roll. Each of the twenty-five students in the room said, "here," when she called their names … including the dark-haired girl, who I knew now was named Ashley Prichard.

Ashley. It was a beautiful name, laden with the flavor of the coast, of Savannah and Charleston and the old South. It was a fitting name for a truly beautiful girl, a girl who was probably as poisonous as she was lovely.

Ashley's friend was named Caitlin Ludlow. She didn't have the flawless beauty of Ashley, though she was attractive. Her nose and chin seemed out of proportion to her small eyes. I rolled the names over my tongue silently. Caitlin and Ashley. I should avoid those two.

Everyone went quiet when the name Sam Roberts was called out, and everyone turned to look at me. I shrank in my seat. "Here."

For the next twenty minutes I held my breath, hoping to not make any mistakes or gaffes that would call attention to me. I was able to escape from the class with a minimum of contact, trailing after the last students.

Hayley was waiting in the hall when I exited the classroom. When she saw me her face lit up with a smile.

Three: Vanished

~~~~~~

Erin

The day Brenna disappeared seared itself into my memory like nothing in my life before or since.

After I realized she wasn't in her room, for the first hour or more I worried, but I didn't panic. Teenagers do stupid things. But I called. And called. And called again. It wasn't like Brenna to have her phone off. She *lived* on her phone. Ninety percent of the time her brain was more hooked into Instagram, Kik, and Snapchat than reality.

Almost ten a.m., I realized I wasn't going to church. Or, I thought, I could just take Sam, then deal with Brenna whenever it was she came back home. It incensed me. For the hundredth time I checked Brenna's location on my phone. No updates—her phone hadn't checked in since midnight.

"Erin, maybe you should sit down," Cole said. "You've been pacing for an hour."

Irritation flashed down my spine. "You could stand to be more concerned."

He set his iPad to the side. "Erin, we were both teenagers, too. How many times did we do something that pissed off our parents? Or sneaked out without telling them where we were going?"

I shook my head. "I never did that."

"Well, I did. I'm worried too, but I'm willing to bet she'll come wandering in any minute, oblivious. Anyway, pacing won't help. Have you called Chase?"

I sighed. Hesitant to admit the possibility she'd snuck out and slept with her boyfriend. "I'll call."

"Okay. I'm going to call in to the meeting."

He stood and walked toward his office. He paused for a second, as if on the verge of saying something … then continued on to his office down the hall.

After Lori told me Brenna was dating Chase, our house had erupted into open warfare, for at least a little while. Brenna refused to stop seeing him, and for months stopped talking to Lori, who had always been her hero. I grounded Brenna, demanding that she promise to stop seeing Chase. Ayanna Walker had brokered a cease-fire, beginning with a demand that Chase meet with me.

Ayanna and I had never been close. Even though I took the kids to church, her open and devout Christianity sometimes made me uncomfortable.

But her husband Jeremiah was Cole's best and only friend. They'd been roommates at Georgia Tech until Cole dropped out. When the kids were younger we'd gone to Atlanta for several years and eaten Thanksgiving lunch with the Walkers before going to Cole's parents. They had stayed with us several times over the years when visiting Washington.

Their girls—twins—were about Sam's age, and Ayanna worked with teenagers professionally. Somehow Ayanna got Brenna to calm down enough to talk with me.

Chase came over to our house on a Thursday evening. Cole was out of town (*of course*), so it was just Brenna, me, and Chase. He'd worn newish-looking blue jeans and a button-down shirt and looked as uncomfortable as anyone I'd ever seen.

"Sit down," I said, with no introduction.

"Yes, ma'am," he'd said.

Once he sat in the leather loveseat, I took a seat on the couch across from him. Brenna was beside him. I didn't like the way we were organized—the seating arrangement implied they were a couple—but it was too late to do anything about it.

"What do you want with my daughter? You're an adult. Why would you date a high school junior?"

Chase flinched a little. Then he met my eyes. "Mrs. Roberts … I met Brenna at the coffee shop. I had no idea she was in high school when we met. Honestly, she seemed a lot older. I swear to you—we haven't—we won't—do anything inappropriate. I would never want to hurt her."

"You're hurting her right now. She should date someone in her school."

Brenna rolled her eyes. "*Mom*. The boys at my school are all idiots. I lo—I like Chase."

A shiver ran down my spine. She'd almost said *I love Chase*. I needed to be careful, or I might lose my daughter while trying to protect her.

I studied him. "Then tell me about yourself. Convince me. Because right now I see an adult who is chasing a high school girl, and that makes me want to call the police."

"*Mom!*" Brenna's voice was hoarse as she nearly shouted the word.

"It's okay," Chase said to her, resting a hand on hers. "I don't blame her for asking questions."

"But Chase, she's being a—"

"Sweetie, stop. Let me do this." His voice was firm, and she stopped talking. I didn't like that. Brenna normally responded to that sort of tone with open combat.

Maybe it was just a sign that this older boy—man—was taking advantage of her youth and inexperience. Brenna liked to act and think as if she was eighteen, but the fact was, she was a fifteen-year-old girl. She knew nothing of the dangers out there.

"So answer my question ... what do you want with my daughter?" I didn't layer any honey on my question—I was angry and suspicious of Chase.

Brenna rolled her eyes at the question. He cleared his throat and shifted in his seat a little, looking anxious. "Mrs. Roberts ... I didn't expect any of this to happen. I didn't expect to meet Brenna, and I didn't plan on getting involved with her. But I won't lie to you. I love her."

He loved her. *Bullshit.* I loved her, she was my daughter. What the hell was wrong with this guy, old enough to be in college, who wanted to date a fifteen-year-old? Who does that?

"In that case, what's wrong with you?" I didn't bother to filter my feelings. "Were you not able to find a girl your own age? Do you have a thing for younger girls?"

Brenna gasped. She stood up, rage on her face. "Mama, you can't say that—"

"Brenna—" His interruption was soft, but once again she listened. It made my stomach twist a little to see her immediate obedience. "Sweetie, sit down. Your mother has a right to ask these questions."

I expected her to storm off. I expected there to be door slamming and rage. Instead, she sat down. She crossed her arms, crossed her right leg over the left, and looked away from us both, foot tapping and chin trembling. A tear ran down her face.

Shit.

"I love her," he murmured. The words were no less offensive the second time around. "But I'm fully aware that she is not old enough for that kind of involvement yet, Mrs. Roberts. I promise you, I wouldn't ever do anything to hurt her."

"Are the two of you having sex?"

He shook his head. "No." His answer was clear and direct. I believed him. That night, I told Cole the same, relaying the entire conversation to Cole over the phone. He had been in San Francisco ... or maybe New Mexico? The last couple of years he'd been traveling so much that it was hard to remember where he was.

It made no difference whether he was here or not. Cole was in town now, yet even with our daughter missing he couldn't leave work long enough to pay attention. Instead, he disappeared to his office for a conference call. Who does conference calls on Sunday mornings?

I paged through the contacts on my phone until I found Chase. I hesitated with my thumb over his name for a moment, and then I pressed it. The phone rang three times before he answered.

"Hello?" His voice sounded groggy.

"Chase, I want to talk to Brenna."

"What ... is this Mrs. Roberts?"

"Chase ... don't bother lying. Please put her on the phone."

"Mrs. Roberts ... Brenna isn't here. I haven't seen her since last night."

Impatience transitioned into panic. "Last night? You saw her last night? When?"

"I sent her home. She showed up at midnight wanting to surprise me. I told her she couldn't do that, that we'd agreed on the rules with you ... and ... we had a fight. Are you saying she didn't come home?" His voice was rising to a high pitch, but all I heard was, *midnight. Midnight. We had a fight.*

"Chase, *where* is my daughter." Panic was setting in.

"Can't you check her phone? She complained about you guys using her phone to track her movements. I told her it was for safety. Can't you check it?"

"Tell me the truth, damn you!"

Cole's office door opened and he poked his head out.

"Mrs. Roberts, I ...I don't know where she is!" Panicky. He stumbled over his words. Was he afraid we would find out something? Had he done something to her? "If she didn't come home, you need to call the police right now!"

For a second or five or a hundred I stood there, with my heartbeat whooshing in my ears. But then it hit me. He said they had a fight and she left at midnight. Either he was lying, and he had done something to her ... or he wasn't lying ... and something had happened to her. My *daughter.*

Cole's name came out in a shriek.

Sam

Where was Brenna?

That terrible morning, I stayed out of the way after my mom asked me if I'd seen Brenna. I moved upstairs to my room, which overlooked the driveway, and slid into the seat at my desk. Despite our age difference, we had some of the same Facebook friends. I searched through her friends and messaged them. Had anyone seen Brenna?

No one seemed to have seen her.

A little after ten thirty, three cars pulled up to the house. Two were Fairfax County police cruisers. The third also looked like a police car but was unmarked, a grey four-door sedan.

My stomach twisted at the sight.

The doorbell rang. I stayed in my seat, no longer paying attention to the computer. I was listening. Footsteps, as my mom walked across the hardwood floor to the front door. Muffled voices. Mom and Dad's voices were recognizable, but I couldn't tell what they were saying. A third voice, low-pitched and gravelly.

I slipped out of my seat and tiptoed to my bedroom door and opened it. From there I could hear better.

My mother was speaking. "... not since last night. We went to bed around ten. She was watching TV in her room."

The deep voice again. A detective? "When did you realize she wasn't home?"

A slight pause. My mom's voice, a little muffled. I had trouble understanding the first few words. "... to get ready for church. Her bed was made, and she wasn't in her room. That's when I checked and saw that her car was gone."

More muffled voices. This was frustrating. Screw it. Brenna was my sister. I had a right to be part of this. I intended to sneak close to the dining room where the voices were coming from, but as soon as I got downstairs one of the uniformed officers saw me. No sneaking around then. I walked into the dining room.

Mom and Dad were sitting at the dining table next to each other. Lately they didn't get near each other, but right now their hands were clasped.

The dining room was usually unoccupied unless Mom and Dad were hosting dinner with guests. In the center of the room stood a polished near-black table that seated twelve. An ugly oil painting covered half the wall, depicting a bare-breasted woman crawling across a wheat field. Brenna called the painting *Christina's Boob*, because it looked like a bad copy of another painting, *Christi-*

35

na's World by Andrew Wyeth. I always thought the painting was terrible, but I'm no painter, so who was I to judge?

Two chandeliers could light the room up like a stage, but not that day. Dim recessed lights highlighted the painting and gave the whole room a creepy feel.

Across from Mom and Dad was a bulky African American man in a dark grey suit. In his right hand he held a small notebook, and in his left, a pen. He looked directly at me when I walked into the room. "Hello. I'm Detective Hunt. You must be Sam."

I nodded and sat down at the table without asking permission.

Dad spoke immediately. "Sam, I think you should wait upstairs—"

Detective Hunt interrupted. "Actually, I'd like to ask Sam some questions if that's all right, Mr. Roberts."

Dad nodded. "Of course."

Hunt turned his attention to me. He was in his forties, with close-cropped hair that showed signs of grey. His skin was dark brown, his eyebrows fierce and unkempt. "Sam, can you tell me when you last saw Brenna?"

I thought for a second. I could see her lying on her stomach on the bed, fingers tapping away on the keyboard of her computer. "About eleven o'clock last night. She was lying on her bed with the door open, typing on her laptop."

His eyebrows raised. "She has her own laptop? In her room?"

I nodded.

"Did she say anything to you when you saw her?"

"No. Wait ... yes. She said good night."

"Does she normally say that?"

I nodded. "Yeah. Almost always."

He wrote in his notebook. How could that be relevant? Why was he sitting here instead of looking for her? After he finished writing, he looked up from his notebook and looked right through me. I felt guilty, and I had no reason to feel that way. "Are you and Brenna close?"

Mom leaned forward. "They're *very* close."

Hunt's eyes darted to her then back to me. "Yes?" he prompted.

"Yes," I said. "She's my big sister. Of course we're close."

"Okay. You know her boyfriend?" He consulted his notebook before speaking again. "Chase Morton. You know him?"

My eyebrows pulled together. I was sure he knew Chase's name without having to look it up in his notes. Checking the notebook was for show. "Yes, I've met him."

Dad frowned. "Are you going to arrest Chase or not?"

36

"It's a little early to be arresting anyone. We don't even know if she's actually missing yet. Is it possible she stayed at a friend's and overslept?"

Mom shook her head. "She always asks if she's going somewhere."

"Always except this time," Hunt replied.

Mom and Dad met each other's eyes. I couldn't tell what they were communicating with each other.

"She's not an idiot," I said.

"Look, we want to find her just as badly as you do. But I need everything I can that might lead to her, all right? Is this Chase guy on the up-and-up?"

Mom shook her head. "I don't know … I thought so. We've given her a lot of rules, because I don't like that she's dating someone older than her."

"Is it possible she ran away? Has she said anything like that?"

"No, of course not!" Mom said.

"Sam? What about you? Did she say anything to you?" His eyes bored into me.

What are you going to do when I'm gone? Don't you think it's time you learned to stand up for yourself a little? I could still hear the words from her mouth. "I … she did say…" I trailed off. She couldn't have run away. Could she?

Mom sat forward, suddenly fierce. "Did she say something to you, Sam? This is serious! What was it?"

I stammered the next few words. "I … she … she said … she asked me what I would do when she was gone. Jake had jumped me again at school, and she stopped him. She asked when I was going to start taking care of myself!"

Hunt looked up at one of the other officers. Then back to me. "Sam, it's important you tell me the exact words she used. What did she say?"

I looked down at the table. Then I said the words in a near whisper. "She said, '*What are you going to do when I'm gone?*'"

Hunt's response was quiet. "Okay. Thank you, Sam." He sighed. "For the time being, we're going to treat this as a runaway situation."

"*WHAT?*" Mom screeched. "What does that mean? You're not going to take it seriously?"

"Mrs. Roberts, we take runaway girls seriously. It's a dangerous world out there. Our procedures are a little different, but that doesn't mean we won't do our best. Do you have a current picture of her?"

Mom turned to Dad and collapsed against him. "We have her school picture," he said.

"That doesn't look anything like her," I said. "Use her Facebook picture. She just took that a couple days ago."

Hunt gave me an appreciative look. "Good thinking, Sam. Speaking of Facebook … we need to examine her computer. Do you have her passwords?"

Mom stood, and the rest of us followed suit. "It's in her room."

Cole

The morning Brenna disappeared may have been the longest morning of my life. In retrospect, it's difficult for me to forgive my initial attitude. When Erin was charging around the house panicking about Brenna not being home, I didn't take it seriously. I mean, I took it seriously in the context of being irritated that my kid had been disobedient. But at that point it never crossed my mind that something had happened to her. I believed that she'd come stumbling back into the house, hung over or still stoned, careless of how her disappearing act had affected the rest of her family.

The week before, I'd been in California for meetings with the IT department of another company we'd acquired. System by system, we were assessing what to keep, what to merge with our own systems, and what to discard. Human resources and some of the other support functions would be eliminated and transferred to the parent company, and it likely made sense to close their data center in California and move everything to our data center in Herndon, Virginia. The discussions were tense. Everyone I met with was worried about losing their jobs, and with good reason.

On the flight home that Wednesday night, I'd written up my plan for the merger and emailed it to my boss. I caught a cab from Dulles, and on the way home, I read an email from my best friend, Jeremiah. He and his wife had just paid off the mortgage on their house in Atlanta, twenty years early. Amazing. Our new place was so expensive that we'd never have it paid off.

There had been a time when Erin would have driven out to the airport with the kids to pick me up, but those days had passed. I hadn't known if it was my fault or hers, but the bottom line was, sometime after we'd bought that mausoleum in Fairfax, we'd grown more and more distant. Was it the travel, or the stress she felt dealing with the kids, or just that there was so much room in that house you could get lost in it? Things got worse and worse, and I didn't think she would ever forgive me for Teagan.

I can't say I blamed her.

When I got home that night, Erin was curled up in front of the television. She gave me a smile, which was rare enough to be remarkable, and I collapsed on the couch next to her.

"How was the trip?" she asked.

"Good. Though I'm getting a lot of resistance from the folks there. What's been going on here?"

"Oh, not much. I had lunch with Angela yesterday."

My favorite person in the world. I didn't voice the thought. Instead, I just said, "How did that go?"

"Okay. She just got back from Europe. We were just catching up." Her voice sounded sad, and I felt a twinge of guilt. Erin and Angela had once been inseparable, and I was part of the wedge that had introduced so much distance between them.

"Also, Brenna brought home a D on her science test Wednesday. Can you talk to her about that this weekend? She doesn't listen to a thing I say."

"Yeah," I replied, "though I don't know that she'll listen to me any more than you."

"I'm worried about her, Cole."

I nodded. "I am too. Especially with that asshole she's dating."

"I don't know. He's not as bad as I thought at first." Her voice trailed off, as if she wasn't sure she agreed with herself.

"He's too old for her."

"True. She's still young. And she thinks she knows everything."

"I'll talk to her about it, I promise. But let's get through her birthday, and I'll catch her Sunday evening. Okay?"

I didn't get a chance, because on Sunday Brenna was nowhere to be found.

My calm leaked away a little when Erin spoke with Chase on the phone. My composure fell apart when Sam informed us that Brenna had talked about going away.

Where was she thinking of going? It had to be with Chase … it's not like she could support herself or feed herself. As soon as Sam said those words, I knew what it was. Brenna had planned to run off with Chase. Maybe they were planning to sneak off and pretend she was eighteen and try to get married? Go to Mexico together? Or just someplace where the age of consent was ridiculously low?

The first person to talk to was Chase. So why were the cops still sitting around my house?

I leaned forward, unintentionally brushing Erin aside. "I'm going to ask you again, Detective—when are you going to arrest Chase? He's behind this and you know it."

Detective Hunt stood up and frowned. "Questioning Mr. Morton will be our next stop, Mr. Roberts. In the meantime, I want you to stay here with your

39

phone lines open. If she's a runaway, the odds are she'll change her mind within the next few hours. You need to be able to take her call when it comes." I stood too.

Detective Hunt had *not* made a good impression on me. Disheveled, his suit cheap, his beard unevenly trimmed. Typical government employee, I thought.

He gave instructions to two of the officers, then said, "I'll return as soon as I learn anything, Mr. and Mrs. Roberts. Please try to stay calm."

Hunt left, followed by the officers. As soon as they got out the door, Erin turned on Sam. "Sam! Why didn't you tell me Brenna said that about going away? Are you keeping her secrets? Why didn't you tell me?" Her voice sounded strained, high-pitched like wind blowing through reeds.

Sam recoiled. Shock spread across his still-childlike features. "I didn't know … I didn't—" With that, he sobbed and buried his face in his hands.

"Erin," I said. "It's not Sam's fault."

Erin turned on me. "No, damn it! It's *your* fault. She wasn't running around with twenty-year-olds before you screwed up our family. She wasn't getting in trouble in school before then. She wasn't—"

"Stop!" Sam cried out, tears running down his cheeks. "Why do you think she always wanted to be out of the house? Because you two *never* stop fighting!"

Sam stormed off to his room, slamming the door loud enough we could hear it all the way at the front entrance.

"I can't talk to you right now," Erin said, then stormed off herself.

I had staggered back to my office, sinking into my desk chair and staring out the window. The need to *do* something was overpowering. I needed to search for her. But *where?* I had no idea who most of her friends were these days. I could ask Marion. But first I needed to make a difficult call. I picked up the phone and dialed my parents.

Four: Dreams

~~~~~~~~~~~~~~~~~~~~~~~~~~~~~~~~~~~~~~~

Sam

The message popped up on my phone at 7:54 p.m.

Hayley: **Hey.**
I texted her right back: **Hey. What's up?**
Hayley: **Nothing u?**
Me: **Homework. Bored.**
Hayley: **Still going to library tomorrow?**
Me: **Yeah.**
Hayley: **Okay. cya ttyl**

I slid off the bed and to my door to double-check the lock. Dinner had been difficult. *How was school? What did you learn? Did you make any friends?*

Boring. Nothing. No. Those were the answers I wanted to give them, but that would only provoke a lot more questions. So I answered, "Great," and told them a story about precalc that was basically made up, and I told them about Hayley.

Mom and Dad zeroed in on that quick—especially Dad, who was always pressuring me to chase girls—but I brushed them off successfully then retreated to my room after dinner.

At least they were talking to each other for a change, and Mom seemed somewhat sober.

I checked the time. Almost eight. I slipped into the chair at my desk, double-clicked on the *Second Life* icon, and typed my login information.

41

Moments later, the progress bar completed and the world began to fill in.

First, my avatar appeared.

She was tall, but not too much so, with long red hair braided into a French braid. She wore a vaguely steampunk outfit: knee-high boots, a tattered skirt, a ruffled rose-colored blouse, and a black coat. A pistol was holstered at her left side and a sword on the right. Above her, the name *Tamara Goldwyn* floated in the air. Underneath my name was the legend *Brigade Sergeant*.

After my avatar was clear, the surroundings began to fill in, starting with the walls of the apartment I rented above a shop in Erie South. I still had a ton of money left over in Second Life … almost one hundred real dollars. But I had no way to convert it back into real currency. So instead of getting the meds I needed, I wasted it here. Not that one hundred dollars would pay for the pills for more than a couple of months.

A loud beep announced an incoming message. Lilya Marjeta was the captain of the Brigade, the faction I was a member of. She lived in the Netherlands and was often online several hours ahead of me. I opened her message.

Lilya: **Tamara, are you on long? Can u come to the hq?**

Tamara: **On my way.**

I clicked on the door to the apartment and it slid to the side, then I made my way down the dark hallway and stairs to the front of the building. My heads-up display only showed a few dots. Probably not friendly: half a dozen different factions with competing and shifting loyalties dominated Erie Isle, and the Brigade was often a minority amongst those factions.

Across the street was the canal, which cut through the island out to the ocean to the south. In that direction were mostly private residences owned by different people who supported the sim. To the north, was the main sim, Erie Main. There I would find the Brigade headquarters and my closest friends in the world.

Crazy, right? That my closest friends in the world didn't even exist? Or they did, but I didn't know their names, or where most of them lived, or anything at all except what went on in our world here.

I didn't care. In real life I was Sam: depressed, outcast, freak. But in *this* world I was a leader. I had friends and people I cared about. Sure, it was a game. Sure, it wasn't real. But maybe that didn't matter. Maybe it was more real than stupid Ashley and her asshole boyfriend Cody. More fun than my high school and my parents. More accepting than my slightly racist and semi-homophobic grandparents.

So I walked, carefully avoiding the dangers in the darkness of my virtual world.

A knock on my door jarred me back to the real world. I minimized the game, my heart suddenly thumping, and opened a Word document with my English report on it. Then I got up and walked to the door and opened it.

Dad stood at the door. His hair was chaotic and his eyes were sunken with deep exhaustion. The uniform he wore, blue polyester with the words Waffle House embroidered on the sleeve, looked like it was soaked. Dad had gone back to the restaurant after dinner … something must have gone wrong.

I stared at him but didn't say anything.

"Sam…"

He didn't sound sure of anything as he said my name.

Hesitantly. "Yeah?"

He looked at me for a second like there was something complicated he wanted to say. Then, it seemed like he sagged in exhaustion. "Just wanted to say good night."

"Good night, Dad."

He half smiled then staggered down the short hallway toward their room. Dad's room, really … it's like they thought I was stupid. That I didn't noticed they never slept in the same bed anymore … that Mom was always on the couch.

Hoping to prevent any more interruptions, I called in the other direction, "Good night, Mom."

"Night, honey…" It sounded like she was watching the ten-thousandth re-run of Law & Order. Her words were slurred, yet another bottle of wine on its way into the recycling. They always talked about how broke we were, but a bottle of wine a day can't be cheap.

Whatever.

I closed and locked my door.

I opened the game back up, my avatar bouncing back into position. I got lucky this time … usually when someone left their avatar idle in the sim, the GMs—Game Masters—would bounce them out. I hadn't been gone long enough for anyone to notice. I continued my walk. On my left was the large hill that overlooked the harbor. On top was the Cathedral, home to the Twilight, one of the less savory factions, and the base for the current Mayor, who I'd long since determined was a sadistic lunatic. Past the Cathedral was the Brigade headquarters. Beyond that, the warehouse district, where it wasn't safe for humans to go.

The Brigade headquarters was a two-story building that might have once been a fire station. It had a pole from the second floor anyway. The basement had been converted to jail cells. In theory, the Mayor was responsible for public safety in Erie, but in practice the Brigade did the job. Vigilantes: violent and effective.

I had joined the Brigade about three months earlier. I was new to Erie and was picked up by the faction fairly quickly. After about a month I'd been promoted to sergeant.

Of course, in Second Life, three months is more like two years.

When I walked into the Brigade headquarters, Lilya was standing there talking with a human male. He was tall, possibly close to seven feet, and well-built with tattoos banded around his upper arms. He had short, shaggy blond hair, and his face showed a five o'clock shadow. A name floated over his head: Gunstock Valor.

Lilya: **Tamara. I'm so glad you're here. This is Gunstock. Gunstock, this is Tamara, our training sergeant.**

I reached for my keyboard, hesitated for a second, then typed: **Is Gunstock a recruit?**

Lilya: **Yes. Can you show him the ropes? I've reached the end of my shift.**

Lilya: **/ooc I have to log off now, it's past midnight here.**

The characters /ooc meant "out of character." Players typed that when they needed to communicate something that wasn't actually part of the game.

Tamara: **/ooc: have a great night, Lilya!**

Lilya: **/ooc: good night, sweetie! Take good care of Gunstock!**

Time to get back into character.

Tamara: **It's nice to meet you, Gunstock. I'm Tamara.**

Gunstock: **Charmed, Miss Tamara. I wouldn't have guessed such a pretty lady would be the training sergeant for an organization like this. Have you been with the Brigade long?**

I felt my cheeks heat up. I ignored that and began typing: **Not long. I'm just very good at what I do.**

Gunstock: **I can imagine.**

I led Gunstock out of the headquarters and along the edges of the warehouse district. As we walked, we didn't chat. In some simulators, voice chat was preferred, but it was disabled here. That made it impossible to talk while maneuvering an avatar. However, it was one of the reasons I liked to play here. When I was online, I preferred to completely put on the role of Tamara. No one in Second Life knew that I was physically male in real life. I was happy to keep it that way. As soon as people knew that, they would begin to treat me differently. And the thing was? In this world, I felt needed. Valued. Confident. In the real world I felt none of those things.

Over the next hour, we stopped in at several locations on the island … the bar, the hotel, the hospital. During that time, out of character, I learned that Gunstock had only been in Second Life for about a month. That was what I had suspected. This was the first roleplay sim he had visited. I explained the rules the best I could, emphasizing that the point was to become immersed in the story, not to get points or achieve a particular end. He seemed to understand.

We were about to find out if he got it. As we left the hospital, we came upon a small grouping of figures.

It was Mayor Kacklick Fromwell, with his assistant Sophie. They were confronting a young woman. The label floating over her head read Ninevah Marvel.

Kacklick was tall and extremely thin and wore a long black overcoat which probably hid serious weapons. He had long sideburns, and black leather boots, and what appeared to be leather pants. He wore a red amulet at his neck. I'd often seen him around over the past three months, and the amulet was new and probably trouble.

Avatars didn't actually have facial expressions except the crudest ones. But somehow Fromwell managed to be menacing without them. He turned to face me.

Kacklick Fromwell: **Tamara. Butting into other people's business, as usual?**

Jerk. I typed: **Just doing my job.**

I turned to the girl and typed: **Hi. I'm Sergeant Tamara, I'm with the Brigade, we're kind of like the cops around here. Are you new?**

The girl took a long time to respond. I found myself checking the clock. I needed to get to bed soon. School in the morning. Finally, she answered.

Ninevah Marvel: ***whispers* help me**

Whoa. I took a step back from Fromwell. Then I typed: **Gunstock, step back a little bit please? Cover me. Mayor, what kind of game are you playing?**

I watched the Mayor closely, even as Sophie backed away from our little tableau, apparently keeping her eyes on Gunstock. If it came down to a fight, I was in trouble. Gunstock was inexperienced, and Sophie deadly. She'd probably take him out in a matter of seconds. I was good, but Fromwell was far more powerful than I was, probably level twenty or higher. He had all the advantages. All the same, I couldn't walk away from this fight.

A private chat window popped up in the corner of my screen. It was Gunstock: **What do I do**

In the chat window I typed: **Follow my lead. If a fight starts, try to take out Sophie with your guns.**

Gunstock: *gulps* **I don't know how to use them.**

Tamara: **Just do the best you can.**

After what seemed like an eternity, Fromwell typed: **Sergeant Tamara, Young Nineveh here is mine.**

Tamara: **Nineveh … get behind me, then run. I've got this son of a bitch.**

As I finished typing this sentence, I drew my weapons. I could feel adrenaline hitting my real life body … I'd never fought the Mayor, but I'd seen him take out high-level players in seconds. As far as I knew, he was the longest standing player on the island.

Fromwell typed: **The Mayor begins to laugh with a menacing tone, then raises his arms in the air. A black cloud begins to form between his hands.**

As the words appeared on the screen, his avatar went into a crouch, arms waving in the air and a black cloud began to surround him.

Crap. Magic.

I jumped high in the air, backwards, hoping to get out of range of the spell as I opened fire with my pistol. Before I hit the ground, the heads-up display showed my hit points beginning to drop. Tiny animated blood-red particles floated away from my body as I hit the ground running. My hit points were dropping fast, and there was no chance of me taking him out with a pistol in that time. I charged forward swinging my weapon.

Another spell: a bright flash of light extended beyond Fromwell's body, enveloping me. I heard the sound of thunder, and a scream. My avatar dropped to the ground.

Words appeared on the bottom of the screen. **Tamara Goldwyn has been defeated by Kacklick Fromwell! Tamara Goldwyn loses 40xp!**

Damn.

I was immobilized and would remain that way for several minutes. The rules said that once you were defeated, you couldn't reengage. Gunstock was also down. We were through.

Fromwell typed: **Nineveh, girl … come with us.**

The girl approached the Mayor. He turned back toward me and typed: **No one will question your courage, Tamara, but one must know how to pick the right battles to fight. When you've recovered, you should consider whether or not the Brigade is the right home for you. We could train you to really fight. And to do other things.**

I shuddered.

Tamara: **I'd never join you.**

Fromwell: **Then I suppose you're doomed to misery and failure. You and all your allies.**

Fromwell, Sophie, and Nineveh walked away.

I sighed and looked at the clock. I needed to get to bed. It seemed like whenever I played, hours could race by without me noticing.

Tamara: **/ooc: I'm out of time for the night. You coming back tomorrow?**
Gunstock: **/ooc: yeah, this was a lot of fun. See you tomorrow.**

I logged out, finding myself, with what felt like a shock, back in my bedroom. I was back in a place where I wasn't a leader; where I was not heroic, not needed, not a woman.

The room was quiet, and through the door I could hear the ticking of Mom's grandfather clock, and from outside, the underlying hum of thousands of insects. But inside, I was reliving the battle. I turned off my computer, turned out the light, and crawled into bed.

I felt empty, so I turned my mind back to the game. Lilya would be upset we'd lost the battle with the Mayor, but I didn't think she'd be mad about us intervening. That was what we did. Protected the innocent. Searched for the missing. Took care of those who couldn't take care of themselves.

In my virtual world, I was all the things I couldn't be in the real world.

I drifted off to sleep and dreamt about the island. In my dream, Brenna was there with me.

Erin

When Sam said the words, "you motherfucker," I almost got up. He was locked in his room, of course, and it was late, and that meant instead of sleeping, he was playing on his computer. Again.

It was almost midnight, and I couldn't imagine what could have caused that outburst. But I knew that he wouldn't welcome my intrusion. What was the right thing to do? Lori and I had talked about it a lot, at least once we started talking again. How much freedom did you allow them? Obviously we allowed Brenna too much freedom. She'd not been like Sam though. Brenna had a very active social life, always out with friends.

Except for whoever he played that game with, it seemed like Sam had no friends at all. When he told us at dinner that he had made friends with a girl named Hayley, I almost didn't believe him. I still wasn't sure I believed him.

My head was muddled, and I was too tired to get up from the couch and go back to the bedroom. Too tired ... *bullshit*. I just didn't want to sleep next to Cole anymore. And so I drifted off to sleep on the couch, the shifting images on the television illuminating the ceiling in shifting patterns of blue and black.

winter flower

My transition to dreaming was smooth and unnoticeable. Almost without warning, I was standing in our old living room when the knock came on the door. It was almost sunset when we opened the door and found Detective Hunt standing there with another man, Stan Wilcox. I didn't know his name then, but in the dream I did for some reason.

In the dream Hunt always said, "Mrs. Roberts, do you recognize this?"

A thousand times he'd held up the plastic bag to show me the iPhone, in its case with the custom Black Flag logo. Who listened to Black Flag anymore? Cole and Brenna did. He'd had the case made for her fifteenth birthday. The phone was cracked, the screen crushed. I staggered when he showed it to me. Cole caught me from behind.

The men came in. In the dream they always shouted. "Why did you let her go?" "Why did you give her a car?" "It's your fault!" Stan Wilcox, the FBI agent, and Hunt, they circled around me.

Hunt sweating, contempt in his voice. "Your daughter wouldn't have run away if you had been a better mother."

Somehow Angela was beside me. "I tried to warn you. Of course she was hanging out with older guys … her father betrayed his family. You should have left Cole when he cheated."

Stan Wilcox said, "Almost three hundred thousand children in the United States are at risk of being trafficked."

Hunt replied, "Because their parents let them go without supervision."

Wilcox said, "You're saying they need better mothers."

Cole's mother Virginia appeared. A crooked line appearing between her brows, she stuck her finger in my face. "If you'd listened to me, this would never have happened."

Hunt said, "It's her fault. Look at her." The disgust in his tone made my stomach cramp.

The phone! The phone! They found it at four in the afternoon, after they'd refused to consider it an abduction all day. They found her car abandoned in a parking lot in Winchester, her phone crushed on the ground next to the car.

Where is my daughter? I screamed it at the two men.

Cole sat there on the other side of the room, inert, stunned. Guilty. Ineffectual. Impotent.

Where is she? I cried.

Hunt shrugged. "It doesn't look good."

Wilcox said, "We'll find her, Mrs. Roberts. But she won't be your child anymore."

Stop, I cried weakly. We drove. Cole wasn't with us. I sat in the front with Wilcox and we drove up and down the highway, looking at the young girls prostituting themselves on the Internet. Here, a fifteen-year-old. The caption, somehow floating above her in the air, read, **I'm your fantasy. $300 / hr.** There, a twelve-year-old, with a bruise on her cheek. Across the street, a girl that looked like Brenna but wasn't Brenna. A thousand girls up and down each side of the street, each dressed more provocatively like the last. The highway had somehow transformed itself into an endless webpage, overflowing with trauma and grief.

One of the girls cried out, "Mama!"

Virginia muttered, "Whores."

I couldn't make Brenna out in the crowd. And Stan kept driving.

"Stop," I said. "I need to get out and look for her."

"We'll find her," he said. "But you have to understand, I'm working all of these cases."

"All of them? All of these girls?" I waved my hand out the window. The faces had become a blur, because he was speeding now.

"Of course."

Help.

The words came out in a whimper. But it wasn't one of the girls.

It was me.

49

Five

~~~~~~

Cole

I struggled to open my eyes and reached out, slamming my hand into the alarm clock, then sat up in the bed. It was 5:30 a.m. Pitch-dark outside, pitch-dark in my bedroom. Slowly, my eyes adjusted, and I saw that Erin had never come to bed. She was most likely asleep on the couch. Lately that had been pretty common.

I stood up and stumbled to the closet and got out a uniform. My suits hung in the back of the closet to the right, more or less out of reach. I hadn't worn one in months. Shower and shave, and by six I was ready to go.

I knocked on Sam's door, and when there was no response, knocked again. Finally, I heard a groan, and the door cracked open. Bleary-eyed, Sam looked out at me.

"School, kiddo. Time to get up."

No answer; instead, Sam nodded and wandered toward the bathroom. I walked through the living room without turning on the light. Erin was asleep on the couch, a blanket wrapped around her. I paused for a moment, looking down at her. Asleep on her side, facing the television, she looked younger. Almost like the girl I'd fallen in love with so long ago. I gave a tired sigh, and went into the kitchen and filled a travel mug with coffee.

Outside, I walked past Erin's Mercedes, which we'd managed to keep only because it was already fully paid for, and over to my car. It was muggy as hell. A warm, unpleasant breeze blew through my uncomfortably short hair. The house we were renting was a one-story, two-bedroom ranch house. Stained carpet, and one of the front windows was cracked and sealed with duct tape. I needed to cut the grass. When we did the math on what the new job was going to pay, minus living expenses, gas, and health insurance, this was the only option. It wasn't the worst neighborhood in Oxford, and it was zoned to a decent high school, which was important. But the entire thing would have fit in our old living room in Fairfax.

I got in the car. There was no point in dwelling on that. Our lives weren't what they had been. Now it was all about surviving, day to day. Somehow I didn't think we were even going to need this much for much longer. Our marriage was utterly wrecked, and as I drove away, I reflected on the fact that the only reason we were still together was Sam and economic necessity. Seriously. If I left, where was I going to go? I could barely afford the rent on this crappy house as it was, much less a hotel room. And Erin wasn't exactly in a position to support herself. Bachelor's degree in economics or not, it had been twenty years since she'd held down a job. And she never missed an opportunity to remind me that it was my fault.

Not to mention, if I left, what about Sam? Would Sam end up staying with his mother? Would that be any good for him? She drank way too much and didn't have a job and Sam was already oddly effeminate. Not that there was anything wrong with that, it's just who he was. But—well, I often thought Sam needed to toughen up. We could go live with my parents, I guess. Dad had warmed up a lot over the years, but Mom was a piece of work. Not to mention that the court wasn't just going to let me up and move. I'd been lucky they let me transfer my probation to Alabama in the first place.

For the ten thousandth time, I thought, *Maybe I should ask Daddy for help.* Except the one time, when we put up the award for information about Brenna, I'd never asked him for a handout. Not once. I didn't want to start. I could picture what it would be like. He'd do it begrudgingly, but would offer a loan. Disapproving. My mother would charge her own form of interest by nosing in where she wasn't wanted, demanding to know how the money was spent and trying to dictate our lives and push us around, just like she pushed Daddy around.

I wasn't ready for that.

Fifteen minutes after leaving the house I parked behind the restaurant. The sun was just beginning to lighten the sky. I took a walk all the way around the building. Linda hadn't swept the parking lot yet, and cigarette butts and garbage scattered the lot.

The building itself was shaped roughly like a shoe box. Old brown brick, dark brown metal panels and glass. Inside, Linda and Dakota were sitting next to each other at the counter talking. I walked in the restaurant. The floor was dirty, and so were the bathrooms.

Without a word, I walked to the register, turned the key, and checked sales. One hundred ten dollars. I raised my eyebrows, then turned to Linda and Dakota.

"Slow night, huh?" I said.

"Dead," Linda replied.

In a sharp tone, I said, "Then why hasn't the parking lot been swept? Why's the floor dirty in here? You're telling me you can't get your job done on a ten-hour shift with just a hundred bucks in sales?"

Dakota and Linda winced, and Linda said, "Sorry, boss. I'll take care of it now." Both of them got up from their seats.

"Good. And this needs to be the last time I have to say this. I'm getting tired of repeating myself."

Shaking my head, I walked down the line, checking supplies and food. I was working myself up into a rage. Eggs pans were dirty, and dishes were piled in the dish pit. Linda had only done a half-assed job of cleaning back here. I could see dirt and grime built up underneath the dish pit, and a fork on the floor underneath was clear evidence she'd only deck-brushed along the line, not bothering to get underneath the equipment. The grills had been done at least, but a glance up close showed the filters were getting dirty again. I'd spent two hours scrubbing them just four days ago, and left instructions to clean them every shift.

I pushed into the back room.

"Morning," I grunted to Julie, one of the first shift waitresses. She stood in front of the mirror next to my office door, doing her makeup. Julie was in her late twenties, an attractive lady with a good smile. She had tied her apron tight enough to emphasize her body's curves, which were pleasant. She hadn't been working here long, but long enough that some of the regulars ... at least the old men who came in here to flirt with the waitresses ... actively sought out her section. That was starting to cause drama with the other waitresses, which was not what I needed. She was leaning into the mirror putting on mascara. I had to turn away.

"Morning," she replied as I unlocked the padlock to the office.

I checked my watch. Twenty to seven. Over the next fifteen minutes I changed the drawer, while Dakota and Linda rushed to finish the jobs they'd had ten hours to complete. Once that was done, I took a minute in the office, leaning against what passed for a desk, looking out through the one-way glass at the restaurant.

Two years ago I'd managed a twenty-million-dollar data center with thirty highly-paid professional employees. People I didn't have to micromanage, because they were excited and motivated to do their jobs. I still sometimes couldn't grasp the transition to this fucking life.

On the other hand, I kept in touch with a lot of my former coworkers, a few of whom were still unemployed after the company's collapse. I'd missed that collapse: I was already gone by then.

A couple minutes before seven, Linda stopped at my office door. "Sorry about that, boss. It won't happen again."

I looked at her and nodded, then said, "Linda ... I just need you to remember, you're supposed to be running this shift, okay? That means you've gotta take some initiative. If Brian had come in here, you can bet I'd be hearing about it."

She frowned at the mention of our division manager. "I know. I'm sorry."

"All right. You ready to get paid?"

"Yes, sir," she replied.

She tapped the numbers on the time clock, and I pulled up the payment module on the computer then unlocked the safe. Her name popped up on the screen, and I tapped through until her pay stub printed.

One hundred thirty-three dollars. I counted out the cash and handed it to her then passed her the clipboard to sign for her check. As she was signing, I glanced over the pay stub. Her check was thirty or so dollars smaller than usual, because she'd been out sick one day, and we didn't have sick leave.

"While you're in there, can you print my last four weeks' pay stubs?"

"Sure," I said. This wasn't an unusual request. Most of my employees were on some form of public assistance and needed to periodically prove their income to whatever county or state agencies they were dealing with.

Linda had two teenagers at home, and raising two kids on less than six hundred bucks a month couldn't have been easy. My *rent* was eight hundred dollars a month. I knew she got a little help from her daughter, who worked for us on the weekends, but that probably only brought in an extra forty bucks a week.

On the other hand, maybe if she did some work during her shift, she'd be making more money. Maybe she wouldn't be stuck working as a third shift cook in a crappy restaurant in the middle of nowhere.

She double-counted the money then put it away in her purse. Less than a minute later, Dakota appeared at my door. She looked sheepish. "Sorry, Cole. Berry was sick and I didn't get no sleep yesterday. I'll do better tonight."

I sighed. The seventeen-year-old was normally one of my hardest workers, and she'd done a lot to improve our third shift sales. In a quiet tone I said, "I know it's hard, Dakota. Just keep trying. I know you normally work hard."

She smiled and clocked out. I'd have liked to have told her it gets easier when they aren't infants anymore. But that's not true. The problems get bigger; the dangers get bigger.

I locked the safe and headed out to the front of the restaurant. Julie was out front now, chatting with one of our coffee-only customers at the bar. Even though shift change was at seven, the other two waitresses wouldn't be in until eight. I had to shave every dollar I could, and bringing them in a little later saved six dollars off my payroll.

I took half the egg pans to the dish pit and started scrubbing them with steel wool. These pans were probably twenty years old and beat up as hell. Carbon tended to build up on the back if they weren't scrubbed every shift.

I listened with half an ear as Julie told her customer, Larry, a story about her last job. She'd been a customer service manager for a custom home builder, but since the recession started, there weren't exactly many custom homes being built around here.

I kept scrubbing. It would be half an hour or more before we started to get many customers.

***

The moment I knew Brenna wasn't coming home was the evening of her disappearance, when Detective Hunt showed up at the door. He'd knocked, and we'd answered together, both of us on the verge of panic.

"Mr. and Mrs. Roberts," he said. "Do you recognize this?"

It was as if he'd designed the moment to be as traumatic as possible. He held up Brenna's phone—it had to be Brenna's, I gave her the Black Flag phone case. The screen was covered with spiderweb cracks.

Erin had staggered back, a gasp turning into a wail. I grabbed her before she fell down, and Hunt came in the room with another man we hadn't met.

"Mr. and Mrs. Roberts—my name's Stan Wilcox. I'm with the FBI's Child Abduction Rapid Deployment Team."

At those words, my chest seized in some kind of a painful spasm. I winced, and I watched as Erin raised her fist to her mouth and bit, hard.

Wilcox continued. "About an hour ago, local police in Winchester discovered a VW Beetle parked behind a pawn shop. It's your daughter's car—the phone was on the ground beside it."

"Oh my God," Erin said. She was starting to hyperventilate.

Through the window, I could see blue lights as more police cars showed up, the flashing illuminating the living room. Hunt got up and opened the door as Wilcox continued to speak.

"The CARD team is going to establish a mobile command post, and we're releasing an Amber Alert for your daughter shortly."

Erin met my eyes. I reached out and grabbed her hand. "We'll get through this," I said, urgently. "We'll get her home."

She nodded, her eyes glassy. I looked around, but I didn't see Sam. Had he gone to his room?

Wilcox began to brief us. Mobile command post. Amber Alert, all-points bulletin. Chase had been arrested and was being questioned already.

Wilcox said, "Her computer showed she'd been chatting with a guy named Rick. His Facebook account has been deleted. Have you heard of this guy?"

Erin swung her face toward mine, eyes wide. I shook my head. "No. Rick? I've never heard of him. What's his last name? Did he go to school with her?"

Wilcox shook his head. "No last name that we can identify yet. Our team is contacting Facebook to try to get more information. We don't even know if we've got the entire conversation. But she's been chatting with him online a lot over the last four weeks or so. Complaining about her boyfriend, among other things."

Erin frowned. "That doesn't make sense ... she's really obsessed with Chase."

I leaned forward, running my hands through my hair. What the fuck was she doing online? Who were these people?

Chase. What if she was talking to this guy, this *Rick* guy, and Chase found out?

Erin

I didn't sleep the night after Brenna disappeared.

In the hours after the Amber Alert was issued, we stayed in the kitchen, listening as well as we could. Stan Wilcox was running the response team right out of our kitchen, staying on the phone and radio with a bunch of FBI agents as well as local and state police. I called my parents, and Cole called his, and we worried, pacing, nibbling at the edges of terror we couldn't wholly digest. Angela arrived with several bags of assorted takeout Chinese, which we spread on the main dining room table. I didn't feel like eating, but the various police could, and Sam needed to eat something; he was so small for his age.

The traffic in and out of the house was more than I could handle. I stayed close to Lori and Sam, anchors in the chaos, while Cole paced around like a trapped tiger. It was loud, at times half a dozen people on the phone at once. Then, less than forty minutes after the Amber Alert was issued, the first news van rolled up in front of our house. Thankfully, Detective Hunt had posted a uniformed officer to guard the gate of our driveway, or they likely would have driven right in. But that van was soon followed by another, and another, until there was a crowd of satellite vans crowding the street outside our fence.

"What do we do?" I had asked Wilcox. "Do we talk to the press?"

"Damned right we do," Cole said. "Get them to put her picture out everywhere."

Wilcox nodded. "At this point I'd recommend it. The first few hours count the most."

This comment brought on nothing but rage. "We're already past the first few hours," I said. "Maybe we'd have her back if you'd taken this seriously to begin with."

Cole ran his hand through his hair, frustration showing on his face. "What about Chase? Is he talking yet?"

Wilcox shook his head. "At this point we're questioning him … he's a person of interest. But we don't have any reason yet to believe that he's involved with her disappearance."

"Bullshit!" Cole's face was red as he blurted out the word. "Who else is there? Of all the fucking incompetent—"

"Cole…" I interrupted. "That's not helping."

He bunched his fists and closed his eyes, leaned his head back, dragging his fingers through his hair in frustration. I'd seen that mannerism before. Once when we were visiting Georgia, his mother had been in a particularly nasty mood and had hectored Cole for nearly forty minutes about nonsense. Cole had finally stood up, his face a grimace, and dragged his fingers against his skull just like this. Then he walked out as she was speaking, mid-sentence. Cole had a reputation at work for being a brilliant engineer and executive, but he wasn't a popular boss. He had too little tolerance for mistakes or anything he viewed as incompetence.

Watching him, Angela's eyes widened. A flash of judgment passed over her face—and for the first time since we'd met on the first day of college, I hated her.

Cole took another deep breath, opened his eyes, and dropped his hands to his side. "Let's do this press thing then."

For the next twenty minutes we sat down and made a plan. Lori came downstairs—she'd been upstairs with Sam for the past hour. Both had red eyes from crying. As we sat down at the table, Lori said, "Mom and Dad are on their way up."

I closed my eyes. I didn't know if that was a relief or not. I didn't have the mental space to worry about it one way or the other. Cole's parents were also on

56

their way from Georgia, and while we had room for everyone, the competing sets of in-laws could be a lot to take. And honestly, I wanted to focus on finding my daughter, not placating parents. They would all have to fend for themselves. But if Virginia started in on Cole, as she was sometimes prone to do, then she and Jim could go find a goddamned hotel.

"The thing you need to remember is that the media will maybe cover thirty seconds of what you say if you're very lucky," Wilcox said. "More often than that, you'll get a maximum of ten to twenty seconds of airtime. It's important that you maximize that time … so you need to focus very carefully on what you're going to say."

"What are the most important things to say?" Lori asked.

"Sometimes families focus on putting up a reward for information. If you're able to do that, it's worth mentioning it. But the key thing is getting the public looking for her. Get their sympathy … ask for their help."

I met Cole's eyes. Most of our money was tied up in stock options that hadn't matured yet, and with our mortgage payments being what there were, we had precious little free cash at any given time. But we did have some investments.

Cole cleared his throat. "We can put up a hundred-thousand-dollar reward."

That was all we had. No … it was more than we had. It would have to be enough. He said quietly, "Daddy will probably put up some of it."

Shock ran through me. In our life together, Cole had never asked his parents for anything. It wasn't exactly bad blood between them—we went to Georgia for holidays some years, and they periodically came to visit us as well. I think it was pride more than anything. Cole had quit Georgia Tech over his father's loud objections. He had to prove he could make it on his own.

But this? It changed everything.

Sam

After the press conference, Mom and Dad disappeared into Dad's office with Lori and Mom's friend Angela, who I hadn't seen in a couple of years. I'm not sure they even noticed I was still standing there—not that my being invisible was unusual—so I followed them back inside and started to my room.

I felt—scared. Numb. Empty. I couldn't get my mind around what they'd said. Her phone smashed, car abandoned. Brenna missing. It was like saying the ground was missing. It just didn't make any sense. How could Brenna be missing? She was my world.

"Sam?" I turned around. It was one of the cops, a white guy with curly hair. He'd been talking as we planned the press conference, but no one bothered to introduce me to him.

"I'm Stan Wilcox. I'm with the FBI."

I nodded but didn't say anything.

"Can I ask you a few questions, Sam?"

"Of course."

He smiled, maybe trying to reassure me. It didn't help. He gestured toward the living room. "Can we sit in here?"

I followed him in and sat down in one of the chairs. He sat down opposite me. He looked tired, his suit jacket gone, tie untucked. It didn't look like he'd slept either.

"Sam, I need you to know that these are routine questions. Part of my job is to explore any possibility for what might have happened to Brenna. Okay?"

I nodded.

He smiled. "Good. I'm glad you understand. So … tell me about your parents. Do they get along?"

I didn't know how to answer that. How do you tell a complete stranger that your family has been falling apart? That you've lost your trust in your father?

Then I thought of Brenna, somewhere out there possibly in danger. If it could help her, I would tell him anything he needed to know. I took a deep breath, then said, "It's not just lately, it's the past couple of years. They've never told us what it was about, but there was a lot of fighting and screaming."

I felt a twist in my stomach. I wasn't going to say it. But then I thought—what if there was something important? What if there was something I didn't know, some tiny detail they needed to find my sister and bring her back to me? I took a deep breath. "I'm pretty sure Dad had an affair."

Wilcox's eyes widened just a little. "I see. Did you and your sister talk about that much?"

"A little. Both of us were tired of them fighting all the time." I swallowed and looked away. "It seemed like … like maybe things were getting better lately. Like … they weren't fighting quite as much. And … they were even nice to each other at the birthday party."

Wilcox made some notes in a small pocket-sized notebook. "Did Brenna get along well with your parents?"

I shrugged. "I guess. She fought sometimes with Mom. Especially about Chase. "

Wilcox tilted his head. "Why was that?"

"Cause … he's pretty old compared to her. He's like, twenty."

"Did those fights ever turn physical?"

I shook my head. "No. Of course not. It wasn't like that."

"And your dad?"

"What about him?"

"Did he fight with Brenna?"

"Not really. He and Mom argued a lot when he was home, but he's been traveling a lot the past couple of years. We don't see him that much."

"Oh, that's tough," Wilcox said in a quiet tone. "How do you feel about that?"

I shrugged. That was a stupid question.

Wilcox leaned close to me. "Listen, I know Detective Hunt has already asked you a lot of questions. And I have too. But if you think of anything, I want you to call me. I promise you, we'll do everything we can to find your sister." As he finished saying the words, he passed me a business card.

So weird. It really said, in all capital letters, FEDERAL BUREAU OF IN-VESTIGATION.

I needed to be alone. "Can I go now?"

Wilcox nodded, and I fled to my room.

Erin

After two years, the days immediately following Brenna's disappearance were a blur to me. My parents showed up in the early morning hours that Monday. I was awake ... we all were. None of us slept the first forty-eight hours. The press maintained their vigil outside, and her picture was spread on all of the networks and cable channels. Her case had all of the sensational elements that the media loves to sensationalize: a young, pretty white girl missing from an affluent family just outside the nation's capitol; the mystery of the crushed phone and abandoned car. The phone rang off the hook all day Monday, and Lori stationed herself next to the house phone to screen calls for us.

By Monday morning, the police presence was mostly gone from the house—the FBI, and both State and Fairfax County Police had moved their headquarters for the search to the FBI field office in Arlington.

It was late Tuesday afternoon when Lori called me to the phone. I'd slept briefly and fitfully the night before, and by this time I was running on empty. Cole was asleep, sprawled on the couch, exhaustion on his face.

"Erin? It's Agent Wilcox."

I flew to the phone, panic rising to my throat. "Agent Wilcox? Did you hear something?"

He sighed. "No, ma'am. Nothing yet. I was actually calling because you'll certainly hear on the news soon—Chase was released by the Fairfax County Police."

"What?" I cried. "Why?"

"At this point, we don't have any reason to suspect him. He voluntarily consented to searches of his apartment and his vehicle. His story checks out. We found nothing to indicate any involvement in hurting your daughter."

I wanted to scream. I wanted to throw something. I scrunched up my forehead, trying to push back the headache that was blooming behind my left temple.

Cole stirred and looked up at me. Concern spread on his face. "Erin?"

I couldn't speak. I gasped and felt tears run down my face for the five hundredth time that day. "They've let Chase go."

Cole's face went cold; his lips pressed together tightly, eyes narrowed. If I'd known then what he had already decided to do, would I have stopped him?

I honestly don't know.

Cole

I still don't know if I regret what happened next. Given the same information, given the same circumstances, I'd probably do the same thing, no matter how awful it was.

It was Wednesday morning. Brenna had been gone since Sunday, and Chase was free. I couldn't wrap my mind around either of those things.

"What can I do you for?" asked the man behind the counter in a thick Southern Virginia accent. He wore a camouflage cap emblazoned with a large logo: a red field with a white pistol on the left, American flag on the right, a cross in the center. The words embroidered beneath read: *Guns, God, and Glory.*

I walked up to the counter, looking through the glass at the pistols beneath. Revolvers. Automatics from Smith & Wesson, Colt, Glock. Two dozen or more were under the glass. Behind the man, rifles were mounted on the wall.

I hadn't fired a gun since shooting at cans with my cousin Lucas back when we were in high school. That'd been with his Dad's old M1911 Colt. I swallowed then said in as casual a tone as I could muster, "Looking for a pistol. A .45, I think."

The man nodded then opened up the back of the case and reached in. "Got a Colt model, it's used. And a Glock 17 here, perfect condition."

"Let me see the Colt?" I didn't care if it was new, long as it worked. And the Colt was more familiar.

He lifted the pistol out of the case and set it on the counter. Its blue metal housing and the wooden pistol grips were near enough identical to Uncle Bill's .45. I carefully picked up the weapon, removed the magazine and pulled the slide back, checking for a chambered round. Daddy taught me a million times to always assume a weapon was loaded until you verified otherwise.

Daddy, Lucas, Uncle Bill. The purveyors of violence from my childhood. Not that Daddy abused me or anything, but after all, his profession was to dispense violence—to kill people. It was something I never forgot. That contrasted vividly with Uncle Bill, whose drunken rages rained down chaos and violence on everyone around him. I struggled sometimes with the memories of that violence, the stink of the beer on his breath, the engorged blood in his face as he attacked his wife and son. I'd promised myself I wouldn't be like my family, and especially, I wouldn't be like *him*.

But this was different.

The weapon felt comfortable in my hand. It even smelled right. I lifted it to the back of the store, raising it to a firing grip with my left hand gripping the pistol, my right hand supporting the left.

"I'll take this one."

The man nodded. "That'll be four hundred. Got some paperwork to fill out," he said.

I started filling out the instant background check paperwork. Once completed, I slid it and my driver's license across the counter. Then I opened my wallet and counted out four one-hundred-dollar bills and laid them on the counter.

Twenty minutes later I was back in the car, headed to Route 7.

Chase lived in a crappy apartment complex on Leesburg Pike not far from Bailey's Crossroads, a mixed urban area bordering Arlington and Alexandria. That stretch of highway was lined with dirty apartments, run-down shopping centers, and partially-vacant strip malls. Perfect place for a sleazebag.

I drove past the townhouse once, scanning for movement. I didn't see anyone, nor did I see Chase's car, an early 1980s Plymouth, held together with Bondo and duct tape. Once again, rage filled me that the police had let him go.

I backed my car in across the parking lot from the townhouse, under the shade of a tree. I had no idea when, or even if, Chase was going to return. But he'd done something to Brenna, and I was going to find out what. I'd wait as long as it took.

61

I slumped down into my seat. The phone rang. *Damn it.* I took it out—it was Teagan. I shuddered. I didn't have time to talk with her right now. I didn't have time to talk with *her* ever again. I declined the call and continued waiting.

I tried to imagine what it must be like for cops on a stakeout. They must get exhausted. I was having trouble keeping my eyes open. But then again, I'd hardly slept in days.

The sound of a cracked muffler was unmistakable. I slumped down further into my seat. Would Chase recognize my car and just keep going? Maybe he'd run, and maybe he'd lead me all the way to Brenna.

The Plymouth came into view as Chase turned too fast into the parking space directly across from me. Even with my door and windows closed, I could hear the music pounding out of his car, some unrecognizable rap. I reached across to the passenger seat and gripped the pistol in my right hand.

Chase's car door opened. I opened mine at the same time. I slipped out as quietly as I could, then bolted across the parking lot. His back to me, he reached back into the car for something.

Without hesitation I reached out and slammed the door as hard as I could, catching his left leg below the knee. He crumpled, half in and half out of the car, and screamed, "Fuck!"

As he tried to whip around, I kicked him hard in the balls and he screamed again. While his mouth was open, I shoved the barrel of the pistol in it, grabbing his shirt in my left hand, and holding the pistol in the right.

He went instantly silent, his eyes growing wide. He started to speak and I shoved the pistol harder, causing him to gag. I could feel the trigger under my finger. I loosened my grip. If I killed him, he wouldn't be able to tell me anything.

"Where's my daughter?"

I pulled the pistol back a little, enough to let him talk. Tears ran down his face. "I don't know. Mr. Roberts, believe me, I don't know where she is."

"You fucking tell me!" I screamed.

He slid down slowly, his ass on the concrete, his back and head against the side of the car. I kept the gun aimed directly at his face.

"I don't know where she is, believe me, I don't!" His denial was a wail. Fucking coward. His eyes were rolling around, searching for help. There wasn't going to be any fucking help for him.

"Tell me, you fucking child molester! Where *IS SHE*?" I snarled.

"I don't know—" he shouted back, starting to try to lift himself up, one hand pressing against the concrete, and the other lifting against the inside frame of the car door.

"Liar!" I screamed. Pistol still in his face, I grabbed the car door with my left hand and slammed it.

He screamed, eyes bugging, face turning red. The door didn't close all the way. I pushed a foot against his arm, then jerked it back and slammed the door on his arm again, crushing bones. His screams turn high-pitched now, shrieking, and tears and snot ran down his face.

I leaned close, pushing the pistol against his temple. My vision had narrowed in; I couldn't see anything else but Chase and my rage.

"*Where. Is. She?*" I screamed.

In my peripheral vision I saw a car screech to a stop, blue lights flashing on its roof.

"Drop it! Police! Drop the weapon!"

"*Answer me!*" I screamed.

"I don't know!" Chase wailed.

I looked up. Blue lights. One police car. Two. A cop crouched behind one of the cars and shouted, "Drop the weapon!"

I raged at the injustice. *I didn't get an answer!* "Arrest him!" I cried out. "He kidnapped my daughter. He hurt her!"

The officer behind the car shouted, "Drop. The. Weapon. Now!"

I closed my eyes, crouched, and set the pistol down.

Then I stood, hands in the air.

One second later, massive hands slammed me to the ground, my face bouncing off the blacktop.

Six

~~~~~~

Erin

I stood at the window, one hand resting against the wall, and watched as the school bus carried Sam away. Cole had been at the restaurant for an hour already, and I had yet another endless day ahead of me. Would today be the day? Would I open my laptop, pick a city, look through the ads and discover my daughter? Would the police call and tell me they'd finally found her body? Would the phone ring, and it would be her on the other end?

Brenna's absence from our lives had left an open wound that refused to heal, a wound that was aggravated every holiday, every milestone, every day we didn't know what had happened to her. Sometimes I hated myself, because there were days when I almost hoped she were dead. At least then we would know. I'd gone through every possible scenario in my mind, from Brenna living it up somewhere happy, to ... well ... the worst.

What was the worst? All too real possibilities. Trafficked. Prostitution. Torture. Drugs. My mind could fill in all the possibilities, all the dangers, all the hideous and unimaginable (but not really *un*imaginable) things.

Maybe today. My eyes dropped to my laptop. The computer sat on the scarred coffee table, waiting for me to begin yet another day ... yet another day that would end with me weeping or vomiting or drinking just a little bit too much.

Not today.

I would search later. Today, I needed to get out of this house.

It's not that I hadn't searched for work before. I had. I'd applied for jobs at Fort McClellan, at the General Dynamics plant, at the car dealerships and a hundred doctors' offices, realtors and accountants. I'd reached out to Jim, Cole's

Dad, to see if he could connect me with someone at Fort McClellan for a job. But so far, I hadn't had any luck. I needed to get out, stop applying for jobs over the Internet, and start walking into places. If for no other reason than to pull myself a step or two out of this despair before I drank myself to death.

I showered, then took extra care putting on makeup and a conservative floral dress. On the way out the door I picked up the leather portfolio which contained copies of my resume. My resume, unfortunately, was sparse. My last full-time job had been with Alliance for Justice, a position I left in 1998, right before Sam was born. I had loved that job. But the economics just didn't work … the job didn't pay that well, and Cole's paid a lot more. When the kids were very young, it just made sense for me to stay home with them, and when they got to be teenagers, somehow I just never went back. I had stayed involved in some things, volunteer work along with involvement at the PTA at the kids' schools. But that was about it.

Unfortunately, that didn't cut it for experience in a depressed job market. Eventually something would come, but in the meantime, we were stuck living on Cole's salary from the restaurant … which wasn't enough.

I drove to the mall first. Most of the businesses in the mall were just opening up for the day or still had their gates down. On top of that, at least half a dozen of the stores in the mall were vacant. The economy here, like much of the rest of the country, was hurting.

For the next three hours, I systematically went from one store to the next, asking for applications and to talk with managers. For the people I spoke with, it was clear this was routine … a lot of people approached them every day looking for work. I didn't get any enthusiasm at all, but I did get applications. I carried them out to the car, got in, and left to drive to the nearby Starbucks. The Waffle House was actually closer, but I really didn't want to see Cole right now.

I hesitated.

Maybe it was time for a peace offering. Things had been so difficult between us for so long, I barely knew how to talk to him anymore. I felt like I didn't even know him half the time. It wasn't just Brenna's disappearance or the months he'd spent in jail right after. It wasn't even the affair, though that, more than anything else, had wrecked our marriage. We were already in bad shape long before he got involved with Teagan Campbell.

I honestly didn't know if I was ever going to forgive him. We went through a lot of therapy together, and I'd gone to plenty on my own. At least until Cole lost his job and our health insurance lapsed.

Waffle House had health insurance, but it was pretty minimal … and it certainly didn't cover therapy.

Okay, then. I would try. Instead of turning left, to go down to the Starbucks, I turned right. Two minutes later, I arrived at the brown shoebox-shaped restaurant with its towering yellow sign. I parked in front of the restaurant and sat in my seat for a moment looking in. Cole stood at the grill, wearing a ridiculous paper hat, his hands moving as he cooked an order.

Sometimes I forgot how big of a change he'd struggled through. Yes, I gave up my career. But he lost his against his will. And as much as he hated this job and was exhausted by it, he still got up and went to work every day. I was feeling more charitable toward him right now than I had in a long time. I grabbed my portfolio and headed inside.

The first thing I noticed walking in was that the air-conditioning had been fixed. For the last three weeks it hadn't been working at all, during the hottest part of the year. Cole's boss was really awful about taking care of maintenance things, even when he knew it was going to hurt traffic at the restaurant. Cole usually tried to stay loyal to the guy, because he'd given Cole a chance despite the felony conviction. While I agreed with that, gratitude only went so far. No one was going to stay and eat in a restaurant where the temperature was over a hundred degrees, and the sales hit would take a big chunk out of Cole's paycheck. And to be honest, Cole's boss hadn't had a lot of choice in giving Cole a chance—not when their senior vice president was Cole's best friend. If your boss's boss called you up and said, "Give this guy a chance," are you going to say no?

The inside of the restaurant had a vaguely 1970s decor: wood paneling, large globe lights, and orange vinyl seats. It always gave me a headache coming in this place.

Maybe more so today than normal. Cole didn't see me. He had his back to the front door as he was cooking. Next to him, standing a lot closer than I would like, was one of his waitresses. She looked like she was in her mid-twenties, with long brown hair. Even though the Waffle House uniforms were tacky and shapeless, she'd tied her apron tight to emphasize the curves at her waist and breasts. She was about an inch from my husband, leaning her head back and looking up at him as she talked. The smile on her face was already starting to piss me off.

"Look, Julie, I said no." *Oh,* I thought. That was Cole's annoyed voice. He continued, "It's a race weekend. Nobody takes off on race weekends. Not you, not me, not our division manager, not our vice president. We're all working that weekend."

Especially in that polyester uniform, the girl looked like a bouncy house—which was slowly deflated. I was happy to hear his annoyed tone of voice with her. She was a little too much like Teagan for my taste.

I slid onto a seat at the counter, just as one of the other waitresses called out, "Good morning!"

Simultaneously, Cole and one of the waitresses shouted, "Good morning!"

Well, that was rehearsed. The only one who didn't say it was the younger waitress who had been pushing her boobs too close to my husband—she flounced off in a huff. I hoped he'd fire her.

Cole completed the order he was working on just as one of the waitresses approached me to lay out silverware. Then he turned around, and there was no mistaking the genuine smile that passed across his face. The smile was followed by a puzzled expression.

"Erin! Hey … I wasn't expecting you to drop in."

"Would you prefer I didn't?"

His face clouded. "No … I'm glad you're here. We don't talk to each other enough anymore. What are you up to?"

Are you checking up on me? Was that what he was asking? Who knew. This was possibly the most conversation we'd had in weeks. At least it wasn't an argument. Yet. I held up my folio. "Job applications. I have some to fill out, and it was here or Starbucks."

One of the waitresses approached me. I guessed, based on the deep lines around her mouth, that she was in her late sixties. Her hair was dyed a rich auburn. "What can I get you, baby?"

"Just coffee."

Cole rested his hands on the counter. "Susan, let me introduce my wife. Erin, this is Susan. Everyone calls her Mama… She's worked here just about forever."

"Oh, it's so nice to meet you, baby!" the woman said. "I was beginning to wonder if Cole was making up his family."

"It's nice to meet you too, Susan. Do people really call you Mama?"

She grinned. "They do. I can't imagine why. Let me give you that coffee. You take cream, baby?"

That "baby" business was a little off-putting, even though I knew it was perfectly normal around here. I guess I spent too many years in the Washington, DC area instead of the Deep South. A moment later Susan came back with a cup of coffee. I declined the offer of food … I just needed to fill out my applications.

I spread them out in front of me, scanning through to see what would be involved. They were pretty simple applications. Of course, these were for hourly retail positions. But at this point I'd do whatever I had to do. I took out a pen and began to fill out the first one. I was halfway through when the door to the back room swung open, and the petite waitress who had been flirting with

Cole—there was no doubt in my mind that's what she was up to—came back out to the front. She checked in with her customers in one of the booths. When she was finished, and she began walking toward the counter, Susan stepped close to her.

"Julie," Susan said. "This is Erin. Cole's *wife*."

The girl's eyes darted to me. She gave an insincere smile. Then she spoke, her accent somewhere between Southern Alabama and trailer trash. "Nice to meet you, Mrs. Cole."

I did not bother to correct her. Instead, I just gave her the nastiest look I could muster. After the past few years, Cole was no prize ... but he was mine, and I wouldn't stand for another humiliation.

For the longest time, I thought the distance in our marriage happened because of the affair. I couldn't begin to describe the devastating punch in the gut it was to find out. I was betrayed. Not just hurt, but somehow gutted. Angry with Cole. I was angry with myself too ... for being clueless. There had been plenty of signs. Overnight trips where he'd been unexpectedly delayed for an extra six hours or twelve hours or two days. Lots of "dead zones" where his phone didn't work while on those trips. And those mostly at night. In retrospect, it didn't take a physics major to figure it out. It was a simple receipt which had forced me to face the truth. I'd picked up his suits at the laundry and the lady behind the counter handed me several small receipts, saying, "I didn't know if these were important." They were. A thousand-dollar charm bracelet purchased three months before, finally made it painfully obvious.

No, our distance started earlier than that by several years. I don't say that to excuse his behavior ... there was no excuse for it. What he did was unforgivable, and I still wasn't sure if I was ever going to be able to trust him again. But for the sake of the years we'd already had, and for the sake of our children, I made the decision fairly early on that I was going to at least give it a try.

If I had to pin down when the distance between us started, I would pin it on September 11, 2001. Crazy, isn't it? The idea that a day which traumatized virtually everyone in America also caused a bizarre cleavage in my own marriage. It didn't start with betrayal or lies or selfishness or money or any of the things that often trip up couples. We had plenty of money, and that was never something that was a problem between us.

What became a problem between us was *politics*.

Crazy, right? Who wrecks their marriage over politics? One of the reasons we'd been attracted to each other in the first place was our differences there. He was conservative; I was liberal. He voted for Bob Dole and George Bush; I voted for Bill Clinton and Al Gore. And that was fine. Occasionally we'd argue

… there were genuine philosophical differences there, especially when it came to social services and things like that. But they were arguments between equals; they were respectful disagreements.

But things changed after September 11.

It was the week of Brenna's fifth birthday. Sam was only three. We hadn't yet bought the mausoleum, and I was at the park with Sam. Sam and a little girl named Megan were playing house underneath the climbing structure at the playground. I was sitting with Lily, the little girl's nanny. Lily was twenty-five and in graduate school. I was twenty-seven and sometimes felt like I was doing nothing at all, even as I struggled, stressed out with the kids.

I felt like the loser in the social wars in Washington. The women I met were always on temporary maternity leave from their six-figure jobs, or in graduate school, or working on Capitol Hill, or some other achievement, and there was a constant air of subtle one-upmanship taking place on the playgrounds near DC.

My best friend and roommate from college, Angela, left Alliance for Justice before I did—not for a pregnancy, but to become senior aide to Congressman Ted Strickland. Angela always knew she was going somewhere. Valedictorian of her class—she was from Woodville, Ohio, a small town in Sandusky County, facts I knew because she relayed them to me within five minutes of our meeting on our first day at Georgetown. "Population two thousand. We export limestone, Republicans, and alcoholics," she would quip when asked about her hometown. Angela was taller than me, almost five feet ten, which often seemed to intimidate guys when we were out clubbing, especially if she wore heels. She usually wore her light brown hair tied in the back and kept her glasses on all the time. By the time September 11 rolled around, she was a full-time foreign policy wonk and was working on her PhD.

When I told people I was a stay-at-home mother, the men gave me curious looks—sometimes envious of Cole, I think—and the women looked contemptuous. But that was a decision we'd made together, because we both felt that someone should be home with the kids instead of putting them into daycare.

Besides, with what I made at the Alliance for Justice? Day care cost more than my salary anyway.

All the same, I missed the job.

The morning of September 11, I'd been at the playground for about thirty minutes. Brenna was in school, her third week of kindergarten. Cole was in New York City for a meeting. I didn't know it at the time, but his meeting was in the South Tower of the World Trade Center. I knew he was in that part of town, so I was understandably panicked when Lily's cell phone started to ring with text messages, and she looked up after reading one and said, "Oh my God, isn't your husband in New York? Somebody flew a plane into the World Trade Center."

It took me several seconds to process the terrible words she had said. The panic paralyzed me, squeezing my throat shut and blacking my vision. Then I reached for my own phone, a brand new Nokia which Cole had bought me two weeks earlier.

It didn't ring. Just silence for a moment, then the message: all circuits are busy.

I had stood up, marched over to Sam and snatched him up. "Time to go, Sam."

Sam waved his little arms and legs, and wailed, "No wanna go! Mama! No wanna go!"

I just ignored him, carrying him on my hip as he wailed.

I got in the car and dialed the radio to WTOP, the all-news station. I was halfway home when they announced that a second plane had hit the South Tower. Sam was still crying in the back seat. I still couldn't get through on the phone, and I started crying too. I turned the car around and drove through snarled traffic to Brenna's school. It felt like the world was ending. I parked at the school at nine thirty in the morning and went in to check Brenna out.

By the time I got back to the car with both kids, a plane had hit the Pentagon.

I still didn't know what had happened to Cole. I waited at home watching the news, unable to tear myself away, calling him every few minutes. It was well after one in the afternoon before he finally got a text message through to me.

Am alive and unhurt. Can't call out. I'll try to reach you when I get back to the hotel.

Even though our kids were still very young then, I mark that day as the beginning of the end of our marriage. September 11 seemed to refine and crystalize people in our country when it came to political issues. Lukewarm positions became hardened, and attitudes which were below the surface came out in a rage.

For a few days or even weeks, it seemed like most of America was united. The night of the attacks, I took Sam and Brenna in town to meet up with Angela. The moment I saw her, I fell into her arms, crying. With thousands of other people, we held a candlelit vigil. I remember seeing the huge clouds of smoke rising from the Pentagon, and the armed soldiers with machine guns parked conspicuously at street corners throughout the city. Every once in a while we could hear the screech of fighter jets flying combat air patrol over the city.

That unity did not last. Rumors that the administration wanted to invade Iraq began to circulate in Washington. By September 2002, one year after the attacks, it was clear that that was the direction. And that was when Cole and I had our first huge political fight. Angela left Representative Strickland's office to work for a large coalition of anti-war organizations being put together by Andrew Thomas, a former US Congressman from Maine. Thomas had hired Angela, who called me and asked if I wanted to come to work with them as deputy policy director.

I was thrilled. By that time Brenna was in the first grade, and it wasn't too late to register Sam for pre-K. Cole had just gotten another big promotion. He was now the director of IT. Which had pushed his salary well into the six figures for the first time. That night I sat down with him and told him about the job.

At first, it seemed like he was going to be supportive. I told him about the of-fer and said that Angela had contacted me about it. He smiled and looked happy for me, and said, "I bet you'll be happy to go back to work. Don't think I don't know how much you've sacrificed for the kids, Erin. So what will you be doing?"

His comment about appreciating my sacrifice felt good. And that's why what happened next was such a slap in the face.

"I'd be working as an organizer for an organization called MoveOn. They're an activist organization … coordinating the Win Without War coalition."

He looked puzzled. "The *what* coalition?"

"It's a coalition of organizations that are trying to prevent an invasion of Iraq."

His face twisted into a disgusted expression. "What the hell for? We need to take out that bastard!"

"Cole, you're talking about going to war against a country with no provo-cation."

His expression and tone of voice were near contemptuous. "Are you *fucking* kidding me? September 11 wasn't enough provocation for you? Don't you know how close I came to dying that day?"

I closed my eyes and took a breath. Of course I knew. Of course I did.

I needed to remember that my husband had been traumatized by the events that day, just like millions of other people.

Quietly, I said, "Cole … Iraq had nothing to do with September 11."

"And you know this because—why? You've got better intelligence sources than the CIA? Are your own inspectors more effective than the United Nations?"

His sarcasm made me wince. I never liked fighting with Cole, because fights invariably led to him talking that way. Yet another thing Dr. Lee later stressed in our therapy was learning how to fight fair. Back then, neither of us had a clue about that. Cole's primary weapon was sarcasm—and sometimes an intimidat-ing rage. Mine was manipulation. We were quite the pair.

71

"Cole, in case you've forgotten, I follow international news a hell of a lot closer than you do. And it's not just me saying it … it's basically every expert in the field. Hon, the president wants to go to war there. And they're making up excuses to do it."

In a biting tone, he said, "Yeah, Erin. You never let me forget that you've got that Georgetown degree and I've just got a high school diploma. You're *always* better informed than me about this kind of thing. But I'll tell you what … this is bullshit. I know enough to know that it was Muslim terrorists who attacked our country and killed a ton of people, *including* some of my *friends*. I know enough to know that my dad was a Marine. You're *not* going to work for some left-wing *traitors*."

Asshole.

"I don't have to ask your permission, Cole. Don't act like *your father*. This is the twenty-first century."

Looking back, I wonder if it would have been better for me to just stick to my guns. If I'd gone to work for Win Without War, and let the chips fall where they may. We'd have fought like hell. I don't even know if our marriage would have survived it.

I didn't do that. Instead, I gave in. I didn't take the job.

Instead, I became resentful.

In some ways, our own little war was taking place, but it was taking place underground, not that different from the way I had seen Cole's parents behave. And I hated it that we looked and acted like them sometimes. Because his mother was a shrew, a manipulative bitch, and his father was a nightmare right out of Jim Crow. I didn't want to be like them.

The argument never really ended. Angela continued to work for Win Without War, and of course I talked about her—she was my best friend and had been since college. We had lunch once a week, went out for drinks in the evening a couple of times a month, and I talked about everything with her.

Cole hated her. Angela returned the favor. Even Lori joined in on the Cole-hating act … she never really stopped, which sometimes made me feel even more isolated, because when I needed someone to talk to about problems with my husband, I needed someone who wasn't pushing their own agenda, who could just listen and nod and not try to push me to do whatever it was they saw would fix it.

Then, in 2006, Cole got another promotion, to vice president. On the one hand it was great—his base pay had more than tripled; he was bringing home almost four hundred-thousand a year, with stock options on top of that. On almost every level it seemed like we were successful, especially after we bought that massive house.

I *hated* that house.

Not when we bought it. Not that early. In fact, I was the one who picked it out. Cole gave me a price range and then went off to travel to San Francisco or San Juan or Oklahoma City or I don't know where else. That year it seemed like he was traveling all the time. When I first saw the house, I loved it. It was ridiculously large, with a whole entertainment suite and guest bedrooms, with more bathrooms in it than we had people. But the view out the back window was stunning, and it was in district for the best school system in the state. The house was so big you could get lost in it for days. I didn't know where my children were half the time. From my bedroom I couldn't even hear the front door open and close, and not long after we moved in, that started to bring on anxiety. With Cole gone all the time, I finally insisted on installing an alarm system.

We fought. Sometimes they were cold and quiet fights. Sometimes our fights were waged across the battlefield of our bed, when I would refuse to have sex with him because he refused to give in on something that mattered to me. After a while, we just sort of stopped. We stopped having sex ... we stopped touching one another.

We stopped *loving* each other.

It was only after all of that happened that he met Teagan.

Teagan Campbell was a new technology sales associate at Cole's company. I had no idea what that job entailed, other than selling things, looking pretty, and working closely with the IT department. The first time I met her was at the company Christmas party in December 2010. Cole and I were standing near the bar, waiting for our drinks to be mixed, when I heard him say, "Oh, Teagan. Let me introduce my wife. Erin, this is Teagan Campbell, one of the new technology sales associates."

As he finished his sentence, the bartender signaled that our drinks were ready and Cole turned away for a second. "It's nice to meet you," I said while I assessed her.

She was petite, maybe five feet two. She wore a red silk blouse with matching lipstick, and a green skirt that was inappropriately short for any kind of business function. The skirt revealed long shapely legs, propped up by three-inch heels. She had brown eyes and dark brown hair, and a too-large nose. Her clothes looked a size too small, showing off a waist that demonstrated half-starvation underneath augmented breasts. At first glance, I thought she was twenty years old and an intern.

From the second I saw her, I didn't like the way she looked at my husband.

She began to blather on. "It's nice to meet you too, Mrs. Roberts. Cole talks a lot about you."

That's funny. He's never said a word about you.

"Is that so? Have you worked here very long?"

She shook her head. "Just a few weeks."

Colt handed me my drink, and I decided to cut this short. "Well, it was nice to meet you. Look, Cole, it's Joe. I haven't seen him in a long time, let's go talk to him."

I didn't wait for an answer, just started walking.

Cole caught up with me a second later, slipping a hand under my arm, and saying in a conversational tone, "That was a little abrupt, don't you think?"

"I don't know, Cole. Her clothes were so tight I was afraid they might bust open, and I didn't want to be standing there when that happened."

He chuckled. "It *is* a bit much."

"A bit much is the opposite of what I'd say. How come you never mentioned her?"

"Because I knew you'd be weird about it. Besides, other than a few meetings now and then, we don't really have much to do with each other. Nothing to tell."

Nothing to tell. *Asshole.*

The thought of Teagan made me look up from my job applications. Cole was back at the grill cooking. Susan (*Mama?*) was at the far end of the restaurant taking someone's order. The short waitress—Julie—was missing again. Probably primping in the mirror in the back.

I closed my eyes. I didn't know anything about that girl.

All I knew was that it was Cole who hadn't been honest with me. It was Cole I still couldn't forgive. And maybe wouldn't ever.

Seven

~~~~~~

Sam

"**S**o how come your family moved to Oxford anyway?"

Hayley whispered the words, because we were sitting in the library together. We'd walked over after school, telling our parents we'd be studying together. We might even do some of that. But mostly it was just so we could hang out.

Mom was picking us up at five. *If she was sober.*

I didn't say that to Hayley.

Should I tell her the whole story? Might as well, I thought. A quick Google search would turn up our family history. "My sister was kidnapped two years ago, and Dad beat up her boyfriend, because Dad thought he had done something to her. Really bad. He went to jail for a while."

Hayley's eyes widened and her mouth opened. After she recomposed herself, she said, "Did she ... did they find her?"

I shook my head. I couldn't express the emotions I felt. "No. It's been ... well, she'll be eighteen next week. So two years."

Hayley leaned forward and took my hand. "I'm so sorry. That must make you really sad."

I shrugged. *Really sad* didn't express much of anything. *Dead inside* might come closer. "It's hard for me to talk about it. I really loved her. She wasn't just my big sister, she was my best friend."

Hayley wasn't finished asking questions. "So your dad went to jail for beating up her boyfriend? He must've really done the guy in."

"Yeah," I whispered. "I think Chase was in the hospital for a while. I don't know for sure, but I know Dad was convicted of assault with a deadly weapon. He went to prison for six months. The judge said it would've been longer, but there were extenuating circumstances. Because Dad thought Chase was the one who … whatever happened to Brenna."

Hayley sank down into her seat, a lock of red curls hanging down over her eyes. "Do you think her boyfriend did it?"

"I don't know. They never found her … they never proved anything with anybody. Dad got fired from his job while he was in prison and they couldn't afford the house anymore. We stayed until the house got foreclosed on, and the cops showed up and threw us out. Eventually we ended up here."

I thought for a minute. Not of Brenna or my family's history, but of the Ashleys and Jake Fennells and Codys of the world. Then I said, "Don't tell anybody. I mean they could find out but … I just don't need any hassle from the popular kids."

Hayley leaned forward, her eyes wide. "I'd never tell anyone anything. I swear to God." As she said the last words, she made the sign of the cross over her shoulders.

That exposed yet another set of bruises on her forearm. I'd seen them earlier that day in class but hadn't said anything at the time. Now I had to. "What happened to your arm?"

She scrunched her eyes together. "What are you talking about?"

As gently as I could, I touched her forearm with the tip of my index finger. "That's what I'm talking about. Those are new ones … the last set of bruises were just starting to heal. Hayley, who did that?"

Her expression was painful to see. "No one did it. I'm just a klutz." She said the words so quietly that it was clear she'd lost any confidence in her own lies. She whispered, "No one hurt me. Stop asking me." Her eyes were wet.

"I can keep a secret too, you know. But I won't bother you about it again."

She closed her eyes, and whispered, "Thank you."

"Can I tell you something?"

She nodded in response to my question.

"You're the best friend I've had since my sister disappeared," I said.

Her skin flushed almost as red as her hair, and her eyes darted away from me. I wish I could tell her the truth about me. But I still didn't know her well enough for that. I didn't know if I ever would. I mean … this was *Alabama*.

Sometimes, I tried to picture how people would react if I were to suddenly start wearing women's clothing. Dad would be disgusted. I'd never forget, years ago, when he talked about how transgender people were mentally ill. Mom?

Who knew? She'd probably just drink a little more to wash it away. Grandpa would probably suggest that I be forced to join the Marines to turn me into a man, and Grandma would turn up her imperious nose and look way down at me. I didn't even think about what people from school would be like.

Don't be ashamed of who you are, Brenna had told me once. *You're beautiful, inside and out. One day the whole world will see it just like I do.*

Well, the world hadn't seen me that way yet.

I missed her. I wished I could talk with her about Hayley. The bruises worried me. Was it her father? I bet it was. She didn't have any siblings; it was just her and her dad, and she hadn't lived with him very long.

"I used to have a best friend in Birmingham," she said. "We still talk on the phone all the time, and online. But I won't get to go back there any time soon."

I swallowed. "So how come you ended up here?"

Hayley sniffed. "Mom's ... she got hurt last year. Hurt her back, and they gave her oxy, and ... she got addicted. She—"

Hayley cut herself off, looked as if she couldn't decide what to do, then she continued. "She overdosed on heroin about three months ago. She's in a halfway house now, but the Department of Children and Families took me. They put me in an emergency shelter for a few days, then Dad came and got me."

"Do you like living with him?"

She shook her head once. With finality in her tone, she said, "No."

I swallowed. I wanted to say, *you gotta tell somebody. You gotta ask for help. What if he hurts you for real?*

I was afraid if I pushed it, she'd walk away. So I didn't say any of those things. Instead, I just listened. And a couple minutes later, she broke down.

Her words were barely audible. "He did it. Daddy. He's got a temper."

I let a slow breath out.

"It's not really his fault," she continued. "I was being sassy. And ... and ... he didn't mean to hurt me. Not really. He just grabbed my wrist."

I nodded. Then I said, "You can talk to me anytime, you know."

I was being sassy. No. I wasn't willing to accept the idea that it was *her* fault her father had hurt her. That wasn't right, no matter what she did. It brought back memories of vaguely heard discussions about my great uncle Bill. Things said behind closed doors, and now I couldn't untangle that.

"Thanks," she whispered.

"Just ... if it gets bad ... call someone? Tell someone? What if he really hurts you?"

She shakes her head. "He won't. He loves me."

I closed my eyes but didn't say anything. I couldn't. I was thinking about men, and rage, and what rage can do to them. I was thinking about Dad, and how he totally fucked up Chase, and ended up doing prison time.

By the time that happened, we were all falling apart. Dad had gone out, and we didn't know where he was. Then the knock on the door, and it was Detective Hunt and Agent Wilcox again, and this time the news they had was just one more piece of hideous, awful news. Dad had assaulted Chase Morton and was in jail. He might be arraigned tomorrow, he might not.

You couldn't really blame Mom for just falling apart. I mean … I understood why Dad did what he did. I completely understood why. But in doing that, he vanished right at the moment when Mom needed him the most. Our lives were already falling to pieces, and he wasn't there to help us put them back together.

Those first days after Brenna disappeared, the atmosphere was frantic. The police interviewed everyone we knew at school, friends, family. They searched Brenna's room twice. The entire time they were searching, I sat in my room shaking, wondering if mine was next. Thankfully that never happened.

I finally returned to school on the Thursday after Brenna disappeared. It was surreal that morning. Dad hadn't been arraigned yet, so he was still in jail. I was used to early mornings when he would be bustling around getting ready for work, and Mom would be trying to get Brenna and me to eat breakfast before school. But he was gone, and she was asleep, and my grandparents had gone back home. It seemed like the house was haunted, as I shuffled around completely alone in the quiet getting ready for school. I almost woke Mom up before I left. I stood there at her door with my hand raised to knock, but then I decided against it. She needed to rest. I left a note on the kitchen table that I had taken the bus to school, then I left the house and walked to the bus stop.

Looking at Hayley now, that was one of the reasons why I was so reluctant to open up at all. From the morning I left for school that Thursday two years ago right up until school started this year, I'd been completely alone. The only time I ever felt needed or engaged in life was when I was online.

Hayley threatened to break that isolation, and I couldn't decide if that was something I wanted or was terrified of.

Cole

On Thursday morning at 9 a.m., I walked into the Calhoun County Courthouse, a large red brick neoclassical structure with white arches at the entrances.

After I cleared security, I walked to the parole office, my shoes echoing off the marble floor. The waiting room had an institutional feel, with none-too-clean tile floors, and a window of thick, almost blue glass, behind which sat the receptionist.

After I signed in, the sour-faced receptionist told me to take a seat until I was called. I sat down in one of the hard plastic chairs. Experience had taught me that it might be a long wait; my monthly visits with the parole officer typically took up an entire morning.

Ironic that I found myself here. Growing up, half my cousins had been in and out of jail. I'd sworn to myself a million times that I wouldn't be like them, that I wouldn't be the kind of white trash that Daddy came from. I kept that promise to myself, worked my way up the corporate ladder, bought a spectacular house in the suburbs of Washington, DC, and yet, except for Lucas, I was the only one of the cousins who ended up as a felon.

After I was arrested, it took four days before I was finally arraigned. I'll never forget the arraignment hearing. The county prosecutor described me in terms I couldn't imagine. He said it was a vicious and unprovoked attack, and that I represented a danger to anyone I thought might have had anything to do with my daughter. *Vicious and unprovoked.* I felt—righteous. I was trying to protect my daughter. I was a fool.

My lawyer fought hard to get bail set, but the last straw was when the arresting officers testified that I had threatened repeatedly to kill Chase. It was true, I had, though it was in the passion of the moment. As a result of that, the judge denied bail. I was to stay in the Fairfax County jail until I went to trial.

I had to hand it to Brent, my lawyer: he was good. Before I had even been shuttled back from the courthouse to the jail, he'd already lodged an appeal with the state court of appeals. The next morning's Washington Post carried the front page headline, *"Father of Missing Girl Denied Bail for Assault."* Apparently it was a slow news day, and Brent was pretty good with the media—by lunchtime the cable networks had gone insane. The talking heads on the cable networks, and the public, seemed to be on my side. It took longer than expected, but far faster than it would have, had I not had access to those resources. Two weeks after my arrest, I was released on bail.

I was grateful to be out. But I'd never forget the disappointment and anger on Erin and Sam's faces when I was home. They'd needed me terribly, and I'd failed them.

Brent spent the next two months maneuvering but with little luck. I was scheduled to go to trial on December 11. The week before that, Brent came over to the house and pulled Erin and me into my office. His face had been grim.

"Cole," he said. "I've done everything I could. The prosecutor's got a hard-on … excuse me, Mrs. Roberts. He's very aggressive, with all his public statements about vigilante justice. The bottom line is, you're not going to be able to avoid going to trial on Monday."

Erin began to cry silently. I'd already been placed on a leave of absence from work; a conviction would surely mean that I'd be fired. I had a golden parachute in my contract, but one of the clauses in that contract said that I lost the parachute if I was terminated due to a felony conviction. And that's where it looked like we were heading.

"What are my odds?"

"Well, you have the jury on your side to an extent. Except that you fucked up that Morton kid pretty good. He'll probably never regain the full use of his hand. The guidelines for assault with a deadly weapon is eight to fifteen years. You'll probably end up at the lower end of that scale, meaning you'll be eligible for parole in three or four years."

I gasped. *Three or four years?* How was that possible? How could I possibly do three or four years in prison?

My next words came out in a rasp. "What are my options?"

Brent shrugged. "We can offer to plea bargain to a lesser charge. You'll still almost certainly get a felony conviction, but we might be able to get them down to vanilla assault. With luck you'll be out within a year. That's really the best-case … if you go before a jury and they wheel Chase Morton into the court-room, you don't stand a chance."

I rested my head in my hands. Even the best-case scenario … we'd lose the house. I'd racked up twenty thousand in legal fees already. We had the mortgage on a two-million-dollar home, three car payments, student loans … we couldn't survive without a sizable salary.

We couldn't leave the house with Brenna missing. *What if she came home and we weren't there anymore?*

Without a word, Erin stood up and walked out. I felt like I'd been punched. But who could blame her? Who could blame her?

In the end, I took Brent's advice and pled guilty to simple assault. I was sentenced to three years, with two-and-a-half of those years suspended. I actually served six months and five days in the Deep Meadow Correctional Center just outside Richmond.

Looking back, sometimes I wish I *had* killed Chase. That might've at least made it worthwhile. As it was, I had wrecked what was left of my family's life for no purpose at all.

I almost hadn't been able to take the job in Alabama, which would've been a real tragedy considering that I interviewed more than a hundred times for different positions after I got out of prison. After Jeremiah got me the interview with Brian, I jumped at the chance, even though I knew that my salary in this job wouldn't be much more than ten percent of what I'd been making before. At least it was enough to buy food and pay rent for a crappy little house in Oxford. Offer in hand, I'd gone to the court and requested permission to transfer my probation to Alabama. Miraculously, it was approved.

So here I was. Waiting to see my probation officer for our monthly visits.

At eleven a.m. I was finally called in to see her. Sergeant Joyce Friendly had once been an Atlanta cop and had readily told me her story when I asked during our first meeting several months before. During a routine traffic stop in South Atlanta five years before, she'd been shot in the face and left for dead. She'd been medically retired from the police department, but after years of therapy and healing, she went looking for work. She finally found a spot with the Alabama Department of Corrections.

When I knocked on the door to her office, she waved me in. She was a physically formidable woman, probably somewhere around one hundred and ninety pounds of mostly muscle. She wore a grey uniform and smiled when I walked in.

She spoke in a thick accent that reminded me of Dad's relatives in the mountains of Georgia. "Cole Roberts. Have a seat, tell me how things are going for you."

I took the proffered seat. "The job's going well," I said. That didn't really answer her question, but I had no plans of getting into discussions about the state of my marriage.

"That's good to hear. Your son's getting settled in school okay?"

I nodded. "You know how it is … moving is a big change. Especially from a big city to … here."

She nodded, eyes wide. "Oh, I know it is. I gotta ask you the routine questions. Have you been out of state?"

I shook my head. "No, but I'm going to ask for clearance to go to Atlanta in the next couple of weeks."

"What takes you there?"

"My parents live there, and it's time we visited."

She nodded. "I don't see that that's a problem. Just make sure you notify me if and when you're going to go. Are you drinking?"

I shook my head. "Not much. A beer sometimes when I get home from work." I didn't say, *Erin does enough drinking for the both of us.*

She nodded. Her face turned serious, and she said, "Have you had any news about your daughter?"

I shook my head. We talked briefly about Brenna during my first meeting with her. Sgt. Friendly had been surprisingly sympathetic. In response to my gesture, she frowned.

"I'm so sorry to hear that, Cole."

I didn't answer. There wasn't really anything to say.

She leaned back in her seat then shuffled in her desk drawer for a moment, pulling out a sheet of paper. "Well, then, that's all I have for this month. I'll need you to take this paperwork to one of the labs listed on the back, it's time for a drug test."

I nodded. I'd been through that routine twice already since we moved to Alabama. I took the papers.

As I stood, she leaned forward and spoke again. "If you do hear anything, whether it's tomorrow or next year, you let me know. I've got a daughter too. I'll do whatever I can to help."

I let out my breath in an exhalation that seemed to deflate my entire body.

Eight: Birthday

Cole

I was in the middle of the church rush when my boss walked in.

Brian Ingram had been with the company for six years. A retired Army Lieutenant Colonel, he was now our division manager, responsible for nine restaurants spread across eastern Alabama from the Georgia border almost to Birmingham.

He'd taken a big chance on me.

When I first interviewed for the job, I'd been desperate. More than a year of job interviews after I got out of jail, and not a single bite. Even under the circumstances of Brenna's disappearance, my status as a convicted felon was a roadblock too hard to overcome for any of the companies I'd interviewed with. We'd completely run out of cash, and the house was in foreclosure. I wasn't even eligible for unemployment, because I'd been fired while in jail, and every company I had talked to declined a second interview.

That's the state I was in when I got a call from Jeremiah. While I'd worked a seemingly glamorous high-tech career at a company that was now nonexistent, he'd taken a decidedly non-technical job, as unit manager for a restaurant. I'd hassled him about it at the time, but he'd risen quickly through the ranks.

"Like it or not, there's a good ol' boy network. At Waffle House, that's the Georgia Tech alumni." When Jeremiah had said that to me years ago, I'd shaken my head. How could he choose that when he had so many other options? But Jeremiah had his own pressures. And that had turned out to be my saving grace after I got out of jail.

winter flower

When he called me to suggest I interview for a job here, I jumped at the chance. Jeremiah set up the interview with Brian, and I was blunt about the conviction, and why it happened. He was blunt at the time: company policy said no convicted felons. But both of them went to bat with the company security department to make an exception in my case.

We'd have ended up homeless if it hadn't been for that. Sometimes you have to be grateful for whatever you can get.

When Brian walked into the restaurant, it was obvious I was in the weeds. Plates were lined up on the sandwich board, the restaurant was full, and all three of my waitresses were calling orders faster than I could get them marked. Brian immediately came out on the floor, washed his hands and put on gloves, and took a position on the grill next to me.

"Morning, Cole," he said, a grin on his face. "Busy?"

"Yeah, it's been nuts the last little while."

"Well, that's a good thing," he replied.

We worked through the rush, and I was grateful for the help. I hadn't been in this business long, and I'd had my own restaurant just a few weeks. I didn't have the skill or experience to keep up with this kind of rush.

Waffle House wasn't the kind of job where managers sat in the back office doing paperwork and watching other people work. As a manager, my job was to be on the grill seven hours a day, six days a week. Paperwork, keeping the restaurant supplied and staffed, scheduling, orders—everything else happened outside of production hours. My usual day started at six a.m. and ended at four or five p.m., and I came back to the restaurant three nights a week, sometimes for hours. I'd been riding on the edge of continual exhaustion ever since I started training, and it didn't look to be getting better any time soon.

The lunch rush ended, though. I cleared the grill area then walked up the line, checking in with customers. Finally, I ducked into the back room. Brian was in my office, looking at the computer. I grabbed the bottle of water off my tiny desk and gulped back a drink.

"You're getting better," he said. He slid off the stool and stepped into the doorway. I traded places, sagging onto my desk.

"Thanks," I said, almost gasping.

"Still, going forward, you need to schedule a second cook on the weekends. Sunday morning's no time to be working alone. Especially on a race weekend."

I nod. "Yeah, I had Jimmy on the schedule to come in at nine and work a double. He was going to back me up, then work second shift," I said. "He called in around 8:55, and by then I was so busy I couldn't get on the phone."

Brian chuckles. "You can take a minute to let me know. That's not just to save your ass. It's so our customers don't get stuck having to wait too long."

I sank onto my stool. They'd start calling orders again any second. I was exhausted, it was only noon, and I didn't have a second shift cook.

"Who you got coming in for second shift?"

I shook my head. "Nobody. I'll start calling."

"You know, you can always work it yourself. Save you some payroll."

I swallowed. True enough. It would be my second double shift in two days: this was a race weekend at Talladega, and our business was way up. Plus, today of all days, I did *not* want to go home.

It was September 15.

Today was Brenna's eighteenth birthday.

"Yeah," I said. "That's a good idea."

I looked through the one-way glass to the restaurant. Everyone was eating except one table, three men. They were regulars, each of them around fifty to sixty years old, and they always sat in Julie's section. She was over there, taking the men's order. You could practically see the old farts salivating.

"So it's been a few weeks since you got your own restaurant. How you holding up?"

I kept my gaze on the restaurant on the other side of the glass. What I wanted to say was, *This is the worst job I've ever had in my life.* I was exhausted, pushed harder than I could really take. But this was the bed I'd made. "It's going well," I said. "I'm not fast enough yet. At anything."

He nodded. "Yeah, that's the way it is. You'll get there, it just takes time and lots of practice. It's a marathon, not a sprint. And this is a big change for you."

I shrugged. "Don't get me wrong, Brian. I'm grateful for the job. When I finally get it down, I'll be the best manager you have. It's just taking some time."

He grins. "I like that. You should be gunning for my job."

"In the long run," I said. Not the least being because he wasn't working a grill forty hours a week. At my level and the one higher, all you did was work to the bone. But if you survived long enough to get a division, the job was very different.

Today I didn't mind staying busy. Today I *needed* to stay busy. I needed it so I wouldn't think about where my daughter was. If I thought about it, I might break down. Again.

I wondered how Erin was doing today. How she dealt with it? Would she sit at home and drink and dredge through all those awful ads? Or would she be keeping busy too? At least Sam had school to keep him busy.

But I knew it wasn't enough.

Julie was heading to the back room.

"Looks like I got an order," I said, slipping off the stool.

"All right," Brian said. "Keep up the good work."

I returned to work.

Sam

On Brenna's birthday, I shut myself in my room and shut out the world. I couldn't do anything else. I'd been online for hours when the incoming chat message popped up on my screen without warning.

Gemini: **I heard you got into a fight with the mayor the other night.**

I replied: **Yeah. It turned out to be pointless. The girl we were trying to help ended up joining his faction.**

Gemini: **That happens. You ought to know that by now.**

I did. Gemini had been one of the first people I met in the sim and had occasionally acted almost as a mentor, even though she wasn't a member of any of the factions. Sometimes she creeped me out, though. She mostly sat at the bar and schemed, only rarely seemed to get out and role-play. I envisioned her almost like a spider, sitting there pulling strings here and there. I was well aware that in her world, I was at the end of one of the strings. But she'd also been a useful source of information. You had to give some to get some.

I wasn't currently on the sim; instead, I was shopping for a new dress and hairstyle. My avatar didn't have a lot of clothing suitable for dates, and tonight I had one coming. The date was *in character* … we would play it out in the sim. That was fine. Everything *had* to be completely in character. It would never be otherwise, because in this world I was Tamara, and to them, that's all I'd ever be.

I was looking at two dresses, one black and one red, trying to decide between them, when Gemini messaged me again.

Gemini: **You didn't answer.**

I sighed. Finally I typed, **I've got a lot on my mind right now. RL stuff.** RL, of course, meant real life.

Gemini: **Want to talk about it?**

I swallowed. There was some safety in the anonymity of being online. And I did want to talk about it. I don't know why, but I hadn't told Mrs. Mullins or Hayley that it was Brenna's birthday. Finally I responded: **It's my sister's birthday. She turns eighteen today.**

Gemini: **And this is a problem because…**

Tamara: **She went missing two years ago, and we haven't seen her since.**

86

Gemini: **Holy crap. I'm so sorry. I wouldn't have asked if I'd realized.**

Tamara: **It's okay. Maybe I need to talk about it. We were really close. Brenna's the only person who treated me like I needed.**

Gemini: **What do you mean?**

I closed my eyes. No one in the world knew. Nobody.

Except Brenna. *She* knew. I wanted to be able to talk about it. But … it's not like this was the *real* world.

I sighed. Then I typed: **Can you keep a secret?**

Gemini: **Of course.**

Well. I might as well. I type: **I'm physically male. But not inside. Inside, I'm a girl. I always have been.**

I picked the black dress, right-clicked on it. The price was $385L, or a little bit more than a dollar in real money. I bought it. Now for some matching shoes. New hairstyle? Yes.

The lack of reply from Gemini was starting to scare me. Had I just made a huge mistake? We'd been talking a lot, but what did I really know about her? But finally she responded. **I didn't realize that. You're transgender?**

Tamara: **I've never put a word on it. Not like that. Gay or transgender or … I'm just … I'm a girl. It's who I am.**

Gemini: **And your sister was the only person in RL who knew?**

Tamara: **Knows. She knows. She's not dead, just … missing.**

Gemini: **Sorry. I'm very sorry. All of that must be difficult for you.**

Tamara: **Sometimes there are good days.**

Gemini: **But you said today is her birthday. I'm guessing this isn't one of the good ones.**

I sighed. It was nice to have someone get it. I typed: **Yeah. It's not. I miss her.**

Then a realization hit me. I'd told her Brenna's name, and that she'd been missing two years. That would be enough information to find us with a simple Google search. To find out who I was *and* to learn that I wasn't even eighteen yet.

People under eighteen weren't allowed in the sim. They weren't allowed on the sim at all. The only reason I was able to get in was because way back when I started playing, I'd stolen one of Dad's credit cards long enough to get my account verified. As far as Second Life was concerned, I was forty-two-year-old Cole Roberts.

Shit. If Gemini Googled my family, that could be awful.

I was shaking. I needed to play it casual.

87

winter flower

Tamara: **Anyway, thanks for listening. I just needed to talk some of that out.**

Gemini: **Any time.**

I checked the time. Twenty minutes before I was to meet Gunstock. I put Gemini out of my mind and teleported back to my apartment.

Shoes. I checked the time. Shit. We'd see. I changed into the dress, my steampunk clothes morphing into a knee-length sleeveless black dress with a high collar. One by one I tried the different hair styles I had, finally settling on one that looked like a French braid.

Perfect. *Perfect.* I checked the time. Five minutes.

In reality, we could do this wherever. We could meet in some other sim in Second Life. But we were playing this one-hundred-percent in character. That was the only way it could ever be, because I wasn't a beautiful woman, and no one needed to know that. So when he asked me to go to dinner and dancing, I agreed. Our characters would be at one of the in-character bars in the sim. Our conversation would be in character. And I was thrilled about it, because it felt like I was really going on a date.

In my heads-up display I could see a green dot moving its way across the sim toward my apartment. That was almost certainly Gunstock. I felt my chest tighten in anticipation.

What if he doesn't like me?

Stop. I wasn't mousy Sam. Here, I was Tamara. I was strong. I was a hero, a member of the Brigade, someone who protected the innocent. I didn't need to let fear rule me.

Words appeared at the bottom of my screen: **Gunstock Valor rings the doorbell.**

I walked to the door and clicked on it. It opened.

Gunstock looked different than the last time we'd played two days ago. He'd been adjusting to the Brigade quickly, and we'd played together several nights. I tried to place it then realized he'd replaced the stock skin with a new one. His face was several shades darker than before and marked with a five o'clock shadow.

Gunstock: **Tamara, you look beautiful.**

I felt myself flush a little.

A knock on the bedroom door yanked me out of the game. *Goddamn it!*

"What?"

"Sam?" It was Mom. "What are you doing?"

"Studying. I've got a test tomorrow."

"Open the door, Sam."

Christ, why now? I quickly typed: **/OOC: I'm so sorry … BRB.** I minimized Second Life on my screen and switched to PowerPoint, which still had a presentation from AP Biology open. Then I got up and opened the door.

"Sam…" Her eyes darted to the computer, where she took in the PowerPoint presentation on the screen then looked back at me. "I just wanted to check in with you. It's Brenna's birthday. Are you … are you doing okay?"

"Mom, I don't want to talk about it."

She looked distressed. "Sam … it'll do some good."

I felt guilty about the pained expression on her face. But right then I needed to get her out of there. "Mom, I need to study for my test and get some sleep. Please?"

Her shoulders sagged, and she looked down at the floor. Then she looked back at me. "If things are bad, will you talk with me? Brenna didn't … and…"

I swallowed. A stab of grief sank through me at her words. I shoved it away. "Sure, I'll talk with you, Mom. You know that."

Mollified, she nodded, and said, "Good night, Sam. I love you."

"Love you too, Mom."

She walked away. I closed and locked the door and rushed back to my computer.

I typed: **/OOC: back. I'm so sorry about that.**

Gunstock: **Shall we?**

The two of us walked toward the Erie Hotel. The building had been modeled after a hotel in the New Orleans commercial district, with wrought iron detailing and rails on a wraparound two-storied porch. On the ground floor were several tables, which were far enough apart to be semi-private. For the next two hours we chatted. Only in character, but Gunstock continued to push. What was I like in real life? Where did I live? What kinds of things did I like? I had to push back and set hard boundaries. *There is no real life,* I said. Only here.

I looked at the clock. Brenna's birthday was over.

A wave of exhaustion hit me. I seated my avatar at a table near the windows … I wanted to crawl into bed. But I didn't want to blow it with Gunstock. I blinked my eyes, trying to decide what to do. I had school in the morning and really couldn't afford to go without sleep another night. Last night, on the eve of her birthday, I hadn't been able to sleep at all.

Tamara: **/OOC: I don't want to blow our fun, but I'm exhausted in RL. Would you be really upset if we picked this up another night?**

Gunstock: **/OOC: Sure, that's fine. I've had a nice time. Get some rest.**

Tamara: **/OOC: Good night.**

Gunstock: **Good night.**

winter flower

Before I could change my mind I logged out. My eyes were aching from staring at the computer for so long. I stood up and stretched, feeling out of place and sad. My eyes went to the picture of Brenna that occupied the corner of my desk.

I turned out the light and undressed in the dark so I couldn't see myself. I slipped under the sheet and imagined I was Tamara, and that I mattered, and that I had my sister back.

I whispered, "Wherever you are, Happy Birthday, Brenna. I love you." I squeezed my eyes shut to hold back tears, but then I gave up trying to hold them back.

That's when I heard them—Mom and Dad arguing again in the kitchen.

Erin

The old grandfather clock I'd bought at one of way-too-many estate sales in Fairfax County chimed twelve times at midnight. The clock was priceless. Dark polished mahogany. Nineteenth century. Incredible craftsmanship. The surface of the clock was highly polished—you could see your reflection in it. You could apply your makeup in the reflection, or shave, or get a good look at all of your shortcomings and faults. The only reason I still owned it was because we couldn't find a buyer for such a priceless item. Although, undoubtedly when it got desperate enough (*it already was*) we'd unload that too, for far less than it was worth.

I'd been sitting cross-legged on the couch, my eyes staring in the general direction of the pendulum as it swung lazily back and forth, back and forth. In my lap was a photo album. Photos of me and Cole and Brenna (and later Sam).

I shouldn't have taken the album out. It was a window to another time, a happier, wonderful time in our lives. The first few pages were mostly baby pictures. We were so young. Brenna was born in 1996, just eighteen months after I graduated from Georgetown. Cole had dropped out of college, opting instead to go to work as a system administrator for a small startup, and we were renting a little two-bedroom in Tyson's Corner.

It was a little ironic. I had a bachelor's degree in economics, but the law of supply and demand meant that my high-school-graduate husband—who happened to have computer skills—made more money than me. So with the kids, I quit my job to stay home. For years I was resentful about that. But now, I was grateful.

Grateful, because I got that time at home with Brenna before she disappeared.

I swallowed the last of my wine and set the album to the side. It was an inexpensive wine, Autumn Blush, from the Bryant winery in Talladega. Undoubtedly, they made moonshine there after hours for the NASCAR crowd, who camped out for days waiting for the races while they played their scratch-off tickets and drank Budweiser.

There was a thought worthy of Cole. I knew better than to stereotype people.

Midnight was past. Brenna's birthday was over. I slid off the bed and stood a little unsteadily. I'd finished off most of the bottle.

Not exactly the first time, now, was it?

I opened the flimsy bedroom door and padded on the crappy carpet down the crappy hall and knocked on the equally crappy door halfway down the hall, then reached down to the handle. Locked again. I could probably push the hollow door open with little effort, but why bother?

"Sam?" I asked.

"Mom, I'm trying to sleep."

I rolled my eyes. I was sure Sam was still on the computer, but I didn't have the energy to deal with it right now. I stumbled through the living room and into the kitchen and dumped my wine glass in the sink, which was piled with dirty dishes. I should do something about that, I thought.

Instead, I shrugged, then looked up at the clock. Where was my husband?

Not like I haven't asked that before.

I shook my head, then picked my phone off the counter to dial it. But I didn't finish, because that was when he walked in.

Cole looked exhausted. Black polyester pants—polyester because they didn't stain with bleach. Not exactly a concern back when he was CIO. Before he fucked everything up. Black leather shoes. A blue, mostly polyester shirt, stained with bacon grease. His glasses were a little bit crooked on his face, and new lines ran down the sides of his mouth. I studied him a second. His hair was turning grey at the temples. We were both too young for that.

"Where've you been?" I asked.

He shrugged and shook his head. "Work. I told you I had to work a double. Stupid problems." His eyes slid over the piled-up sink and cluttered counters, and looked away. He didn't say anything about it. "I need to get some sleep," he said.

He started to turn away again, and I said, "Cole?"

He stiffened then turned back. "Yeah?"

"It's her birthday," I said.

I swear to God I wasn't going to say anything. I wasn't going to mention it. I wasn't going to do this.

His face clouded, and he looked to the floor. "I know," he said in a rasping voice. "Eighteen."

I crossed my arms over my chest. It was too much to think he'd come over and hug me. And I didn't know how to approach him. Not anymore. I wasn't even sure I wanted him to.

"Do you think she's still alive?" I asked.

"Of course she is," he replied. His tone had an edge in it. "Don't ever say otherwise. She's out there somewhere."

I swallowed. "Then why doesn't she call?"

"I don't know."

Bitterly, I asked, "Do you care?"

His eyes widened slightly as he recoiled from me. "How can you ask that?"

"Because I don't know, Cole. You never talk to me."

"I never do anything but work and sleep," he replied.

Poor him. It was the same thing I heard from him constantly, and it was true. He certainly didn't do anything around the house, or with our remaining child. On the rare occasions he was awake, he was planted in front of the television with a beer.

"Is that supposed to be my fault?" I asked.

He leaned against the wall. "I didn't say that," he said. "Although it wouldn't hurt if you got a fucking job."

"I've tried," I said. I was defensive, and I hated that. "I've tried the Army base, and the General Dynamics plant, and the fucking school system. I've tried at the department stores, and at the mall. You saw me this morning. All I hear is, I've got no experience."

"You gotta start somewhere," he said. "You could always wait tables. In case you hadn't noticed it, Erin, we're pretty goddamned broke, and all you do is sit around here and drink all day. You should start buying that shit in the box. At least then it's a little cheaper."

I wanted to hit him. I wanted to smash his smug face in. But then I heard it. A high-pitched, sad voice coming from down the hall. "Please stop arguing. I'm trying to sleep."

I closed my eyes and sighed.

Brenna had once asked us to stop fighting.

"I'm going to bed," he said. His voice sounded dejected. "I've got to be back at the restaurant at six thirty."

He turned and walked down the hall, his shoulders slumped.

I didn't follow. I watched him walk down the hall and wondered how I'd ended up here, in the middle of nowhere in the Bible Belt, married to a defeated man.

Nine

~~~~~~

Erin

It took me four days after Brenna's birthday before I finally came out of the deep emotional hole I'd fallen into. But I finally got up. I had to. I lectured Cole on the fact that he was never home and never did anything with Sam. But I *was* home, and I hardly ever did anything with Sam. I called Lori that morning, and after a hard cry, I made a promise to reengage with my son and get moving.

I had to do something, anything to break the depression. So I started in the kitchen, windows open, fan going. Mechanically washed the dishes, rinsed them, racked them up. The counters were filthy. I sprayed them down and began scrubbing. Sugar was encrusted on the counter near the coffee pot. Gross. I couldn't do this anymore. I couldn't live like this anymore.

I was on my hands and knees, cleaning some god-awful spill from the floor, when my phone rang. I leaned back on my knees and wiped my hands on a paper towel, then reached in my pocket, my mind running through who it could be. My sister again? Cole, calling from work?

He rarely, if ever, called from the restaurant, unless it was to tell me he was going to be late. Sam's school?

I wasn't prepared for the number I saw, but I recognized it immediately. My heart instantly started pounding in my chest, my throat closing up in fear.

It was the number for Stan Wilcox at the FBI.

I fumbled, dropping the phone. It landed on the floor with a loud crack and I dived for it. It rang again, and I hit the answer button.

"Hello?" I said frantically.

"Mrs. Roberts? It's Agent Wilcox."

"Yes," I choked out.

"I've got some news."

Time froze. In less than a second, my mind ran past all the incidents where Wilcox had given us news. When they found her car, with the broken phone. When they found the bracelet Lori gave her in Chase's apartment. The weekly calls for a year, then less often since then. But he still called, and he almost always prefaced those calls with the statement, "I don't have any news, I'm just checking in."

Today he'd said, *I've got some news.*

"Yes? Tell me."

"Three weeks ago, a young woman going by a, uh … street name … of Strawberry … she was picked up in Portland, Oregon. Arrested for prostitution. Apparently there was some kind of mix-up, the links to the National Crime Information Center were down, so the fingerprints didn't get matched up until this morning. But, Erin, it was Brenna. She's alive."

I swallowed and sank back against the cabinet, my numb legs splayed out in front of me. I couldn't breathe. I tried to say something. Anything. Tears ran down my face.

"Mrs. Roberts? Erin?"

"I'm here," I whispered. She'd been arrested for prostitution. One of my worst fears had come alive, but I didn't care. I just wanted her back. I just wanted her back.

"Did you understand what I said?"

"Brenna's alive. And in Portland. Can I talk to her? I can fly up today."

He was silent for just a moment, taking a breath, and replied, "Erin … she was released on bail. We've alerted the Portland PD, and they're treating it as a trafficking case now. They didn't know she was a minor when they picked her up, and … well … we don't know exactly where she is."

I screamed into the phone, *"My daughter's alive after two years missing and you can't tell me where she is?"*

"I'm sorry, ma'am. But I promise you, we're putting every resource we have into the search. We'll find her."

"Who bailed her out?" I demanded.

"I'm working on getting the details."

"I'm going to Portland."

"Mrs. Roberts, I don't think that's a good idea."

I hissed into the phone. "I don't care anymore what you think. My daughter's been missing for two years and she turns up alive and you can't even tell me where she is? I'm going to Portland and finding my daughter."

I hung up the phone, unable to think clearly. I'd have to fly to Portland, it was too far to drive and get there in a reasonable period of time. We didn't have money, not any money at all, but maybe my sister or Cole's parents could help. I tried to get my mind in order then took out my phone and dialed Cole at work.

He didn't answer, so I moved to the bedroom and began wildly throwing clothes into a suitcase, not paying any attention to what I was putting in there. It didn't matter. What mattered was getting to Portland as quickly as I could.

I dialed again five minutes later. Still no answer. Damn it.

I threw the suitcase into the back of the minivan then went back in and changed into clothes that weren't completely filthy from cleaning. On the way back out to the van, I dialed again.

This time he finally answered.

"Hey," he said.

The second I heard his voice, I fell apart again. My knees let go, and I sank to the ground. For just a second, I wanted nothing more than to have my *husband* back, because I needed him. I needed to be able to lean on him; I needed him to be able to help.

"Cole?" I wailed.

"Erin? What's wrong?" he asked, his voice suddenly panicking.

I broke down instantly, sobbing. Then I said the words. The words I'd been desperately wanting to say, to hear, to believe.

"Cole. She's alive. Brenna's alive!"

Brenna

In my dream, I was six years old.

Daddy would be home from his business trip tonight. Mommy ran around, getting the house ready. I sat with Sam in the living room. I had a book, a really awesome book, called The BFG, and it was about a giant. Only Daddy said it was about a GIANT, and whenever he said that, he growled and made claws with his hands.

I read The BFG to Sam. He couldn't read, but I was going to teach him.

I acted out the parts. I stood up and walked around, leaning this way and that. I made up funny voices. I growled. Just like Daddy did when he read it. I missed him and wanted him to come home from his trip.

Sam threw his head back and laughed, a smile showing all of his teeth, and we went upstairs and played in my room. We dressed up in princess dresses, and Sam looked so happy, so I put my purple wig on her and I wore the pink one.

Mommy made us change back before Daddy got home, and that's okay.

When Daddy got home we ran outside and threw our arms around him. He smelled warm and like coffee, and he put his arms around us and I felt safe. I climbed up one leg and Sam climbed up the other, and he knelt down and lifted us both over his shoulders so we faced his back next to each other, and squealed our brains out. He spun in a circle, and we both screamed and let go, letting our arms fly out in front of us, the room spinning around in a whirl, and I got dizzy. When Daddy put us down, we walked funny and me and Sam fell against each other. I laughed and threw my arms around him to hold myself up, and we both fell over giggling.

Mommy put her arms around Daddy and they smiled and then kissed. They looked in each other's eyes, and me and Sam followed them back into the house for Daddy's surprise.

A banner hung across the living room. Me and Sam made it. Mommy helped. It said HAPPY BIRTHDY DADDY, and Mommy told me earlier it's okay I misspelled BIRTHDAY.

Daddy laughed. Mommy gave him her present, a new phone that he wanted. I gave him lip balm for when he flies, because it's windy in the sky, and Sam gave him a drawing of a silly pig with wings.

We played and laughed and we were happy, and there were no bars on the windows, and no grey, and no fear. That's where I went when I slept.

Part Two

Ten

Sam

While I dialed the combination on my locker, I spotted Ashley Prich-ard to my right, standing near Cody Hendricks. She was holding her phone out in front of her at a weird angle, taking a selfie. As she took the picture, she crossed her eyes and sucked in her cheeks.

Weird.

I tossed my precalculus and English books into my bag then zipped up the bag and slammed the locker shut. I had about four minutes to get to the bus, so I threw my bag over my shoulder and started to hurry down the hall.

Just as I was about to pass, Ashley stepped backwards, still shooting selfies, directly into my path. I jerked back, trying to avoid her, but it was too late. We collided, her right elbow hitting my side.

Horror sank into me as I heard the loud *smack* of her phone hitting the floor.

Ashley let out a screech then dropped to her knees, scrambling for the phone.

"What the fuck!" Cody shouted as I stepped back.

"I'm so sorry!" I blurted. "I didn't mean to—"

"You asshole," Ashley screamed. "If you broke my phone I swear to God you'll—"

She cut herself off when Cody reached out with both hands, grabbing the front of my shirt and shaking me back and forth. "What the fuck is wrong with you? Are you fucking suicidal?"

I tried to pull away. "I didn't do anything!"

From across the hall, a loud male voice called out with a tone of authority. "Cody! Let go of him!"

With a deliberate motion, Cody let go of me and took a step back. Ashley gave me a death glare and spoke in a petulant, nasty voice. "The screen is cracked. You owe me a new phone."

The man who had spoken was a teacher I didn't recognize. He was a tall man, with a muscular wide build not all that different from Cody's. If I had to guess, I would have picked him for a football player. Maybe he was one of the coaches?

The man spoke in a thick rural Southern accent. "He don't owe you nuthin', Ashley. You stepped right into him, he was just trying to get to the bus."

Cody opened his mouth, flailing his hands around. "Coach Braddock, that kid's got a thing for Ashley. He was giving her pervy eyes on the bus last week. You didn't see it but he tried to grab her ass, that's what happened." He gave me an angry look and started to raise his fist.

"Cody! Put your hand down and step back. Right now."

Cody's eyes swiveled to the coach. Then, grudgingly, he said, "Yes, sir."

"If you plan to keep playing for my football team, you for damn sure better keep your hands to yourself and your mouth under control. Got it?"

Cody swallowed, his Adam's apple bobbing down and back up again. "Yes, sir."

"My dad is going to be so mad," Ashley said. As she said it she gave the coach a vicious look. I knew she was kind of a bitch, but I couldn't imagine talking and looking at a teacher that way.

The coach said, "I don't care who your daddy is, Ashley. I'll do my job the way it's called for. Both of y'all get out of here."

The coach had intervened and saved me ... but at what cost? Was I going to be dealing with even worse problems from Cody later? I bet I would.

"What's your name, kid?"

I froze at the words. "Sam." I hated how my voice rose at the end of my name, like I was asking a question.

"You new here, Sam? I ain't seen you around."

"Yes, sir."

The coach hitched his thumbs in his belt and looked at me as if I were a bug. "Well, let me give you a piece of advice. Keep your distance from Cody Hendricks. And Ashley too. They ain't the nicest kids in the school, if you know what I mean."

I tried to smile but failed. "I kind of sensed that."

The coach frowned. "God don't like a smart-ass, kid."

I nodded. "Yes, sir. Can I, uh ... can I go? I'm going to miss my bus."

The coach waved a hand at me in dismissal and turned away. I ran for the bus, but by the time I got outside, it was too late.

Oh, man. I had planned on joining a role-play that was being organized by the Europeans in the Brigade. There's no way I would be home in time for that. Whatever. It probably wouldn't be the last time Cody and Ashley ruined something for me.

Dad's restaurant was only about half a mile from the high school. I would head over there and do homework until he was ready to go home from work.

I threw my backpack over my shoulder and began walking away from the school. I wasn't even off the school property before I saw an oversized black pickup with gleaming polished wheels pull up to the corner, driving away from the school. Cody was at the wheel, and Ashley sat beside him in the cab. That explained why I hadn't seen either of them on the bus in the last several days. Cody either just got his driver's license or the truck. As Cody turned left out of the school he spotted me and shouted, "Faggot!"

Where did people like Cody come from? I couldn't understand why people were so cruel. I'd have to really keep my eyes out. Cody wasn't going to let this go. A dull sense of dread settled in on me.

As I walked along the six-lane road, I wanted to sneeze from the pollen and dust in the air. I was sweating before I'd made it a quarter of a mile. I guessed it was ninety-five degrees out, and there wasn't a cloud in the sky.

I fucking hated Alabama.

I made it to the Waffle House without any further incidents. The parking lot was nearly empty. Where was Dad's car? It wasn't parked in the usual spot, and he didn't typically leave before four or five. I pulled the door open and walked into the restaurant. The air-conditioning blew over me with beautiful waves of ice cold air. I shivered.

I recognized the waitress who was at that moment making salads behind the counter, but I couldn't remember her name. She had dark hair and was probably in her early fifties. She walked with a limp, as if her left leg were slightly shorter. She was always friendly, and when I walked in she waved at me.

The restaurant was almost empty: the only customer an old man sitting at the counter, his head hunched down between his shoulders.

The waitress spoke. "It's … don't tell me … Sam, right?"

"Yeah," I responded. I leaned to look in the open door to the back. "You seen my dad?"

"He had to leave early … some kind of emergency. Brian came over and covered for him."

"Brian?"

"Oh, he's your dad's boss, the division manager."

He had to leave for an emergency. Weird. Really weird.

I sighed. I didn't want to bother Dad, especially if there was an emergency. But there was no public transportation. I sat at the counter, as far from the old man as I could get, and dialed Dad.

It rang twice, then he answered. From the background noise, I knew he was driving as soon as he said, "Hello?"

"Dad? It's Sam."

"Sam? Hey. Did you get the note we left?"

"What note?"

Dad sighed. "On the kitchen table."

"Oh … I'm not home. I missed the bus. I was calling to see if you or Mom could pick me up. I'm at the Waffle House."

Silence. For ten long seconds. Then Dad said, "Sam, your mom had to take an emergency trip. We're halfway to Atlanta, I'm taking her to the airport. I won't be back until pretty late."

I swallowed. *Emergency trip?* "What … what trip?"

"I left you twenty dollars so you could order a pizza. It's on the kitchen table with the note."

I sighed. Why didn't he answer? "Okay. I'll walk, it's not that far."

"Christ, are you sure?"

What choice did I have? I felt a lump in my chest. What could be so important that they dropped everything to rush Mom to the airport? Urgently enough that they wouldn't even bother to make any provisions for me other than leaving some money on the table.

Brenna.

That's all it could be. We didn't have the money for anyone to be traveling. If Mom was flying somewhere, and they were keeping it a secret, then it had to be Brenna … and it had to be bad news. Why else would they hide it?

I choked back tears. "I'm sure." I hung up the phone. I waved and said, "Thanks," to the waitress, whose name I still didn't know. Then I got out of there as quickly as I could.

It wasn't *that* far. I guess. Three miles? It felt like longer in the heat, as I walked past Oxford Mall, with its empty parking lots, then crossed the overpass over I-20. I stood in the middle of the bridge for a minute looking down as the traffic raced by underneath. The cars moved so fast from this perspective.

I kept walking, past the giant Indian mound, which was tied up in controversy. My history teacher had talked about it the other day. Part of the mound had been excavated to make space for a Sam's Club, and an entire archeological site, once a village, had been bulldozed.

Alabama.

All told, the walk home took an hour. Not bad, all things considered. As I walked, I thought about Brenna. I thought about Cody and Ashley and what had happened today.

What had happened was that I'd behaved like a mouse. She bumped into me and dropped her phone, but *I* was the one who apologized.

Brenna would have said I needed to own it. That instead of keeping to myself, slinking through life with my eyes on the ground and my arms across my chest, that I needed to flaunt myself, own my own style, take charge.

But I wasn't Brenna, I never had been. It made me feel guilty sometimes to think about it, but often I thought she didn't know what the hell she was talking about. Confidence and flash only goes so far. There were very real dangers out there: dangers she'd had no idea of until two years ago, when she vanished off the face of the earth. I'd have done anything to have my sister back in my life. But whatever happened to her, it had to have been bad. It had to have been truly awful for her to never so much as send a text message, contact us online, call, nothing at all.

In my heart, I knew my sister was probably dead. But the thought seized me up, tightened my throat, made me want to fall apart. Our lives had all frozen in the moment she disappeared. Life seemed to go on around us, but me and Mom and Dad? We were all dead to the world. And I was afraid we'd never recover, never learn to live our own lives, never move on. And I didn't want to. I didn't want to move on. I wanted to find her, rescue her, hug her, give her life back.

My sister was perfection. Her confidence and talent. Her porcelain skin. Her infectious smile and laugh, her sense of humor. She protected my secrets. She protected me. But I wasn't able to return that protection.

So I kept to myself. I didn't look up, I didn't interact, I didn't say a word as I trudged through life.

When I finally got home, it was broiling inside the house. I turned on the air-conditioning and went to dump my books in my room.

The note was on the kitchen table.

Sam,

Your father is taking me to the airport for an urgent trip. He'll be home very late.

Love you,

Mom

Why would they keep whatever it was so secretive? What happened?

105

winter flower

My parents didn't trust me at all, they hadn't since Brenna's disappearance. After all, she'd hinted to me that something was happening. *What are you going to do when I'm gone?* And I didn't tell them. So it was my fault.

And then I did tell, and that delayed the investigation. My fault again.

As if I didn't know that already.

How late was late? It was more than two hours to Atlanta in one direction. Plus maneuvering the airport. Traffic. I suspected late meant very late indeed.

Was it wrong for me to hope so?

I took a sharp breath. Shaking with anticipation, I closed my eyes for a few seconds. I wasn't thinking straight. I should call. Find out how long. But I didn't want to make them suspicious. I didn't want to give my father any cause to wonder what I was up to. And calling them would do that.

It would be hours, whatever happened. I opened my eyes and walked to my closet. In the back, a stack of cardboard boxes contained my life from before we lived in this tiny place. I slid the top box off of the stack. The second box was labeled books. I took it out into my room and reverently laid it on the bed, carefully removing the packing tape. I hadn't opened this box since we'd left our house in Virginia.

Opening the box revealed chapter books, books that I'd read in middle school. Carefully I took them out, setting them to the side, revealing what was underneath.

On the very top. A silk dress. Brenna had taken me shopping for it. "It's for a costume party," she told the women in the store. But I think maybe they knew. From the way I shook, from the way I stared, wide-eyed, at myself in the mirror.

I didn't care.

Shaking, I quickly undressed. The dress was wrinkled, but I didn't care. I put on the panties from the box, but I almost screamed in frustration when I couldn't get the bra on. It didn't fit anymore. I pulled and stretched, and finally got it on, though it cut into my ribs almost painfully. Then, slowly, I slid the dress over my head, almost getting stuck pulling it down over my shoulders.

I felt ... conflicted, angry, confused. Reaching behind me, I pulled the zipper up. It was far too tight; two years had gone by and I'd grown a lot. I turned toward the mirror and cringed. I looked ... ridiculous. Rage filled me when I saw that my shoulders were broadening. I'd taken the hormones until they ran out, but run out they had, and there was no money to buy any more, nowhere to have them shipped even if I could, and I wanted to scream because ... I was starting to look like a boy.

I blinked my eyes, trying to shut out the cascade of emotions. The dress didn't look right, too tight in the shoulders and chest, too loose in the hips. It

106

was painfully obvious my breasts were nonexistent. I sat down at my desk in front of the mirror, still shaking in anger, and began to brush my hair, parting it high above my left eye. It was almost shoulder-length now. My eyes fell to my legs. The dress had been knee-length when Brenna bought it for me. Now it was at least four inches shorter. It had been a couple days since I'd shaved my legs, but I didn't have time right now.

You need to get a haircut, Sam, you're starting to look like a girl.

Dad said that to me the other day. I wished. I wished I looked like a girl, but a glance in the mirror showed I didn't. I reached in my bottom desk drawer. In the very back was my makeup case.

Slowly I began to apply mascara. My eyes, a deep blue, were probably the only feature I was happy with. Very carefully, I applied eyeshadow and eyeliner, choosing a pale blue eye shadow that complemented my eyes and the dress.

I almost froze at that point. I closed my eyes, and I could feel the silk of the dress against my skin. It felt right. The last time I'd worn this we'd still lived in a fifteen-room house, and my parents would never come looking for me anyway. I didn't think they'd seen my bedroom more than twice in the year after Brenna disappeared. But here we were living in a shoebox, and I was lucky to even have a room.

If my father came home now, I'd never have time to change and remove the makeup.

I swallowed. I stood, my heart racing, and looked at myself.

I wanted to cry. When my eyes were closed I could imagine it was the way I wanted to be. Beautiful. Or even simply pretty.

With my eyes open I saw … a boy, dressed in comically small girl's clothing.

My eyes started to water. My hair hung all wrong. Somehow in the past two years my Adam's apple had appeared. No matter how much makeup I wore, no matter what I did with my clothes, no matter how much I wished, it didn't change what I was. What everyone else in the world would see me as.

A tranny.

A pervert.

A freak.

I sank back into the chair and put my head in my hands. Who was I kidding?

Some people wanted to grow up to be stockbrokers, or astronauts, or the President, and every good parent in the world would say, "When you grow up you can be whatever you want to be."

Except mine.

Because the one thing in the world that I wanted to be was an impossibility.

Erin

I checked the time on my phone again. It was almost six p.m., and I had just an hour before my flight departed. I swallowed nervously then looked over at Cole.

"You'll make sure Sam is doing his homework? He gets all wrapped up on his computer and forgets."

"Yeah," he said, nodding. "Don't worry about us." He pulled the car to a stop in the check-in lane. We were surrounded by traffic: people rushing into the airport to catch their flights, police, airline employees.

I was shaking as I opened the car door. Cole got out and opened the trunk then set my suitcase on the ground. After my call to him, his boss had taken over the restaurant for the day, and Cole came home. While I got myself ready, he'd taken his laptop and pawned it, then dropped the money in the bank. It was just enough to pay for the ticket to Portland.

We met at the back of the car. I took a deep breath and looked up at my husband. He had dark circles under his eyes and a mix of anxiety and exhaustion on this face.

"Soon as I get home, I'll put the clock on Craigslist. We should get a thousand for it ... maybe more. That'll keep you going for a while. Then I'll ... I'll come up with something."

I nodded. It was the only option. Hotels and travel cost a lot of money ... money we didn't have.

Tentatively, I reached my left arm out. To hug him? Our marriage had been a wreck for so long, we hardly ever touched each other. But I wanted to. I wanted to touch him.

I wanted *him* to touch *me*.

He caught the tentative motion and pulled me to him. In a rough voice, laden with emotions too complex to dissect, he said, "Find her if you can. I'll take care of Sam."

I swallowed back tears, wrapping my arms around him. For a second, it felt ... like Cole. Like things were the way they should be.

But they weren't. They couldn't be.

"I'll call. Keep you updated."

We parted, both of us full of words we couldn't express. Cole's eyes met mine for a moment. I didn't have any words for that moment, I wasn't equipped for it. I turned, grabbed the handle of my suitcase, and walked away.

I was a mess of free-floating anxiety. It had been three weeks since she'd been picked up by the police in Portland. *Three weeks.* A lot could happen in that time. She might have been moved. She might ... I couldn't think of the words. I couldn't form them in my mind. For nearly two years there hadn't been a word, hadn't been any news, there'd been *nothing.* Now, everything was thrown out there in bright relief, and the thought of what my daughter might have endured for the past two years was too horrific to contemplate.

I waited impatiently in the line to check-in, then even more impatiently in the security line. But finally I was through and on my way to the gate. The Atlanta airport was huge, staggeringly huge, and it took a while to figure out how to find the train to take me out to the gate. But finally I was there, and just in time. My flight was boarding. Thank God I'd only brought the one carry-on bag. I didn't have time to mess with checking bags. With a last-minute ticket, I was stuck in a middle seat in the back row. I squeezed into my seat, in between a heart-stoppingly beautiful teenage girl who sat looking out the window, and a man in his early forties in the aisle seat.

I sat up straight in my seat. My chest hurt, and it was hard to swallow around the lump in my throat. I didn't have a car in Portland, and we didn't have credit cards anymore, so I couldn't rent one. I'd found a cheap motel to stay near the airport, but I still didn't know anything really. In the morning I'd have to find the police station and talk to whomever had arrested her. I needed to find out where she'd been picked up, how she looked, who she was with, and who had bailed her out. What if they wouldn't help me? If they treated me like I was interfering? How would I handle it?

I closed my eyes, trying to focus. I'd call Wilcox back in the morning at the FBI. Maybe a push from him would help. Or maybe they'd be cooperative. Maybe I was borrowing trouble. I didn't know. And that's what it came down to. I didn't know anything.

I was so wrapped up in my thoughts I paid little attention to the plane taxiing to the runway, until suddenly we were accelerating and the plane took to the air.

I closed my eyes. It'd been years since I'd been on a flight. I thought back. Brenna was five and Sam three, so that would have been around 2002. Cole had just gotten another promotion, and with the promotion came a hefty raise and a bonus. We took our first lengthy family vacation. We flew to Disney World and spent a week there.

Cole and I were still crazy in love then. But the cracks were showing. The trip was wonderful, but the flight had been laced with anxiety, my first flight since the hijackings that had turned the world upside down.

Today, Cole hadn't hesitated when I'd called him. He'd immediately done everything he could to get me on this plane. It reminded me of when we were partners. I missed that. I missed holding hands. I missed feeling like we saw each other as equals. I missed dinner and looking into each other's eyes across the table.

I remembered the night we met. I was a junior at Georgetown, and Angela had dragged me to a party at a friend's house just a few blocks from campus. It wasn't an out of control party—that wasn't our style—though there was plenty of alcohol and loud music. Not long after we got there, Angela ran into her ex-boyfriend, and the two of them camped in a corner most of the party, leaving me to fend for myself.

I knew some of the people at the party, but it really wasn't a crowd I ran with, so I found myself edging closer and closer to the window. I turned to the nearest small circle of people, unobtrusively joining in their conversation.

Cole caught my attention immediately. He stood on the opposite side of the circle from me. They were all women but him, and they were hanging on to his every word, which was no surprise. He was tall, well-built, dressed in casual clothes, khakis and a black polo shirt that made his shoulders look strong and sexy. He was making a point about the midterm elections which had just gone by, his hands gesturing as he spoke.

He was the same age as the other people at the party. But more confident somehow, more himself. From his clothes to his demeanor to his pale blue eyes, something about him just screamed confidence.

And of course, I was one of five girls hanging on his every word. But that didn't last, because the next thing he said was so obnoxious that my mouth just dropped open.

"All welfare does is increase poverty," he said. "People get trapped in a cycle where we reward them for not working. It's a self-fulfilling negative trap and creates a whole culture of dependence."

I raised an eyebrow as all the girls cooed around him.

"And you base this opinion on … what exactly?" I asked.

I think he liked the challenge. Because he started spouting statistics and opinions right out of the Heritage Foundation's playbook, most of which was a load of bullshit. He ended by saying, "Look, the bottom line is, we have a level playing field. Everyone in this life has a choice to work or not work. And if you work, you get ahead, and can have a decent life. Some people just choose otherwise."

I said, "And you don't think there's anything about being a white male that helps you get a leg up?" The other girls in the group gave me hostile looks.

"No," he replied. "In fact, if anything it penalizes me. Companies get tax breaks to hire blacks and the disabled and to have affirmative action." As he said the last two words, he used his fingers to make air-quotes.

I shook my head. "You've got no clue what you're talking about."

By this time, the girls in the group were looking at me with daggers in their eyes, because Cole's attention was one-hundred-percent on me. It was as if he'd forgotten any of them were there.

Actually, I'm pretty sure he had, because he moved a little closer to me, which put two of the girls almost at his back.

"I know exactly what I'm talking about. I'm not in some insulated academic ivory tower, I'm out there working for a living."

"Oh, yeah?" I asked. "So what do you do?"

"UNIX system administrator. I work for a startup in Northern Virginia."

"Oh yeah? So where did you learn about computers?"

He shrugged. "I'm self-taught."

"Nice," I said. "I like that, and it fits your whole everybody can bootstrap their way up narrative. Where'd you get the computer to teach yourself on?"

His eyes widened and he grinned. "Okay, you got me there. When I was in high school, my parents got it for me for Christmas. So I guess you would say that's a sign of what, white privilege?"

"Middle-class privilege maybe. Home computer, what are we talking, two thousand dollars?"

He nodded. "It's not like my parents didn't make sacrifices to make that happen, though. My Dad served in Vietnam, I'm a military brat. And for the record, my roommate at Georgia Tech was black. He got *exactly* the same education I did."

"I'm sure he did," I said.

He moved closer to me again. "What's your name? I don't think we've been introduced."

"I'm Erin."

"I'm Cole. You go to Georgetown, Erin?"

Two of the girls walked away, disgusted. Cole didn't notice.

"Yes. I'm an economics major."

A grin appeared on his face, then he leaned back his head with a full-throated laugh. "It figures I'd get into a debate with an economics major from a liberal arts college."

I grinned. "Does that intimidate you?"

He grinned back. "Not in the least. Should it?"

"Yes. Because I'm clearly a lot smarter than you."

He threw his head back and laughed. I won't lie; I found his confidence insanely attractive. I wasn't any different than the other girls who'd been surrounding him, fawning. Except they were all gone now, and somehow I was still here.

"Can I have your number?"

I laughed, a little disbelievingly. "Excuse me?"

"You heard me. I want to take you out to dinner."

"We'd better not talk politics."

"What fun would that be?" he asked.

I rolled my eyes. And then I gave him my number.

A few minutes after that, Angela gave me *the signal* … the signal we'd worked out when it was time to leave a party together. We walked back to campus, and she talked for thirty minutes straight about her ex and what an *asshole* he was. Then abruptly, she said, "Who was that guy *you* were talking to?"

"His name's Cole. He thinks too much of himself," I said.

She laughed. "There was a crowd of girls around him. But they all left, leaving just you. You were like a dragon slayer."

I shrugged and smiled.

"Oh my God," she said. "You like him?"

"A little. I gave him my number."

She cheered.

A week later, Cole and I went out for the first time, to a play at the National Theatre, and then dinner. We did talk politics … debated them all night, in fact. We also talked careers and jobs and about our families. Cole was brilliant and erratic. He'd attended two years at Georgia Tech before dropping out to go to work for a tech startup in Northern Virginia. When he talked about the job, he was excited, his eyes gleaming. He was a believer, going on about how their work was going to revolutionize how people interacted in business. He tended to talk with his hands, waving them around in an animated fashion. It was a wonder he didn't knock anything off the table.

Sometimes it was hard to connect those days with now. It's like we were different people. We'd been so optimistic, so happy. Cole traveled a lot for work, even then, but when he was in town we would go out dancing or to dinner. He took me horseback riding in the Shenandoah Valley, and I took him to lectures on campus and to book signings.

We laughed all the time and made love all the time.

I took Cole to meet my parents on my twentieth birthday, right before Christmas that year. It was a five-hour drive from DC to Cary, North Carolina, where I grew up, a town derisively known in the area as the *Containment Area for Relocated Yankees*. The weather that Saturday morning as we drove was pleasant, unusually warm, and we rode most of the way with the windows down in Cole's new Mustang, listening to the audiobook of *The Witching Hour* Cole had bought me as an early Christmas present. He knew I was a fan of Anne Rice. I'd actually waited in line for hours at Politics and Prose to get a signed copy earlier in the year.

It was early afternoon when Cole pulled the car to a stop in my parents' driveway in North Cary. The house was on top of a hill, a two-story, white clapboard home with dark green shutters and a wide wraparound porch. Mom was a professor at NC State, and Dad a doctor on staff at Duke University Medical Center. Cary was almost halfway between the two, a nice, rapidly growing suburb.

Dad opened the door first, before we were even completely out of the car. He had a big grin on his face and walked toward me, pulling me into a big hug.

"Erin, I've missed you so. Happy Birthday, sweetie. And this must be Cole."

Cole approached and put out a hand to shake. "Cole Roberts," he said. "It's a pleasure to meet you, sir."

"Pleasure to meet you. Call me Carl." He looked around, mystified, then said, "The wife is still inside. I think she's making some kind of … um … thing … in the kitchen. Come on in."

I grinned at Dad. My parents were unusually progressive for the Deep South. They were hippies, throwbacks to the sixties, though that didn't interfere with their education, and they saw each other as equal partners. But my father had spent my entire life pretending he didn't understand anything in the kitchen. He'd go in there willingly, burn food, cause things to boil over, and make a disastrous mess. My mother finally gave up and ended up taking a more traditional role in the kitchen.

As we hung up our coats, I smelled waves of garlic, and, less prominent, butter and spices. I walked into the kitchen and found my mother at the kitchen island chopping garlic.

She smiled, wiping her hands, then wrapped her arms around me. "Erin. Happy birthday. This is Cole?"

"Cole, meet my mom."

Mom hugged him too, then said, "I hope you like garlic chicken."

Cole grinned. "I love it, ma'am."

My dad walked in behind us, saying, "She's putting enough garlic in there to make sure you two don't so much as kiss while you're staying here."

I blushed horribly, and Cole chuckled and said, "My intentions are completely honorable."

That was when I heard the footsteps thundering down the stairs. Lori came flying around the corner and into the kitchen and threw her arms around me. Five foot four, just shy of eighteen, her hair was dyed a deep blue-green that clashed with her bright pink lipstick.

I squeezed her back, feeling tears prick my eyes. I missed my little sister. Flamboyant where I was conservative, Lori was gregarious and unconventional. "I missed you, sis," she said. "We've got so much to talk about."

I introduced her to Cole. Dad grabbed a couple of beers out of the refrigerator—he never had any problem finding those—and passed one to Cole. "Come on outside, Cole. I want to show you the garden."

Dad wasn't exactly subtle.

Lori and I sat down at the kitchen table, and she started filling me in on her senior year in high school, which sounded like it consisted of nothing but music, art, and boys. So very different from mine. I'd dated, of course, but my focus was academics and career. To be honest, none of the guys at my high school really interested me. Too much football, too much drunken partying, too many drugs. It had never been my scene.

It didn't take long for Lori to convince me that the football crowd wasn't a problem for her. The drugs might be another thing, but I didn't want to push.

As Lori and I chatted, I glanced outside periodically. Dad was standing, one foot casually resting on the top of the foot-high fieldstone wall we built together when I was twelve. His face was open and friendly as he spoke with Cole. Cole had his back to me, but I could tell when he was talking, because his arms waved wildly as always.

Both of them laughed, throwing their heads back.

Lori followed my eyes and smiled. "You really like him, don't you?"

My mother, still standing over the stove, looked over at us when Lori asked that question.

I took a deep breath and nodded. "Yes. Yes, I do."

Looking back, Lori at that age was so like the young woman Brenna would become. When my daughter hit her early teens, Lori had been a confidante and friend to her, something I was grateful for, because she'd stopped trusting me, stopped talking to me for a long time. But all that changed when Lori broke her trust to keep her safe.

Since then, Lori and I had talked about it often enough. We'd torn it apart. We'd second-guessed ourselves and each other. For nearly six months we didn't even speak, until Mom and Dad brought us back together. And still, I wondered if only we'd done something different, said something different, would Brenna still have trusted us? Would she have been safe? How did Cole and I possibly fail so much as parents that this happened to our daughter?

My eyes felt hollow as I stared out the window of the plane. The teenage girl next to me was watching the in-flight movie, her headset in her ears, laughing. Relaxed. Happy. Everything Brenna should be.

Two more hours to this flight, and then I'd be on the ground in Portland.

I was going to find my daughter. No matter what it took.

Eleven

~~~~~~

Cole: Now

I waited to drive away until I saw Erin disappear into the doors of the airport and head for the escalator. I'd wanted to park and walk her in to the security gate, but both of us recognized that we didn't have the money to pay for airport parking on top of everything else. At this point, every dollar made a huge difference.

I so badly wanted to be getting on that plane with her. I needed to do something: something for my family, something for Brenna, something for Erin.

I couldn't remember the last time she had called and asked for my help for anything. The sound of her voice on the phone, a mix of panic and shock and joy and devastation all at the same time, had left me confused and filled with an urgent sense of need to do something, anything, I could for her.

The thing is … we hadn't just lost Brenna. We lost our whole family. I'd spent the past two years watching my wife slowly kill herself, watching my son become isolated and depressed, and I bore the guilt of knowing that much of it was my fault.

As I pulled out of the airport, I dialed Jeremiah.

In some ways the two of us had oddly parallel lives. My dad was a Marine Vietnam veteran, his was an Army Vietnam vet. Both of us were military brats and traveled all over the country, and both of us spent our high school years in the Atlanta area … me in Marietta near the Atlanta Naval Air Station, and Jeremiah in East Point near Fort McPherson. Both of us had grown up interested in engineering and had earned scholarships to Georgia Tech.

But there our similarities ended. He was black; I was white. He was a Democrat; I was a Republican. He listened to hip hop and jazz, and I listened to punk and southern rock. We quickly became best friends.

One time, I dragged Jeremiah to the site of the former Metroplex in Atlanta. Long since closed down, the club was a shithole in an old warehouse in an area surrounded by other old warehouses and had burned down in the late eighties. But someone had rented a warehouse down the street for Columbus Day weekend for a revival of the old club. A lot of the old bands came, like the Sex Pistols, Rotten Gimmick, and Henry Rollins, and a couple new ones on the scene like Blink 182.

Before it burned down, the Metroplex had been like an awakening for me. At the end of ninth grade, I'd told Daddy I didn't want to go spend any of the summer with Lucas. He was my oldest cousin on my father's side of the family, the younger son of Daddy's sister.

"Why the hell not?" he'd demanded.

I'd squirmed but finally told him. "It's bad there. Big Bill's always drunk and he's real quick with his fists. Ain't nothing to do there but sit around and get messed up. I hate it."

"Quick with his fists?" Daddy asked.

"With Aunt Donna. And Lucas."

A quick flash of anger crossed his face. Donna was Daddy's sister, and I didn't think he cared for Big Bill. "You ain't gonna sit around the house all summer playing video games."

"I'll get a job."

"All right."

I did end up working—mostly cutting lawns and yardwork, going door-to-door in our neighborhood most of the summer. A lot of the houses in the area were occupied by current and former military, men who served at Dobbins or Atlanta Naval Air Station, and they were particular about their lawns.

It afforded me freedom I'd never had. On Saturday nights I'd take the bus into Atlanta then the train downtown. I walked the streets, mouth hanging open like a tourist, staring at the high-rises, drinking up the energy of the city. This was an entirely new world.

I stumbled across the Metroplex by accident, walking up Marietta Street one Saturday night right before I turned sixteen, passing a shitty-looking warehouse covered with graffiti. From inside, the pulsing of drums made windows rattle in their frames.

A girl like no one I'd ever seen before sat out front of the building. She had spiked hair, shaved on one side, and wore a jean jacket with tiny metal spikes embedded in the shoulder. Half a dozen earrings shone on her left ear. She was leaning back against the building, smoking a cigarette. She was remarkably pretty.

"You lost?"

I looked around. At the corner were two guys who might have been skinheads, black leather with heads nearly shaved, both wearing what looked like combat boots.

I had short hair, but it was my dad's preferred high and tight. I was wearing sneakers and blue jeans and a sky blue T-shirt and probably looked right out of the 1950s. So I just shrugged and said, "Yeah. I guess I am."

She grinned and stood. "I'm Faith."

"Cole."

She held out a cigarette to me. I took it, and she lit it, and I coughed and she laughed at me.

That summer, Faith became my first girlfriend. I ended up, by default, being part of the punk scene for a while. I'd spend my week cutting grass and stacking wood and doing whatever else I could to earn a few bucks, and on weekend nights we'd go see shows at the Metroplex: the Dead Milkmen, Gorilla Biscuits, Flipper, and the Circle Jerks. It was an awakening. I'd never imagined a world like this: colorful and loud, music blasting, the smell of pot smoke, and screams into microphones.

It didn't last past summer. Faith had dropped out of school and wasn't interested in anything other than partying. I already knew that life wasn't for me. The Metroplex closed then burned down, and that part of my life came to a close. I'd occasionally run into her in other clubs or around town, but the magic was over.

But freshman year at Georgia Tech—when I saw the flyer for the Metroplex Reunion—I knew I had to check it out. I also knew I had to drag along my best friend and roommate.

"Nah, man. I'm not into that scene," was Jeremiah's first reaction. We were in our room in Cloudman Hall, an early twentieth century red brick edifice decades overdue for renovation. Jeremiah was at his desk, an Introduction to Engineering textbook in front of him. I sat across the room, flyer in one hand and a wine cooler in the other.

"Come on, dude. I need my wingman! Besides, Henry Rollins is going to be there. You'll love it."

"Why is that? Is this Rollins guy a jazz virtuoso I've never heard of?"

I laughed. "Trust me, you'll love it. The man's a poet."

He grunted. "You know how much I love poetry."

The next evening we caught the bus from campus to Five Points, which ran right down Marietta Street. The reunion was unmistakable as we approached. Three girls in their late teens and early twenties were standing outside an old building wearing tattered clothes. Two of the girls had fluorescent spiked hair, and the third had a spectacular mohawk, its foot-long spikes radiating from the top and back of her head like the rays of the sun.

After we passed the girls, Jeremiah asked in a falsely innocent tone, "Friends of yours?"

I chuckled. Secretly, I had hoped we'd run into Faith; that she'd gotten her life together maybe just a little; that I could introduce my best friend and the girl who had been my first, and thus far only, girlfriend.

She was nowhere in sight. We entered the temporary club, got our wrists stamped ("UNDER 21" in bold letters) and wandered toward the mosh pit.

In retrospect, it occurred to me once again how good a friend Jeremiah had always been. He was correct that this was, in fact, not his scene. Reserved, conservative, studious Jeremiah was far more comfortable in a jazz club or a public library than a mosh pit filled with teenagers slamming their bodies into each other. But he was game to try anything. Both of us were exhausted by midnight when we left the club.

We walked side by side through the dark downtown streets after leaving the club, headed for Five Points and the train station. We didn't make it more than a block before three guys stepped out of the darkness.

Two of them barely registered on my consciousness, smaller and less visibly hostile, but the guy in the center scared me instantly. Tall and strongly built, a pale man wearing a sleeveless vest with spikes embedded in it, he had a swastika tattooed on his shoulder. His head was shaved clean.

"This the asshole who bumped into you, Ray?" the one in the center asked.

"Yeah," said the youngest of the three—a kid really, no older than fifteen. "The *nigger*."

This guy looked punk, but he *sounded* white trash. "Hey, man, we don't want any trouble," I said. "We're just headed home."

"You found trouble," he replied. "Your nigger friend bumped into my brother in the club."

My heart was beating a thousand beats a minute. Back in the day, there'd been a small group of skinheads who hung out across the street from the Metroplex and sometimes caused trouble. I didn't recognize these three, but I recognized the type. They might not be homicidal, but they'd be willing to hurt us. I scanned the sidewalk quickly, looking for a weapon.

As the big skinhead unhooked a long chain from his belt, I grabbed a bottle from the gutter and hit it against the curb. The end of the bottle shattered, leaving a jagged nasty weapon. The sound startled all of us. Jeremiah raised his fists.

The big skinhead said, "That how you want to play, motherfucker? You gonna fuck with me?" He swung the chain at me. I jerked back, waving the bottle in as unpredictable a pattern as I could, trying to force the guy back. But his friends were circling around behind us. As they did, I knew we were screwed. But I couldn't take my eyes off the fucker with the chain. He swung it in a wide arc, fast, and I had to jerk back, almost bumping into Jeremiah.

Then I had my chance. Asshole swung too hard and lost control of the chain. As he wound up to swing again, I jumped forward, slashing at his face. He screamed and fell back, dropping the chain and grabbing at his face. I spun, just as the other two guys started to grab Jeremiah. I ran at the bigger one, swinging the bottle, just as Jeremiah punched the young one in the face. Both of them stumbled back, the younger kid falling on his ass on the sidewalk.

I caught Jeremiah's eye. Neither of us had to say a word—we took off at a dead run for the train station. The skinheads didn't pursue, and finally we reached the relative safety of the MARTA station.

"Jesus Christ," I said, staggering as I tried to control the rushing breaths. I was shaking.

"Man, that would never have happened if we went to Blind Willie's," Jeremiah said, laughing. He was shaking too.

"That was crazy."

He shook his head. "Thanks for bailing us out there, Cole. That was savage. But don't ever ask me to a concert again."

I laughed, loud, making light of it. But the incident tied us together. Since then, it'd been Jeremiah who bailed me out of trouble, way too many times. Jeremiah had argued persuasively that I should stay in college and not accept the job at RalCom. I had tried to convince him to come with me. While he worked slow and steady—graduating early, then working his way up in the restaurant business, I'd been busy doing mergers and acquisitions.

A few days before I dropped out of college, I'd taken up the job offer with him. "Dude, they're starting me at sixty-five thousand. I'm twenty years old! It's like a gold rush up there. Stock options, fast promotions. You gotta come with me."

He shook his head. "Nah. My mom's sick, Cole, you know that. I can't leave her. If I dropped out of school, she'd check herself right out of the hospital and come kick my butt. And seriously—*you* might be able to drop out of college and just start your career, but it's not so easy for me."

"What, because you're black? Come on, it's the nineties."

He scoffed, shaking his head. "Yeah, that don't mean shit. If I want a leg up, I've got to work twice as hard. And that means I have to finish college. You go on, and let me know how it goes."

Later, when I screwed it all up? It was Jeremiah who showed up. He made sure Sam and Erin had a Christmas when I was in prison. He found me a job when no one else would hire me.

I owed Jeremiah everything. That's not something I could ever forget.

He answered on the second ring. "Cole, what's going on?"

"I'm going to be driving past your place in about twenty-five minutes, I'm just coming back from the airport. You busy?"

"Come on by. Ayanna will be happy to see you. Is Erin with you?"

"No, I just dropped her at the airport, actually."

"I got beers in the fridge," he replied.

Twenty minutes later I pulled up in front of Jeremiah's house in Douglasville. I remember how astonished I was that he'd taken the job with Waffle House after graduating from Georgia Tech. I'd been baffled by his decision to work at the restaurant, but he had made his way up higher and higher in the company in the intervening years. I didn't know exactly what regional vice presidents made, but I was pretty sure that by now he was doing very well indeed. He and Ayanna maintained a modest lifestyle, buying a three-bedroom ranch house when he first became a district manager. I'd bought a gigantic house and a flashy car and gone way too deep in debt. Jeremiah had been careful, hadn't taken out any debt other than his home loan, and that was long since paid off.

I'd once thought his progress was plodding, overly careful. Now I only wished I'd emulated him, because he and Ayanna had security that I could only dream of.

I parked in the front of the house and walked up the driveway to the front door. Three years ago, Jeremiah had added a wraparound porch to the house, giving the place a stately look. The boards creaked under my feet as I walked to the front door and pressed the doorbell.

The door opened, revealing Ayanna. She was a tall, elegantly dressed woman with tightly curled shoulder-length hair, skin a rich brown. Her dress and the string of white pearls she wore made her look as if she were getting ready to go to a party.

"Cole!" She smiled and reached her arms out. We embraced. Then she stepped back and said, "You'll have to forgive us ... Jeremiah will be free soon, but right now we're having a *talk* with the twins. You're welcome to join us." At the last words, she had a twinkle in her eyes.

121

I could do that. "I'm game."

I followed her into Jeremiah's office, a dining room he had converted years before. Jeremiah sat in his office chair. Across from him, side by side on the love-seat, were Kelly and Antoinette, their fifteen-year-old twins.

Jeremiah stood as I entered the room and grabbed me in a bear hug. "Hey, roomie. Give me just a minute."

He turned back to his daughters and said, "This discussion is over, ladies. You leave this house, you wear appropriate clothing. Are we clear?"

Kelly rolled her eyes, and Antionette opened her mouth to talk.

They didn't get a chance. Ayanna interrupted, saying, "That will be quite enough. Let's leave your father alone with Mr. Cole. Say hello, girls."

Both of the girls approximated well-mannered greetings to me, despite their age. I complimented the latest news about their grades and they went on their way with their mother.

"You want a beer, or something stronger?"

I thought about it for a fraction of a second. "I think maybe something stronger."

"Well, come over here to the bar." Jeremiah maintained a well-stocked bar in one corner of his office. Within a couple of moments he had mixed both of us scotch and sodas. Then he led me outside, where we took seats in the rockers on the front porch.

For a few moments we just sat in silence taking in the smells and sounds of the neighborhood; cicadas hummed in the woods and the frogs and other animals cried out in the darkness. It was the first time in weeks I had done anything resembling leisure. Sitting and listening immediately unlocked a flood of memories of growing up. My childhood had sounded and smelled like this.

I sipped the scotch and closed my eyes. "This is good."

"What brings you by, Cole?"

I looked over at my oldest friend. "Brenna's alive."

He set his scotch down on the small wicker table between our chairs and said, "And you're just telling me now? I can't believe you didn't say that the second you came in the door. Or called me earlier. Tell me what's happened?"

In short, clipped sentences I told Jeremiah about the phone call to Erin and what little we knew about Brenna's situation.

Jeremiah instantly zeroed in on what was making me uncomfortable. "How come you aren't going out there?"

"Sam. It's been three weeks since they saw Brenna. She could be anywhere. We can't leave Sam alone and I can't lose my job ... not again. Not to mention, I can't travel without permission. Technically, I shouldn't even have brought Erin to Atlanta—I don't have a travel pass."

He nodded. "Yeah, that's a problem. Jesus. I'd love to get my hands on the son of a bitch that let her slip through the cracks."

I nodded. I'd been struggling with rage ever since I learned she could have been safe in police custody, and instead, they'd treated her like a criminal.

"So now we wait?"

I nodded. "Erin's going to the Portland police in the morning, and hopefully we'll know more then. In the meantime, Sam has school and I have work, and I'll try to keep life as normal as possible for him."

Jeremiah frowned and shook his head. "Life ain't been normal for that boy since the day his sister disappeared." He took a deep breath then a slow sip of his scotch. "How are *you* hanging in there?"

"I'm all right." I shrugged.

He frowned. "Don't bullshit me, Cole. I've got eyes, you know."

I sighed. "I'm doing the best I can, Jeremiah. This job will kill you."

"I know it. Hang in there, and before too long you'll be set to flipping papers instead of burgers and take home real money. Just gotta be patient."

"What about you?" I asked.

"Well, you know how it is. Busy as hell. Ayanna's going to run for city council, and we're working on figuring out how that's going to go. I kinda wish she would wait until the girls graduate from high school, but you know how useful wishing is."

"I bet Erin might want to help. She's always loved political stuff." As I said the words, I knew they weren't really true. Once it might have been, but with her drinking and depression—I couldn't imagine her bothering to get involved in something political now.

He eyed me carefully. "How are things with her? With the two of you?"

I took a sip of the scotch. Then another. It had a faintly earthy smell. It felt good going down. I didn't know how to answer his question.

"That bad, huh?"

I felt my eyebrows pulling together as I struggled to find words. "I fucked things up bad. After Teagan, she can't trust me. When Brenna disappeared, she didn't have anybody to turn to."

Jeremiah snorted. "Except her sister."

"Right. Lori's advice is consistent if nothing else. I'm pretty sure she still tells Erin that she should just leave me."

Jeremiah let out a deep sigh. It sounded like one he'd been waiting to release for years. He cleared his throat then took a sip of his whiskey. "Maybe she should."

I was stunned by his words. Stunned and betrayed. "What the hell is that supposed to mean, Jeremiah?"

He frowns even deeper, deep lines appearing on both of sides of his mouth. "Chill, chill. How long have we been friends?"

"Twenty years. A little more."

"Do you trust me?"

I nodded, a little dazed by the direction the conversation had taken. "Yeah, I trust you. You're damn near the only person in the world I trust."

"Then listen to me. You can't fix your marriage by sitting around whining about how she doesn't trust you. I saw how it was then … you were all dazzled by the money and the power and the pretty salesgirls. And I know you try in your own way. You've taken a job you hate to keep your family supported. I get that. But she's not gonna trust you until you trust her. In there." He pointed at my chest.

"I don't know what you mean—"

He interrupted. "How often do you talk to her about your fears? About things that go wrong? About how you feel about Brenna?"

"That's not really who I am, you know that."

"I *do* know that. And I pay attention. Erin didn't marry someone to provide a paycheck … she married someone to be partners with. You used to understand that. And it seems to me that as time went by, more and more you were focused on providing *things* instead of love."

I shook my head. *Christ,* that was harsh.

But was he right?

When I looked back to those heady days when Erin and I first met, things were so different. And one of the biggest differences was that we'd always talked about our dreams. It's funny how our dreams had reflected our lives. With her hippie parents, Erin dreamed of saving the world, of making a difference, of leaving the world a better place than she'd found it. It's one of the things I admired the most about her—most people couldn't see past their own comfort and security long enough to consider anyone else. But even in college, Erin was fully engaged in the world around her.

My dreams had been shaped by my childhood moving from one base to another before my dad's retirement from the Marine Corps. I'd wanted to give my family stability, a home, a place they could remember for their entire lives. I'd wanted to give them one thing I'd never had as a kid or as an adult … roots.

Like everything else, I'd failed at that too.

My voice was rough when I spoke again. "I don't even know when we stopped talking."

Jeremiah stretched, a long luxurious stretch. Then he punched a hole through the silence. "Do you really want to stay with her?"

I almost answered with a simple knee-jerk, *Of course I do*. But this was Jeremiah, my best friend who had always been able to see through me. So I considered. I thought about what things were like now ... Erin drinking herself to sleep on the couch almost every night. The smell of death in our house. The despair.

Then I thought about how she'd looked the other night, asleep on the couch, much like the girl I'd fallen in love with. About her beautiful smile, her outrage when she talked about injustice in our world. I thought about the four of us laughing and giggling together in our living room before we bought that stupidly large house.

I missed her terribly. I missed my family.

"Yes. I want her back." Unexpectedly, I felt my eyes begin to water. My voice choked up as I said, "I want her to be happy again. I hate seeing her so miserable."

Shit! I quickly wiped my face with the palm of my hand to erase the tear that had run down my cheek.

Jeremiah put a hand on my shoulder. "You gotta tell her that, man."

I spoke in a near whisper. "We had everything ... and I fucked it up. I fucked it all up. It's my fault Brenna disappeared. She wouldn't have been hanging around with older guys if I hadn't gotten mixed up in the affair. And then when Erin needed me the most I got myself locked up in prison."

Jeremiah nodded. "Yeah, you screwed up. I don't think you can blame yourself for Brenna, at least not all of it. Screwing things up is nothing special ... that just makes you part of the human race. But here's the thing, Cole, you've got hope. She's alive. And I don't think it's too late to save your marriage, either. But you've got to be the one to make it happen. You've got to want it bad enough to make some changes."

Both of us went silent, sitting and listening to the night sounds. Night sounds that took me to an earlier, simpler time, a younger time, a time when I hadn't lost my daughter and my marriage.

winter flower
Cole: January 1994

"So what are your parents like?"

When Erin asked the question, she had no idea what kind of can of worms she was opening. But we'd reached that point. After our pre-Christmas visit to her parents, visiting mine in January made sense. I had accumulated way too much vacation, so taking a few days off wasn't a problem, and she didn't go back to school until almost the end of January. Atlanta was a considerably further drive from Washington than Raleigh-Durham, and we'd been switching off the driving for some hours, listening to music and talking before Erin broached this particular question.

I smiled. "Nervous?"

She snorted. "Of course."

I shook my head, my eyes on the road and scanning the countryside as we drove, now through South Carolina. It was greener here than it had been in Washington. "Don't be. They'll love you."

"I don't have that kind of confidence."

I grunted. "Seriously, Erin, my bigger worry is that you'll realize what throwbacks my parents are and you'll have second thoughts about *me*."

"Not possible," came her quick reply.

"You haven't met them yet," I responded. "My parents—Daddy especially—aren't exactly ... um ... politically correct."

That was an understatement.

Daddy had always been a throwback to an earlier era, and not necessarily a good one. Mom was all Southern charm and gentility, nose in the air, her whole family too good to see most of the white trash that surrounded them. Which was the main reason her family always hated Daddy. Brash, bold, and loud, Daddy grew up as a scrappy kid in the mountains of North Georgia in a time when literacy rates were still low and high school graduation rates lower still. The Great Depression came early to the mountains of North Georgia, and its effects lingered long after World War II ended—especially for poor families. And while the mountains of North Georgia had never been big slaveholding country, there were plenty of old racists who were mean as snakes.

Daddy never talked about growing up that much—what I knew, I knew from Mama, or from stories he sometimes told when he'd had too much to drink. James Roberts—everyone called him Jimmy—left home for Riverside Military Academy in Gainesville at the beginning of the seventh grade. Mama said it was to get away from his father, a drunken and bitter man who had seen

126

his entire World War II service inside the gates of Camp Oglethorpe, Georgia, where he trained recruits to go overseas and fight. The hour or so drive between Canton and Gainesville was just enough distance to keep his father from visiting very often, and the academy's endowment provided enough financial aid that he was able to continue attending even when his father refused to pay.

In those days, Riverside maintained a winter campus in South Florida. For the two coldest months of the year, the entire campus decamped and relocated, occupying an old school on land that had been purchased by the Academy a number of years before. During the rare times when I was growing up that my daddy talked about his own childhood, it was invariably stories from the winters he spent in Florida. They were sometimes humorous stories, stories of practical jokes and friendly harassment among the cadets. But there was often a darker edge to those stories. In the fifties and early sixties, Riverside was, of course, all-white. Jim Crow was still fully in effect, and the general poverty of rural mountain Georgia was even worse for the black population. More than once he told me of the Riverside cadets going as a group into black neighborhoods "*to teach the niggers a lesson.*"

When my father said such things, Mama would always cringe. Not because she was any less racist than he was; rather, it was because to her, a sophisticated vocabulary, good posture, and a neat presentation meant far more than substance or character. Mama grew up in the dying world of the Charleston royalty, eking out the last vestiges of their antebellum status in the few square blocks of Charleston they still occupied. In those few square blocks, the Civil War (or, as they called it, the *War Between the States*) might as well have never happened.

Virginia Carolyn Roberts (née Grady) was a sixteen-year-old debutante when she was swept off her feet by my father, at that time a naval ROTC cadet at Georgia Tech. Despite the dire predictions of his own father, Daddy had graduated from Riverside with honors and was accepted to Georgia Tech with a full scholarship.

The two of them married the day after Daddy graduated college and received his commission as a Second Lieutenant in the United States Marine Corps. Nothing in his experience up to that time had changed his perspective about women, politics, or race. He was fundamentally a mountain boy, mean as a snake, and even less predictable. The only thing that had changed over the years was the polish. After decades of trying, my mother's rough tongue and genteel Southern upbringing had worn Daddy down just like flowing water smooths out the edges of a stone.

I'd struggled to explain some of this to Erin without directly saying my parents were racists. To be honest, it was a little embarrassing, in this day and age, to hear my father talk.

"By *not politically correct*, what do you mean?" Her tone sounded a little wary.

I shrugged. "They're from the Old South, Erin. Not academics like your parents ... Daddy was a Marine."

"They'll hate me, won't they? I'm too liberal."

I brought a fist to my mouth and coughed. "Karl Marx would think you're too liberal."

Erin gasped in mock outrage then took a verbal swipe right back at me. "Cole! Being knowledgeable and caring about people doesn't make me too liberal."

I laughed. "Don't worry. Even my parents care about people. Mama mostly cares about her bridge club, and Daddy cares about the Marines."

"So, what you're saying is, we should avoid talking politics."

"Yeah..." My voice trailed off. Avoiding politics was necessary, but I doubted it would be enough.

Nearly fourteen hours after we left Washington, we drove into my parents' semi-circular driveway in North Atlanta.

My parents didn't live in the house I grew up in. Daddy was in the Marine Corps until 1989, so I grew up floating from base to base, year by year. I was lucky enough that he spent his last years in the Marines at Atlanta Naval Air Station, which gave me enough stability to attend the same high school for four years. During those years we lived in a rickety house not far from the base, south of Marietta.

When Daddy retired from the military, he was quickly hired by Lockheed for three times as much as he'd made as a Marine Lieutenant Colonel. The year before I met Erin, he bought a five-bedroom brick colonial in a much better neighborhood than he'd ever lived in as a Marine.

When I parked, it was behind a beautifully maintained '76 Corvette. Daddy was going all-out with the midlife crisis.

The lawn was shockingly verdant for January, the landscaping precise. Red brick contrasted with the black shutters and front door, and all of it gave the impression of a carefully manicured golf course. The beautiful, almost serene setting was ruined by the appearance of a foot-high figure on the lawn not far from the front entrance, depicting a black boy in a red and white outfit and cap. The skin on the figure was very dark, the eyes oversized and white, standing out only slightly less shockingly than the bright red oversized lips.

"Oh, my," Erin said.

"That's new," I murmured.

"You know my godfather's African American, right? And that the twenty-first century is right around the corner?"

"I know these things. My father does not."

She closed her eyes. "Well, let's do this."

"Hey," I said.

"Yeah?" Her voice was pensive.

"Give them a chance, okay? They shocking anachronisms, but they're also my parents."

She gave me a smile that I supposed was intended to reassure; in fact, it only increased my apprehension. "Of course."

The front door opened as we approached. Mama stood there, wearing a green dress with long sleeves which might have easily appeared in a catalog from the fifties. Her hair, still black as always (I suspected she had it dyed, but she would never tell), was bound up in a complicated fashion. She wore a lengthy necklace of white pearls and bright red lipstick.

"Cole," she said, holding out a hand to mine.

"Mama," I said. "This is Erin Bennett. Erin, this is my mom."

"It's nice to meet you, Mrs. Roberts."

"Erin, you must call me Virginia. *Mrs. Roberts* makes me feel dreadfully old. Come in! Come in!"

We followed Mama into the house.

Erin sucked in a breath as her eyes scanned the entryway. The front atrium was floored with polished cherry, and an awe-inspiring crystal chandelier hung over the entry. French doors opened on either side of the entryway, the formal dining room on one side and the family room on the other.

"This is amazing," Erin said. "I love your home!"

"Thank you, dear," Mama said. "Cole's father worked very hard for it."

Lest Erin think I grew up in these polished circumstances, I said, "They moved here three years ago. Most of my life we lived in base housing."

"It's true," Mama said, her voice dripping with ennui. "I don't know what your father does for a living now, but it certainly pays better than being a Marine officer."

I said to Erin, "He left the Marines, so now he sells things to the Marines."

"Don't be crass, dear."

As always, Mama put me in my place.

"Where's Dad?"

I swear her eyes showed a wrinkle of amusement. "Oh, he's around here somewhere. Maybe check out back. In the meantime, why don't you help your lady friend with her bags? We put her in the front room upstairs. You can stay in the guest room next to the library."

Mama turned to Erin. "Come with me to the kitchen, sugar. You must be exhausted from the drive. Would you like some sweet tea? Or … I daresay it's not too early for a glass of wine."

Erin murmured, "A glass of wine sounds wonderful."

As Erin followed Mama into the kitchen, I went out the front door to the car to gather our bags. Undoubtedly, Mama would subject Erin to the third degree, but she'd probably do it in such a painless way that Erin wouldn't even notice. In the meantime, I unloaded my one bag and Erin's three and got them inside and to our rooms. No surprise that Mama put us at opposite ends of the house. Anything to avoid the appearance of impropriety.

The front room where Mama had put Erin—I didn't fool myself into think-ing Daddy had anything to do with it—had a decidedly feminine cast. The bottom half of the walls was paneled with white wainscoting, and the top half had a somewhat girly flowery blue and white wallpaper. The window was framed with white lace curtains; the double bed was piled high with comforters and blankets, all white.

Erin would be amused. Her own taste tended toward hippie Americana. Her dorm room was festooned with incense burners, a statue of Buddha, and a poster featuring the cover of Joseph Campbell's *The Hero with a Thousand Faces*. It was charming and quirky and somewhat adolescent. I secretly hoped she would grow out of that by the time we got more serious or moved in together … or if we got married.

After putting Erin's bags away, I wandered downstairs to the guest bedroom in the back. This room, squeezed in next to the library, was clearly not intended for the important guests. A single bed was jammed up against the wall next to a three-drawer bureau. Between the bed and the opposite wall there was maybe a foot and a half of space to maneuver. It was perfect for me. Even better, Daddy was visible in the backyard, bent over a bed of flowers.

I stepped out the back door, down the steps, and walked along the red brick pathway to where my father crouched.

He glanced up at me, raised an eyebrow, then said, "Pass me the clippers from over there." A few feet away, in the wheelbarrow, were the hedge clippers he indicated. I walked over and got them then carried them back to my father.

He took them and began carefully trimming the tiny bush next to the flow-er bed. "You had a good drive down?"

"Yes, sir."

"I thought you were bringing a girl."

I nodded. "Erin. She's in the house undergoing interrogation."

Daddy winked at me. "Well, Godspeed to her, then."

"You want to come in and meet her?"

Instead of answering, he handed me the clippers then began to pull tiny weeds from the flower bed. "You bring her on out here."

I nodded. I understood … no matter that they had been married for many years, my father assiduously avoided his wife whenever possible. I couldn't say that I blamed him. Mama was much easier to bear in the abstract.

"Lucas got arrested again."

I raised an eyebrow. "What for this time?"

"While you're standing there jawin' why don't you throw on a pair of gloves and help me weed?"

"Sure." I grabbed another pair of gloves out of his wheelbarrow. "What did he get arrested for?"

The creases on either side of Daddy's mouth deepened until it looked like his mouth might break. Then he spit out the words, "Heroin. Possession with intent to distribute."

I crouched down next to Daddy. "How am I supposed to tell the good ones from the weeds?"

Daddy gave a low chuckle and said, "The flowers or your cousins?"

"Well, let's not get into philosophy right now."

He let out a laugh like a bark then pointed at a flowering plant. "Them there is the ones you want to keep. Pull up everything else."

This is how it was with Daddy. He was usually a pretty closemouthed son of a bitch, but if you could catch him while he was doing something, like gardening, he would talk. I wasn't looking forward to dinner, because guests or not, my mom and dad were rarely able to contain the tension between them. For that matter, I couldn't be near them for long either. I hadn't finished college like both wanted, nor had I joined the Marine Corps like Daddy wanted. It didn't matter that I was making almost six figures at twenty-two years old. I'd dropped out of college, and in their eyes, that made me a failure.

An hour before dinner, Erin and I were able to regroup for a few minutes. Outside, of course, on the porch, because Mama was not going to let us be in the same room alone.

"How bad was it?" I asked her.

She laughed. "It was fine. Your mom asked me ten thousand questions. She was thrilled to learn that Dad's a doctor and Mom's on the faculty at Duke."

"Does she know they're old hippies?"

She giggled. "I left that out."

"What else?"

"She told me about you as a little boy. Showed me pictures."

I started. "What? Pictures? Of what?"

"You with your dad. Others with your cousin. You never mentioned cousins."

"That's because they're all white trash."

She flinched. "Really, Cole?" She wasn't asking if they were really white trash. She was asking if I'd really said it.

"Actually, yes, really. Dad just finished telling me about Lucas, he went to jail on a heroin rap. Dealing, not possession."

"Ouch," she responded. "Pretty harsh."

"Yeah, well." I didn't have anything good to say about Lucas. "Anyway, after dinner, I want to get out of here. Take you to meet Jeremiah."

"Does he know I'm coming?"

"Yeah. And, he's got a girl he's serious about, and I haven't met her yet."

"Does she require your approval?"

I grinned at her. "No more than you require his."

"Smart-ass," she replied, grinning. "Okay. I'm looking forward to it."

"Just ... do me a favor? Don't mention Jeremiah around my dad."

She raised her eyebrows.

I leaned close. "Jeremiah's black. Daddy ... he's just ... he's not much changed from the past."

"Your mom didn't say anything horribly or blatantly racist."

"Yeah, her manners would preclude that. But my father doesn't have any manners."

Reluctantly, she agreed. But her silence was pointless. As we were finishing dinner, when I told my parents we were going out, Daddy said, "Going to see that nigger roommate of yours?"

Mama reproved him immediately. "James, we don't use that word..."

Erin frowned. "Mister Roberts ... you've made such a good impression up until now, I'm so sorry to see it spoiled."

Silence instantly fell on the room.

Erin plunged ahead. "First, you should know my godfather is black. Second, you should know it's the nineties, and we left slavery and Jim Crow behind decades ago."

Red spots were beginning to glow on Mama's cheeks. It didn't matter that she constantly harped and bitched at Daddy—she would *never* put up with another woman doing it.

Daddy leaned forward in his seat, a frown on his face. "Now see here, Miss. I'll make allowances for you because it's clear Cole really cares for you. But you don't come insult a man in his own home."

"I'm sorry, Mister Roberts. But *my* father told me to always tell the truth and to confront bigotry when I see it."

A flash of displeasure on his face. "I'm no bigot. I've got friends who are black. I served with blacks in Vietnam—in fact, one of 'em saved my life. There's some people who are black, and they're okay in my book. Then there's some people who are *niggers*. And that's just the way it is."

Mama tried to salvage the situation. "James, maybe we should just drop the subject?"

I just sat there, admiring Erin more and more every second.

Erin didn't back down. "Let me ask you, sir. Who are the ones most deserving of that label?"

Anger flashed through my father's tone. "Well, the ignorant ones. The ones who don't know how to talk or how to act. The ones who go around with guns and killing good people."

Quietly, Erin persisted. "You mean, the ones from poor neighborhoods, with lousy schools? The ones who come from broken families? Families whose histories of being broken go right back to when husbands and wives and sons and daughters were often sold away without so much as a word? The ones that *we* prevented from voting, or learning to read, or having decent jobs? Are those the ones you mean?"

"Well, my appetite is ruined," Mama announced. "I believe I'll retire to my room now."

"We should go, too," I said. I took her hand and practically pulled her out of there, with none of the ceremony you might have expected.

That might have been the end of it. Not long after that, we got out of there and spent the evening enjoying ourselves with Jeremiah and Ayanna. Jeremiah took us all to Blind Willie's, where we listened to a jazz quartet that almost put me to sleep (the three of them loved it).

Ayanna was enchanting. She was a senior at Georgia State, planning to go straight into graduate school, and had a beautiful smile. Poised and cheerful, she had an electric laugh. Halfway through the show, I leaned over to Jeremiah and whispered, "I'm impressed, buddy."

133

We high fived, looking mystified when Ayanna and Erin asked what it was about.

The next morning, the funniest thing happened. Everyone pretended nothing had happened at all, and we had a pleasant breakfast. But before we headed back to Washington two days later, Daddy pulled me aside.

"Just wanted to tell you, Cole … don't let that one go."

"What?" I sputtered. "I assumed you hated her."

He chuckled. "What, because of our disagreement? Naw. Maybe I learned something from her. Maybe not. But she's got spirit, that one. You treat her right, and she'll make you happy."

You treat her right, and she'll make you happy.

Those words stayed with me, that hour, that month, that decade.

Sadly, more than anywhere else in my life, treating Erin right was the one area where I failed the most.

Twelve: Two Years Ago

Brenna

When I look at the devastation of my life, I still can't blame Chase for what happened. I wish I could. But it wasn't his fault. I loved him. Back when I believed in love, when I was nothing but a dumb teenager who thought nothing bad could happen. When I believed love could solve anything, that it could give you anything, that it wasn't just another thing to be twisted and broken, another weapon to be used against you until you couldn't even recognize your own face in the mirror.

I thought I knew so fucking much. When my mother got in my face and yelled that I was putting myself in danger, I just rolled my eyes and ignored her. When Chase told me he didn't trust Rick, I didn't listen.

The only person I ever really listened to was Grandpa. Everyone else saw this old guy who puttered around in the garden after he retired, but whenever we talked it seemed to me there was a world of hurt going on behind his eyes. He never talked about it—if I asked him about growing up, he'd tell me a funny story about poverty in the North Georgia mountains. When I asked about Vietnam, he'd say, "It wasn't what you see in the movies. War is mostly boring."

I wish I could see Grandpa now. Crazy.

My dad? He was a hypocrite who had an affair. Mom? She didn't understand. Her whole life was college and being perfect and impressing her parents. And Sam was too young to understand being in love.

Maybe that's the curse of being young. You think you know everything. You think nothing can ever hurt you. You think you're invincible.

If so, then I'm not young anymore, and I never will be again. Now I live in hell. Now I know just how badly I can hurt, and just how much I'm not invincible.

If it wasn't for Nialla, I'd be dead. And I don't mean that in a *oh, isn't that lovely* way some people talk about their girlfriends. I mean reality. She taught me how to avoid pissing Rick off too much, enough that he's only seriously hurt me a few times. She taught me how to shut down emotionally. How to protect myself. How to stay huddled inside in the few places left where they couldn't touch me.

Nialla taught me how to guard myself.

She taught me what to do to humor Rick, to keep him happy, to keep him satisfied.

She taught me how to take myself to faraway places in my mind when real life became too painful to bear.

She taught me how to be numb.

Now? I don't feel anything for anyone, except my parents and Sam, who I'll never see again, and Nialla, who I love.

The first time I saw Rick and Nialla I felt immediate tension. It was a few weeks before my sixteenth birthday, and I was hanging out at Scott Towson's house with Chase.

We often hung out in the basement drinking, and when Rick walked into the room with Nialla, Chase tensed suddenly, the muscles running up his thighs where they touched me flexing suddenly. I responded to his tension, putting a hand on his knee, looking where he was. I was a little light-headed. Light-headed from a couple of drinks, but mostly light-headed from Chase.

Rick was tall, with short cropped hair and frightening brown eyes. I guess if I looked at them alone, they'd seem warm. Or maybe they were just colored by my memories. But I remember being scared by his cold expression, by the tense, bunched muscles of his tattooed arms exposed in a sleeveless shirt. He walked into the room with his arm on Nialla's. He held her arm in a possessive, almost controlling way. Her eyes moved everywhere in the room in a way that made my skin crawl. She was terrified of something and seemed to be clinging onto Rick for dear life.

"'Sup, Chase?" Rick said.

"Hey, man," Chase replied. But his tone was lifeless.

Rick looked at me, his eyes hooded, then looked at Chase. "Introduce me to your girl?"

Chase spoke in a low, careful tone. "Brenna, this is Rick. Rick, Brenna." No one introduced the girl who was with him, the girl I would later know was named Nialla, the girl who would become my savior.

His tone scared me. I didn't know what was going on here. I'm not sure I wanted to know. Abruptly, Chase said, "We gotta get going."

Rick's mouth curved up in an amused half smile. "Later, Chase. Brenna." There was a pause before he said my name, a tension-filled pause as his eyes rested on me, and it sent a shiver of fear down my neck. But I'm ashamed to say, it also sent down a shiver of ... fascination? No one had ever looked at me that way. Chase loved me. But a look of naked lust? It was disturbing, frightening ... and a little thrilling.

Whatever it was, I followed Chase out, his hand tightly clamped on mine. So hard that it hurt a little bit. I could feel Rick's eyes on my ass and legs as we walked away, and my neck flushed.

We got to his car, and Chase said, "Promise me you'll stay away from Rick."

I swallowed then gave him a surprised look, one eyebrow raised. "I have no intention of being around Rick. You're my boyfriend, Chase. I love you."

He turned his head toward me and leaned close. "I'm not saying this out of jealousy, Brenna. He's ... that dude spooks me like no one I've ever met. He just started hanging around, nobody knows where he came from. It's ... I don't know. Just ... I don't want you coming here without me."

What the hell? Did he think he owned me? I gave him a glare. "If you don't trust me, just say it, why don't you? I've been hanging out at Scott's since before we met, in case you forgot."

He closed his eyes. "Brenna. Please."

"Fine." I leaned back in my seat, crossing my arms over my chest. I was still a little drunk, and a lot angry. I stared out the window as he put the car in gear and backed out of the parking lot. He pulled out into traffic too quickly, the tires squealing, and I heard another car honk at us.

I gritted my teeth a little. "Just because you're angry with me doesn't mean you can risk my life."

He was silent for a full minute or two, aggressively changing gears and shifting through traffic. Too fast. My heart beat quickly, and I gripped the door with my right hand. Finally, he took a deep breath and slowed down.

"Brenna, I'm not angry with you. I just don't trust that guy at all. I worry about you. You're so damn young."

"What the *hell* does my age have to do with it, Chase? We've been through this."

He looked away from me, his jaw clenching. "It has everything to do with it. You're fucking fifteen years old, Brenna."

I closed my eyes and sniffed, blinking back tears. Was he backing out? Because I was younger than he was? Is that what this was all about? "I'll be sixteen in two weeks. And you *promised*."

"I know I did, baby. But that doesn't change the fact that even after your birthday ... I could still go to prison if we do what you want."

I swallowed. "You know I wouldn't tell anyone," I whispered.

"Yeah? What about your mom and dad? They can't be fucking thrilled about us dating."

"I can handle them."

"Fuck," he muttered, shaking his head.

"You don't want me."

"I want you more than I want to breathe. I want you so badly I could die right now, Brenna. But you gotta admit this is all fucked up."

I felt tears rolling down my face. And that pissed me off. Nobody made me cry. Nobody. "So ... what? This is it? Thanks for the good times?"

"No!" He slammed his fist into the steering wheel. The car horn sounded a short blast in response to the first.

"Then what?"

"I just want you to fucking listen to me, Brenna. Rick is dangerous. That's it! Everything else is the same, including the fact that you're too stubborn to listen to anyone else but you. But I'm asking you to listen to me on this one, okay?"

I felt my lips twitch around my mouth and held my teeth together in a tight grip. Trying to compose myself. I swiped at the evidence of tears on my face, looking out the window. Finally I said, "Yeah. I'll listen. I don't give a shit about him anyway. It's just ... Scott's house is like, I don't know, it's always been a safe haven. It's like you're telling me I can't go home."

I didn't have to tell him that we'd met and become friends there. That our romance had begun there, in that basement. We'd told my parents that we met at a coffee shop, because it was unspoken in our circle that Scott's basement was never talked about. His parents were never around, and even when they were, they stayed clear of the basement. Scott had turned it into a rec room, filled with beanbags and old secondhand couches, a big-screen TV, and a no-questions-asked policy with weed and alcohol. I didn't smoke it much, but the vibe there was good, and I didn't get a lot of questions about my age or anything else. And that was what I wanted, right?

I didn't know what I wanted. I didn't know anything, did I? Because if I'd had a clue what was coming, I'd have run like hell. I'd have curled up at home with my mother and never left the house again.

Hindsight is like that. You look back and think about how it could have been. If only. If only I'd never gone to Scott's house. If only I hadn't met Rick and Nialla there. If only I hadn't accepted Rick's friend request on Facebook when it came three days later.

If only I had listened to Chase's warning.

Brenna

Tuesday night.

Sam had finally left my room, where we'd spent thirty minutes going through my makeup. Dad was out of town, and Mom was doing whatever, so I was finally free. My room was clear on the other side of the house from hers, so I was pretty much guaranteed all the privacy I needed, unless Sam came back in, and I never really minded that.

I booted up my computer then hopped on Facebook. It's not that I was doing anything really secretive. I just didn't like Mom and Dad snooping in my business. And snoop they often did. Dad knew a lot about computers, so if I wanted any privacy at all, I had to be careful.

I froze, though, when I logged in. New friend request. From someone named Rick Sutton. I studied the picture. That was him. The guy I'd met the other night at Scott's. The picture looked a little younger than he looked the other night. Younger, and somehow less frightening. He had a friendly, engaging grin.

It was just online, it's not like I had to see him. So I did the stupidest thing I'd ever done in my life. If there was moment that sealed my fate, this was it.

I clicked yes.

Less than thirty seconds later a message box appeared.

Hey there.

I froze. Jesus. What did he want? I wrote back: **Hi! What are you doing?**

His answer was immediate. **Thinking about u. The other night was a little weird, and I wanted to apologize.**

Well, that was weird. **What for?**

He replied, **Nialla was really upset about some family stuff. So we were both a little off. Anyway, you gonna be at Scott's any time soon?**

My heart was thumping in my chest. I didn't know anything at all about this guy, and Chase thought he was dangerous.

Chase liked to act like he owned me. He thought I was a little girl who didn't know shit. I loved him, but I didn't like being treated that way. And besides, chatting with someone online couldn't hurt anything. In a flash of mixed emotions, I typed back, **Why do you want to know?**

I think you're pretty.

My heart started thumping. Who the hell was this guy? I clicked on his profile, but there wasn't a whole lot there. It looked like he was new on Facebook, just a few pictures, a few posts, very few friends, and they were all people I knew. It couldn't hurt to be nice. I could feel heat on my face and neck.

I typed one word in response: ***blushes***

And that was how it started. Rick and I chatted for an hour, then again the next night. I was so flattered by his interest. And I never realized that while he was drawing out information about me, about Sam, about my life, he never told me a single thing about himself.

I was so stupid. Rick played me like a musical instrument, tuning me up, then forcing me to sing whatever notes he wanted. It's not that I wanted to dump Chase. I loved him. And if I'd listened to him, my life wouldn't have ended up where it was.

At the same time, Chase wasn't *there.* He wasn't on Facebook. He rigidly controlled when we could see each other. He worked all the time, so we hardly ever saw each other. I wasn't cheating on him. I never even considered it. But I won't lie. Rick's attention excited me. It made me feel wanted, desirable, when sometimes I felt like I had to beg Chase to kiss me. Chase, who loved me. Chase, who was all hung up over my age.

It was Thursday night when Rick messaged me again.

Going to Scott's tomorrow after school?

Yes, I answered, my pulse pounding in my temples.

See you then.

So Friday after school, I caught a ride from Scott and went back to his place. His parents lived in a big house just down Leesburg Pike from ours. It was large but not one of the new McMansions that seemed to be covering all the nearby Northern Virginia neighborhoods.

It was strange. I felt far more comfortable at Scott's. Ever since my parents bought the monstrosity, it seemed like our lives were more distant. Dad traveled so much I hardly ever saw him. Mom was more and more preoccupied with the PTA and volunteer stuff, but it seemed hollow. Like she was doing it for her benefit, not mine. Scott's house seemed more homelike. Oddly safe.

Not that Scott's parents were at all involved in his life. He was a nice guy, a little goofy. Always had a funny smile and a kind word to say. I think he'd been

140

bullied in middle school—he was a little overweight—but his general kindness to everyone had become a bubble protecting him. It helped that he surrounded himself with people like me. People who would go to the mat to protect a friend.

When we got down to the basement, he said, "Want to smoke one?"

I nodded, and we sat down on the couch. He slid the cigar box out from under the couch, where he kept his stash hidden in a half-assed way. His parents never came down here anyway.

Two minutes later, he passed me the smoking joint and I took a long drag, my throat burning. Then I coughed loud and giggled. He grinned and said, "Lightweight."

I giggled again.

"So you doing anything for your birthday?"

I leaned back, already feeling light-headed. "My parents are having a party for me. Dorky."

"Nah," he said. "That's cute. And hey, maybe you'll get a car."

"I doubt it. But maybe. They did promise to take me to get my license though. Only two weeks."

"Fucking awesome."

A second later the back door opened. And in walked Rick, his arm gripped around Nialla's. Her eyes darted all over the room as they walked in.

My pulse immediately began racing. What was up with Nialla? Why was she so scared all the time? Where the hell had they come from anyway? Rick had just ... shown up, two or three weeks ago. It was a little weird. He had to be in his mid-twenties, but Nialla was a lot younger. Eighteen, maybe.

"Scott, my man," Rick said. He reached out and clasped hands with Scott, his eyes sliding over me. "What's going on?"

Scott shrugged and passed the joint to Rick.

Rick took a long toke from it. "Good stuff." His eyes dropped to me, and he gave me a lopsided grin. Then he passed me the joint. Our fingers touched for just a second, and I shivered. I took a long drag, desperately trying not to cough. Nialla's eyes continued searching around the room. Looking at everything. Except me. She never once looked at me.

Scott's phone rang. He looked at it, rolled his eyes, and said, "Hello?" He got an impatient look on his face. "Mom, I've got friends over."

He listened a second longer. I could hear her voice even though the phone was against his ear. Whatever she was saying, it was in a pretty shrill tone of voice.

"All right, I'll be right up." He hung up, then said, "Well, that blows. I gotta go. My uncle's having some kind of dinner tonight, and they said I have to go."

He reached into the open cigar box, took out a bottle of eyedrops, and leaned his head back, dropping one in each eye. "Feel free to hang out. I'll be back late."

Then he stood up. And my throat closed. Fear? Apprehension? Anxiety? I don't know what it was, but I felt like I couldn't breathe. I took another long drag off the joint then passed it to Nialla. Her hands trembled as she took it. My head was swimming.

I stood up. "I gotta go, too."

Rick stood up. "Hey ... you don't have to go anywhere."

I was woozy from the weed. The sharp edge of fear that ran through me seemed to make me more alert.

"Hey, Scott. Wait up ... do you think I can get a ride home?"

I caught up with Scott at the top of the stairs and followed him into the kitchen. I had never been up here before. Scott's friends all came and went through the basement door.

"Dude! You *know* it's not okay to come upstairs. If my mom sees you stoned—"

"Just let me out the front door, okay?"

Scott smirked. "Is Rick scaring you?"

"Who is he? I don't remember ever seeing them before a few weeks ago."

Scott shrugged. "Friend of Gearbox, maybe?"

I whispered urgently. "You mean you don't even know?"

A moronic chuckle erupted from Scott. "I know he's got the hots for you. His eyes were all over you. He didn't *care* that his girl was looking."

Even though Rick scared me, maybe because he scared me, I felt a flood of pleasure at those words. I swallowed. "Look, can I just get a ride?"

"Scott! I told you to come!" The call came from somewhere down the hall.

Scott shrugged and spread his hands wide. "Sorry," he mouthed. Then he pointed toward the front door.

I really didn't want to get Scott in trouble, and his parents were so cool about people hanging out. So I carefully tiptoed to the front door. People were talking down the hall ... not just his mother, but three or four people. Whatever. Very carefully, I opened the front door and slipped out.

Scott's parents owned a house in an old wooded neighborhood. Their driveway stretched around the back, where Scott's friends usually parked. But his parents' cars were in the front. When I heard a car start in the back, I ducked down behind one of the cars in the front drive. Less than a minute later, Rick's gleaming Hummer drove by and turned right out onto the street. I stayed low as I watched him drive away then began walking toward home.

Some things about Rick just didn't make sense. Why was Nialla so scared? And where did a twentysomething who had no apparent job get the money to drive a car like that? I didn't know much about cars, but I knew enough to know that a brand-new Hummer with custom detailing must cost at least thirty or forty thousand dollars. Maybe he had a good job and it was just easy hours? Because he showed up around here at all hours of the day and night.

Or maybe he sold drugs?

For that matter, why did he only have a few friends on Facebook, all people who were in Scott's circle?

It was going to be a long walk home, probably more than an hour. Before Dad bought that ridiculous house, we had been neighbors with Scott and his family. I missed the neighborhood. I missed our old house, it was only one block over. I'd loved that house.

I was going to have to live with the walk. If I called my parents they'd see I was stoned, and if I called Chase he would be pissed that I went to Scott's without him. The walk would give me time to clear my head anyway. God, I couldn't wait until I got my driver's license.

Two weeks seemed like forever.

The walk also seemed like it was taking forever. But fifteen minutes into it, my phone rang. It was Chase.

"Hey! I didn't think I was going to hear from you until later! Did you get off work early?" My words came out in a jumbled mess, because I was so happy to hear from him. But that happiness was fleeting.

"I thought I told you to stay away from Scott's if I wasn't there with you." His tone was cold.

My reaction was instantaneous and instinctive. "Chase, you don't own me. You don't get to tell me what I do with my time." *Asshole.*

"I thought I explained—I'm not trying to control you, Brenna. I'm just worried. Something about Rick freaks me out."

Something about Rick freaks me out, too. But that doesn't mean you get to dictate where I go.

"Chase, it's not like I was alone with him. Scott was there, and his parents, and Rick's girlfriend."

In a patient tone, Chase said, "Scott told me that you urgently asked for a ride when he had to go." I closed my eyes. It figured Scott had called.

"Well … I forgot I had to write a paper."

Chase actually chuckled. "Really? That sucks, because I got off work early and I was hoping to come get you and take you out."

"Really?" I felt myself grinning and relieved.

"Yeah. I miss you, you know. With this job we don't get to see each other that much."

A momentary flash of guilt reminded me that I had been thinking exactly that when I spent so much time chatting with Rick on Facebook. But it wasn't like I had cheated on him. I didn't even want to be around Rick. "I'd really like that."

"Where are you? I'll come get you."

By the time I got home from dinner with Chase, my scare at Scott's house had faded to nothing much in my mind. Fear brought on by little more than my own imagination.

When I walked into the house, I was greeted by the sound of shouting. I sighed and wandered toward the kitchen. Mom and Dad's room was far away from the front door … if I could hear them yelling, this was a hell of a fight. I made out Dad shouting, "*I don't know what you want me to do. I've apologized. I've gone to therapy with you. I've done everything you asked, and it's not enough!*"

A stab of anger ran through me. I knew about the affair, not that they had told me, but it was hard to miss when people screamed things at each other. I didn't know any details, just that it was some woman from work.

But I did know that it had been a long time, and Mom still hadn't let it go, or forgiven him, or even given him a chance to make it up to her. It would be one thing if he lied about it. But from what I could tell, he admitted the truth, and apologized, and did everything he could. And Mom? Sometimes I could see why Dad might have gotten so distant from her. She was always sniping at him, making little comments or complaining. You could see the tension between them most of the time. Did that justify him cheating? No. But I could see how it happened. A moment of weakness while he was traveling. But the thing was, I had heard him practically begging her to forgive him. They went to therapy all the time, and it seemed like he was doing everything he could to make up for it. And she just wouldn't give him an inch.

Sam disagreed with me. Every time we talked about it, she took Mom's side. I couldn't figure out why. But she blamed Dad for everything.

I wanted to ignore them. I wanted to not hear the fighting anymore. I was tired of it.

But I couldn't stop listening. It was like watching a disaster happen, like that tsunami the year before, where I kept watching the videos on YouTube of the waves coming in and lifting up cars and washing buildings and people away to the ocean. I figured eventually Mom and Dad were going to get a divorce. But unlike a sudden disaster, that particular flood rose only an inch at a time, so slowly that we almost didn't notice it was happening, until suddenly you find out you are treading water and can't breathe and you're being washed out to sea.

I shuffled around in the kitchen, making myself a snack—Graham crackers with peanut butter and toasted marshmallows—and in the process, I slammed all of the doors and the oven and generally made as much noise as possible.

Where was Sam? She always made herself scarce whenever Mom and Dad were fighting. Was it any wonder? I'm guessing that she couldn't hear me because she'd have music turned up, headphones on, to shut out the sounds of the fighting.

Now it was Mom. It was harder to make out what she was saying. Except for one shout: *"How am I supposed to trust you ever again?"*

I wanted the fighting to end.

Thirteen: Two Years Ago

Brenna

The next weekend, Chase picked me up on Saturday morning. We had made plans to spend the day together, and I had also asked him to take me to the post office to pick up Sam's packages. It was the perfect September morning: clear sky, not too hot, and a beautiful breeze.

Chase walked into the post office with me. I fished out the key to the post office box and unlocked it. I had rented the box a year earlier, after Sam had begged me for weeks. I could never say no to Sam, especially about something this important.

Don't you know these drugs are dangerous? I had asked.

Yes! But what happens when I start growing in my shoulders and grow an Adam's apple and get a man's face and my voice lowers? Don't you understand that once that happens, there's no going back? Brenna, please, I'm begging you. I'm so afraid of what's happening to me.

In the end I had relented. But it had turned out to be even more complicated than Sam had imagined. Ordering black-market hormone blockers from Mexico had required significant effort, not the least of which was the post office box. But we'd gotten them, a six-month supply, and had ordered twice more since then. It had become routine, and it was clear the drugs were working. Sam was fourteen years old but looked closer to twelve. She stood out when lined up with the other ninth grade boys, all of whom were going through various stages of puberty.

A postal worker had placed a yellow slip in the box, informing me that an object too big for the box needed to be picked up at the counter. We waited in line. While waiting, Chase asked, "What are we picking up anyway?"

I didn't need to look around to know that this was not the place to discuss it. We were surrounded by people in line. My heart was thumping with anxiety. "I'll tell you later."

Chase looked annoyed. But he didn't make an issue of it.

The postal worker handed over the package with no questions asked. As I turned away I felt the anxiety drain out of me, and I realized I'd been holding my breath. I was always afraid that when I showed up to pick them up, DEA agents would appear out of nowhere and arrest me. But for the third shipment in a row, the drugs had passed through customs without being inspected.

Back in the car, Chase said, "You gonna tell me what this is about?"

I nodded. He put the car in reverse and pulled out of the parking lot.

"You have to promise to keep what I tell you an absolute secret. It's a matter of life and death. Literally."

Chase's eyebrows seemed to scrunch together. "That's dramatic. Of course, Brenna. You know you can trust me. I'm a little upset you felt like you had to ask."

"This isn't my secret, it's Sam's."

"Okay…"

I swallowed. I had to tell him. "Sam is a girl."

Chase glanced away from the road, giving me a quizzical look. "Your brother, Sam?"

I shook my head. "No. My sister. Sam was born a boy, but she is my sister. She wants to get a sex change as soon as she turns eighteen."

"*Whoa.* Are you serious?" He looked over at me, eyes wide. Then he nodded. "You are. You think *he's* serious about it? That's crazy."

"Not really. It's not common, but it happens. And I'll do whatever I have to take care of her. If that means helping her with this, then that's what it means."

Chase shrugged, looking confused. "You gotta admit it's a little whack."

"You don't get to decide that."

He shrugged then shook his head. "Okay … he's your brother … er … sister. Anyway, what's in the box?"

"Blockers … hormone blockers … they're drugs to delay puberty."

Chase exploded into words. "Are you fucking kidding me? Drugs? Your parents sure as *shit* don't know about this, or you wouldn't be the one picking them up! What, did you order them from Mexico or something?"

"Yeah. I did."

Chase looked pale. "Do you know how much trouble you could get in? Not to mention, the drugs might be laced with heroin or sawdust or motor oil or something. That is insanely dangerous. It's … it's irresponsible!"

I flinched at his shouts. I hated when people shouted at me. In response, I felt a rush of defensive anger, and I shouted right back at him. "Yes, I know how dangerous it is! You know how many transgender kids commit suicide if they don't get treatment? Do you know that if she goes through puberty the changes are irreversible? That the later she gets treatment, the more male she will look?"

"So he should go to a doctor. You don't do something serious like this on your own. That's nuts! You could kill him! And what if he changes his mind, when you started a sex change all on your own? What then? Is what you're doing even reversible?"

I sigh. "Chase, these don't start a sex change. All they do is buy her some time to be sure."

"Stop saying *she*. Sam's not a *she* yet."

"Stop being an *asshole*!"

Chase looked shocked. I crossed my arms over my chest and looked out the window. He drove, and we spent the next several minutes in silence.

It seemed like lately all we did was fight. Is this what happened when you loved people? That's all Mom and Dad did. They fought and yelled and raged and cried. If that's what I had to look forward to, maybe I should just go live in a convent or become a crazy cat lady.

Who was I kidding? Cats were nasty creatures, and I loved Chase. I felt my eyes water and I blinked them angrily, unwilling to let him see them. I sniffed and wiped furiously at my eyes.

"I'm sorry." His words were quiet and calm. "I still think you're nuts, but I didn't mean to shout at you."

I didn't answer right away. Because I wanted to punch him in the nose. I *hated* when I cried. I hated when we fought. I hated shouting and yelling and conflict.

"Can you forgive me?"

I turned toward him. His eyes were on the road, as he turned onto the Dulles Toll Road. "Of course I forgive you. Just ... can you understand why I have to help Sam?"

He shrugged, and said, "Understand ... not really. But yeah, I can accept it. It's between you and him—her. Just ... be careful. You're getting into some really serious shit. I don't know what would happen if you got caught having that stuff shipped into the country illegally."

"I will," I said. "I promise I'll be careful."

Brenna

When I got home that night, I waved at Mom and Dad, who were sitting mindlessly numbing out in front of the television, and headed upstairs to Sam's room.

I knocked on the door then tried to open it. Locked. It didn't matter: she opened it seconds later.

"Hey! Did you get it?"

"Yeah," I said. I slipped into her room and closed the door, rummaged through my bag, and took out the package. Her eyes were bright as I handed it over, and she sat down on the edge of her bed and began to tear open the wrapping.

I studied Sam for several seconds as she tore open the packaging. Chase had raised fresh doubts about whether or not I should be helping Sam with this particular problem. But there was no denying the happiness I saw. Nor was there any denying that it had prevented her body from undergoing the kind of rapid changes the other eighth and ninth grade boys had been going through around her.

Sam wore a plain white T-shirt and athletic shorts. Her legs were smoothly shaven, which might have been a clue to our parents that something was up, if they had bothered to pay any attention. But they were too wrapped up in their own problems to notice us. As she began to lay out the bottles one by one, checking the labels, I noticed that she wore mascara and the faintest eye liner.

I guess she could get away with it. Some of the guys who hung out at Scott's occasionally wore it. Guy-liner. The same guys who wore black and pretended to be cynical and oh-so-above-it-all, but who took a hundred selfies a day and posted them online. I didn't have much patience for those guys, to be honest.

Sam opened the bottles and checked them.

"Looks okay?" I asked.

Sam nodded. "Same pills as last time." She slipped off the bed and walked to the closet then rummaged around in there. A few moments later she came out, without the pills. Sam walked over and put her arms around me.

"Thank you," she whispered.

"Just be careful. If you feel weird or anything, say something. Right away, okay? I worry about you."

"I will."

Was I making a mistake? What if Chase was right? Or what if the drugs were bad, or like, laced with something? I was so worried about her. There was no winning in this situation. Sam had a tough life ahead of her. I was hyper-aware of news about transgender issues because of Sam, and the news was almost never good. Dad listened to Fox News all the time, and for days they'd been all up in arms about some judge ruling that a prisoner had the right to a sex change at the state's expense. I didn't know the legal issues. What I *did* know was the hate that just dripped from their mouths whenever they talked about it. Mom and Dad had argued about it. Not like a real argument, but a political argument.

Dad had said, *They don't have a physical illness. It's a delusion, and they need to see a psychiatrist, not a surgeon. I don't see any reason taxpayers should pay for surgery for some pervert who wants to change their sex.*

Sam had been sitting at the table when Dad said that, and she flinched when he said the word *pervert*.

I love Dad, but I wish he knew how much he was hurting her. Someday Sam would run away or get hurt or hurt herself because of how alone she felt.

"Listen," I said. "I love you, you know that?"

Sam smiled. "I love you too."

We hugged again, then I said, "Good night."

"You too."

I unlocked the door and headed down the hall to my own room. Minutes later a message popped up on my phone.

It was Rick.

Rick: Hey, what ya' doing?

Brenna: Hanging out. Just got home.

Rick: Out with Chase?

Brenna: Yeah.

Rick: Want to get together with me and Nialla?

I stared at the screen, my heart suddenly racing. He couldn't be all that bad, after all, Nialla hung out with him constantly.

No. Chase would be upset. And … just no. I didn't even want to. I didn't know why I wanted to.

There was something just a little thrilling about the pursuit.

Brenna: I can't tonight.

Rick: Maybe we'll get a chance some other time. Take it easy.

My stomach hurt.

I let out a slow, slow breath, then put down the phone.

Fourteen: Two Years Ago

Brenna

"Are you and Mom getting a divorce?"

I hadn't planned on asking Dad that question. We were sitting side by side in his car on our way to the Department of Motor Vehicles, where, with any luck, I would be getting my driver's license in a few hours. I didn't know why I asked ... I guess because I knew that absolutely nothing could burst my bubble that day. I was sixteen years old, I was in love, I was getting my driver's license. I didn't have a thing in the world to be upset about.

Despite that assurance, or maybe because of it, I blurted out the question.

Dad visibly took a deep breath when I asked the question. His hands moved restlessly, as if he wished he were driving. "What makes you ask?"

I stared at him in sort of a slow-motion disbelief. Did he really even ask that? Did they think we were oblivious?

Maybe he did.

"Uh ... because you guys fight all the time? Because you're never home? Because half the time when I get up for school, one of you is asleep on the couch?"

His face crinkled with a look of fierce concentration, as if he were screwing up his courage. "Brenna, in the last couple of years I made some horrible mistakes. Some really, really bad decisions."

Like having an affair?

"We're not out of the woods yet. I'm not going to lie to you. But your mom and I are in therapy. We're trying. So ... no, I don't think we are getting a divorce."

Not a definitive *no*. But I wouldn't have believed that anyway. This was better because it had some hope.

"Things have actually been better between us. I know you might not believe that, but it's true. It really is."

Unexpectedly, my eyes watered. I took my right hand off the wheel and with my palm, I quickly tried to rub away any hint of tears. "Thanks for not trying to bullshit me."

He tactfully didn't point out the obvious, that I was starting to cry. Instead, he said, "Up to the right … do you see it?"

I nodded. The entrance to the DMV was only a block away. I switched on my right-turn signal.

"You're old enough to hear the truth from me. And … whatever happens with your mom and me, you've got to know that we both love you. No matter what." As he said the words he rested his left hand on my shoulder. I glanced over at him, but he ordered, "Eyes on the road."

When he said, *You're old enough to hear the truth from me*, it made me feel warm inside. It had been a long time since I wanted to be around my mom and dad, but that comment made me want to be with them. Crazy. Ever since that disastrous sit-down when Mom interrogated Chase, I'd been daydreaming about convincing him to run off with me. The more we fought about things like whether or not I was following the rules at home, the more I wanted to do it.

I tried to imagine what it would be like. Running away with him, then writing home from Mexico or Belize or someplace where they couldn't find me. We could do it. We could be happy.

The voice in the back of my head, the one I wanted to tell to shut up, asked, *What about Sam?*

What *about* Sam? Wasn't it time she started taking care of herself? I'd kept her secret ever since the day I walked into my bedroom after coming home early from a field trip and found Sam in my room wearing one of my dresses. I could never forget that day. Sam had fallen to her knees, blubbering, begging me not to tell our parents. I was so shocked that all I could think of was to protect her.

I *still* felt a responsibility to protect her. I always would. But when did I get to have my own life? I was practically a grown-up, and I couldn't exactly stay and watch over Sam forever.

I made a promise to myself then that I would talk with Chase about it that night. About our future. Surely he'd be willing to come pick me up on my birthday.

I parked the car in the DMV parking lot.

Dad smiled at me. "You ready for this, sweetie?"

"Hell, yeah!"

He opened the passenger door and started to get out. Then he ducked his head back in. "Watch your language, sixteen or not."

A little over two hours later, I walked out of the DMV with my own driver's license. I wanted to hug everybody in sight. I wanted to jump up and down and scream. I was so excited. "I know you guys have plans for me tonight, but can I borrow the car tomorrow? Can I?"

Dad hesitated, and I threw my arms around him.

"Pleeeeease." I drew out the word like it had a hundred e's in it.

He smirked. "I'm sure we'll figure something out."

"Dad!"

He just chuckled in response.

Less than an hour later I understood why. I literally screamed when I saw the car.

I circled around it when I first saw it, almost afraid it was a mirage. It was a brand-new VW beetle, white with pink and purple polka dots. They must have had it custom painted. I was crying when I got in. The interior had black leather seats, carpets and steering wheel, but the dash was a shiny bright red. To the right of the steering wheel, a tiny plastic flower vase was built into the dashboard. A purple aster with a bright yellow disk cheered the interior.

"Oh my God." I think I said it fifty times.

I asked Mom and Dad if I could take it for a ride. They just smiled, and I hugged them and maybe cried just a little bit more. My friend Marion, who I didn't get to see often enough anymore, got in the car, Sam got in the back seat, and I started the car.

It was really quiet. Brand new. I couldn't believe this. Dad rolled up the garage doors, and I put the car in reverse and backed out.

"This is so great," I said. I turned on the music and we drove.

Brenna

At a quarter after eleven, Sam knocked on my door. I was lying in bed with the lights out, watching Netflix on my phone. I was still dressed, because it wasn't long before I was planning to sneak out of the house to go see Chase.

"Yeah…"

Sam opened the door. "Can I come in?"

I paused the show and said, "Sure."

Sam sat down on the end of the bed. "I just wanted to say happy birthday. And to thank you for yesterday."

"Yesterday?"

"With Jake."

Right. That little prick. When I exited the gym yesterday afternoon, I was already in a bad mood because Chase had let me know we wouldn't be able to go out on Saturday evening. I didn't understand why he couldn't ask for the night off from work, considering it was my birthday. When I came out, I saw Sam pushed up against the wall.

Jake was about twice Sam's size, and he had harassed and bullied her all the way through middle school. When I saw him, it raised every fear I had for Sam. And the truth was, I was afraid of a *lot* of things for Sam. I was afraid that Mom and Dad would find out and that Dad would reject her. I was afraid of someone hurting her. I was afraid that the agony of feeling like she was in the wrong body would eventually get to be too much. That she might hurt herself. Or that some bigot would beat her up, or worse.

"I'll always watch out for you when I can," I said. I had to be careful how I said this. "But you need to remember that I won't always be here. You need to start learning to take care of yourself."

Sam whispered, "I know."

She stared at me for a minute then spoke again. "What's it like? You know … having a boyfriend? Do you love him?"

Sam's question had an ache of loneliness behind it. "I do. I do love him. But you know, it's not all roses. We fight a lot, and I don't get to see him very much. Sometimes he treats me like I'm a kid."

Sam shifted position, lying on her stomach next to me. "But he makes you happy?"

"Yeah. He really does."

Sam was quiet for a really long time. I could tell something was eating at her. So I sat there and didn't say anything, just waited. After several minutes, she took a breath, started to speak and then stopped. Her eyes shifted to mine. "Do you think … I mean … will … will I ever have that?"

Oh, Sam. "I'm sure you will. You're beautiful. Inside and out."

"Mom wants to take me to the doctor. She's worried about me not having gone into puberty yet. I heard her talking about it with Dad. What happens if they find out I've been taking hormones? What happens if they make me stop taking them? I'll end up looking like a boy in a dress, and no one will want me."

Jesus, I never thought of that. Would hormones be detectable in some kind of a blood test? I had no idea. "It's going to be okay, Sam. It's going to be okay."

Sam shook her head. Tears were starting to run down her face. "I don't think it is. I don't think it is at all. Even if I can find some way to somehow pay for my transition, how will I ever tell someone I'm dating? *Oh, by the way, I used to be a boy.* Can you imagine the reactions?"

Tears were freely running down Sam's face then. I reached out and pulled her to me, whispering, "It's going to be okay."

Her words were so full of pain and fear and loneliness it was overwhelming. She whispered, "I'm so scared, Brenna. I'm so scared."

Brenna

Sam went back to her room about half an hour later, sheepishly apologizing for falling to pieces. I told her several times it was fine. A few minutes after that, I peeked in her room. She was already out cold, wiped out by her tears.

My heart ached for Sam. Because even though I kept saying *Everything will be okay*, I didn't know if that was true or not. If she couldn't even tell our own father who she was, how could she tell someone else? Her fear was real and well-grounded. What if she did date some guy for a while, then had to reveal she'd been born male?

A lot of guys were assholes. A lot of guys would beat her up for that kind of surprise. It happened, in shockingly high numbers.

At the same time, sometimes it was so frustrating that everything had to be about her. It was my *birthday*. I just got my driver's license and a car, and yet here was Sam in my room, crying.

Whenever I felt like that, it made me feel like such a bitch.

Once I was sure she was asleep, I padded further down the hall then down-stairs.

Silence. No light under my parents' bedroom door. I stood in the darkness for a long time, waiting. Were there any movements, any sound? None. I tiptoed to the front door, far enough away from Mom and Dad's room I wasn't worried about waking them as long as I was careful. I opened it and slipped outside.

The air outside was heavy with humidity and the scent of flowers. A cool breeze tugged at my hair. I checked my phone. A little after midnight.

Our house wasn't exactly on a hill, but it was at the top of a gentle slope, almost a hundred yards to the street. I had parked my car facing out, knowing that I was going to try to get out tonight. I walked to the car and unlocked it, put the keys into the ignition and turned them halfway, then put the car into neutral and released the parking brake. Then I got out and pushed on the driver's side doorframe.

Oh. I had assumed it wouldn't be too hard to move. But it was *very* hard. I pushed, bending over and planting my feet wide apart. I strained, squeezing my eyes closed and pushing with all my strength.

The car moved slowly. Half an inch. An inch. It started to pick up speed as it began rolling down the slope, and I was walking, then running to keep up. *Oh my God, it's getting away from me.* I almost panicked and lost the car entirely, but I grabbed the steering wheel and dragged myself in, then slammed both feet on the brake just as I reached the street. The car came to an ungainly stop.

Oh God. My heart was thumping. I sat there, catching by breath, suddenly wanting to laugh. What if it had kept going? All the way down the street and into Old Georgetown Road with its heavy traffic?

I could have killed somebody.

I couldn't even think about it. I looked back up at the house. All dark, except for the exterior lights near the front door and garage. I was far enough away. I turned the keys in the ignition and began to drive, so excited I could barely breathe.

Traffic on Route 7 was heavy, even after midnight. I drove carefully, both hands on the wheel, music turned off. Around me were cars moving in the darkness, six lanes of traffic moving through Bailey's Crossroads, flanked by a constant flow of mini-malls, diners, office buildings and hotels, gas stations and apartment buildings.

The silence enveloped me inside the car, not broken but dulled by the low rumbling of other cars on the road. It was strange being out this late by myself. I'd been out with friends before, of course, though rarely this late at night. But never on my own. Having my driver's license gave me freedom I'd never had before. I didn't want to squander it.

It took half an hour to get to Chase's from our place. The drive felt magical, even when a truck got so close to me that I had to swerve out of my lane to avoid it.

I parked in the guest spot underneath the tree across from his apartment. When I got out of the car I looked up at the sky. No stars ... there was too much light here. I felt a tiny thrill as I walked up the stairs of the apartment building and to his door. Chase lived on the second floor in a small one-bedroom apartment that he only rarely let me in. *We have to be careful*, he would say. I was sick of being careful all the time.

I reached up to knock, hesitated, then knocked on the door. I immediately heard movement on the other side—he was awake.

"Who's there?" The peephole went dark.

I stood on my tiptoes and waved. "It's me!"

156

After a clatter of sliding chains and locks, Chase yanked his front door open. "Brenna … what are you doing here? How did you get here?"

I felt my shoulders sink down a little at his almost angry tone. "What, no 'happy birthday'?"

Chase winced. "Shit. I'm sorry. I just wasn't expecting you."

He didn't move to wave me in or even to give me a kiss. I was starting to feel really hurt. I could feel my eyebrows pushing together and had to fight the beginning of a tremble in my chin. Forcing a smile, I said, "My parents bought me a car for my birthday! So … I thought I'd come over and see you."

I waited through an uncomfortable delay. What the hell? Was he keeping a girl in there or something? "Chase, aren't you going to invite me in?"

He licked his lips and looked away from me almost nervously. Then he muttered, "I didn't want to do this on your birthday. Come on in."

Chase's apartment looked unfinished. Textbooks were stacked next to the couch, even though he wasn't in college anymore. He had a twenty-gallon aquarium, but he hadn't replaced the fish after they died. The coffee table was cluttered with a stained pizza box, napkins, two open cans of beer, remote controls, and envelopes that looked like bills.

"What didn't you want to do on my birthday? Be kind? We were going to make love on my birthday. Are you going back on that?" My eyes shifted down to two cans of beer. I pointed at them. "Is someone else here?"

He shook his head. "Jesus, Brenna. Slow down."

He scrambled to clear a spot on one of the chairs that sat at an angle from the couch. "You want something to drink? A soda? Both of those beers are mine, I drank them earlier."

I shook my head. "I just want you to tell me what's going on."

"Well, sit down, and we'll talk about it." His tone was slow, quiet, an intentional effort to calm. Condescending.

His condescension made me want to punch him. But I knew Chase well enough to know that he wasn't going to talk until I sat down. So I did, crossing my arms over my chest and one leg over the other.

"Baby, listen. I've been thinking … a lot. About us. About everything."

Oh, God. He was doing it. Chase was breaking up with me. He was breaking up with me *on my birthday.* A tear ran down my face, and I savagely wiped at it. I sat with my back straight, not touching the seat, and kept my hands tucked under my arms to avoid hitting him.

"I don't want to hurt you, Brenna. But I can't do this anymore."

The words that burst forth weren't exactly a shriek, but they weren't very calm either. "You can't do *what?* I thought we loved each other."

157

"Of course I love you. But that's not the point."

Of course he loves me. But that's not the point? What the *hell* did that mean? "You aren't making any sense."

He didn't respond to my statement. Instead he just continued. "I can't do this ... this hiding things from your parents. Always trying to push the boundaries. Trying to get me to sneak out with you at night. Did you even think about the fact that if you get caught picking up those drugs from the post office, then you might get a slap on the wrist or get grounded, but if I got caught, I would go to prison? Did you even fucking think about that before you involved me in a felony? You just show up in the middle of the night. Do you know what kind of trouble I could get in for having a fifteen-year-old girl in my apartment at one o'clock in the morning?"

"*Sixteen*, asshole!"

He closed his eyes and took a deep breath, his shoulders rising a little as he did it. Then, eyes open, he said, "That's the point, Brenna. I love you. But you act like a child, and nothing I say will persuade you to behave otherwise. I'm not willing to risk ruining my life. Or yours, for that matter. Your mother is right. You should be dating someone your own age."

Tears were running uncontrollably down my face now. I felt so humiliated, I wanted to sink down into the floor and die.

"You don't have to do this." I hated how my voice sounded, hoarse and desperate. I hated that I was beginning to sob. "I didn't realize you were so upset about it. I just wanted to surprise you. I thought you'd be happy. I won't try to push the rules anymore. I won't."

He leaned forward, placing his elbows on his knees, resting his face in his hands. In that position, he murmured, "This is not easy for me, you know."

It's not *easy* for him.

I hated him.

I stood up, shaking uncontrollably, and unable to control the tears that I didn't want him to see. "I'm fucking out of here."

He stood up too, grabbing at my wrist. "Wait..."

I yanked away from him. "Don't touch me!" I pulled away and ran to the front door, throwing it open and running out into the hall blindly. I had to get away from him as quickly as I could. As I flew down the stairs, I heard him shout, "Brenna!"

I unlocked my car and got in, starting it before he made it out the front door of his building. I got one last good look at Chase as I pulled out into the parking lot and drove away.

I couldn't go home like this, not yet. I drove as carefully as I could, while letting the tears flow freely. I finally stopped at a gas station and sat there for a long time crying in the car. I didn't want to be seen. What if a cop drove up while I was like this? I needed to calm down.

Then I realized. Lori's bracelet, the one she just gave me. It was gone.

Oh, *crap*. It must have fallen off at Chase's, which meant I was going to have to call him. And endure further humiliation.

That's when my phone lit up. New message from Rick. I considered turning the phone off. But then I thought again. What the hell, why not? I didn't have Chase to order me around and tell me who to be with and where and when to be there. I unlocked my phone.

Rick: **Hey, u awake?**

Brenna: **yeah.**

Rick: **Me and Nialla are hanging out with a couple peeps. Want to join?**

I didn't have to think about it. I needed to talk with someone. I was humiliated and rejected and angry, and I didn't want to feel that way anymore. I didn't want to go home.

I texted back: **Yeah. I got a car for my birthday. I'll come to you.**

Fifteen

~~~~~~

Cole

I left Jeremiah's at seven thirty. From his place it was not quite a two-hour drive back to Oxford, which meant that Sam would likely still be up when I got home. That was good news ... we needed to talk sooner rather than later. I wondered how he would take the news that Brenna was still alive, but still missing.

I had a gnawing regret that I hadn't picked him up from school and brought him along to the airport. What was the right thing to do? The walk home wasn't that bad, but I'd been reluctant to tell him what had happened over the phone. Would he be stuck on his computer as usual? Or fretting, worrying about what had happened and why we'd gone to the airport?

I had failed both of my children so profoundly that I didn't even know where to begin. As I drove west, Jeremiah's words roiled through my head. He was right. I hadn't been there for Erin, not when it counted. Not for Erin, and not for the kids. I've been so focused on success at work, on affording the flashy cars and that god-awful huge house that I lost sight of everything that really mattered.

It made my stomach hurt to think about it. It was crazy. I grew up wanting nothing more than to be the opposite of my father. He'd been a remote figure who dragged us from one place to another, sometimes leading us into different states during the same school year. No stability, no warmth, just constant warfare between my parents. It wasn't a hot war, the kind of parental battles that involved screaming and flying dishes. No, my parents were Russia and the United States during the Cold War; the tactics being my father's distance and my mother's constant sniping, the proxy wars being conducted through their

160

children. The front lines rarely moved, our lives locked in a stalemate between my father's territory—the garage, the outdoors, the basement—and my mother's—the living and dining rooms. They met for battle in the dining room.

I ended up as the only casualty.

Ironically, I've ended up just like Daddy. I'd been so focused on providing economic stability that it never even occurred to me that my marriage had turned into a ghastly parody of my parents.

No more.

I didn't know if I could ever expect Erin to forgive me. I doubted I'd ever be able to forgive myself. My actions had brought ruin on my family.

I couldn't fix the past. But I could try to do better for the future. I wanted my family back. I wanted to put my arms around them and beg for healing and forgiveness.

Brenna was alive. I wanted her home.

Traffic began to ease up as I finally got past the exits for the mall in Douglasville, but I stayed exactly at the speed limit. I didn't think that traffic tickets could affect my probation, but I wasn't taking chances on it either.

As I drove, I thought, maybe I should send a thank-you card to Jeremiah. This wasn't the first time he had shared some hard truths in our friendship. In fact, Jeremiah had been the very first person to visit me at the Deep Meadow Correctional Facility in Southern Virginia.

I could never forget the horror and shock of those days. During the weeks I'd been awaiting trial, my company put me on paid family leave. Of course that only lasted until my conviction—I lost the job permanently the day I went to prison. I remember sitting in the courtroom, helpless as my attorney and the prosecutor talked with the judge.

The judge, a stern Asian American man with grey hair, had said to me, "You understand that in accepting this plea bargain, you are pleading guilty to felony assault. You will lose your right to vote. Until your probation is over, you won't be free to travel, and you'll be periodically monitored, checked for drug use, and called in for interviews. You are waiving the right to a jury trial in accepting this. Is all of this clear?"

"Yes, Your Honor."

I felt like a bug as the judge looked down at me. "Mr. Roberts, I understand that you were in extreme circumstances, and I sympathize deeply with the disappearance of your daughter. But my sympathy doesn't extend to you becoming a vigilante. You committed a serious crime and did permanent injury to an innocent bystander. I'm sentencing you to nine months in prison plus five years' probation. If you screw up during probation? God help you. Do you understand, Mr. Roberts?"

I told the judge I understood. But I didn't really. How could I? I didn't even understand what was going to happen to me the next hour, much less the next several months. Almost without a chance for a breath, a court bailiff handcuffed me then led me out of the courtroom. I didn't get a chance to kiss Erin goodbye, or to say anything other than a quick, "I love you!" before I was shoved out the door. A few moments later I was in a small room standing in front of a counter while a bored officer sat with one eye on a security monitor and the other occasionally drifting down to his cell phone.

The bailiff removed my handcuffs, then said in a curt tone, "Remove your tie and shoelaces."

I was panicking. "Can I get a drink of water?"

The officer behind the counter looked at the bailiff incredulously. "Pace, did you tell him to talk?"

The bailiff hooked his thumbs through his belts and gave me a scornful look. "Nope. Let me give you a word to the wise. When you get to the state lockup, don't open your trap unless you're invited to. You might have been a big cheese where you came from, but here you're just another convict. Understand?"

I didn't know shit about prison, just what I'd seen in bad movies and television. Gangs. Rape. Savagery. I needed to learn quickly if I was going to survive.

"I understand." I began to undo my tie.

It took a little over three hours to drive from Fairfax County to Deep Meadow, riding in the back of an unmarked white van. Seven convicts, including me, were seated on two hard metal benches that faced each other in the back of the van. The ride was rough, every pothole and bump sending shock waves up my spine. It was dim in the van, the darkness flooded with the acrid shock of sweat from the men.

I would have done a lot to have been able to change out of my suit before getting in the van. Four of the men in the back already wore prison uniforms. The man on my right wore jeans and a white T-shirt that strained against bulging tattooed biceps. He desperately needed a shave and stank of body odor. To my left was a kid, who couldn't have been more than twenty-two years old. The kid had slightly too long hair and a hipster beard, and wore brown corduroy pants with a button-down white shirt. His eyes were red from crying, and he turned his face away from everyone else in the van as best as he could. The five across from us, all of them in prison uniforms, were a study in contrasts. Three of them were African American, two of them in their early twenties or late teens, the third my age or older. The first man on the bench across from us would have looked at home at an accounting convention.

One of the young guys across from me, his face twisted with scorn, looked at the kid next to me and made a kissing motion with his lips. Then he winked and chuckled. The older man next to him elbowed him. "Leave the kid alone. He's obviously in way over his head."

I stood out in my suit, but there was nothing I could do about it now. Except maybe salvage what I could.

I had a dull sense of dread in my stomach, knowing that I was going into a situation far more savage than the business world I'd lived in for the past decade. I needed to somehow reabsorb everything I ever heard from my cousin Lucas's dad, who had done his own time in prison.

I always knew: I was never going to end up in prison. I wasn't going to be like Uncle Bill—or Lucas, for that matter. The violence that characterized their lives wasn't part of my life.

I was better than they were.

But nevertheless, here I was.

I wondered, briefly, what my parents thought. Daddy would understand, I thought. He would likely have done the same thing if presented with the same set of circumstances. Mother, however, would refuse to speak of it, now or ever. She would raise her nose in the air and go play bridge and pretend I was off on a work trip for the next nine months.

What I really knew was this: I would be tested, probably within twenty-four hours. They were going to find out if I was a victim, and if I failed that test I might not survive prison. I had to pass that test, no matter what it took.

The guy on my right with the bulging biceps muttered, "What are you in for?"

This was no time to fuck around. "Assault with a deadly weapon. I pleaded down to assault."

The guy looked at me skeptically and said, "You don't look the type."

I shrugged. "I'm not. But the guy fucked with my daughter."

The guy smirked. "I can respect that. Man's gotta protect his family. Name's Paul Vance. I'm up for armed robbery. But there was extenuating circumstances."

"Yeah, me too."

"Shut up back there." The words from the corrections officer in the front of the van were harsh.

163

I wondered what kind of extenuating circumstances there were for armed robbery. It didn't matter. What did matter was that I find allies quickly. Because I was in more danger than I'd ever been in my life.

It was incredibly frustrating sitting in the back of the van, with only the vaguest idea where I was going and no way to see outside. Every once in a while, the kid on my left would start shaking as he struggled to contain his tears. It was almost evening when we arrived, stepping out of the van into a brisk cold breeze. The sun was setting, but I couldn't see it anyway, because the view of the horizon was blocked by a thirty-foot high wall and a confusing array of chain-link and razor wire fences between several buildings. At intervals along the walls, guards stood with rifles.

Only then did it sink in how serious this was. I barely heard the corrections officer order us into the building and walked zombie-like through the process of exchanging my suit for a pair of prison jeans, a too-small T-shirt, and a ridiculously large short-sleeved blue shirt. During the in-processing, I learned the kid's name: Kyle Pawlenty.

Immediately, I recognized the kid's name; he'd been all over the news. He'd been a senior at George Mason University who drove home drunk from a party and killed a family of four in a violent accident when he ran a red light and hit their car without slowing down. Not malicious, just careless and stupid. But all the same, an eight-year-old boy and his four-year-old sister were dead along with their parents. His trial, much like mine, had occupied the front pages of The Washington Post.

Our heads were shaved, and we were sent through showers with a terrible chemical smell. Delousing. Despite my own fear, I felt for the kid. He stood in the shower, turned away from the rest of us, his head low. Vance, showering next to me, muttered, "Kid's gotta man up or he's going to get all fucked up."

When it was all over, we were led to our new cells.

It was a week later that I got my first visitor. A corrections officer escorted me to the visiting area, a large room that vaguely resembled a school cafeteria, with small tables lined up in rows. The walls were painted a pale blue, almost the same color as the uniform shirts. Half a dozen guards were scattered around the perimeter of the room.

Jeremiah Walker sat at one of the tables. When I saw him, I felt an immediate exhalation of relief. It wasn't Erin and Sam. I didn't want them to come here, I didn't want them to see me like this. Jeremiah looked good. He wore khakis and a black shirt, and was sitting calmly when I entered the room.

I walked toward him. He stood up and wrapped his arms around me in a bear hug. "Good to see you," he muttered.

We sat.

Jeremiah seemed to study me, his brown eyes looking me up and down. "How you hanging in there?" he asked.

"Trying to grow eyes in the back of my head. But so far, so good. Have you talked with Erin? Sam?"

He nodded. "Erin's ... well, you know. She's pretty broken up, too much has happened. But she's trying to stay strong for Sam. Erin and Ayanna have been talking a lot lately."

"I'm glad. She needs someone to talk with."

"Whatever happened to Angela?"

Jeremiah's question was a tough one. Over the years the two women had grown further and further apart, and I often had the uncomfortable feeling that I was the cause of that distance. I just replied, "They don't talk much anymore."

Jeremiah grimaced. "That's too bad. Everyone needs close friends. Especially at a time like this."

I nodded. Then I said, "Has there been any word about Brenna?"

Jeremiah shook his head. "Nothing. I'm sorry."

I leaned forward and rubbed my eyes with my right hand. "I hate that I'm stuck in here instead of out looking for her."

"Well, keep your nose clean and don't get your sentence extended. You got any friends yet? Anyone to help protect you?"

"Yeah. Guy named Paul Vance. He robbed a liquor store. He's ... dangerous. Biker type. Lots of tattoos. I wouldn't fuck with him in a million years."

"Good," Jeremiah replied. "You want guys like that on your side."

"I don't know what I'm going to do. You know I got fired?"

"I expected that. You didn't really think they were going to hold your job for you while you went to prison?"

I shook my head. "No. But..." I shrugged. "I have no idea what to do from here."

"You stay tough and get through the next few months. That's all you do. Erin's got things under control at home. Look, Cole ... if you'd had a different shade of skin standing there with that gun, Erin would probably be a widow. Consider yourself lucky. If you can't get a job when you get out, you've got a standing offer from me."

Back then, I couldn't see that ever happening, but the offer meant a lot. Looking back, I want to kick myself in the ass. Even there, sitting on the wrong side of prison bars, I thought I was too good for the career he'd chosen.

"Thanks, Jeremiah. I think I'll be okay, but I appreciate the offer."

I was such an asshole.

Not long after that, visiting hours had ended and Jeremiah left to make his way back to Georgia, and I went back to my cell to what would be a months-long struggle for survival.

Tonight's talk from Jeremiah had shown once again just how good of a friend he was. I had never returned that kind of friendship. Yet another area where I had failed. But I wasn't going to fail anymore. Not when it came to the people who mattered in my life.

It was almost ten when I drove up to the house in Oxford. I surveyed it critically for a moment, noting the rotting wood on the front porch and the duct-tape repair to the picture window in front. This is what we'd been reduced to. But it wasn't the house that mattered, or the cars, or the paycheck, or any of that.

As I got out of the car and walked toward the front door, the sound of insects swept over me, a chorus of buzzing that might have been in a jungle it was so loud. I could smell the cow manure from across the street.

I opened the front door. It was quiet, but every single light in the house was on. *Typical.* Sam didn't have to pay the electric bill, so he didn't think about it.

Let it go.

Okay. I took a deep breath. And let it go. I *really* let it go. We had a much more important conversation ahead of us. I surveyed the scene. An open pizza box was on the kitchen table, half of it eaten. At least he'd ordered dinner. I walked to the hall and knocked on his door.

"Sam?"

He opened the door. "Hey, Dad."

"Can I come in and talk for a few minutes?"

Sam sucked in a breath and flinched a little. What was he expecting? He looked *terrified.* "Okay."

He opened the door all the way and sat down on his bed. I noticed he'd taken some of the boxes out of his closet, books and other stuff that he hadn't gotten around to unpacking since the move.

I sat down next to my son and looked closely at him. He looked so much younger than sixteen. Was it just that I couldn't remember what sixteen-year-olds looked like? I didn't get them anymore. I hadn't understood Brenna, and I didn't understand Sam. It looked like he was wearing eyeliner or mascara or something. Why? I guess guys did that sometimes now. I'd seen some of the goth kids wandering around the mall, trying to look like vampires. I didn't think Sam moved in that crowd.

"What is it?" he asked, his voice trembling.

"Sorry," I said. I didn't know how to begin. I swallowed.

166

"Just get it over with." As he spoke the words, his voice began to quaver. "She's dead, isn't she? That's why Mom left and you're hesitating. Brenna's dead and you're afraid to tell me."

My heart sank. Oh, God. We should have taken him out of school for the drive, so we could explain things. He must have been sitting here terrified all night. "No. That's not it. Sam … listen…"

His eyes widened and he seemed to shrink in on himself.

"Your sister is alive. We don't know where she is now, but about three weeks ago, she was, um … picked up by the Portland, Oregon police."

"Portland!" he cried.

"Yeah. Anyway, the police didn't know she was missing, and the links with the FBI were down or something, and they didn't put it together until today. You remember Agent Wilcox? He called your mom this morning."

As I spoke, Sam just sat there, eyes wide, trembling. Silent. Tears began to run freely down his face.

"When … what—"

"Sam … we don't know where she went from there. Mom is flying to Portland to look for her. It's the best lead we've had since she first disappeared."

Sam's shoulders rose and fell as he took a deep breath. He wiped at his face, smearing the makeup or whatever it was. So strange. With his hair the way it was, he looked so much like his sister I felt my heart cry out.

"Why aren't we all going to look?" He wiped at his face again but only cried more. "When can we go? Why aren't we all going?" Each sentence came out slightly higher pitched, his voice beginning to tilt toward a wail.

I put a hand on his shoulder. "Hey, it's okay. We can't all go. I can't leave work … and you've got school. And I'm not … I can't legally travel to Oregon anyway."

Sam jerked away from my hand and came to his feet. "*Fuck* work and school. It's *Brenna!* Can't you get them to let you go? Can't you … can't you talk to your probation officer or boss or someone?"

I swallowed. I wanted to so badly. But then we'd lose what little we had left. My voice was rough as I said, "It won't do Brenna any good if we're homeless."

"Let *me* go, then. You stay here and work, and I'll go find her with Mom!" Sam looked like he was in agony. He was, really. He sniffed back snot that was running down his face.

"Sam. I would let you go if I could."

The wail that came out of him seemed to come from the bottom of a well. "I want her back!" he cried, breaking down into sobs.

167

winter flower

I pulled Sam to me, wrapping my arms around him. "We'll do our best. I promise. We'll do our best."

Sixteen

~~~~~~

Erin

When the alarm went off at 6 a.m., I didn't know where I was. My thoughts immediately ran back to the phone conversation with Sam right before I went to sleep, and that placed me in time. The devastation in Sam's voice made my heart ache. I wanted to hold him in my arms like he was still a little boy. I had failed my son just as much as I failed Brenna.

That phone call, and maybe the sudden distance away from Oxford, made me see things in a much starker perspective than before. I pictured Sam coming and going to and from school, into his room, locking the door … while I slept or sat despondent. How lonely he must have been.

I had to stop that. I had to stop the drinking, and if we couldn't find Brenna while I was here, I needed to stop dragging myself through the muck so much that it destroyed my ability to be a parent. Sam was sixteen, and so alone.

Somehow my children had always seemed like they'd been switched, that Sam was the gentler soul, and Brenna the more assertive and outgoing. But did she have the internal strength to survive whatever she'd experienced in the past two years? It was difficult to imagine or even comprehend what that might be.

I sat up in the bed and turned off the alarm clock. Then I reached out and pulled the chain to turn on the dim lamp. The lamp illuminated a depressing hotel room, with faded wallpaper and a slightly dented steel door. The ceiling in the corner was stained, and the tile in the tiny bathroom was worn and faded. The room stank of mildew and cigarette smoke. I had never stayed in a hotel this disgusting before. But it was forty-five dollars a night, which meant I'd be able to stay in Portland longer. Right now, that was all that mattered.

winter flower

I checked my phone for messages. There was a text message from Cole from 3:15 a.m. It read, **Good luck this morning. Please keep me in the loop. I love you**.

I stared at the message. He must have sent it right before leaving for work. Unexpectedly, the message blurred, the letters becoming unintelligible, indistinct.

I wiped at my eyes then stood up to go to the shower. I couldn't remember the last time he had said "I love you." Such things were the currency of marriage: expressions and actions of love, doing things for each other, considering each other. We hadn't even given each other birthday gifts this year. Or last? I couldn't remember. A message like that was unsettling.

I tapped the response: **I will**.

I wasn't ready to respond to the "I love you."

I didn't wait for a response—it was eight o'clock in the morning in Alabama, which meant he was busy with the breakfast shift at work. Instead, I got up and went to take my shower and get ready. The shower was gross, with mold in the grout and unidentifiable stains on the shower curtain. Of course. There was no shampoo or soap, nor would there be any at the front desk. This wasn't the sort of place you could call and ask for complimentary toiletries. I sighed and resolved to just take a shower in hot water. At least I would feel a little refreshed.

I didn't want to look like a slob when I went to the police station, but I also didn't want to draw attention, so I settled for my softest jeans, a button-down blouse, and my walking shoes. No amount of brushing could bring any life to my hair though, after not using shampoo or conditioner. I would need to pick up groceries, at least bread and peanut butter or something, but in the short-term I needed to get some breakfast before I went to the police station.

The motel lay in a blighted section of downtown Portland, less than a quarter-mile from the police station. Nearby were pawnshops and a rundown building with a sign that read "*Girls Girls Girls* Lingerie Modeling" not far away from a strip club. A block away was a small diner. I double-checked that my room was locked then began to walk. As I walked, I opened the online banking app for our bank so I could check and see if Cole's deposit had cleared yet.

I stopped cold, not understanding what I was seeing. That couldn't be right. Our bank balance was $20,192.

Not possible. Last night, after we paid for the ticket and the hotel room, we had $238 left. It had to be some kind of a bank error.

The sky was threatening rain, so I walked quickly, getting to the diner just as fat drops started to drop from the sky.

170

Inside the diner, it was nearly empty. A bored waitress stood talking with a cook behind the counter, and at the far end from the door a woman sat hunched over a cup of coffee. She had hair in her face, but I had a clear enough view to see an ugly bruise on her cheek.

The waitress approached as soon as I slid into a booth. "Coffee?"

"Yes, please," I said, scanning the menu. A moment later she returned with the coffee and I ordered, then went back to looking at the bank account.

Last night. Electronic banking deposit of $20,000 even. There was maddeningly little information, just the one line that said, "ELN ID:408001 TRNSFR."

Well, that was helpful. I texted Cole: **There's a big deposit in our bank account from last night. Do you know what it is?**

I hit send, and that's when my phone rang.

Angela Gallo.

My eyes widened and I stared at the phone in shock. It rang a second time. I almost didn't answer. We'd barely spoken in years, and not at all since a few days after Brenna disappeared. My hand shook a little as the phone rang a third time.

"Hello?"

"Erin? It's Angela." Her voice sounded hesitant. As if she knew I might hang up on her any second. Which I still might.

"What is it?" I asked.

"Erin, I called … I … *oh no.* I knew exactly what I was going to say before I called, and now I'm losing it."

It sounded almost like she was crying.

"What's wrong?"

She hesitated again. Then she said, "I just … I was looking at the calendar, and I realized it's been two years since … since…"

"Since Brenna disappeared?" I asked.

"Yeah," her response was quiet. "That and … well, since I screwed things up for our friendship."

I didn't argue with her. I still remembered the hurt and anger of that day. Cole had been arrested—it was all over the news—and Angela called from London, where she'd been attending a conference. We'd talked about Brenna of course, and I'd cried. Then somehow the conversation moved to Cole, and Angela had said, *If this doesn't prove you should leave him, Erin, I don't know what will. He savagely attacked that kid—*

I never found out what else she had to say. Ever since I'd turned down the job with Win Without War, she'd harped about Cole. What an asshole he was. How he was a throwback. How dare he try to control where I worked? And yeah, I felt that way sometimes too. But it got old. And right then, when my life was completely falling apart, when everything, *everything* was darkness, my best friend didn't offer comfort, she offered judgment.

I hung up on her mid-sentence. She called back and I ignored her call. She called the next day, and the next, and then a few days after that, then a week later, and then a long time passed.

So I didn't respond to what she said. I just listened as she awkwardly continued. "Anyway … I just … I called to … offer my apologies. I can't imagine how difficult it's been for you. I check the news for you all the time. I worry about you. And about Brenna."

Now I stayed silent, and she kept trying to fill the silence.

"I, um … Erin, listen—" Then she sniffed, loud. "I'm sorry. I'm so sorry. I didn't mean to be such a shitty friend. I just wanted to ask if … well, if you'd forgive me. If it's not too late. I promise I'll never say anything bad about Cole again. But I want my friend back."

Damn it. I sniffed then had to wipe my face. "Yes," I whispered. "Yes, of course I forgive you." Did I really? Could I so easily forgive her after all this time? I didn't know. Maybe I just had to try. Because … I needed someone to talk to. I needed someone to listen to me. I was so sick of being alone.

"Oh…" She broke down on the other end of the line. I waited and listened. Finally she pulled herself together and said, "I drove by your house, like fifty times. Then I got the courage to go up, and I knocked on the door, and someone else answered."

"Oh no," I said. "We lost the house."

"Oh God, really? I didn't realize. Maybe we can get together for coffee some time? Or—"

"Angela, we live in Alabama now. But I'm actually in Portland, Oregon at the moment."

"*Alabama*? Holy *crap*. And … what are you doing in Portland?"

"Yeah, um, the FBI called yesterday with a lead. Angela, Brenna's still alive. She was here in Portland three weeks ago. I flew out last night to look for her."

Three thousand miles away, Angela sucked in a breath. "That's incredible. Do you think … I mean … how much…"

I sighed. "I don't really know anything yet. It's just a lead. But it's the most we've had since she disappeared."

The waitress approached, dropping off my food and refilling my coffee.

"I was a lousy friend." Her voice sounded sad.

Had she been? I thought so at the time. We had grown more and more distant over the course of several years, mostly because of Angela's unceasing campaign against Cole. But she'd been right, hadn't she? Cole had been arrogant, bossy, and worst of all, unfaithful.

"You were trying to look out for me."

"I pushed too hard. And it couldn't have been worse timing. I promise I won't ever suggest you leave Cole again."

"I've missed you."

Both of us were silent for a long time. I couldn't help but think how ironic it was. Ironic that I'd broken off my friendship with her because she kept suggesting I leave my husband, but now, I wanted nothing more than to leave him. Actually, I didn't know if that was true. I didn't know *what* I wanted. I was still confused after Cole hugged me at the airport, not to mention him saying *I love you* in the text message.

The truth was, I wanted things to go back to the way they were. Before Brenna's kidnapping, before the affair, before our lives fell apart. I wanted to go dancing with the man I had fallen in love with. I wanted to laugh. I wanted to feel joy again.

I just didn't see how that would ever be possible with him again.

"Angela, I've got to go. Can we talk this evening? I'd like to catch up."

We said our goodbyes just in time for my breakfast to arrive. I had just taken my first bite when the phone rang again. It was Cole. I answered immediately.

"Hello?"

"Hey. How was the hotel? Did you get any sleep?"

"It was okay. The hotel room's kind of gross, but I guess it could be worse. I'm headed over to the police station in just a few minutes."

"Okay. Let me know how that goes. I got your text."

"Any ideas? It's got to be some kind of bank error right?"

"I called the bank after I got your text. The money was transferred in as an electronic funds transfer, from another Bank of America customer. Did you know you can deposit money in anyone's account if you have their account number? They wouldn't tell me who did it, but I've got a pretty good idea."

"I don't understand." I pointed at my coffee cup as the waitress passed by. She topped it off.

"I stopped and saw Jeremiah last night, on my way back from dropping you off at the airport. We talked for a while, and I updated him, told him you were headed out to Portland. If I had to take a guess, I'd say that he gave us the money. Or Ayanna did."

My eyes widened. His voice had started to choke up as he said the last words.

I shook my head, feeling my eyes welling up. "Twenty thousand dollars?"

"I don't see how we can accept that," he said. "We would never be able to pay it back."

"I'll call Ayanna. Jeremiah wouldn't tell you the truth if he's the one who gave us the money."

"All right. And ... Erin?"

"Yeah?"

"Thank you for doing this. I'd do anything to be there with you looking for her."

Emotions too complex to get my mind around flooded through me. I didn't trust him. He'd been just as solicitous when he'd been having the affair with that woman. At least some of the time.

"I'm going to get going," I said. "I'll call Ayanna. Talk to you later."

"Okay. I love you."

I didn't answer. I couldn't. I disconnected the phone, angry at his presumption. I didn't know what kind of game he was trying to play, but now wasn't the time. Still angry, I dialed Ayanna Walker.

She answered on the third ring.

"Erin, I thought I might hear from you."

"You deposited that money, didn't you?"

I heard a soft chuckle at the other end. "I guess I knew you'd figure that out pretty quickly."

Of course I figured it out. When Cole was in prison, Ayanna had given me some cash to help me get through. She'd refused to consider it a loan and just explained that they had too much anyway.

"I can't accept that, Ayanna. I can't. It's too much."

Silence for several seconds. Then she spoke in a firm voice. "Now you listen to me. I didn't send it to you and Cole. I sent it to Brenna, all right? Jeremiah told me you were headed to Portland to look for her. You don't need to be worrying about whether or not you've got a place to sleep, or can you afford to rent a car, or whatever. All you need to worry about is doing whatever you can to find that girl, okay? Because she must have been through some kind of hell."

"But, Ayanna—" I was fighting tears. Again.

"*No.* Don't let your pride do this. Listen, me and Jeremiah, we got plenty of savings. The Lord didn't give us money so we could sit on it. He gave it to us to help others. You just take care of that girl. I don't want the money back, not today, not tomorrow, not in ten years. It's not a loan. Some day when you've got your life back together, you can pass it on to someone else who needs it. And if you run low, you call me. Okay? You *call* me. If a friend can't help you with something like this, then what's the good of having any friends at all?"

Jesus Christ. Tears were running down my face. I sniffed then blew my nose on the rough napkin on the table.

"Okay. Okay." My voice choked, and I whispered, "Thank you."

We said our goodbyes and I leaned my face in my hands while trying to regroup. My nerves felt like they were on fire, jagged and raw, exposed to every possible stimulus. Between Cole's weird behavior and an incredibly unexpected gift, I felt like I might never stop crying.

The rain outside was coming down hard now, drumming against the roof of the diner and leaving deep puddles along the edge of the street. I stared out into the grey.

My daughter was out there somewhere and I was going to find her.

I checked the clock on the wall. 6:50 a.m. When I called last night, the dispatcher told me the precinct captain would arrive at the police station around seven. Time to go. I waved down the waitress to pay her and walked toward the door.

"You going out in that? You ain't walking, are you?"

I looked back. The words had come from the forlorn-looking woman at the other end of the counter. She had lifeless brown hair and a gaunt face with sunken cheeks. Wrinkles around her eyes made it difficult to determine her age, but the black and purple bruise surrounding her left eye was unmistakable.

"That's okay, I just need to walk over to the police station."

The women shook her head. "You'll catch your death out there. Take my umbrella." Words that were slurred, though it was impossible to tell if it was from being under the influence or if she was just tired or sick. Whatever it was, the kindness from someone who was clearly way down on their luck nearly brought me to tears again.

"Thank you. It's not necessary, I'm going to get one later today anyway."

I had a sudden urge to ask her if she knew Brenna. After all, my daughter had been picked up in this police precinct for … prostitution. I didn't know the circumstances of the arrest, but she might have been walking on this block. The thought put a golf ball in my throat, but I fought down the nausea and reached in my purse. I carried a four by six photo of Brenna everywhere I went. I took the picture out and said, "Are you from around here? Do you … do you know this girl? Have you seen her?"

As I asked the question, the waitress slowly approached. The woman at the counter reached out her hand to take the picture. I passed it to her.

The woman's eyes peered at the picture. "Your daughter?"

I nodded, trying to hold back the tears that had been threatening me all morning.

175

"She's pretty. I used to be that pretty."

The waitress said in a warning tone, "Jasmine…"

"It's true," Jasmine said. "Is your daughter working the track?"

I flinched at the words. I recognized them from my research. Every city had a track. The track was where the streetwalkers worked. My hotel, the diner, and the nearby police station were all on the track. Late at night, or even during the day, cars would be circling the track. Men, looking for sex.

I swallowed, then said, "I don't know. Maybe."

Jasmine frowned, deepening the already dark furrows on both sides of her mouth. "This is no kind of life for a young girl. Get her out if you can. I don't know her. You seen her, Kristi?"

The waitress took the picture. She studied it for several minutes. Then she slowly shook her head. "I don't know. She looks familiar, sort of. Is this a recent picture?"

I shook my head. "No. It's two years old."

Kristi set the coffee pot down on the counter. "There's a girl who looks kind of like that. But older. A lot older."

"If she's working the street, that'll age her quick," Jasmine added.

Her frank words made me want to lash out.

The waitress continued, "Anyway, I've only seen her two or three times. Maybe a couple months ago? If it's the same girl, and I don't really know the answer to that. I don't know if she is or not." She looked up at me with sad eyes. "I'm sorry. I wish I could tell you for sure."

"Maybe I can get a newer picture." I was thinking about the possibility of a mug shot. After all, Brenna had been arrested three weeks ago. "I'm going to go now. Thank you."

"Take the umbrella!" insisted Jasmine. "I'm not going out there anytime soon."

"At least let me pay you for it?"

She shook her head. "Just take it."

I took the umbrella.

I was grateful for it within sixty seconds of leaving the diner. If I hadn't brought it, I'd have been drenched right away. As it was, I didn't stay dry, but at least I wasn't drowning. I walked the two hundred yards to the small police station and walked in the front door.

Behind the counter near the front door was a young man in his mid-twenties. His uniform was immaculate, his upper body defined with well-conditioned muscles. His left arm was in a sling.

"Help you, ma'am?"

"I'd like to see Captain Ramos, please."

The young officer stretched and looked mildly annoyed. "Captain's busy. If you'll tell me what this is about, then maybe I can help you."

I considered holding out until I was able to speak with the captain but I ruled that out. They could stall me all day. "My daughter was kidnapped two years ago. Someone at your precinct picked her up while she was still a minor, and instead of getting her help, or calling her parents, or calling the FBI, you put her in lockup and then let her go. I need to speak with Captain Ramos, please."

The officer sat there for a full ten seconds, absorbing what I had said. Then he picked up the phone and dialed a number. "Captain ... woman here to see you. I know, sir ... I know ... I think you'll want to see this lady. Yes, sir."

He hung up the phone.

"The captain says he's in a meeting right now, but he can see you as soon as it's over. Someone's on the way down to escort you there."

I felt a stab of anxiety. I didn't know what I was going to learn from this meeting. I didn't know if they were going to be willing to offer any genuine help. Part of me was terrified that I would find Brenna and it would be too late.

Five minutes later I was sitting in a hard plastic chair outside the captain's office. The office was to the side of a wide open room with a dozen or so desks. About a third of the desks were occupied, but as I sat watching, the officers in the room left in singles and pairs until there were only two people left.

A moment later the office door opened. A young female cop left the office and walked quickly down the hall.

"I'm Ed Ramos. I understand you asked to see me?"

I stood up and faced the man in the doorway. He looked like he was in his early forties, with close-cropped tight curly black hair and bushy eyebrows. His nose was crooked; it looked as if it had been broken at one time.

"I'm Erin Roberts. I'm here to talk with you about my daughter Brenna."

His eyes widened for just a second. "Come in. Have a seat, Mrs. Roberts. What can I do for you?"

"I need to know everything you can tell me about my daughter. Where and how was she arrested? What kind of health was she in? And what are you doing to find her now?"

He nodded. "Of course I'll help. Understand, this is an ongoing investiga-tion, and there are some things—"

I refused to deal with any stalling. "I've been looking for my daughter for two years," I interrupted. "She was kidnapped. She was on the National Miss-ing Persons registries; her fingerprints were on file. She was a minor when your people arrested her instead of rescuing her. I don't want to hear your ongoing investigation *bullshit*. I want help finding my daughter now."

My heart was thumping wildly. I didn't know those words were going to come out of my mouth until they did. But rage was beginning to boil over that she'd finally been in the hands of someone who could help her, and instead, they treated her like a criminal.

He nodded. "I understand, ma'am. Give me just a minute." He picked up a microphone and spoke into it. "Sgt. Mackey, Detective Michelson. Still in the building?" After muffled affirmative answers, he spoke into the microphone again. "Need both of you in my office, ASAP."

He stood and opened the office door. "Sergeant Mackey was the arresting officer, and Detective Michelson is in charge of the investigation. Understand, Michelson won't have much yet. Until we got the flag from NCIC yesterday, this was a simple prostitution bust. We're now treating it as a trafficking investigation."

I winced a little—I don't know why. I already knew those things. But hearing them in such blunt terms was akin to being punched in the face.

A moment later, two officers entered the room. One was in uniform, a man in his thirties. He looked fit, but blotches marred his face, the burst blood vessels of a heavy drinker. His name tag read Mackey.

The other officer was an Asian woman. She wore jeans and a sweatshirt; I couldn't tell her age, maybe early thirties, or younger.

The captain spoke. "Mrs. Roberts, this is Sergeant Mackey and Detective Michelson. Mrs. Roberts is the mother of the girl who came up as a NCIC match yesterday. I'd like you to tell her everything you reasonably can."

Sergeant Mackey looked distinctly uncomfortable. He shifted on his feet and said, "Well, Ms. Roberts, some details are police procedure—"

"You can tell her everything." The captain's voice was firm. I felt a sense of relief in response. I'd been half expecting to get the runaround.

The sergeant twitched, and his eyebrows scrunched together. "Captain, are you sure? Some of the details…"

"Everything."

The sergeant shook his head. Then he said, "Ma'am, I don't work vice. I'm a supervisor, and I was out on a routine patrol. This stretch of Portland, some people call it the track. It's where the … the whores and johns hook up."

I flinched. The detective rolled her eyes and tapped the sergeant on the shoulder. "Please don't use that word, Mackey."

"What word?" He looked genuinely confused.

Ramos shook his head. "What the sergeant's trying to explain is that this is an area with a significant level of street prostitution."

Mackey gave the captain a look that I read as, *Isn't that what I just said?* I wanted them to get on with it. He did.

"Anyway … one of the spots they go to is behind the First Baptist Church. Every morning there's a bunch of condoms out there. Behind a church, if you can believe it. So around three a.m. I swung through the back parking lot, and there they were. A big Cadillac Escalade, and…" He looked suddenly uncomfortable again. "The subject was in the vehicle with … a john. They were having sexual intercourse."

I tried to maintain a stone face, even as I wanted to scream or throw up. This was beginning to turn into confirmation of my worst terrors. "What happened then?" I asked.

The sergeant shrugged. "Got them both out of the vehicle, questioned them. She didn't tell me her name. So I took her in and booked her."

"What about the man?"

He shrugged. "I gave him a warning and sent him home."

Rage flashed through me. "You're telling me that you came upon an adult male who was sexually exploiting a child, and you let the guy go? And arrested her? What the hell is wrong with you?"

A flash of anger swept across the sergeant's face. "There's no call for that kind of talk, and she weren't no child either."

Ramos said in an angry tone, "That will be enough editorializing, Sergeant. Had you seen the girl before?"

He shook his head. "No. She wasn't a regular on the track. Dressed better, and not quite as run-down."

My mind flashed back to the woman in the diner, Jasmine. Was that how this cop saw things? He classified Jasmine as a "run-down whore?"

Some of this must have passed across my face, because the detective put her hand over mine. She didn't say any words, but the touch reassured me.

"You questioned her?" the captain asked.

"Sure. She wouldn't tell me her name, or who her pimp was, or where she was from or anything else. I don't know what else to tell you, ma'am. It seemed like a routine prostitution bust."

I closed my eyes and silently prayed for patience. I opened them and looked him in the eye. "Sergeant Mackey, for just one minute can you imagine yourself in my position? And put the same kind of concern into this that you would if it were your own daughter?"

The sergeant shook his head. "Sorry, ma'am, I can't. I raised my daughter better than that."

I came to my feet without consciously willing it, my hands balling into fists. I wasn't the only one. Detective Michelson nearly shouted, "Mackey, get out of here. How dare you speak to this woman that way!"

Ramos shook his head. "Mackey, come see me later. We need to discuss how to talk to the public, understand? For now, you can go."

Looking angry—as if *he* had anything to be angry about—Mackey stood and left without another word to me.

I closed my eyes. I needed their cooperation. I *needed* their cooperation.

"Ma'am, I'm sorry about that." The words came from the young detective.

"Me too," Ramos said. "Please … accept my apology. Mackey's very rough around the edges. But he means well, he's a good cop."

Bullshit. A *good cop* doesn't arrest a *child* who is being sexually assaulted. But I didn't say it.

"Anyway," Ramos said. "I assigned the case to Detective Michelson because she's on the Portland Human Trafficking Task Force. If anyone can help locate your daughter, it's her."

I swallowed. "Okay. Tell me … what do you know?"

Michelson sighed. "Not much so far," she said. "As the captain said, he assigned the case to me yesterday afternoon. I've done an initial assessment of the case and requested her file from the FBI and Fairfax County police."

"Have you gotten an answer yet? I can give you the number of the FBI agent in charge. Stan Wilcox."

Michelson smiled. "Thanks. I've met Wilcox, actually. I expect to get whatever they're willing to share this afternoon."

"What else?" I asked.

She took a deep breath. "Mrs. Roberts, I don't know how much you know about sex trafficking…"

"More than I ever wanted to. I've read a lot."

"Okay. Well … we don't *know* anything yet. But what I suspect is that Mackey is correct, that she doesn't normally work the streets. From her mugshot, I would speculate that she was being trafficked on the Internet—Backpage or some of the discussion boards. I'm guessing she hadn't made her quota that night and that her pimp dropped her down here to make it up."

I winced. "Her quota…"

Michelson nodded. "Most of the women and girls I've encountered since I took this on, their pimps expect them to earn … hundreds of dollars, or more, per night. They can be pretty brutal if they don't get their money."

I sighed. Then I whispered, "You said … you have pictures."

Captain Ramos opened a file and passed over a color printout. A mug shot.

I took it in my hand, and for the first time in two years, I laid eyes on a current photo of my daughter. Immediately her face blurred, and I blinked to bring her back into focus. I held the mug shot in my right hand, but my left hand gripped the arm of the chair so hard it hurt.

Brenna looked tired. Exhausted. And … she looked *hard.* Her hair hung shoulder-length, her natural brown color, but lifeless. Eyes which once glowed with joy on Christmas morning looked dead. Tiny crow's feet beside her eyes aged her by ten years or more: in the photo she looked like she might be twenty-five or even thirty years old. She wore a grey sweatshirt that left one shoulder exposed. She looked like a caricature, not my daughter at all. Like a dead person wearing a Brenna costume.

A stylized tattoo marked the left side of her neck, it looked like a dragon. An ugly round white spot marred her collar bone. I couldn't make out what it was at first. A scar?

A cigarette burn.

It was Brenna. It was my daughter.

Against my will, a series of images flashed through my mind.

Brenna sitting on the floor in our first house, wearing a pink onesie with tiny pigs and angels, her arms wide out beside her, a translucent yellow cloth tenting over her head as she giggled.

Brenna stumbling through her first ballet recital when she was four, as she went twirling in circles away from the other girls, totally uninterested in what the rest of them were doing, laughing and smiling as if she were the only girl on the stage.

Sitting across the table from her when she was nine as she held a handful of UNO cards, a sly look on her face. She always got that look on her face when we played cards, a look of playful competition.

Brenna and Cole leaving for the fifth grade father-daughter dance. He'd rented a tuxedo for the dance, and she'd worn a silver princess dress and sparkling one-inch heels. Both of them had looked so happy.

I couldn't hold the tears back anymore. I choked back a sob, setting the photo down and balling my other hand into a fist. But then more tears came, and I sobbed again.

Michelson knelt next to me and said, "I'm sorry, Mrs. Roberts. I know. It hurts."

That was all it took. A moan escaped me, as I hid my face in my hands and sobbed. Two years of grief and terror poured out of me in a torrent of tears. I struggled to hold back but couldn't. For five minutes or an hour, I don't know which, I wept.

Finally, I was able to pull myself together. Barely. I looked at Detective Michelson, studying her compassionate brown eyes.

"Will you help me find my daughter?"

Seventeen

Sam

Mrs. Mullins came to a stop on the track and said, "Sam, what is *wrong* with you today?"

I slowed down and stopped beside her. I'd been dragging behind through the whole run. It was a beautiful morning, the first time since the school year started when the heat wasn't so oppressive I wanted to crawl under anything I could just to get some shade.

"I'm sorry. I didn't get much sleep last night."

"Why not? Something going on at home? You want to talk about it?"

I hadn't told anyone yet except Hayley. But Mrs. Mullins was different than any teacher I'd ever had. She understood in ways no other adult I knew was able to. I took a breath and said, "Please don't say anything to … well, anyone? But, my sister—she turned up alive in Portland. Three weeks ago. We don't know where she is now, but Mom flew out there yesterday to look for her."

Mrs. Mullins' eyes widened and a broad smile spread across her face. "Oh, Sam, that's wonderful!"

I said in a quiet voice, "I hope so. She … see … she was picked up by the police," my voice dropped even quieter, to a whisper, "for prostitution."

Understanding swept across her face. "I see. Well, Sam. She's alive. That's the important thing. We'll pray for her. I'll ask my church to pray for her."

I gave Mrs. Mullins a half smile. She was the sweetest lady I'd ever met, but I couldn't imagine her church would have anything nice to say about Brenna, and even less so about me. But that wasn't important. Right now what mattered was *her* kindness.

"Well," she said. "I'm not in the best shape either. Let's head back to the office and call it a day."

"Okay," I said. "Thanks."

We turned and began walking back toward the main building.

Across the field, the class I would have been in was doing calisthenics. Ashley was in that class. I could see her standing near the other students, one hip extended to the side, her hand resting on it, doing nothing while the rest of the class worked out. Was it because she was a cheerleader? Or because she was a walking stereotype? I'd heard her dad was a city councilman or the mayor or something, and she dated the biggest dickhead—I mean football player—in the school. I *hated* her.

And, to be honest, I wanted to *be* her.

As we walked, Mrs. Mullins said, "Did you give any thought to my suggestion about the clinic in Anniston?"

I had. A week earlier, she'd asked again if I was in any kind of therapy. When I told her no, she'd given me the contact information for St. Michael's Medical Clinic in Anniston, a sliding scale clinic which she thought might be willing to see me for free. I just couldn't see doing it. "I really appreciate it, Mrs. Mullins. But I don't think I need therapy."

She chuckled. "*Everyone* could use a little therapy."

I smiled. "I know. But really, it's okay."

I tried to picture the reaction I'd get. I'd be labeled. A transvestite. A freak. And what if they told my parents? I couldn't risk anything like that.

"Well, Sam, I'm not going to push. But you know I'll need some kind of good explanation to keep you out of PE next semester. And you still haven't told me what the problem is."

"I *can't*," I whispered.

She stopped in her tracks and put a hand on my shoulder. "It's okay, Sam. I won't push. I just care about you and want you to be okay. You must be going out of your skin knowing she's alive but not being able to do anything."

We started walking again, and I said, "I am. I'd do anything to be able to go to Portland with Mom and look. But Dad says I have to stay here and go to school. And ... well, Dad can't travel. He's on probation."

She nodded. "I'm so sorry you can't go. But your parents are right. You need to stay in school."

Like *Brenna* had a chance to stay in school? The bitter thought ran through my mind before I could think of anything to say. But I wasn't going to say that to her.

184

Back in Mrs. Mullins' office, I tapped out a quick text message to Mom. **Did you find out anything?** An alert popped up from Snapchat, a message from Hayley. I opened it. She was in first period history, and the picture showed her with her eyes crossed and her tongue sticking out of the right side of her mouth. The caption said, **SO BORED I DIED.**

I laughed. Mrs. Mullins raised an eyebrow, and I showed her the picture. She chuckled. "You and Hayley are pretty good friends, right?"

I nodded. "We're BFFs." *Best friends forever.*

"Can I ask you a question? The other day, Hayley had a pretty good bruise on her wrist. Did you see that?"

Jesus. Guilt flashed through me, even though I hadn't done anything. Or maybe *because* I hadn't done anything, and I knew I should.

"She said she fell. On the steps at her house."

"She lives alone with her dad, right?"

"Yes, ma'am."

Mrs. Mullins nodded. "Sam … if something ever put Hayley in danger, would you tell me? To protect her?"

Hayley had made it *very* clear I couldn't tell anyone.

"Sure," I said. "But I don't think it's anything. I really don't."

"Okay. Just … keep your eyes open, okay? I worry about you kids."

"I will."

"Okay, Sam. You can go change."

I walked down to the faculty bathroom next to the counselors' office—it had an actual locking door—and Mrs. Mullins had let me use that room to change every day after PE. I really loved her. She understood teenagers. She had a huge bowl of candy on her desk, but it was an open secret that she kept condoms in it. Real sex education was frowned upon in Alabama, but she was looking out for kids, not her career.

Two hours later, I was sitting in English, texting back and forth with Hayley. She was sitting three rows behind me, but our English teacher, Mrs. Gottlieb, rarely bothered anyone with their phones out unless it was during a test. For the last week, we had been reading short autobiographical essays at the beginning of class, followed by a writing prompt. I rarely felt confident about anything in school, but I had enjoyed this unit a lot. I had written essays before, of course, but this was different. Somehow it was difficult to pin down exactly why, except that like when I played in Second Life, it was a chance to express myself. And I never got to express myself.

Hayley: **did u hear back from ur mom?**
Sam: **she said she would call me l8r.**

winter flower

Mrs. Gottlieb began to write on the whiteboard in her spidery, barely legible cursive. Her message read: *Select an important memory in your life. Write about what happened. Describe the smell, taste, sounds, texture.*

Hands shot up across the room. Mrs. Gottlieb pointed to Ashley first. Naturally.

"How long does it have to be?"

"Length isn't the point, Ashley. What matters is that you give a clear and vivid description. James?"

"Does it have to be real?"

Mrs. Gottlieb looked impatient. "I want you to write about something you remember, something that is important to you. It can be happy, it can be sad. It can be last week or last year or when you were three years old. Stretch yourselves. I want to feel why it's important to you." Several hands slowly dropped, and she picked one more person.

"What happens if we don't finish in time?"

Mrs. Gottlieb rolled her eyes. "No more questions. I want you to take the first five minutes to pick a memory. Then I want you to start writing."

She checked her watch. "Begin. Put your phones away. I don't want to see anything on your desk but paper and pencil."

I dropped my phone in my backpack and took out several sheets of paper.

I tried to think of a significant memory. My mind immediately turned to Brenna's birthday and her disappearance. I thought of the raw terror I'd felt when the police told us they had found her crushed phone.

No. I didn't want to write about that. I reached further back. Birthdays. Fights between Mom and Dad. Brenna teaching me how to put on makeup. I sure couldn't write about that. I sat there with my eyes closed, digging in my past.

A vision of Brenna laughing.

I remembered. I must have been eight or so, Brenna ten. Mom and Dad had taken us camping for three or four nights in the Shenandoah Mountains. It had to have been in the fall, because I remember the leaves, brilliant oranges and reds and yellows everywhere.

I took out my pencil and began to write. I started with a simple detail: the turtles. Mom and Dad had rented two canoes, and we spent a long and lazy afternoon floating down the river. The canoes occasionally scraped over gentle rapids and in and out of shoals and curves. At one point we had rounded a corner in the river and came into view of two trees that had fallen and were floating on the west side of the river, still barely attached to their stumps. Lined up in rows on both trees, heads and necks extended far out of their shells, were at least two dozen turtles sunning themselves.

Brenna had pointed, shouting, "Daddy, look!" Two dozen tiny heads turned slightly toward us, but the turtles stayed in position, apparently deciding that we weren't a threat. Mom and Dad stopped paddling and let us drift for a few minutes, our canoes floating side by side. Mom leaned back, basking in the sunshine, then looked over at Dad and said, "This is heaven. I love you."

Dad smiled. "It is pretty nice, isn't it?" Then he paddled our boat right up next to Mom and Brenna's. He leaned toward Mom. "I love you, babe." I involuntarily let out a squeal as the boat tilted slightly, and Mom said, "*Cole*, you'll tip the boat!"

"Just one kiss."

Mom rolled her eyes and leaned toward him, then he leaned a little further, and then I let out a scream as our canoe capsized.

The water was a shock, but it wasn't that cold, nor was it particularly deep. My feet touched the bottom and I kicked off, my life vest taking me back to the surface almost instantly. Dad reached out and pulled me toward him. He had a huge grin on his face, as he grabbed for the boat with his left hand while holding me with his right. Brenna was hysterically laughing and pointing. Mom tried to look annoyed then stern, but she couldn't maintain the look: she cracked a smile.

Dad said, "Whoops." That started Mom laughing.

I was half asleep when, a few hours later, Dad slowed the car to a halt on Skyline Drive. We were on our way back to the campsite.

"Oh my God."

Something in Mom's tone made my eyes pop open. Brenna said, "It's a baby bear!"

Fifteen or twenty feet away, on the side of the road, a black ball of fluff was rolling on its back, paws extended in the air. It was a baby black bear.

"Can I pet it?" I asked.

"No way!" Brenna shouted.

"No, Sam. Mama bear is around here somewhere, and she won't let anybody touch her baby. This is as close as we can get, and we stay in the car."

I think I pouted for just a minute. But then I stopped. Because a massive rumbling in the bushes beside the road signaled something coming, and the next thing I saw was a full-size adult bear wandering into the road. She pushed the baby along with her snout, and the baby sprawled, then ran ahead, off the road. The baby bear wrapped its paws around a tree and scooted right up the trunk. Then the mama bear followed.

winter flower

"Holy cow," Dad said. He put his arm up, resting his hand on Mom's shoulder. She looked at him and smiled, and they leaned toward each other and kissed.

"Ewwww!" Brenna screamed.

"Gross!" I yelled.

Dad laughed maniacally and said, "I'll show you gross!" Then he kissed her again.

A car behind us honked, and Dad broke away, and Mom giggled a little as we began driving up Skyline Drive again.

Concentrating on the smell of the fall woods, the feel of the water, the sounds of the bear rustling in the trees, I wrote my essay for class. And I remembered. And I wondered. Could Mom find Brenna? And if so, could she bring her home? For a second, I imagined Mom was like that bear we saw all those years ago: cute, but dangerous as hell. At least that's what I hoped for. Because I wanted my sister back.

I wanted my family back.

Sam

The text message from Mom was stark: **I have some leads I'm working on, but we don't know anything for sure yet except that she was here. I promise I'll keep you updated. Call me before bed?**

I immediately texted back: **I will.**

Mom: **School going okay?**

Me: **boring**

Mom: **Can't you come up with something more expressive than boring?**

Me: **it was soul crushing.**

Mom: **That made me smile. Love you**

I was so wrapped up in texting Mom, I had forgotten my surroundings on the school bus. Normally that could be hazardous, but as I looked up from my phone I breathed a sigh of relief. No one seemed to be paying any attention. I had spent the day alternately ecstatic about Brenna and terrified about my run-in yesterday with Ashley and Cody. I didn't know what form it would take, but I knew bullies well enough to know that at some point, today or tomorrow, next week or next year, Cody and Ashley would get their revenge. My guess from my encounters with him so far was that Cody had a short attention span and primarily only went after targets of opportunity. Ashley, however ... *she* would keep him focused on target as long as it took. I needed to watch my back.

Whatever. I couldn't spend my entire life freaking out about when and how I was going to have to deal with bullies.

I picked up my phone and opened Snapchat, bared my teeth in a growl, then took a quick selfie. I sent it to Hayley with the caption: **mall tomorrow?**

A response came immediately, a photo of her, smiling, with her smile stretched and exaggerated. I laughed.

It was a couple of minutes later that the giggling at the front of the bus began to get louder. Three of the girls were laughing and looking back toward the back of the bus. I sat about halfway back. Were they looking at me? I felt heat on my face. Across the aisle from the girls, two boys suddenly burst out laughing. They were all looking down ... laughing at something on their phones. Whatever the joke was, I wasn't included. The laughter spread to the back of the bus, and the driver shouted, "Pipe down! Or some of y'all will be walking home."

I looked down at the floor then fiddled with my phone so I could at least look busy. But then Billy, sitting next to me, burst into laughter. He doubled over, then looked at me and back to his phone, laughing even harder.

What the hell? "What is it?" My voice came out in a croak.

Billy just shook his head, murmured a muffled, "Oh my God," then started laughing hysterically. I twisted over to get a look at his phone and froze. Then I reached out and grabbed it, stunned.

"Let go, freak!"

I didn't listen. I stared at the phone in shock. It was a picture. My face, a little blurred but clearly me. I was red-faced, with hair in my eyes. It must have been taken by somebody when I was running with Mrs. Mullins. Someone had crudely Photoshopped my face onto a pornographic picture of a naked woman who was being held down on a desk with no clothes on. A muscular man with extremely dark brown skin and a large penis was fucking the girl from behind. Mrs. Mullins' face, a black and white yearbook photo, had been Photoshopped in place of the man's face.

I barely heard Billy shout, "Let go of my fucking phone!" I felt a twisting in my stomach as nausea swept over me. But then he grabbed the phone out of my hands and stood over me and began throwing punches.

The first connected with my nose, knocking my head back against the glass with a loud crack. The second hit was in the eye, and my vision went white. I threw my arms up in front of my face as he continued to wildly throw punches.

The bus jerked to a stop, and a moment later Billy was pulled off of me. I stared up in shock, feeling hot wet liquid running down my face.

"What the hell got into you, Billy?"

"Freak tried to steal my phone, sir! He wouldn't give it back!"

winter flower

The driver whirled on me. "Is this true, boy? You stealing on my bus?"

I shook my head rapidly, unable to speak.

The driver gave an expression of disgust. "Billy, get to the back of the bus and keep your hands to yourself. And you, boy, you ever try something like that on my bus again and you'll be walking the rest of the year."

Nobody said a word. I rode the rest of the bus ride home in silence, holding my face in an effort to stop the bleeding from my nose.

Eighteen

~~~~~~

Cole

My alarm went off at five p.m., waking me from what had been a sadly short nap. When I came home Sam had been in his room doing homework. I'd knocked, told him I was going to take a nap, then stumbled into the bedroom where I collapsed onto our uncomfortable discount mattress we'd bought at Big Lots when we first moved to Alabama.

I yawned. Naps rarely left me feeling refreshed, but I was so consistently short on sleep that I sometimes needed them just to function. I sat up, then got up from the bed. I hated having a mattress on the floor. It reminded me of summers in the North Georgia mountains when I was a kid. It reminded me of being poor.

I hadn't bothered to change out of my uniform when I got home, because I had to go back in for shift change. Three nights a week, go in for shift change. Work six days a week. Sleep every once in a while. Last night third shift had called (at two in the morning) because they couldn't figure out where the damned to-go cups were, and apparently their eyes weren't functioning enough to spot them in the place where I put them *every single day*.

Sitting here and bitching to myself wasn't going to do me any good.

I got up and walked down the wood paneled hallway. All it needed was orange carpet to finish the look of 1970s working-class near poverty. As I walked into the kitchen I reminded myself to call the landlord again tomorrow to complain about the broken front window and the rotting wood on the front porch. We had rented this house sight unseen before moving from Virginia, and the photographs shown by the management company had artfully concealed those shortcomings. Not that we could afford much better. But still.

I knocked on Sam's door as I passed.

"Yeah?" Sam's tone of voice was annoyed. When did teenagers become so antisocial? Was it just built into their DNA that when they turned fourteen they became unfit to live around other human beings?

"I'm going to make dinner, you'll have to come out of your cave soon."

"Okay." For a second I put my hand on the doorknob and thought about pushing Sam to open the door. No ... I would give him a few more minutes. Then we could have dinner, clean up together, and maybe I could persuade him to play a game of chess before I headed off to work.

I sighed when I entered the kitchen. My coffee cup from this morning. Sam's plate from last night, three pieces of pizza crust still on it. Sam never ate the crust. Yesterday's breakfast dishes, all were piled in the kitchen sink. In the middle of the floor was a bottle of Mr. Clean, a scrub brush, and a towel. Half the floor had been scrubbed clean, and the other half still had a slight layer of grime.

I smiled slightly as I picked up the cleaning supplies from the middle of the floor. That explained why Erin had smelled vaguely of citrus as we drove to the airport last night. She'd been scrubbing the kitchen. Not that I wanted to see her on her hands and knees scrubbing anything, but it was good that she was doing something. She'd been so hideously depressed, and truth be told, so had I. I felt almost as if a cloud had been lifted by Jeremiah's words last night, a cloud of despair.

I quickly washed the dishes, scrubbing the rings of coffee at the base of yesterday's mugs. Then I filled up the pot with water and began preparing dinner.

Every day we were in Oxford, I was vaguely reminded of my years growing up. Not because of the landscape—Oxford was largely flat—but because of the poverty. The gun stores and pawn shops and title pawn and check-cashing places; the liquor stores and beat-up pickup trucks took me back to summers in North Georgia. With the exception of his year-long deployment in Lebanon, Dad spent most of my childhood at sea six months out of the year. Whenever his deployments carried into the summer, Mama would pack me off to his relatives in Banks County deep in the back woods.

Daddy's family owned a five-acre plot of mostly woods at the end of a three-mile-long dirt road with ruts deeper than drainage ditches. Grandma lived in a rounded steel single-wide marked with large swaths of rust and peeling paint. I had often been reluctant to go over to her place. Aside from the six chihuahuas she kept fenced in the kitchen causing the entire place to reek of urine and shit, she also hoarded everything from newspapers to tin cans, all of it in stacks and piled to the ceilings in the tiny rooms.

Daddy's brother-in-law Big Bill lived in the double-wide next door with his wife (Dad's sister) Donna. Big Bill didn't do much. Like his deceased father-in-law, his primary contribution to the economy was the purchase of Budweiser and moonshine. Somewhere along the years he had built a rickety front porch attached to the double-wide, and most summer days he could be found on that porch lounging in a metal-framed lounge chair, shirt off, a beer resting on his rounded belly. Bill was prone to using his fists on people too small to defend themselves, like his wife and son. I remember him lecturing about being "in the big house." Lucas followed in his footsteps and was in prison much of his adulthood. Sadly, I ended up using a lot of Big Bill's lessons when I went to prison.

I never knew if Mama realized what her brother-in-law's behavior was like when left alone. In polite company he generally behaved well enough, and Donna certainly wasn't going to say anything to anyone. I still vividly remember one summer night when I was twelve years old, Big Bill burst into the trailer, raging and so drunk he was stumbling.

The second he came through the front door, Donna realized how things were. She screamed, "*Run!*" at Lucas. We didn't hesitate. Both of us ran for the back door even as Big Bill yelled, "I'll kill you, you little shit!" as he lunged at Lucas. We made it out the door and scrambled between the cinderblocks underneath the double-wide. For the next twenty minutes or maybe it was twenty hours, we heard Donna screaming. Lucas covered his ears and buried his face in the dirt, sobbing. I lay on my back, looking off into the darkness, swearing that I would never live like my family.

Three years later, I was fifteen when Lucas got his driver's license. That summer, Daddy was in the Persian Gulf again, and a week after school got out I was on a Greyhound bus bound for Georgia. Usually Donna picked me up at the bus station, but that summer it was Lucas, sitting behind the wheel of an ancient Ford pickup. I grinned when I got in.

"You got your own truck?" I scanned the interior, with ripped upholstery and an obviously broken eight-track player.

"Hell, yeah," he replied. "Got it for just five hundred dollars. Still needs work, but it runs."

"Awesome."

"You getting a car when you turn sixteen?"

"Not unless I can find a job. Daddy sure as shit ain't gonna pay for it."

"We're gonna swing by the house so you can say hi to Mama before Big Dick gets home."

I snickered at Lucas's name for his Dad. "Things been better? With him?"

Lucas shrugged. "Shit." He pronounced it *shee-it.*

193

Aunt Donna was, as usual, tired and looked overwhelmed, when we came in the house. But she paused long enough to kiss me on the cheek. "Good to see you, Cole. Your Mama doin' okay? Yeah? Y'all skedaddle, I'm tryin' to get this floor clean. Dinner's at six."

Big Bill ignored me when he got home, which I far preferred to him paying attention to me. By eight, he was asleep in his chair, a beer perched precariously on his stomach. Lucas tiptoed over to his dad, apparently in an effort to extract the beer and place it on the side table. But when he touched the can, Big Bill stirred and put his hand on the beer.

Lucas stepped back. "Mama, we're headed out."

"Where you going this time of night?" she asked.

"Party over at Brian Wilkes' place. Don't worry, his mom don't tolerate no pot or nothing."

Donna looked doubtful. But she nodded. "Y'all go on. Behave yourselves."

We were halfway out the door when Big Bill stirred, letting out a grumble. Then we heard a loud curse. "Son of a *BITCH!*"

My eyes swept back to Big Bill, who was sitting up, eyes wide now, beer running down the bottom of his shirt and pants. His face contorted with rage, eyebrows coming together, lips scrunching together in a mean look, like an old man with no teeth. His eyes fixed on Donna.

She started backing toward the kitchen. "Let me get you a towel," she mumbled.

"Bitch!" he cursed. "Why the hell you let that happen?"

"*Bill*, we tried to get the can from ya. Lucas here tried to get it and put it on the side table. But you wouldn't let go."

He stalked toward her. "Are you talking back to me?"

Dread was sweeping over her face. "Bill, you leave me alone."

Lucas, standing next to me, let out a curse. "Fucking asshole, leave her alone. It was your damn beer."

Big Bill froze in place, his back suddenly tense. Then he turned toward Lucas. "What the *fuck* did you just say?"

Donna grabbed at him. "Bill! Leave him alone—"

Her words were cut off in a gurgling scream when he elbowed her in the nose. She fell back onto her ass in the kitchen, blood spurting from between the hands she held to her face.

"Asshole!" Lucas shouted. Then he charged at his father.

Big Bill might have been a drunk and flabby, with a giant belly, but he was strong, with the strength of a boa constrictor. He swung at Lucas, connecting

194

with Lucas's cheek with a loud *crack!* Then he swung again with his left hand, connecting with Lucas's other cheek.

"I'll fucking kill you, boy," Big Bill threatened, his voice low and full of rage. He shoved the dazed Lucas up against the wall.

I looked around in a panic, urgently, as Bill's hands closed on his son's throat.

Baseball bat. There was an aluminum bat in the hall, leaning against the corner next to Lucas's door. I ran for it and hefted the bat then walked back into the living room. Bill was holding his son against the wall, Lucas's face turning bright red at the neck where his father gripped him.

Donna grabbed at his arm, screaming, "Leave him alone!"

In five quick steps, I approached, bringing the bat behind me like I was ready for a grand slam. Then I yelled, "Big Bill!"

Bill turned his head toward me, rage on his face.

I swung.

The bat connected at Bill's temple with a loud *pop*, bouncing his head back like a bowling pin. Big Bill collapsed to the floor.

"Oh my Lord, you killed him!" Donna screamed, dropping to her knees next to Big Bill. *"You killed him!"* She leaned over her husband, crying, apparently losing any interest or concern for Lucas, who was now standing off to the side gasping and sputtering as he tried to regain his breath. "You killed him!" she accused again.

Lucas, recovering, muttered, "He ain't dead. He's too damned mean to die."

He wasn't dead, but he did end up spending a week in the hospital. And for the rest of that summer, the bastard kept his distance from me, and I kept myself armed with a six-inch knife at all times.

I *hated* the Deep South, and I'd been perfectly happy living in Metro DC. But the loss of my job had brought me back down here, not far at all from those mountains in North Georgia. I never wanted to come back, I never wanted to do a lot of things. But here I was. I had to make the best of it, and do the best I could for Erin and the kids.

The *kids.*

I closed my eyes and unusually, said a quick prayer. Unusual because I never prayed. But for Brenna, I could do it.

Where was she? Every day for two years I had asked that question. I'd never realized what it meant to be a parent who had lost a child. Missing. Not knowing if she was dead or suffering or … what? It changed everything. I had a gaping wound that never scabbed over, never healed, never stopped hurting. It was made that much worse by the fact that for most of the first year she was gone, I was unable to do anything, locked away in a cell.

I ached to go now, to leave everything, to walk away from our jobs and school, take Sam and drive to Portland. Never stop until we found her.

Instead, I strained the spaghetti and put it on the plates, put them on the table, and called out. "Sam? Dinner!"

Sam's door opened, and he came shuffling down the hallway. I had my back to him, pouring glasses of lemonade as I asked him, "How was school today?"

When I turned around, I saw his face and froze. His nose was swollen and red, and he had a nasty bruise forming underneath his left eye. I set the drinks on the table and approached him. "Christ, what happened to you?"

Sam seemed to shrink into himself as he slipped into one of the chairs. "I got in a fight."

The words that came out of my mouth were worthy of my father. "Well, I sure hope the other guy looked worse."

Sam's face went through a progression of expressions, ending on a hurt look.

"*Shit*. I'm sorry, Sam. That's something my father would have said to me. I didn't mean it." I sat down in my seat. "Are you okay? Who was it?"

My words seemed to sink in, but he didn't answer right away. I waited, watching. Finally he said, "Nobody. It doesn't matter."

Both of us started to eat, but I pressed the issue. "It does matter, Sam. Are you being bullied? Tell me what's going on."

Sam didn't respond. He just sat there eating and ignoring me.

"Come on, Sam. Talk to me. I can't help you if you won't tell me what's going on."

"I didn't ask for your help." His tone had a sense of finality to it.

How was I supposed to respond to that? I didn't at first. I ate and studied my sons face. He was so small for a sixteen-year-old, it was a little unnerving. It begged the question, what kind of an asshole beat up a kid half his size? Because I seriously doubted there was anyone Sam's size at his school.

I decided to try again. "Listen, I know I haven't exactly been the most available lately."

At the word lately, Sam's mouth curled up in a look of contempt. I paused for a second, knowing that *lately* was probably the understatement of the decade. "Look … I screwed up bad after Brenna disappeared, and I work so much lately we hardly ever do anything together. I'm sorry about that, Sam. But give me a chance. Tell me what happened."

Sullen. "Leave me alone."

Crap. I took another bite of my food then chewed, not knowing what to say. Or if there was anything I could say. I swallowed, and I thought. Like I often did lately, I felt like a failure. Sam's reaction reminded me so much of Brenna in the weeks and months leading up to her disappearance, it made my heart ache. Hollow, empty. I sighed. I wasn't going to be able to force Sam to communicate. I would just have to be patient and keep trying.

We ate the rest of the meal in silence. Finally, he said, "May I be excused?"

"Yeah," I said vaguely waving. "I've got to go back to work in about forty-five minutes. Want to play a round of chess first?"

"Nah, I'm tired. Thanks, though."

Sam left his plate at the table and walked away. Normally I might have prodded him to scrape it off and put it in the sink, but now wasn't really the time for that, was it?

Instead, I stood up and washed the dishes, sprayed down the counters and wiped them, and then checked my watch. I didn't have to leave for twenty minutes, but that was an awkward amount of time. I sat down on the couch and picked up the book I had been starting and stopping for the past two weeks. I read two pages but stopped when I realized that I hadn't comprehended a word.

My eyes drifted to the shelf under the coffee table. I hadn't realized that Erin had put our photo albums there. I slid the top book off the stack and lifted it up, laying it on top of the coffee table. It was brown faux leather with fake gold etching, and the words, Family Memories, stamped in the center. I opened the album.

It was like being punched. The first photograph was an eight by ten of Brenna and Sam running side by side on the sidewalk in front of our old house. Not the huge house ... no, our first home. The one we loved. Our *old* house. Brenna was dressed all in black, with long flowing sleeves, and a peaked witch's hat. Her face was painted green, and in the midst of the makeup her smile gleamed, except for the one missing front tooth. In the picture, she was seven years old. Her left hand was gripped around Sam's right as he ran beside her. Sam had dressed as a ladybug, an occasion which had provoked an argument between me and Erin. In retrospect, I felt like an asshole. I'd argued that he should have a *boy* costume.

Why couldn't I just let the kid be a kid? In the photo, Sam had a fiendishly large smile for a ladybug, and both of them looked thrilled as they carried their plastic jack-o'-lanterns on their way to collect candy.

I didn't realize I was crying. But somehow, while I sat there staring at the picture as it blurred, Sam walked in the room and said, "Dad? Are you okay?"

I looked up, and my vision blurred, and for a second Sam looked like Brenna, then he looked like the little boy he had once been, and I choked a little as I said, "Yeah." But it was obvious that wasn't true, because more tears were running down my face.

197

winter flower

I couldn't remember ever having cried in my adult life except the night after they found Brenna's smashed cell phone. "Shit. I'm sorry. I didn't mean to ... I miss her too."

Sam swallowed and looked anxious, like he just didn't know what to say. I didn't either. There was nothing in the parental manual my dad passed down that gave any precedent or instruction for this. Finally I said, "I've got to head into work. I'll be about an hour, you want to come with? I can get you some hash browns or something if you want."

Sam shook his head. "I'm really tired, I want to head to bed. I just came out to say ... I'm sorry for being rude at dinner."

I wiped my face with my left hand and stood, placing my right hand on Sam's shoulder. "It's okay. I love you, you know."

He ducked his head in acknowledgement.

Five minutes later I left for the restaurant. I was hoping to get in and out of there relatively quickly, but that would depend somewhat on my staff. I needed to do an inventory in the back, and that could be time-consuming.

I drove with the windows down, savoring the cool breeze that portended the end of summer. I caught the faint scent of honeysuckle as I left our neighborhood, the smell reminding me of my childhood. The flower hadn't grown in our area of Virginia, and so I'd never shown my kids how to pluck them and suck the juice out. I felt oddly sad about that. There were so many things I wanted to show them and teach them. And the flowers ... I remembered them from before adolescence, before hearing Big Bill beat up his wife, a time when things were simpler.

It took ten minutes to get to the restaurant. After I pulled into the parking lot, I sat in the car and looked through the windows at the scene inside. Second shift was still on the floor, and the cook was busy scrubbing the floor behind the counter. Two men who appeared to be in their late forties or early fifties sat in one of the booths. They looked vaguely familiar ... I must have seen them on another night during shift change. Hunched over the low counter was an older man in his late seventies named Harold. Harold came in twice a day, at one p.m. and eight p.m. He always ordered the same thing: a sausage biscuit, the biscuit cooked on the grill so long that it was as hard as a hockey puck. Harold liked to tell stories and often talked about local politics and scandal, as well as long-past races at Talladega. Even though I was from the South, his Southern accent was so thick, and he spoke so quietly, it was difficult to understand anything he said.

I got out of the car and did a quick once-over of the parking lot. It had been swept, and it looked like second shift had washed the windows. I entered the front door just as Linda Poole, the third shift cook, came out of the back room. She was working with Dakota tonight.

I waved as Linda called at a near-shout, "Hey, boss!"

I checked out the restaurant. Second shift had actually done a great job, it was very clean. I thanked them then got started with the process of changing out and counting the drawer. As I entered the back room carrying second shift's register drawer, I saw Dakota standing at the mirror tying on her apron.

"Hey, Dakota. How are things?" I only half expected an answer.

But she surprised me when she gave me a huge smile and said, "Guess what?"

"What?"

"I passed my GED!" As she said the words she smiled even wider.

I set the drawer down on the surface of my desk and said, "That's great!" I gave her a high five. Then I sat on the stool in my office. Before I started counting, I said, "So what are your plans? You going to apply at the community college?"

Doubt immediately clouded her face. "I'm wouldn't even know where to start."

"If you need some help figuring that out, I'm happy to talk you through some of it," I said. "You're a smart kid and your baby will be a lot better off if you can get any college at all under your belt."

Her face crinkled up in a surprised smile. "You'd do that?"

"Yeah. I'll bring my laptop in some afternoon, and we can sit down here at the restaurant and look at the local colleges. I bet you could get a Pell Grant to pay for your classes. But for now, it's shift change, head on out front."

Once the drawer was changed, I headed to the back room and began my inventory. Along with everything else, one of my job requirements was to inventory everything in the store three times a week. When I first started, the process would take a couple of hours. But I had it down to a science now and could usually finish the job in under fifteen minutes.

I was standing in the deep freezer, wishing I had brought a coat to work, when I heard Linda's voice. "Boss? Can I talk to you for a second?"

I held a finger up in the air and said, "One moment." I only had three items left on my checklist. I got them written down then stepped out, latching the freezer and then the walk-in refrigerator behind me. "What's up?"

She squirmed a little. "You know I don't like to make trouble..." she trailed off.

"What is it, Linda?"

She jerked her head towards the front of the restaurant. "It's those assholes in the booth again. They're bothering Dakota."

199

I shook my head. "What are you talking about?"

"They come in about once a week. If she's working, they always give her a hard time." I had a sinking feeling.

"What kind of a hard time?"

"They just say mean things to her."

I stepped out of the stockroom and look toward the small window in the door to the front of the restaurant. I didn't see Dakota out there. I turned around, about to ask Linda where the hell Dakota went, but then I saw her, standing near the lockers, her back to the room. She had her head down, shoulders hunched over, hands at her side bunched into fists.

I motioned to Linda to get back out front—we didn't leave the front of the restaurant empty when there were customers in the building. She went without saying anything.

"Dakota?" I asked.

She spun around, a fierce expression her face. But the expression was belied by the tears that marked her cheeks. She was crying. "Cole, I know the customer's supposed to always be right. But I'm not waiting on those two anymore. I won't do it. I don't care who they are, you can fire me."

"Jesus. What happened? What did they say?"

Her expression twisted into anger. She spoke in an accent, mocking the thick Alabama twang that was common in the area. "How's your crack baby, *SHANEEKWA?* Or is to Toowanda? How's your little nigger baby?"

She burst into open tears.

"Are you kidding me?" I said.

She shook her head. "No. They come in here all the time. It's always something."

"Not anymore," I muttered. "You stay here, I'll take care of that bullshit."

I walked through the door to the front of the restaurant, accidentally banging the swinging door into the counter. Linda jumped. I approached her.

"Listen," I said. "Can you just verify ... they say those kinds of things regularly to her?"

"All the time, Cole."

I frowned then nodded and walked around the counter to the two men at the table.

At a closer look, I could see one of the men was younger than I'd originally guessed. He had greying hair, but his skin was smooth. I'd guess he was in his late thirties. The other man was at least fifty. They looked up from their food as I approached.

"Excuse me, gentlemen. I'm afraid I'm going to have to ask you to leave."

Both men started in shock. The older one said, "You've *got* to be kidding me."

The young one said, "Hey … we were just having some fun. It didn't mean nothin'."

I took a deep breath. It wouldn't do anyone any good for me to lose my temper. "You can go have fun somewhere else. You aren't welcome here anymore."

The older man slid out of the booth and stood up, facing me. "Son, you don't get to decide that. You just fucked up a lot worse than you realize."

"Sir, if you don't leave right now, I'll call the police. As of right now, you're trespassing."

I shook with anger and anxiety. Who the hell behaved like this?

The older man's lips curled up in a contemptuous snarl. "Good luck with your career, son. Because you just ended it here." He turned and walked away, the younger man running to catch up. Both left out the front door in a hurry.

I sighed then turned around. Linda was staring at me in open astonishment. "What is it?" I asked.

She shook her head and smiled. "We told our last manager about it plenty of times. He wouldn't do nothing about it. Honestly, I didn't think you would either."

I shrugged. "It's my job to take care of y'all, okay? Nobody's going to come in *my* restaurant and treat people like that."

She grinned.

"All right," I said. "Back to work."

Erin

It was seven in the evening when I finally walked back in to the motel room. It had been an exhausting day, both emotionally and physically. I set down the two plastic bags filled with groceries—peanut butter, bread, microwavable food along with necessary toiletries. Then I went back outside and took the cardboard box out of the passenger seat of the car I had purchased that afternoon.

I wasn't squandering the cash that Ayanna had given me. But I *would* use it strategically. I had paid five hundred for the 1996 Datsun with a rusted undercarriage and a malfunctioning muffler. It was highly unlikely the car would ever pass state inspection, but I had thirty days before the inspection would be due. Hopefully I wouldn't need the vehicle that long. In the end it was far cheaper than renting.

winter flower

I had made the decision to stay in this hotel, despite the apparent presence of drug dealers and God only knew who else. It seemed possible that if Brenna was to be found in Portland, it might be in this neighborhood. Back in the room, I set the cardboard box down and lifted the lid.

Inside was a flyer. Under the bold headline, *HAVE YOU SEEN THIS GIRL?* were side by side pictures of Brenna: one taken on her sixteenth birthday, hours before she disappeared, the other a mug shot from three weeks ago. I was still devastated by the contrast between the two photos.

But I also had new information. If pictures of her were being published in ads on the web, they might show the distinctive tattoo on her neck, or the cigarette scar on her collarbone.

I wanted a drink very badly. On the way back to the motel, I had pulled into the parking lot of a liquor store and sat there. Four, maybe five minutes. I didn't get out of the car. Finally, I backed out and drove away.

Leaving that parking lot was one of the hardest things I'd ever done.

The clock on the microwave said 7:15. Time to call. It would be 9:15 in Alabama.

I dialed Cole's number and waited through three rings. Finally he picked up. "Erin? Hey, give me a second, I'm just leaving the restaurant."

He must have held the phone at his side because it sounded like he was at the bottom of a well as he gave instructions to someone to make sure the underside of something called the "dish pit" was scrubbed clean. Then, a moment later, he was back on the line.

"Sorry about that. So ... tell me what happened. Did you learn anything?"

I hardly knew where to begin. I started to tell the story of my morning—the waitress in the diner who thought she *might have seen* someone who looked like Brenna. I'd gone back to the diner in the afternoon, but the waitress was gone until tomorrow morning. The visit to the Police Department and my disastrous interaction with Sergeant Mackey. I almost didn't repeat the contemptuous words he had used. *I raised my daughter better than that.* But I was still so hurt and outraged by those words I had to say something.

"I can't fucking believe he said that to you. Jesus Christ. Does he think she voluntarily got kidnapped?" His voice cracked as he said the words, a level of emotion I hadn't heard from Cole in a long time.

"I did like the detective who has been assigned the case now, though. She's young but seems to know a lot, and she's on the sex trafficking task force here. We're meeting for breakfast in the morning. I ... I think she's going to help."

There was silence on the other end of the line for several seconds, then Cole asked, "Did you see a mug shot?" He sounded incredibly hesitant as he asked the question.

Tears started to run down my face. *Damn it!* I answered in a low, quiet voice. "She's been through hell. She ... she has a cigarette burn scar on her collarbone. And the tattoo on her neck ... and wrinkles around her eyes. She looks a *lot* older, Cole. Like ... thirty? But she was here. *She was here.*"

At the other end of three thousand miles of wires, Cole sniffed. He inhaled like he was going to say something, stopped and hesitated for a few seconds, then spoke in a rough, emotion-laden tone. "I was afraid our daughter was dead."

After he said the words, Cole let out a deep cry of pain like I had never heard from him before. "I'm sorry," he said. "I'm sorry I ever thought that."

His statement was layers upon layers of pain and regret and fear, and the raw torment in his voice made me sob.

"Now is our chance," I spoke through the tears. "We might find her. We might bring her home."

Neither of us spoke for a very long time. But we didn't hang up. I could hear him breathing on the line as he drove ... home? That awful place in Alabama didn't resemble a home in any meaningful way.

And maybe that was my fault. Maybe it *could* be home.

"How's Sam?" The question came out in an awkward whisper.

Cole took a deep breath, and the change in subject seemed to give him a chance to collect himself. *Jesus,* I thought. In twenty years of marriage I had never seen my husband cry. The sound confused me, it made me want to run to him and comfort him, no matter how badly he had hurt me in the past.

"To be honest, I'm a little worried about him. He got in a fight at school today."

"Sam?" As if there were another child we could be talking about. But when did Sam ever get in fights? "What happened?"

"He wouldn't tell me anything. He got really defensive when I asked him and basically begged me to butt out." Now *that* sounded like the Sam I knew.

"Was he hurt?"

"Swollen nose and the beginning of a black eye. I think he'll have a pretty good shiner, but no permanent damage."

I sighed. "Do you think we should talk to the school?"

"His counselor, maybe. He likes her." Cole's response was interesting. I didn't know Sam's counselor, nor did I know that he liked her. I couldn't think of a time in our marriage ever when Cole had known more about the kids than I did. A flash of shame swept through me. I thought back to the past few months.

203

I'd gotten worse and worse, hadn't I? I'd been drinking too much. I'd hardly spent any time with Sam. What the hell was wrong with me?

"Maybe you should try that. Let me know what she says?"

"I will. Call me tomorrow after your breakfast?"

I didn't know how to feel. Not because there was anything shocking about his request … it made sense. There was something else going on here.

"Okay. Can I talk to Sam? Are you home?"

"Yeah, hold on a minute. I'm still in the driveway."

I waited as he got out of the car and into the house.

I heard Cole knocking, then he said, "Sam? It's your mom on the phone." Silence.

A moment later Cole was back on the line. "He's fast asleep. You want me to have him call you after school tomorrow?"

I felt a pang of disappointment but pushed it back. Sam needed his sleep.

"Yeah. I'll talk to him tomorrow."

"Erin…"

"Yeah?"

I heard nothing but breathing at the other end of the line for several seconds. Then he said, "Good night."

A flash of anger swept through me, irrational I knew, but there all the same. What was I supposed to do with his behavior? Did he think a couple of phone calls was suddenly going to change his years of destruction in our marriage?

"Good night." My response did not have the same warm tone as his. I didn't wait for a response, disconnecting the call. Then my eyes shifted to my bag in the corner of the room, where my aging laptop was tucked away. For all I knew, she was being sold on the Internet right now. Right here in Portland.

I stood up and almost stumbled to the corner of the room, scrambling to get my laptop out of the bag. Once opened, I began my search. I started with Backpage, because that's where most of the ads in the country were posted. But there were other sites I would check too, and there were probably local discussion boards. Over the years I'd searched through so many layers of filth and muck that I was almost numb to it.

Or at least the wine helped me feel like I was numb.

My mouse hovered over the link *Escorts and body rubs* for several seconds, then I clicked. The ads immediately filled my screen, most of them with photos of young women. Would I find her in here?

The language turned my stomach. I began my search. It was immediately overwhelming. More than a hundred ads were listed in the previous two hours alone. Girls and women of all shapes and sizes. The same kinds of ads as always.

** BBW Busty Girl for You $60 **

** Sugar and Strawberry Here For Your Needs * Double Your Pleasure *

** New in Town * College Girl * 18 * Two Nights Only * 180 **

I hated this. I scanned through the photos, getting angrier and angrier. Then I slammed my laptop shut.

Nineteen

~~~~~~

Brenna

The night of my sixteenth birthday wasn't the worst night of my life, not by a long shot. But it sent me spinning in that direction. That night was right before the dividing line in my life, the moment before I fell off a precipice that led me straight into hell on Earth.

But I didn't know that yet. I didn't know I was sliding down to the edge. Instead of scrabbling for purchase, reaching out for help from Sam or Mom and Dad, I turned toward the abyss and leapt.

I drove that night to the address in Leesburg Rick had texted me. Leesburg seemed to be a nothing of a town, just an extension of the vast suburbs that surrounded Washington, DC where I had grown up. The drive out Route 7 seemed to take forever as I passed mini-mansion developments, strip malls, and industrial parks. I would have never made it at all had I not had the GPS on my phone, which unerringly gave me directions to the end of my childhood.

The parking lot was empty, except for a gleaming black convertible Mustang at the far end. My headlights swept across the parking lot, illuminating little other than faded painted lines and garbage here and there. Rick and Nialla were sitting on the hood of the Mustang. Rick was holding a glass bottle in his hand.

I parked my car and got out. Nialla waved, although she looked as grim as ever, and Rick said, "Hey, Brenna. How's it going?"

I didn't expect to respond the way I did. I wasn't going to say anything about Chase. I was going to show some bravado; I was going to have fun with my friends and forget all about *him*. But instead, my chin quivered, and I said, "Chase broke up with me."

Nialla's eyes flashed in dismay. Rick's expression didn't change, but he slid over, away from Nialla and patted his hand on the hood of the car in between them. "Oh, that sucks. Come tell us about it."

I sat on the hood of the car in between them. I was intensely aware of Rick's thigh touching mine. In halting fits and starts I began to tell them the story of how I met Chase, fell in love with him, and ended up there with them that night. I felt like I talked for a hundred years. Midway through my story, Rick handed me the bottle. I took a too-large drink of it then gasped and sputtered. "What is that?"

"Jack Daniels," he said. "You gotta take it slow, don't swig it. Just a small swallow at a time."

I tried again, this time just taking the barest sip. It tasted awful but made my throat warm as it went down.

"So that's the story. I'm such an idiot. I can't believe he dumped me on my birthday."

Rick shook his head. "If you ask me, he's a fucking idiot. I'd make love to you in a heartbeat. You're seriously pretty."

I shivered, feeling a warm rush through my body that wasn't from the whiskey. Rick's frank attention made me nervous, but I was also flattered. No one had ever paid that kind of attention to me before, and sometimes Chase, with his reluctance to even make out, much less kiss, made me feel utterly undesirable.

Rick began to ply me with questions. He asked about Sam and my parents, and I found myself telling him about Dad's affair and my anger with both of my parents. I was sick of hearing them fight all the time, and their marital troubles meant that they basically just ignored me and Sam. Sometimes I wanted to stand in between them and their television and scream, *"I'm here!"* Or go live with Grandpa, where at least I could go out to the garden and get away from everything.

Rick murmured sympathetically, while Nialla sat there silently. I kept wondering what the deal was with her. Was she Rick's girlfriend? If so, how did she feel about him complimenting me the way he had? Surely it made her jealous? I didn't get it. I checked the time and was dismayed to see it was nearly three a.m.

"Oh no, I've got to go."

I felt an almost electric tension split the air. "Wait just a second, I've got something for you," Rick said.

He dropped down from the hood of the Mustang and walked around and opened up the car door. He started to rummage inside for something.

winter flower

I felt Nialla tense beside me. She leaned close. She met my eyes, spoke in a perfectly calm tone, as quiet as a whisper. "Run now while you still have a chance. Go."

I stared at her in shock. She *was* jealous.

I was still staring at her when Rick reappeared. He had a box in one hand, about the size of the palm of his hand. In his right hand was the bottle.

"Here, the Jack is almost gone. You drink the last of it."

I turned away from Nialla and took the bottle, which had only a splash left at the bottom. I looked Rick in the eye with what I thought was a mature, flirting glance, and tossed the Jack Daniels back, the liquid scorching my throat as it went down.

I coughed again but not as much as before.

So *what* if she was jealous? What kind of a relationship did they have anyway?

"Here. Open it." He grinned.

I took the tiny box from him. It was wrapped in silver wrapping paper. My heart started to thump. As I tore it open, he said, "Happy birthday!"

I gasped when I saw what was inside. A jewelry box. I opened it up and was stunned to see a delicate pearl bracelet. In the moonlight, the pearls were luminous.

I was starting to feel very woozy. "Oh my God, is that for me?"

"Sure is," he said. I barely remember him placing it on my wrist, because I felt like I needed to curl up on the ground and go to sleep. I didn't know why I was so tired. I just knew I so badly wanted to take a nap.

I barely felt his hands as they shoved into my pockets, as he took out my phone and keys. My eyes were half closed when I heard my phone hit the ground with a loud crack. Had he broken it? Why?

I was too tired to care.

I stumbled as he pushed me into the back seat of the Mustang and lay me down on my side.

"Just go to sleep. Everything's going to be fine."

Brenna

I woke up with a throbbing headache. My face felt rough, where my cheek had been resting on thick carpet. It was dark, but a thin sliver of light underneath a door illuminated the room I was in.

Not a room. A closet. I was in a walk-in closet. A shelf ran along one wall above me. The light under the door was faint, but clear. I swallowed, fear suddenly gripping me. Where was I? I could only barely remember last night. I'd gone and met Nialla and Rick after Chase broke up with me? I remembered talking with them but not much else.

I slowly sat up, groaning. I needed to pee. I needed to get out of this closet. What was happening to me?

I stood, panic surging me into full wakefulness.

I turned the knob, but the door didn't budge. "Hello?" I cried out. "Hello? Is anyone there?"

I turned the knob again, desperately. It turned freely. But the door wouldn't budge.

"Hello? Hello?"

As I shouted the words, the headache, starting somewhere in the center-left of my forehead, turned sharp. I winced but banged on the door with my fists anyway. "Come on, guys, this isn't funny."

There was no response. I was becoming afraid. I had to go to the bathroom, and no one was answering the door, and I couldn't get out. For just a second, a series of possible nightmarish scenarios ran through my mind. Rick was a serial killer or a perv or … what?

I couldn't catch my breath. Because I didn't really know anything at all about Rick or Nialla. I didn't know where they came from, or why they had been hanging around, or … anything at all. I thought of every warning I'd ever been given in my life, about every time my parents said to be careful, or *Make sure you check in and let us know where you are*, or *Don't talk to strangers*. I remembered Grandpa saying *It's a dangerous world out there. Stay close to your family.*

How could I have been so *stupid*?

Tears ran down my face. I called out again. "Hello? Is anyone there?"

I banged on the door with my fists. I was starting to panic, and my pleas for help were getting higher and higher pitched. Finally, I began to scream. I screamed as loud as I could, calling for somebody, anybody to help me.

When the door opened, it happened so fast that I didn't have time to react before a man's fist hit me in the right eye. Instantly everything went white and I fell to the ground. I cried out, "Stop!" But by the time I finished the word the man who had hit me was kneeling on my back, his knee crushing my spine.

I gagged, my nostrils flooded with sharp-smelling cologne and my own terror. My fear almost instantly grew worse … I knew the cologne. It was Rick.

He yanked my head back by my hair. I felt something sticky against my face, and it tightened and tightened over my mouth. It was duct tape. I was screaming as loud as I could now, struggling as hard as I could, but I couldn't make any sound. My nose was clogged up with snot and I shifted to a new terror … that I wouldn't be able to breathe and that I'd be left alone to die here. I struggled, but then felt an incredibly sharp pain in my lower back. I'd been punched in the kidney. I doubled over, weeping and grabbing at the tape that was wrapped around my head.

Rick's voice, when he finally spoke, was almost clinical. "You need to be quiet in here. No one can hear you anyway."

I froze. His weight lifted off of me and the closet went dark again. During the melee I'd pissed all over myself; my jeans were soaking wet and my nostrils were flooded by the stink. I scrabbled, desperately trying to get my fingers under the tape, to tear it open. With each breath I felt my nose clogging more and more.

I was making animal whining sounds as I tore at the tape and my face, and finally I was able to tear a tiny corner. I yanked at the tape, getting greater purchase, and finally was able to pull a significant piece of it loose. Unable to stop myself from moaning in terror, I slowly unwound the tape until my mouth was free.

Then I just lay there, sucking the cool air into my lungs.

I didn't call for help anymore.

I stripped off the soaking wet jeans and balled them up in one corner of the closet, then I curled up on the floor in the other corner and cried. I tried my best to stay silent.

Brenna

I never found out how long I was locked in the closet. Hours? Days? I know that the crack under the door went dim, then bright again, then dim, so it was at least one night and another day. But I'm not sure if it was more than that.

I didn't move the second time he opened the door of the closet. My lips were cracked from dehydration, my stomach hurt so bad from hunger I hardly understood the sensation: it was nothing like I'd described as simple *hunger* in my life before.

He looked down at me with an expression of pity. His eyes took in my condition as I lay on my side: the pile of feces that I'd finally lost control of sometime on the second day, the stinking mess of my clothes.

He sighed and said, "There's fresh clothes for you out here. And a shower. But clean up that mess first."

I cleaned it up the best I could, but it was in the carpet, the smell permeating it, no matter how hard I scrubbed. The more I scrubbed, the more it seemed like I was just spreading the stain, and I began to shake, my chin trembling. Was he going to be pissed? Would he lock me in the closet again? Or worse?

The clothes he had put on the bed were … not enough. A too-short blue mini-skirt. A sleeveless black tank. No underwear.

I kept my soiled underwear, took the clothes and went into the bathroom without a word. There was a window. It was small, but it was there. I started to close the door, but he put a foot in the way.

"Leave it open. We've got things to discuss, and we can't do that if you're trying to climb out windows."

I swallowed and looked away.

His lips curled up in a sad, knowing smile. I continued to stand there, holding the skimpy clothes in front of my body, and I said, "What am I supposed to do?"

"Go on and take your shower. Just leave the door open."

I was going to be sick. My stomach hurt, and I couldn't stand the way he looked at me. I backed toward the shower and turned it on, then did my best to get in and undress without him being able to see me. He just looked amused.

I stayed in the shower until the water got cold. But no matter how much I scrubbed, I didn't feel clean. I knew he was out there waiting, and I didn't know what was going to happen. It wasn't going to be anything good … that much was sure. I wondered where Nialla was. I wondered where my parents were, and Sam, and how long it had been. When the hot water finally ran out, I reached outside the shower curtain and grabbed a towel and began to dry off.

I carefully wrapped myself in the towel then stepped out of the shower.

He was sitting on the bathroom counter, leaning against the mirror and looking at his phone when I stepped out. "Feel better?"

He sounded like he was actually concerned.

"I want to go home."

He shook his head. "Your home is here now."

Dread and anxiety overwhelmed me. "What are you going to do to me?"

He shrugged. "That's completely up to you. You cooperate and make me happy, I'll make sure you have everything you've ever dreamed of. You get into trouble, you'll have to be disciplined." He stood up and approached me. Then he pointed a finger directly at my nose. "Betray me, and you'll die."

I swallowed. "Please, just let me go."

He shrugged. "That's the one thing I can't do. Now or ever. You might as well get used to it."

He reached toward me and tugged at the towel. I grabbed at it with both hands, but he pulled harder, yanking it off of me. I tried to shrink, covering myself the best I could with my hands, but he just shook his head. "Get on the bed."

I started to cry. I couldn't help it. I'd never been so afraid in my life. I shook my head, *no*.

Rick exploded into violence.

I can't talk about the things he did.

Twenty

~~~~~~

Brenna

"It won't always be this bad, you know. Sometimes he can even be gentle. But it's easier if you don't fight."

At Nialla's words, I curled myself into the tightest ball I could. I wanted to be invisible. I wanted to go back in that horrible closet. I wanted to be anywhere but where I was. My stomach was churning, and I felt weak from hunger and thirst and despair.

"Let me get you some water," she said. She slid off the bed, and a moment later I heard the door open and then close. From somewhere outside of the room, I heard his voice murmuring, the words indistinct. Nialla's response was sharp in tone, but I couldn't make out the words.

The sound of his voice made me flinch.

You're nothing but a whore, now, he had said. *You work for me now. You can make it easy or hard on yourself, but in the end it doesn't matter. No one is coming to get you. No one is going to rescue you. Me and Nialla … we're all you've got.*

He had made me say it. *I'm a worthless whore.* When I didn't say it convincingly enough, he hit me and made me do it again. And again. And again.

I hated him.

I was alone only a few minutes. When she came back in, she spoke in a gentle tone. "Sit up, drink some water.

She had to help me sit up, which made me more ashamed than ever. I winced at the sharp pain between my legs. I was bleeding. She wrapped a blanket around me then handed me the water. "Drink it slow. If you drink too fast after going so long without water, you'll puke it all up."

winter flower

I took a sip of the water. It felt like lead in my stomach. I wanted to curl up and hide, but I took another drink instead.

"That's good," Nialla said. "You're doing good."

Her kindness made me resent her. I thought of her telling me that I should run while I had the chance. I swallowed and spoke my first words to her. "I thought you were just jealous. You tried to warn me."

She looked away from me. "Not soon enough."

"Why?"

She looked puzzled. "Why what?"

"Why did you warn me?"

She shrugged. "It's too late for me. But this is no life for a kid like you."

The bitterness in her tone was unmistakable. I asked her, "What happens now?"

"Now you whore for him."

I flinched. Fear was settling in on me down to my bones. I slowly shook my head. "I'll die first."

She gave me a sad look. "You might. If you don't make him happy."

I needed to survive. I needed to somehow escape from this place … wherever it was … and get in touch with my parents. I didn't answer Nialla. Instead, I drank more of the water … slowly. Finally I said, "I'm really hungry. Can I have something to eat?"

Rick let me eat a little, just enough to take the edge of the hunger. Then later that afternoon, he raped me again. Then he locked me back in the closet. I was beginning to believe that he was just going to kill me, but it turned out, he had much worse in store than that.

Brenna

On the third day of my imprisonment, Rick burst into the closet. He threw new clothes at me. "Get dressed in this."

It was a dress that amounted to little more than a long shirt, sheer and silvery reflective material. It would barely cover me.

"I don't—"

"I didn't *ask*. I *told* you. You're gonna get used to this one way or another. Understand?"

He turned and walked out of the closet, shouting, "Nialla! Get your useless *ass* in there and get her ready to work. I'm done waiting."

"But Rick—" Her protest was cut off by a loud crack. He must have slapped her, and hard. She went silent instantly. A moment later she appeared at the door of the closet. A bright red handprint marred her face, with white spots in the center.

"Come on, Brenna. You gotta get up off the floor. You gotta get dressed, or he's gonna fuck both of us up."

I stared at her, feeling dead inside. "Why do you listen to him?"

Nialla shook her head. "You don't get it, Brenna. He'll kill you. Or me. He *owns* us. It's better to just go along now. You'll see. Someday it'll get better. We're saving for a place."

I shook my head, not understanding.

"*Please,*" she said. "Just get dressed."

I shook my head. "I won't do it. I won't be his whore."

Nialla started to cry and looked back toward the front of the apartment. I still hadn't seen past the boundaries of this closet and the room and bathroom beyond.

"Brenna—" she whispered.

The shout made both of us jump. *"Are you fucking kidding me? She's not ready yet!"*

Rick appeared suddenly, but he didn't come after me. Instead, he ran at Nialla, shoving her up against the doorjamb. "Why the *fuck* isn't she ready?" he screamed. As he shouted the word *fuck* he shoved her against the doorjamb, slamming her head back. "What the *fuck* is wrong with you? You think you can be my bottom *bitch* if you can't control a fucking new *whore?*"

With each emphasized word he slammed her against the doorjamb again. Her eyes were starting to dull, and I could tell this was real; he was really hurting her. I stood up and started to run toward—

I stopped. Without pause, he'd pulled a pistol from his waistband and pointed it at my face.

"Were you going to run at me, *bitch?*"

I shook my head, suddenly even more terrified than before. "I'll get dressed. I'm sorry. I'll get dressed. Just don't hurt her anymore."

He stared at me, nodding his head. His eyes were wide, his nostrils flaring. "Good. Good. You do that."

He shoved Nialla against the doorjamb again, but with no real force, and then he walked away.

She stood there catching her breath. I peeled off the senselessly tiny skirt and shirt and changed into the ... dress? It wasn't deserving of the word. It was too tight, and the fabric irritated my already raw nipples.

215

But what was I supposed to do *now?*

Nialla was crouched down in the doorway, crying silently.

I whispered, "I'm sorry. I'm sorry. I didn't mean to get you hurt."

She shook her head. In a rough voice she said, "It's fine. Just come on."

She stood up and led me into the bathroom. She broke open a makeup case and spread boxes across the counter. She picked through it, selecting one thing, then the next.

"Okay. We're going to make you look pretty."

I swallowed and felt my chin quivering as the dread sank back in. "I don't want to. I don't want to do this, Nialla."

She sighed and closed her eyes. After a few seconds, she reached into her bag and took out an unmarked prescription bottle, opened it, and extracted a small blue pill. "Here. Take this."

"What is it?"

"Valium. It'll help. Trust me."

I couldn't do this. I *couldn't*. But what the fuck was I going to do? I reached out and took the pill and dry swallowed it. It caught in my throat, and I almost gagged, then leaned forward and drank directly from the faucet.

The valium hit me almost immediately. I'd hardly eaten in days, and suddenly felt woozy as hell, like a fog was lowering over me.

I stood there quietly while Nialla put heavy makeup on me. Lipstick. Dark blue eyeshadow, and more mascara than I'd ever worn in my life. She put some perfume at the base of my neck.

"Hopefully it'll be someone nice," she muttered. "I asked him to wait, to give you a few more days. But he said if we didn't turn you out tonight, then he'd have to … have to … sell you."

I closed my eyes. Sell me? What the fuck world was this? Who would he sell me to? How does someone go about selling a person?

I wanted to go home.

"Is she fucking ready?"

Rick's shout from the front of the apartment barely penetrated my consciousness. Everything seemed so fuzzy.

"Let's go." She led me to the living room. Rick looked at me dismissively then jerked his head toward the front door.

I followed Rick out of the room and down what seemed like a mile-long hallway, then down an elevator. He kept a hand on my elbow the entire time.

As we came out of the elevator, I saw someone entering the nearly featureless lobby. A man, maybe twenty-five, in a suit. I tensed and immediately felt him increase the pressure on my elbow.

"Don't even think of it," Rick whispered. "You'd be dead and I'd clear out of town and that would be that."

The man walked past us, and I felt, more than I saw, his eyes scan me from head to toe.

In the car, I sank into the bucket seat, the leather feeling almost sticky against my skin. The stupid dress rode up my butt when I sat down. I tried to pull it down. Looking out the window, the lights in the parking deck were fuzzy with wide halos.

I didn't recognize where we were. Unfamiliar urban streets. Washington, DC? Rockville or Bethesda? Arlington? It had to be one of those. We stopped in the parking deck of another large building and Rick keyed in a number. The gate opened, and then we were going down a long row of cars until he parked.

It was all too loud, too unfamiliar. Another car drove by, fast for a parking deck, the wheels screeching on the smooth concrete. Then we were headed down another long hallway, and Rick unlocked a door.

He looked around, leaning into the room, then pulled me in. He pulled me close to him and said, "Now listen to me. I'm gonna be right there in that room. I can see everything that's happening. You try to run away, you try to fuck with me in any way, you'll pay. You understand?"

I nodded, helplessly. He probably could see everything. Did he have cameras? Peepholes? One-way mirrors? I looked around, wondering.

He put a hand under my chin and jerked my face back toward him. "Look at me when I'm speaking. You're Strawberry now. Tell them that if they ask your name. You don't have any other name, not anymore. Understand?"

"I understand." I was *Brenna*, no matter what *he* said.

A knock on the door.

"Listen!" he said urgently. "Go answer it. When you wouldn't cooperate, the only people I could reasonably get were folks who didn't care if you fought a little. So just cooperate and maybe you won't get hurt."

He walked away, shutting a bedroom door behind him. I looked around. There was a small living room, and another bedroom.

Another knock on the door. Maybe I could open it and run. Maybe I could talk to them. Convince them to leave me alone, and go call the police and set me free.

Yes. That's what I would do. They wouldn't hurt me if they knew I'd been kidnapped. I opened the door.

A man stood there. He was tall and wore a suit. Forty maybe, with sculpted hair and glasses. He looked like a banker, or somebody's father. He was my father's age. He wore a gold wedding ring.

Folks who didn't care if you fought a little. Was that true? Could it be true?

I froze. I didn't know what to say.

"You gonna invite me in?" he whispered, urgently.

I nodded. "Come in," I said. "Um … we're in here."

He followed me in, closing the door behind him. Then he looked me up and down, his eyes lingering a long time on my breasts. "In there?" he asked, pointing toward the bedroom.

I took a deep breath. Through the haze of whatever pill Nialla gave me, I knew I should be terrified. But I felt muffled, like a heavy blanket was draped over me and the entire world had lost its sharp edges. I walked into the other room. He followed, closing the door and locking it behind him.

I turned toward him. His eyes were sweeping over my body now, wide. His mouth opened slightly, like he was barely breathing through it.

"You look familiar," he said. "You were on the news, weren't you? You're that girl from Fairfax County."

I was on the news?

Jesus. I nodded, tears welling up in my eyes, fear punching through the numbness. "Please help me," I whispered.

His eyes widened. "What?"

"Please," I begged. "I just turned sixteen. I was kidnapped. Please don't hurt me. Call the police? Tell them I'm here?"

His jaw set in anger. "Are you fucking kidding me? You want me to call the police? What should I say? *Hi, I'd like to turn myself in for screwing a minor?* Is that what you want?" His voice rose to a shout at the end, and he surged toward me.

No! I cried out inside, wanting to scream as he grabbed me.

That was my sixth time being raped.

Brenna

Nothing but a whore.

Nobody else will ever want you.

Your parents would be ashamed.

Nowhere for you to go but here.

I heard it all. Every day. I was a worthless whore.

After a while, when you hear something long enough, you start believing it.

Within a couple of weeks they were letting me out of the room and into the remainder of the apartment—though not close to the front door. I'd even been able to watch some television, enough to see the news of Dad's arrest for beating up Chase, along with the coverage the media gave of my own disappearance.

Rick snickered during one of the news stories about ten days after they abducted me. "If they only knew, they'd never want you back. I should send them your movie, huh?"

I gasped and ran out of the room, into the bathroom—which I wasn't allowed to visit without permission—and vomited. The movie Rick referred to was a porn film—I guess you could call it that—though I don't know who could ever get off on watching a sixteen-year-old being raped by three men. He made me watch it after.

I hated him. But so much more than that. I despised him, but he'd somehow become the very center of my life. Whatever mood he was in, it controlled me. When he was angry, I was afraid. When he felt expansive, I was relieved. It was like I wasn't even a person anymore, just an extension of his rage and lust and greed.

I didn't know where we were. But after three weeks, without warning, Rick ordered us to pack our things. We were leaving.

"Where are we going?" I asked Nialla as I packed my meager belongings. All I had were some awful clothes Rick had bought. My own clothes were long gone.

"Atlanta," she said. "Rick's got a place he works with. It's okay. We don't ever stay anyplace too long."

So we moved out. I rode in the back of the Mustang during the drive to Atlanta. As we pulled out into traffic, Rick began to lay down the rules.

"You don't look at anybody. When we stop at the rest stop, we walk in holding hands. Nialla goes with you into the bathroom. If you talk to *anyone*, you're dead. Understand? Don't forget, I know where your parents live."

I nodded.

"You're going to wear sunglasses at all times. Between that and the hair, I think you'll be mostly invisible. You make sure you stay that way."

I told him I understood. But I was planning to run the first chance I got.

It was a cold and wet day outside, and the drive was punctuated by the sounds of the windshield wipers with their monotonous motion back and forth, back and forth, back and forth, a hypnotic rhythm that lulled me into a vacant stare.

I wanted to go home, but I didn't know how.

We were almost halfway through the trip when Rick pulled the car into a truck stop in the middle of nowhere.

Despite the rain, he parked at the opposite end of the lot from the main building. I was in a lot of pain by then—he'd refused to stop until *he* was ready.

219

winter flower

Across the hundred yards between us and the building, a lake of a parking lot spread out before me, raindrops drumming against it.

Rick turned toward me. "You're going to try to run, aren't you?"

I froze, my eyes instantly on him. Of course I was going to try to run. I had to escape. I had to get away from him, get back to my family, call the police, run away. It had been just a few weeks and I felt like I was dead. I didn't see how I could possibly go on any longer. I didn't see how I could survive. But like always, every bit of my attention was locked on him.

"You see this?" he asked in a casual tone. He took out the pistol that he sometimes played with. "If you run, I'll kill *her*. Understand?"

"Rick—" Nialla started to say.

"Shut the *fuck* up!" His shout was like a gunshot in the interior of the car. She went silent.

"Do you fucking understand me?"

"Yes," I whispered.

"Are you going to try to run?"

I shook my head.

He slowly rested the muzzle of the pistol against Nialla's forehead. "Say it," he said. "Out loud."

"I won't try to run," I whispered.

"Very good. Remember the rules I gave you."

"I will."

I didn't run.

Twenty-One

Sam

Mrs. Mullins took one look at me and motioned for me to sit down in the chair nearest her unkempt desk. "What happened?"

I knew this was going to happen. I *knew* it. "Nothing, really," I said. "It's no big deal."

"You didn't get that black eye from *nothing*." She raised one carefully shaped eyebrow as she said the words.

I looked down at the floor. I didn't have a good answer. But I wasn't going to snitch. They'd never let me live it down if I did. If they let me live at all.

I thought bitterly about Billy's words to me on the first day of school. *Don't mess with the populars.* Instead, Billy was the worst kind of brownnoser. This morning, right before homeroom, I'd passed him talking with Cody. Cody was laughing, and as I passed I heard someone mutter, *"Faggot."*

Mrs. Mullins sat back in her seat, studying me. "Just tell me this," she said. "Did it happen on school property?"

That I could honestly answer no to, so I did. Or mostly honestly. It wasn't *at* the school.

Her eyes seemed to be looking right through me. She raised an eyebrow. "On the school bus?"

I looked away. *Christ.* Now she knew. I couldn't answer. I wasn't going to lie to her. Other than Hayley, she'd been the only thing good in my life this year.

"All right," she said. "I'll let it go. For now. You ready to run?"

I was, and we did, and thankfully she didn't bring it up again. At least not then. An hour later, I sat down in biology next to Hayley.

221

"Let me see it," she whispered. Mr. Bernard was already calling the roll. I turned my face toward Hayley and she winced. "Billy didn't kid around, did he? *Asshole.*"

"It looks worse than it is," I whispered. My eyes dropped to her wrist. Her forearm was marked up with an ugly set of bruises.

She met my eyes, looked away and pulled her sleeves down to cover her forearms. I didn't ask her where she got the bruises. I knew the answer to that. I thought about Mrs. Mullins the other day. *Sam ... if something ever put Hayley in danger ... would you tell me? To protect her?*

"Here," I responded when Mr. Bernard called my name.

I didn't tell when Brenna was saying mysterious things about being gone. Not until it was too late.

Hayley would never forgive me if I told.

I'd never forgive myself for not telling. What if something happened to her? What if next time, instead of twisting her arm and bruising it, what if he broke it? What if he got drunk and killed her? It's not like that kind of thing didn't happen all the time.

It would be my fault.

"You need to tell someone," I whispered.

Hayley recoiled. "Like *who?*" she replied.

Mr. Bernard's voice boomed from the front of the room. Normally he was one of my friendliest teachers, but today he had a pugnacious look. "*Mister* Roberts. Miss Briggs. Is there something you'd like to share with the rest of us?"

Hayley gave me a death glare, her eyes narrowed, her chin set. "No, sir," she replied.

"Good. Then please, turn your attention to the board."

We did. But moments later, Hayley scribbled a note. *What the hell are u talking about?* She slid the paper toward me.

I wrote on it: *I'm worried about u. What if he hurts u? Like RLY hurts u?*

She responded in a scrawl so hard it tore the paper. *He WONT.*

I sighed. Closed my eyes. Then wrote, *Okay. Sorry.*

She wrote, *You won't say anything?*

No.

Slowly, she took the sheet of paper and put it into her notebook.

After class, as I was walking out into the hallway, I saw Mrs. Mullins standing there. She had a sour expression on her face.

Uh-oh. She didn't look happy at all. "Sam, can you come with me, please?"

I looked at Hayley, then back at Mrs. Mullins. "I've got ... class..."

"I'll send you with a note. For now, I need you to come with me."

I felt like a prisoner being led to the execution chamber as we walked down the long hallway toward the offices. The other students crowding in the hallway parted as if by divine intervention. We were halfway there when I heard the word *snitch*.

This was a disaster.

My stomach was a pool of acid by the time we finally reached her office.

"Sit down." She closed the door behind her and took a seat at her desk. "Since you wouldn't give me any information, I had to look into it myself. I'm told you were in a fight with Billy Townsend on the bus yesterday."

I nodded. Miserable. "Yes, ma'am."

"Don't *'yes, ma'am'* me, Sam. You don't seem much like the fighting type. You know that I'm required by school policy to bring this to the attention of Mr. Flowers. And then they'll have to drag in Billy and maybe the other students on the bus, and pull the video from the bus. I'm hoping this isn't that big of a deal, but you were really hurt."

I felt tears pricking my eyes. "You heard them in the hallway. Calling me a snitch. All this will do is get me in trouble. It will make it so much worse."

She looked sad, and her eyes had love in them. "Sam, I can't help you if you won't tell me what's going on. Are you being bullied?"

That provoked a bitter laugh. I'd never been anything *but* bullied in school. "Not really. Billy had a picture on his phone that upset me and I grabbed at it. I didn't let go when he asked me to, and he started throwing punches."

"Do you have a copy of the picture?"

I shook my head violently. "No."

"Can you tell me what it was?"

I shook my head. No way was I telling.

She sighed. "Sam, you know that your safety ... everybody's safety at the school ... is part of my responsibility."

I nodded, thinking of Brenna and Hayley. Thinking of responsibility and having to do things that might seem to hurt someone in the short-term in order to help them in the long-term. "Yes, ma'am. I do understand."

She smiled at me. "Wait here then. You can read something or do homework until I get back."

When my boss stalked into the restaurant with a manager trainee in tow, I was startled. I hadn't been expecting him, although he often dropped in unexpectedly. But today he was in no mood to chat.

"Take over the grill." His words were directed at Jim Ryerson, the manager trainee. "Cole, come with me."

He barked the orders like the retired Army officer he was. I quickly showed Jim what I was cooking then followed Brian to the back. He walked right past the office to the stockroom, then approached the cabinet that contained the security computer.

"What's going on?"

Brian didn't answer. Instead, he logged into the computer and quickly changed the time on it to the previous night. He was fast-forwarding through the videos captured by the six cameras mounted throughout the restaurant.

I watched on the cameras as I walked into the restaurant and began doing my inventory the night before. There was Linda coming to the back, and Dakota crying near the office door. Brian paused the video on a frame showing me standing at the table talking to the two men.

Brian shook his head in apparent disbelief. He looked at me and pointed at the screen. "Do you know who that is?"

I shrugged. "I know it's a guy who was harassing one of my waitresses with racist comments. Both Linda and Dakota reported that those two do it routinely."

Brian shook his head, his teeth showing. "That is the *mayor* of Oxford and one of the town council members. Need I remind you that you run a restaurant *in Oxford*? Last night you kicked out the *mayor* of this town from your restaurant."

A rush of anxiety flooded through me. What did this mean for my job?

A rash of thoughts ran through me all at once. I remembered how Erin had stood up to my father all those years ago about his racist attitudes, and how ultimately that had transformed the man. I thought about the search for Brenna, and how Erin needed me to be earning enough money to support her search. I thought about all the months of unemployment, the hundreds of interviews, the humiliation and fear of losing my career and not knowing if I was going to be able to feed my family.

Then … I thought about Dakota crying in the back room because of those two men.

I took a deep shuddering breath, trying to calm my inner turmoil. In an outwardly calm voice, I said, "When you were training me, you made it very clear that our company policy is to never tolerate harassment of employees. I didn't know that was the mayor, but that doesn't change the fact that he's no longer welcome in this restaurant."

Brian's hand slapped down on the computer console with a loud snap. "I think you're forgetting just whose restaurant this is, Cole."

I needed to de-escalate this. I couldn't afford to lose my job. But I was severely troubled and ... what? Disappointed? Yes. My respect for Brian had just fallen a long way.

"Unfortunately, I already told him to leave. What exactly is it you want me to do?"

Brian studied me. "This is a business we're running here. I thought you understood that. What I expect you to do is to personally apologize to the mayor, tell him it was a misunderstanding, and invite him back. Is that clear?"

I couldn't believe this. "So you're telling me our *zero-tolerance harassment policy* doesn't apply to local political figures?"

Brian shook his head. "It's not that cut-and-dried. There are grey areas, and maybe you aren't the best judge of what's racist and what isn't."

"It was harassment, Brian. Dakota was back here crying."

"When I took a chance and went to bat for you, I expected you were going to maintain some loyalty."

Christ. When I went to work for him, I expected him to be someone with some integrity.

"Brian, please rethink this. I know he's the mayor, though I didn't then. If he wasn't the mayor we wouldn't be having this discussion."

Brian frowned even more. "You're going to apologize."

I'd never been a praying man, but at that moment I wanted to pray for forgiveness from my family. "No, I won't."

Brian's face went bright red. "Jim is going to take over for you for the rest of the day. I'd like you to go home and think about what you're doing, Cole. And then come back tomorrow and do the right thing."

That was rich. Brian wanted me to do *the right thing*. At that moment I felt like *the right thing* would be to punch him in the face. I closed my eyes and took a deep breath. In half a second a childhood of occasional casual violence ran through my mind. Hitting Uncle Bill with a baseball bat. The assholes at the Metroplex running at Jeremiah. Chase's agonized screams.

I had violence in me. But if I were to respond to that instinct I'd land myself back in prison.

225

I took another deep breath to compose myself then opened my eyes. "I'll go home if you want, sir. But I'm going to ask you to reconsider as well. I know I'm a brand-new manager in this company. But you are asking me to basically throw one of my employees under the bus. Do you know what they said to me? Linda and Dakota? They said they hadn't thought I would do anything about it, because their previous managers had ignored it. Is that really who we want to be?"

Brian's face was red, his mouth set in a straight line, rigidly controlled. But his rage was clear enough from the red spreading across his cheeks, the narrowed eyes, and the hand he raised to point at my chest. "You are going to have a very short career if you don't learn some loyalty. Go home."

The energy of anger seemed to drain out of me. I felt exhausted. "All right."

I took off my apron, balled it up, and threw it into the laundry bag. Then I walked to my tiny office, grabbed my car keys, and headed for the door.

Sam

It was almost forty-five minutes before Mrs. Mullins came back. This time, she was accompanied by Mr. Flowers, our assistant principal. They both took seats facing me.

Mr. Flowers was a trim man with close-cropped hair, slightly longer than the buzz cuts most of the male teachers favored. His olive complexion was pockmarked with acne scars, and he typically had a frown on his face. Everyone I knew avoided him as much as possible—he had a reputation for handing out Saturday detentions and suspensions at the drop of a hat.

"Sam, I'm Mr. Flowers. I don't think we've met before?"

"No, sir." I'd learned that here in the Deep South, "sir" and "ma'am" was the preferred mode of address for adults, whatever the circumstance.

He continued. "Sam, we saw the video from the bus yesterday, and as you can imagine, we pulled Billy in for questioning and the bus driver as well. That led us to question the other students on the bus, which led us back to Cody Hendrix and Ashley Prichard. Have you had some kind of run-in with them recently?"

My eyes darted to Mrs. Mullins. I hadn't told her about what had happened the other afternoon. I nodded and reluctantly spoke. "Yes, sir."

"Can you tell us about it?"

At this point there wasn't a lot of point in trying to keep anything secret. I told him about the incident in the hall the other day.

Mr. Flowers nodded. "It appears that Ashley Prichard did the Photoshop job. That's a nasty little bit of revenge. Was the bus the first time you saw it?"

Ashamed and unable to look at Mrs. Mullins, I looked away and nodded.

Mrs. Mullen said, "Sam, I'm sorry that happened. As far as anyone else is concerned, it was the security video that prompted us to ask the questions."

Yeah, right. I could hear the whispers now. *Snitch.*

"What happens now?"

Mr. Flowers' response was quiet. "Obviously I can't talk about the specifics of the punishment for another student, but let me assure you we're taking this seriously. Ms. Prichard is unlikely to do anything like this again in the future."

Adults didn't understand *shit*. If they suspended Ashley or gave her detention or something, Cody would take ten times as much revenge on me.

Within the hour, I knew just how serious it was. Miss Mullins and Mr. Flowers might not have told me anything, but you couldn't keep something like that a secret for long. Word spread instantly via text message that both Billy and Ashley had been suspended for three days.

I was screwed. While I couldn't blame Miss Mullins—she'd done what she thought was the right thing—there was no question in my mind that this was going to make things very difficult for me.

I continued through the next couple of hours expecting the attack to come at any second. Something humiliating or possibly painful. I sat in my classes, not hearing a word, not taking notes, unable to think of anything but how they were going to get their revenge.

But it ended up not being me at all.

Between fifth and sixth periods I usually cut through the courtyard, at least if the weather was nice. It cut several minutes off the time it took me to get to class and sometimes made for a pleasant breath of fresh air before my final class of the day. The added bonus was most days I ran into Hayley there and we would stop for a minute or two and talk.

This day was different.

On the edge of the courtyard, just out of sight of the windows of the main office, a small crowd of students had gathered. I didn't know most of them, but I did recognize Cody's bulk in the crowd. What were they surrounding? What were they looking at?

It was stupid, foolhardy. But I had to know. I walked that way, pretending to mind my own business and not notice them.

As soon as I was in clear earshot, I knew I needed to get away. The crowd was taunting someone. Cody's vomit-worthy voice blared out the words, "She's so broke I bet her dad whores her out at night."

That comment caused the group to erupt in a chorus of laughter, two of the girls clutching each other as if it were the funniest thing they'd ever heard.

I need to get out of here now. Or I was going to be the next target. I started to turn away, but then I heard Hayley's voice.

"Just leave me alone, you assholes." She sounded like she was on the verge of tears.

I didn't think, not even for a second. I stooped down and dug a small rock out of the lawn. I spent enough time skipping rocks with Dad and Brenna in the mountains that I knew I was a damn good shot. The rock sailed in a perfect spin that would have skipped four or five times had I thrown it on the river. Instead it whacked Cody Hendricks right on the back of the head.

Cody staggered forward, and let out a scream. "Motherfucker! What the fuck was that?" His hand flew to the back of his head, and he spun around looking for his assailant. His eyes fixed on me.

It was too late to pretend. I cried out, "Why don't you pick on someone your own size, you big, fat fucking slob?"

Immediately I heard the voice of twenty or more teenagers say, "*Oooooh...*"

For a fraction of a second my eyes fell on Hayley, who gaped in shock. Then they went back to the biggest source of danger. Cody Hendricks, who looked as mad as a nest of wasps.

"*FRRRREEEEEAAAKKKKK!*" He barreled toward me as he screamed the word out. I spun and ran as fast as I could, my feet digging into the damp soil of the courtyard. As soon as I ran, I knew I was in full view of the main office, but I didn't know if anyone in there was looking. I wasn't taking any chances. I ran like one of the NASCAR racers at Talladega. I ran like I'd never run before. I ran like my life depended on it. At the end of the courtyard I reached the breezeway between the main building and the gym. I shot across the breezeway, scanning for an open door.

One of the doors to the gym was open. I sprinted, praying that one of the coaches would be in sight inside. Immediately the cool air inside the gym enveloped me. I didn't slow down, but I heard Cody scream, "*I'm gonna kill you, freeeeaakkkk!*"

I was running too fast to make sense of my surroundings. I blew past a man—Mr. Flowers, I realized too late—who was standing in the middle of the floor holding a microphone. There were loud gasps as I ran by him and then tripped over something, I don't know what it was, but I scrambled up and started to run again before someone grabbed me.

Behind me, Cody charged into the gym, bellowing, his face bright red with venom. "*Motherfucker! I'll killlllll you!*" he screamed.

He ran directly into Mr. Flowers, who spun and knocked Cody to the ground. "You ain't killing nobody."

The gym exploded into the voices of a hundred students speculating, gesturing and gawking at the scene on the floor.

I stopped struggling, seeing that Cody was no longer chasing. A crowd of students who had followed me and Cody through the courtyard was at the door of the gym, but they started to melt away.

"All y'all stay right there!" That shout came from one of the assistant coaches.

All at once my brain took in the scene. One set of bleachers was pulled out, with maybe two hundred freshmen or sophomores sitting on them. One of the coaches and Mr. Flowers had been speaking to an assembly when I came charging in, interrupting it.

I swallowed. I had a feeling I was in trouble.

Cole

When the assistant principal finished telling the story, I looked back and forth between him, Sam's counselor, and Sam.

"So what's the bottom line?" I asked.

I had been home no more than fifteen minutes when the phone call came, and I drove back to this side of town to the high school. I was having some difficulty imagining the scenario that had been described to me: a large crowd of students bullying a girl, and Sam coming to the rescue by attacking the biggest kid in the school?

The assistant principal looked profoundly uncomfortable. "Sir ... the thing is, as much as I admire your son for standing up for that girl, I can't condone him throwing a rock at another student or starting a fight. Our penalty for fighting is a three-day suspension. Normally the student would get zeros for any work missed during the suspension, but in this case we'll waive that. Sam will be able to make up the work. And, we're going to reduce it to one day. But this is the only time. If it happens again, the penalties will be much more severe."

To the vice principal's left, Sam's counselor closed her eyes in apparent relief. When she opened them, I saw Sam mouth at her, "Thank you."

I sighed. Erin would be furious, of course. But I could talk her through that. I raised my eyebrows. "Is there anything else?"

The vice principal shook his head. "No, sir."

"Mr. Roberts, here's my card if you ever have any questions." The counselor handed me a business card as she said the words. I looked down at it. Patricia Mullins.

I didn't really have any, but it would be good to have her information. Plus … there was something in her expression that led me to think she wanted me to call.

"Let's go, Sam."

Sam hadn't said a word through the entire discussion. He threw his backpack over his shoulder and followed me out of the building. We walked to my car in what felt like an awkward silence. When we got in, he sat down beside me, and twisted around, tossing his backpack on the back seat. "Am I grounded?"

Is he grounded? That never even occurred to me. I took a deep breath, trying to decide what was the appropriate fatherly thing to say. Should I tell Sam that violence was wrong, and he should have gone and found a teacher to intervene? That seemed like the responsible thing to do.

But then I thought of Dakota crying in the back room last night because a grown-up version of a bully had been treating her like dirt. I thought of my aunt screaming as Uncle Bill punched her in the face.

I shook my head. "No. You're not grounded. Instead, I think I'm going to take you out for ice cream. You still like ice cream? I can never tell anything with teenagers."

Sam's eyes widened, and a smile spread on his face. A beautiful smile. "You're not mad?"

I looked over my glasses at my son. "I'm giving you a stern lecture right now that violence is wrong, and you should find an adult when you see something like that. That said … Sam, I'm very proud of you."

Sam blinked his eyes rapidly and looked away. Then he said in a voice almost too quiet to hear, "Thank you."

I looked at my watch. It was almost 2:15. "School's almost out. You want to bring your girlfriend?"

Sam blushed. "Hayley's not my girlfriend."

I grinned. Blushing was a good sign, I decided. It reflected—what—some level of innocence? When I was sixteen I was so angry at the world, I couldn't imagine myself blushing back then.

"Have it your way, kid. Anyway, do you want to bring your friend?" I made air quotes at the word *friend*.

Sam gave me a wry expression. "Can I? I'll text her right now."

"Yeah," I said.

I wanted to meet the elusive Hayley, and in truth I was more likely to find out details of what happened by listening in on their conversation than asking questions. Sam was a teenager, after all. I pulled to the side and waited. It took just a minute to get a response. Sam looked up with a rare smile on his face and said, "She says she can come, but she has to be home by four to do her chores. Can we give her a ride home?"

"Yeah, of course." I checked traffic then pulled the car out into a U-turn and headed back to the high school. I found the pick-up lane, and parked the car behind a newish grey Dodge minivan sporting a series of bumper stickers. One bore the question, *Where will you go when you die?* On one side of the bumper sticker were pretty clouds, on the other side were flames and a comical-looking devil waving what appeared to be a bullwhip. That was subtle. Another one said in, PRO-LIFE. The window sported a National Rifle Association membership sticker. Seeing the bumper stickers made me tired. I'd been an active Republican most of my adult life, much to Erin's irritation, but in the absence of Brenna, it all seemed like so much bullshit.

It wasn't really relevant to me anymore anyway. Thanks to the felony conviction, I'd lost my right to vote.

"Dad?"

"Yeah?"

Sam's voice cracked a little when he said *Dad*. He was so small for his age, but it sounded like his voice was starting to change.

"Didn't you have work today?"

I nodded, debating on how much to tell Sam. He had so much uncertainty in his life, he didn't really need to be worrying about whether or not I had a job. I looked over at him. He was still so young.

In the end, I decided that Sam had pretty much gone past the bullshit stage of life. All lying would do would be to make him distrust me.

"To be honest, I kind of got suspended today too."

Sam gaped. I continued. "Last night some asshole was harassing one of my waitresses ... racist stuff. It was pretty ugly, and I kicked him out of the restaurant and told him not to come back."

"Whoa. That's legit. But why are you in trouble? Isn't that the right thing to do?"

I exhaled. "It is, unless the person you kicked out turns out to be the mayor. My boss is pretty pissed."

Sam gave me a stare for a long time. I couldn't tell if it was disbelief or astonishment or admiration. Finally he said, "Mayor *Prichard*? That's Ashley's dad."

Ashley wasn't a familiar name. "A friend of yours?"

Sam shook his head and gave a bitter sort of chuckle. "Hardly. She's the one who sent out that awful picture. She got suspended this morning because of it."

Huh. That was unexpected. A selfish part of me tried to calculate how much that might have an impact on my job situation. I tried to push that to the side.

Students were now streaming out of the building. The school day must be over. It quickly became apparent that there was a semi-uniform. The boys almost all had crew cuts, T-shirts bearing mostly corporate logos, and they all wore baggy khaki shorts. The girls either wore skirts that were too short, or white T-shirts and blue jeans with flannel shirts carefully tied around their waists.

"It seems like they all dress the same."

"Morons." Sam's judgment was quick.

"You don't ever get the urge to run with the pack? Follow the same kind of fashions as your friends?"

Sam shakes his head. "I hate flannel anyway."

Weird, the boys weren't wearing flannel. I didn't have time to give it any more thought, because Sam gave an excited wave to a girl who was approaching the car.

She was about five foot three with golden-red hair and extremely pale skin with freckles, lots and lots of freckles. She wore a threadbare blue dress. She got in the backseat of the car, slamming the door shut behind her, and immediately said, "Hi, I'm Hayley."

I twisted around in my seat and offered my hand, which she shook. "Cole Roberts."

When she shook my hand, I noticed that her wrist was badly bruised with what looked like handprints.

As if someone had grabbed her wrist and twisted and squeezed. I'd seen that before, on my aunt.

I made a mental note to ask Sam about it later; I didn't want to make Hayley uncomfortable.

I drove toward the Baskin-Robbins as Sam twisted around in his seat to face Hayley. The two of them immediately began gossiping and laughing as they ran through a succession of stories about people I didn't know. I kept my ears open for clues about my son's life. Most of it I didn't understand, but I did catch the frank admiration in Hayley's voice when she said, "I can't believe you went after Cody like that."

Sam smiled. "I know, right? Did you see his face? I thought he was going to kill me."

"I did too," she said quietly.

There was no mistaking it. That girl was falling hard for Sam. She couldn't take her eyes off of him, and it was clear she noticed nothing else about her surroundings.

Sam, for his part, seemed oblivious.

Over ice cream—Sam had butter pecan and Hayley had mint chocolate chip—I asked Hayley some strategic questions. I learned that she'd only recently moved from Birmingham and in with her father. I didn't ask, and she didn't say, why she wasn't living with her mom anymore. Custody changes could be messy, and I didn't want to be intrusive. I asked what her dad did—construction—and how she liked Oxford.

At that question, her eyes shifted over at Sam. "I like it okay."

It was painful, seeing how oblivious Sam was to Hayley's longing gaze. Intentional? Who knew. Maybe he just didn't want to blow a good friendship. He'd had few friends in Virginia, and since we'd moved here, even less (none, if I was honest). It was clear that she adored him.

Back in the car, Hayley gave me directions to her neighborhood. I guess it wasn't much of a surprise, given how threadbare her clothes were, that she lived in a run-down trailer park on the edge of Oxford. Four rows of rusted single-wides crowded about two acres of land. Overgrown weeds peeked out through cracks in the pavement. She grew quiet as we pulled into the neighborhood, her only words directions to the fourth trailer on the left.

I came to a stop in front of the rickety-looking building. It was raised on cinderblocks, with no skirting to hide it, and a simple wood and steel staircase leading up to the door. The side of the trailer was clearly old, with marks of rust and other damage apparent.

"Oh no," she whispered as we came to a stop. I glanced over at my shoulder and followed her gaze to the ancient Dodge Charger parked near the trailer. The right front fender and the hood were grey with primer paint, and fabric from the underside of the roof hung down into the interior.

I didn't know what was wrong. But that became clear enough when a man came bursting out of the house just as she stepped out of the car. He was in his forties maybe, or fifties. It was hard to tell—he had the sunken cheeks of a man missing a lot of teeth, and his skin was rough. Heavy smoker, probably. His shirt bore a confederate flag, waving above the head of a nearly nude woman with stars covering her nipples. What a charmer. This must be her father.

"Where the *hell* have you been?" the man shouted.

"I—I—" she stammered.

I swung my door open and stepped out. "Sir? I'm Cole Roberts."

The man swung toward me, rage in his eyes. "You been messing with my daughter? I'll have your—"

"No," I responded in a firm tone, not sure what I was going to say.

Sam burst out, "Sir, Hayley was helping me with my calculus homework and we missed the bus. My dad offered her a ride."

I didn't condone lying. But in this case? I just nodded, verifying Sam's lie.

The old man frowned, his eyes darting back and forth between my son and the girl. "Get inside," he spit at her.

She nodded, her eyes watering, and ran inside.

"I guess ain't no harm done," the man said, seeming to moderate his tone.

I suspected otherwise. I had the feeling this guy could do a *lot* of harm, especially to that kid. This whole scene reminded me so much of my aunt and uncle I wanted to be sick.

I didn't really have time to think any more about it though. She was gone, into the house, and the man was standing there, staring at us, waiting for us to leave.

I let out a breath, my shoulders sagging, and said, "Come on, Sam."

Moments later, we were on the road, heading back home. Both of us were silent for a long time. But finally, as we crossed over the interstate headed south, he said, "Dad? Can I ask you a question? If … if I knew that someone was being hurt. By their parents. But they'd made me promise not to tell. What would be the right thing to do?"

I didn't answer right away. It was obvious what he was getting at.

"Is Hayley's dad hurting her?"

He didn't respond at first. But finally his head jerked in a nod. "Yeah," he whispered. "She comes into school bruised sometimes. But she made me promise not to say anything."

I needed to be very careful how I answered this. The knee-jerk reaction of course, was to say, you should *always* tell. Domestic violence wasn't something to fool around with. I'd seen how serious it could get, when I watched my uncle beating the crap out of his wife and son.

On the other hand, how much did we really know?

I thought about the raw anger of the man who had boiled out of that trailer. We knew enough.

I sighed then began to speak. "You never met cousin Lucas's parents, did you?"

Sam shook his head. "I've only met Lucas once."

234

Of course. I'd avoided Lucas since before Sam and Brenna were born. Dad and Big Bill didn't talk, not since Big Bill went to prison, and the kids didn't need to be around that kind of life.

"I used to spend summers there when I was a kid. Right up until the late eighties. Out in the middle of nowhere in the woods."

Sam looked puzzled. Like he wanted to ask what this had to do with anything. All I could do was keep talking.

"The reason you never met Big Bill—Lucas's father—is because he's in prison for murder. Way back when, when I was in middle school and high school, he used to beat his wife up sometimes. When we were younger, me and Lucas would hide. But one time, the last time I spent the summer there, he went after her. Busted her nose, and when Lucas tried to intervene he started to choke him. I knocked him out with a baseball bat."

Sam gasped and said, "Holy shit!"

I didn't bother to correct his language. "By that time, I hated spending summers there. I knew I was planning to go to Georgia Tech, and the only plans Lucas had post-high school were to deal drugs. But the thing was, they were so isolated, no one ever called the police. No one ever tried to get any—I don't know—intervention. It was a long time ago. One day in 1991, Big Bill got drunk and went on a tear. Lucas was away from home, and there was no one to protect her. He strangled her."

By the time I finished the story, we had reached the house. I turned the engine off but didn't open my door just yet.

Sam looked distressed.

"I'm not saying that's what's going to happen. I'm not saying that happens in most abuse cases. But ... it's pretty rare that abuse gets better over time. Most of the time it gets worse. And—" I hesitated to continue.

I didn't have to. Sam completed the sentence for me. "A lot of women die that way."

"Yeah. Too many."

"I don't want to lose her," Sam said, his tone despairing. "I haven't been close to someone like that since Brenna. But I have to. What kind of friend would I be if I didn't do what I could to protect her?"

235

Twenty-Two

~~~~~~

Erin

My alarm went off at two a.m. I turned over, peeking at the alarm with one eye, and pressed the snooze button. Then my eyes closed again and I drifted away.

In my dream I was walking on a dark street late at night. Moonlight reflected off puddles, and shadowy figures seemed to hover just out of sight, obscured by swirling black smoke or fog. Across the street stood a huge pile of stones, a church, with peaked towers and a high doorway with a pointed arch. The doorway was sealed shut; a double wooden door with planks nailed into it to hold it closed. The paint peeled, red and green flecks scattered on the steps in front of the door.

Tendrils of fear twisted around my spine and nerves all the way down to my feet. I approached the church and walked around the side of it, my feet knocking aside beer bottles and wrappers and paper. In the parking lot I saw a used condom. In the darkness, almost out of sight, a huge black SUV.

No sooner did I see it than I was standing at the fogged window, looking in. I couldn't see anything at first, but then I saw the glowing green lamps of the dashboard softly illuminating the interior. Nothing … then I felt, more than heard, a thump.

My daughter appeared, hands pressed against the glass, her face in the window. She looked twelve, her hair still cut with bangs and long over her shoulders. She wore blue overalls, blue overalls that made me want to cry out and scream, because I remembered the overalls, with their *High School Musical* logo. She'd refused to change out of them, sometimes for days at a time.

I grabbed at the car door, trying to yank it open, but it was locked. I screamed and pounded on the glass.

A dark figure appeared from behind her. Huge, imposing, but ill-defined, more of a cloud than a man, it grabbed her around her waist and pulled her away from the glass with the ease of plucking a dandelion.

Brenna screamed and struggled, her arms and legs flailing ineffectually, and the faceless man looked out at me with nothing but a grin. The SUV pulled away slowly as I screamed, scrabbling against the metal and glass trying to tear it open with my bare fingers.

She was gone.

I woke up with a scream, suddenly sitting up, my hair gripped in my fingers. I struggled to take a breath, my hand pressed against my pounding chest, and I suppressed the whine that wanted to force its way out of my throat. My face and hair were damp with sweat.

I looked at the clock. *Shit.* It was 2:25. I'd planned on being on my way by now. I got out of bed and threw on clothes. I'd get a shower later. I grabbed a stack of flyers, my phone and car keys, and stepped outside. It was chilly, but not cold, and the rain had stopped. The ground was still wet, puddles in the parking lot reflecting the streetlights.

Before I let the hotel room door close behind me, I scanned the area. At the end of the row of hotel room doors, two men sat in plastic lawn chairs smoking and talking quietly. Both of them wore jeans and T-shirts, and the larger of the two had a round belly that he rested his hands on. He chuckled at something the other man said. Neither of them took any notice of me. No one else was in sight.

I gripped my car key in my hand. I'd already established yesterday that the remote didn't work. In four quick steps, I walked to the car, my eyes scanning everywhere, especially the two men, as I unlocked the door of the car, threw my things inside, and got in. I didn't breathe again until the doors were locked.

Neither of the men had looked up or paid any attention as far as I could tell.

My hope was tenuous. The night before I had searched through the regional discussion board on the *UtopiaGuide,* one of the many discussion boards where so-called *mongers* compared notes on sexual services, strippers, and prostitution.

Sometimes the self-righteousness and ignorance of the men on those boards filled me with rage. They called themselves hobbyists and mongers and expressed no concern at all for the welfare of the women they exploited. They shared photos of the women and stories of their exploits, all of it completely in the open on the Internet.

I had, however, gained important knowledge from the board. Several posters on the Portland discussion board had commented that recent law enforcement activity had driven the appearance of street prostitutes into later and later hours, between two and five in the morning.

I had mapped out my routes after struggling to decode the half-disguised stories of the men on the board. They were trying to tell each other where and how to find sex. I was hoping to use their information to find my daughter.

First I drove down the broad boulevard past the diner, the strip club, and the police station. Dark houses, some of them with boarded up windows, were interspersed on both sides with used car dealerships, pawn shops, dry cleaners. In the darkness on the right, overlooking a dirty parking lot, was a billboard with the words, *Jesus: Your Only Way To God.* Three blocks further on the left was the church where Brenna had been arrested.

Half a block before the church, across the street from me, I spied a woman walking in the darkness. From behind, all I could see was her dark shoulder-length hair. She wore jeans and a sweatshirt, and other than the fact that it was a time of night when you rarely saw women walking alone in the darkness, there was no indication of what she was doing.

But then it was clear enough. A car rolled slowly past her and she turned and waved. I slowed almost to a crawl as I saw the woman approach the car. Now I could see her face. She looked as if she were in her thirties or forties, with deep furrows on both sides of her mouth. Her expression was devoid of any emotion. The car slowed long enough for the driver to get a good look at her, then it sped up and drove away. The woman screamed and cursed at the driver.

There was the church. It wasn't the huge stone edifice I had seen in my dream; instead, it was a simple brick structure. I turned left, pulling into the driveway and sweeping my headlights across the parking lot where Brenna had been arrested.

No one was there. I sighed. It's not that I had any expectation I would find her here, but maybe deep inside I had hoped it would be that simple. That I could drive here, pick her up. and take her home.

I turned around, pulling to the end of the driveway. I put on my blinker but didn't pull out, because the woman was approaching rapidly.

As she approached, I rolled down the passenger side window.

"Hey, baby," she slurred. "You looking for a date?" Then she got a good look at my face, and said, "Sorry…"

She must not have realized I was a woman.

"Wait." I scrabbled for one of the flyers. "Hey, wait … have you seen this girl?"

The woman looked terrified. She started to back away, and I called out, "Wait … *please!* I'm not a cop. I won't hurt you. I'm just looking for my daughter."

She looked around. Looking for her pimp? Who knew. She approached the car and leaned close. I held the flyer out to her.

As the woman studied the picture, I looked at her. She was younger than I had initially thought. It was hard to tell. She was missing some teeth and had a nasty scar on one side of her face. A tattoo on her forearm, in stylized lettering, read *Property of Poppa Jake*. I shuddered. Was that her boyfriend? A pimp? Was it like a cattle brand?

"I ain't seen her. She don't work this area."

I sighed. "She was arrested next to the church three weeks ago. In the parking lot."

The woman's eyes darted up from the flyer to me. "I'm out here most days, but not all. If she's been working the block, she's either new or part-time. Or an indoor ho, out here to make her quota."

Indoor ho. That meant a girl who worked out of hotels or the Internet, not the street.

I winced at her words. "You're sure?" I said.

"Told ya, didn't I? Why you wasting my time?"

My heart was breaking. This woman might be twenty-five or might be forty-five. But she was somebody's daughter. She might have been just like Brenna years ago. I said, "Can I get you anything? Coffee? Or … *anything*?"

"Crazy bitch," the woman muttered. She stalked away into the darkness.

I took a breath, trying to get ahold of myself. The blinking clock on the dashboard said it was five minutes after three. I took a right turn out of the church and drove exactly the speed limit. A hundred yards ahead of me, a BMW changed lanes suddenly, pulling up to the curb in front of a white-haired woman. This woman wasn't wearing a sweatshirt and jeans … she wore a tight miniskirt and a crop top that exposed her belly, with a bra that pushed her breasts high. She tottered toward the BMW on her six-inch heels and leaned close, speaking rapidly with whoever was in the car. Then she got in. The brake lights went off and the car took off in a hurry.

Another woman, just past there. I was almost at the police station. This woman was African American, also dressed in revealing clothes, her bronzed hair trailing all the way down to her butt. I pulled up beside her.

"Hey…" As soon as she saw me inside the car, she started to walk briskly down the sidewalk away from me.

"Wait!" I called out. "I'm not a cop. I'm looking for someone. Maybe you've seen her?"

"Ain't seen nobody," the woman said. I had to take my foot off the brakes and let the car drift forward to keep up.

"Please just take a look? It's my daughter. *Please?*"

The woman stopped. She swung toward the car and held out a hand. I passed her the flyer through the passenger side window. She stared at it, a frown on her face. Finally she said, "Might have seen her. Once or twice in the last month. Never before."

My heart started to thump. "Where—where did you see her?"

"Walking the track. She got a mean-looking pimp. White guy with lots of tattoos. I don't know her name though."

I took a deep breath. "Walking the track. Here?"

She nodded. "Yeah. Late night. First I thought she was a renegade, but when Mack K went to bump her, this guy come out of nowhere waving around a gun. Her pimp. Mack say she was reckless eyeballing, but her pimp don't give a shit. I ain't seen her since."

Jesus Christ. I didn't understand half of what the woman had said. Except the key point: Brenna had been here.

"Listen," I said. "If you see her, can you give her a message?"

The girl looked annoyed. "Do I look like a messenger service to you?"

"*PLEASE!* Just ... tell her I'm here, looking for her. I'm her mother. Tell her I'm not leaving until I find her."

A bitter look passed across the woman's face. "I'll tell her. Wish my mama had come after me." She took the flyer and folded it up, then stuffed it in her back pocket.

Then she cursed and began walking away fast. I took my foot off the gas and started to drive, but blue lights suddenly flashed in my rearview mirror.

Damn it.

I sat there with my hands on the wheel, and I wanted to curl up in exhaustion. I'd only talked to two women, and I was exhausted and didn't see how I could continue.

I heard her say the words again: *Wish my mama had come after me.*

I was dispirited, and I wanted a drink. The police car behind me hadn't moved, and the lights were still flashing. I leaned my head against the steering wheel and closed my eyes.

Almost a full minute later I heard a knock on the window. I looked up. An officer stood outside, shining his flashlight in. He motioned for me to roll down the window. I hit the button and the window slid down.

"License and registration, please."

I reached over to the passenger seat, where the folder containing the car's paperwork was still located. Of course I didn't have registration, but I did have the bill of sale. I passed that over, along with my driver's license.

The officer was standing just slightly back from my seat and still shining the flashlight in the car, making it impossible for me to see him. I knew another officer was out there, because another flashlight was roving over the interior of the car. It came to rest on the stack of flyers.

"You just purchased this car yesterday?"

"Yes, Officer."

"Did you just move to Portland?"

"No. I don't think I'll be in town very long. But I needed wheels while I was here."

"What brings you to Portland? And ... what brings you out here on this street at three o'clock in the morning? If you don't mind my asking."

I didn't see any point in circumlocution. I said, "I'm looking for my daughter." I passed a flyer to the officer. He shone the flashlight on the flyer for a moment, then the light dropped down. For the first time I was able to clearly see his face. He was young ... very young, maybe twenty-two or twenty-three years old. He looked over at his partner on the other side of the car.

"You recognize this girl, Bill? I don't think I've seen her."

The other officer, apparently deciding that I didn't represent a threat, walked around to my side of the car.

The other officer, considerably older than the first, took the flyer and studied for a minute. Then he looked at me. "The picture on the left is a mug shot?"

I nodded. In a quiet voice, I said, "She was arrested on this street three weeks ago."

The younger cop's face went through a series of expressions that were difficult to interpret. He shook his head and said, "Oh man, I'm sorry."

The older cop looked at me with a grim gaze. "You related to her?"

"My daughter. She was abducted two years ago. We didn't have any signs or clues until she was arrested. As soon as I heard, I flew out here."

The officer looked around the street. Then he said, "The odds of you finding her like this are pretty slim."

I shrugged. "I don't care what the odds are. Would you if it was your kid?"

He shook his head slowly. "No, ma'am. So here's what I can advise you ... first, be really careful. It's dangerous out here, and if one of the pimps thinks you're messing with one of their girls, they won't hesitate to hurt you. Stay on well-lit streets. And while I can't advise you to arm yourself, since it's highly doubtful you've got a permit, at the very least get some Mace or pepper spray."

I took a deep shuddering breath. I don't know what response I'd been expecting, but that hadn't been it.

"Can we take some of the flyers?" the younger officer asked. "I know some places where we can hand them out and put them up."

A rush of gratitude flooded through me. I nodded and passed him a stack of the flyers. As he took them, the older officer took a card out of his pocket and passed it to me. "If you're going to be out along the stretch early in the morning, you'll probably get pulled over again. Here's my card if you run into trouble."

I glanced down at the card. *Sergeant Bill Clayton.* The younger officer—his name tag read Reynolds—passed me my driver's license and the bill of sale for the car. "Good luck."

They walked away from my car. Almost immediately, I began to get a bad case of the shakes. The police car backed up and then did a U-turn. As I watched the taillights recede in my rearview mirror, I put my own car in gear and began to drive. Two minutes later, I approached the diner on the left. It looked far busier than it had yesterday morning … at least a dozen cars filled the parking lot. There were a few spots left; I pulled in and took one of them.

I grabbed a small stack of flyers and went into the diner.

The diner seemed almost bright after coming in from the inky black night. But my eyes quickly adjusted to the surroundings, and restored the place to its original grubby look. I scanned the room, noting that all of the corner booths were taken. I decided to sit in the same spot as the woman I'd spoken to yesterday, because it had the clearest view of the entire restaurant. I wondered if that's why she'd been sitting there. I made my way to that side of the diner, carefully maneuvering my way around the men and women who crowded the place.

I sat down and waited, while scanning the people.

The taller counter, to my right and facing the grill, was occupied by two men who sat a fair distance away from each other. One of them was in his twenties, with a crew cut and a bitter expression. He sat there staring at the wall in front of them, not even making a pretense of drinking the cup of coffee in front of him. The man a few seats down from him was easily twenty years older, and obviously drunk. He was saying something to the younger man, his words so slurred I couldn't understand him from where I sat.

Not far away from them, facing each other in a booth, were three young women. They were chatting with each other and laughing. They wore revealing clothing, but none of them so much that I would guess they were prostitutes. Or if they were, they certainly didn't work the streets. The sad thing was, they might just be teenagers or college girls out with friends for the night. But with this location, I could only assume the worst.

Maybe they worked at the strip club down the block. They didn't look rundown like the women I'd seen on the street.

242

There was little question, however, about the next table over in the corner. A mean-looking dark-haired man with a thick five o'clock shadow leaned back in the corner of the booth. He wore a sleeveless white T-shirt that revealed powerful shoulders and a series of tattoos, some of which looked as if they'd been done at home or in jail. He wore a gold chain studded with what appeared to be diamonds. Two women sat in the booth with him, both of them scantily dressed. Both of the women were young … one of them might have been eighteen. Or possibly less. How could you tell? They were heavily made up and had dull eyes which made it difficult to guess their age.

The younger of the two girls threw her hands up in the air and said, *"Fine!"*

With no change of expression, the man leaned toward her and grabbed her chin between his finger and thumb and squeezed. He said something, but it wasn't loud enough to hear clearly.

She looked terrified.

After a few seconds, he released her.

He shook his head, his face still set in anger. The girls slipped out of the booth and he followed, throwing a twenty on the table.

A waitress approached—the same one I'd had the day before. I hadn't noticed then, but her name-tag read "Kristi." She approached me, putting a napkin and some silverware on the counter in front of me.

"Hey, you're back. Can I get you something? Coffee?"

"Coffee, please," I said. I slid one of the flyers across the table at her and continued in a much lower voice. "And maybe you can take a look at another picture?"

She looked down at the picture then at me. She nodded.

I leaned closer. She rotated the flyer to get a better angle. "That's her for sure. I recognize the neck tattoo. She was here with another girl, and some guy. At least twice."

I began to shake. "You're sure? When was it?"

She nodded. "Yeah. I remember the guy. He was an asshole. He got into it with one of the other pimps. I almost had to call the cops. I'm thinking it was about two weeks ago, but I'm not sure. I can talk to my manager, we could maybe check the security tapes. But he won't be in until tomorrow."

She leaned close. "Give me your number, and I'll call you right away if they come back in."

"It's right here," I said, pointing to the number on the flyer. "That's my cell phone."

In an unexpected moment of kindness, she put her hand on mine. "If I see her, I'll call you immediately."

My throat felt raw. I croaked the words, "Thank you."

I still had three hours before I'd be meeting Detective Michelson. I finished my coffee and paid, and on my way out the door I put two copies of the flyer on the bulletin board near the front door. I decided that later that day I would stop at a hardware store and pick up a staple gun so I could attach it to the telephone poles in the area. In the meantime, it was time to get out there.

I'd given a lot of thought to the flyers. What happened if her trafficker saw them? Would it be putting Brenna in more danger? Would they leave town? There was no way to know. I couldn't quantify how serious the danger was—but I knew that without the flyers, she'd been tortured and burned at least. If there was a chance of getting her home, I was taking it.

For the next several hours I drove the length of the track. All in all, it was about ten blocks in a rough square. I wasn't the only car circling those blocks, not even close—at any given time I could see four or five cars circling along, either in front or behind me. They would slow down anytime they approached one of the prostitutes, brake lights flashing as the men inside examined the women. If the drivers came to a stop, the woman would lean in the passenger window, a few words would be exchanged, and either she would get in and the couple would drive off together, or the car would move on.

The women I saw and spoke to over those hours ranged in age from their teens to their forties. They were every race. Some of them looked young and beautiful, and some looked like they might have been grandmothers. Everywhere I looked, hovering in the darkness or some circling in cars, were men. Pimps. Johns. Even police, who were patrolling the area regularly. Some of them talked with me willingly. Some shied away, backing up and refusing to talk. One pimp threatened me. *If you don't get off the damn track, I'll turn you out myself, bitch.*

I was still shaking from that encounter at seven a.m. when it was time to meet Detective Michelson. It bothered me that I didn't know her first name. I'd remedy that as soon as we met. But I pulled to a stop when my phone rang a moment later—the name on my phone sent immediate tension through me.

"Mrs. Roberts? It's Stan Wilcox."

"Agent Wilcox. Thank you for calling. Do you have news?"

"Actually, I'm wondering if you decided to fly to Portland after all."

"I'm here now."

After an almost imperceptible pause, he said, "In that case we should meet. I arrived late last night."

Stunned, I blurted, "You're in Portland? I didn't expect that."

"It took some convincing the Bureau. But I'm here, and at least for the next little while, I'm exclusively on your daughter's case."

I closed my eyes. "You know where Dave's Diner is on Eighty-second?"

"I've heard of the place."

"I'm meeting Detective Michelson from the Portland Police there for breakfast in a few minutes. Want to join us?"

"Michelson? I know her. It'll take me a while to get there."

"That's fine, I'll wait."

We disconnected and I drove on toward the diner. Wilcox being here was a relief, provided he didn't try to shut me out of looking for Brenna. I was ready to fight. I'd taken too passive a role when she first disappeared, and that wasn't happening again.

Now, with the sun coming up, the diner was far less crowded. I got out of the car and locked it, carrying a few of the flyers inside with me.

Inside, I scanned the restaurant. She was in the back booth. Kristi, the waitress, waved when I walked in. I smiled at her, then walked to the booth and slid in across from Michelson.

"Good morning," she said.

"Morning," I replied. "Listen, you'll have to forgive me. But I never learned your first name yesterday."

She smiled. "It's Melody."

"You can call me Erin. I wanted to let you know, I just got a call from Stan Wilcox at the FBI. He was the investigating agent on my daughter's case."

"From the child abduction unit? I know him actually, we've worked together."

"He told me that. He got into town last night—he said he's working her case exclusively at least for the next few days."

Melody brightened. "That's good news. He'll have access to a lot of resources beyond what I can do."

"What have you found so far?"

Melody shook her head. "Not a lot. I started by getting and reviewing the FBI file. I've got some questions I'm going to ask you there, just to clarify some things. We might want to wait until Wilcox gets here though. So we're not asking you the same things twice."

I nodded. "What else?"

She sighed. "I want to be realistic with you, Erin. The odds are significant that they're no longer in Portland. Which is not to discourage you. We're going to do absolutely everything we can. I just need you to know that it's a long shot." Her expression was grim.

"I get it. But this is the best shot we've had in two years. I'll do everything I can."

"Okay. For what it's worth … I'll do everything within my power to find her."

I studied her. She met none of my stereotypes of what a detective would look like. And I had met my share of detectives, unfortunately. She had a trim athletic figure and wore conservative clothing: a navy suit with wide lapels and a white shirt. She wouldn't have looked out of place in a corporate office in Silicon Valley or New York City.

"How did you become the resident expert on trafficking?"

Melody winced. "Are you sure you want to hear that story? It's not pretty."

I felt my eyebrows drawing together. "There's nothing pretty about any of this. I would like to know, if you're willing to talk about it."

Melody waved at Kristi and pointed at our coffee cups. She did it with a friendly smile. But when she looked back at me, her expression was sober. "I grew up in a family with five kids. My parents took us all with them as missionaries to Central Africa when I was really little. When we came back home, Mom was— what do you call it—a tiger mom? She was always in our business. Getting a B on a test was an occasion for scorn. Anyway we were kind of a stereotype, and all of us went to really good schools."

I nodded. "I get it. I went to Georgetown."

Melody said, "Cornell. But after I graduated, I didn't want to go the same route. Both my brothers are doctors, one of my sisters is a surgeon, and the other works for Google. I came back home and applied for the Police Academy."

I smiled. "I bet your mother was thrilled."

Melody laughed. "Not exactly. Not at first anyway. She's come to accept it, and she knows the work I do is important. When I first joined the force, I took a whole lot of ribbing from the guys. Because I was a woman, because I'm Asian, because I went to Cornell. But I can outshoot two-thirds of these guys. I made detective four years ago. My very first case was a missing child."

I felt a chill when she said those words. The chill wasn't for me … it was from her. From her eyes. She continued.

"She was an eleven-year-old girl. Her family lived in a poor neighborhood, not ten blocks from here. Her mom was struggling to make ends meet and had a shit for a boyfriend who I'm pretty sure abused the kids. Anyway, the girl—her name was Grace—they thought she was a runaway. The cops who were initially called didn't escalate it—they figured she had run away and would turn back up."

246

She paused, and I found myself dreading the rest of the story. Melody looked away from me, unable to meet my eyes. She stared out the window. "I couldn't find her in time. They sold her. I don't know how many times. But she was trafficked initially in a little house up Eighty-second Avenue, getting raped for twenty or thirty dollars a time by I don't know how many men. Three weeks after she went missing, a confidential informant told us he'd heard about this girl. She was being trafficked by someone she knew, a friend of the family. But when we raided the place, she was gone."

Tears were running down her face now, and mine too. I reached out and took one of her hands.

"She finally did turn up. She was dismembered, cut up into little pieces and thrown in a trash bag and dumped in the woods."

Jesus Christ. I felt a sudden panic attack coming on; my chest tightened, a sharp pain right in the center. I pressed my hand against the center of my chest and tried to breathe.

Melody took a long shuddering breath and said, "I went to the Chief of Detectives after that and we started work on the Trafficking Task Force. My husband's an assistant district attorney, and we've been trying to put together a network of places that can help these girls get off the streets. It's heartbreaking what happens to them. But then we've still got assholes like Sergeant Mackey, who thinks of it only in terms of the girls being *whores*. They don't get it. We estimate that there's anywhere from fifty to a hundred children being trafficked every single night in Portland alone."

I had become so wrapped up in Melody's story, I completely forgot that Stan Wilcox was coming. So I was startled when he appeared next to our table. I stood up, hitting my knee on the edge of the booth and wincing.

We shook hands all around, and Melody said to Stan, "It's nice to see you again."

Wilcox ordered a cup of coffee and said, "Sorry it took me so long to get here."

"It's fine," Melody said. "We've mostly been talking background stuff, getting to know each other."

"So what do we have?" Wilcox asked.

Melody told the story of Brenna's arrest. Over the next few minutes we caught up on the details of my own questioning along the track.

"Do you mind if I ask you both some questions about Brenna's original disappearance?" Melody directed the question at me.

"Whatever you think may help."

"I understand the original prime suspect was her boyfriend. Why was that?"

247

Wilcox answered. "He was an adult dating a sixteen-year-old... fifteen at the time they started. But the damning thing was the bracelet."

"Found in his apartment, right?" Melody asked.

"It was a birthday gift from my sister Lori," I said. "She had just gotten it that day, which meant that she'd been in Chase's apartment after the last time we saw her."

Wilcox said, "In the end, there just wasn't any evidence he'd been involved in her disappearance. We knew she had been there, but that was consistent with his story. But her car and her cell phone were found almost twenty miles away."

Melody opened the folder and paged through it. She stopped and looked up. "Was there ever any hint of who this guy Rick was?"

Wilcox shook his head. "The Facebook account was registered to a Gmail address that was opened at a public library. We know that she received a few text messages around one a.m., and she wasn't at Chase Morton's apartment—that's based on the cell phone towers that carried the messages. The messages came from a prepaid burner phone."

All three of us sat quietly, considering for a few seconds. Then Melody said, "I think we can make some assumptions based on what little we know. She's not been working the streets except maybe on an occasional basis. We don't know where she's been between Virginia and here, but I think it's safe to guess that she hasn't been in Portland very long.

"Why is that?" I asked.

"Mainly because of Kristi over there. At the very least, they've not been on this stretch before a few weeks ago, and this is the only twenty-four-hour place on Eighty-second or close to it."

That explained the three a.m. traffic. "So where do we start?"

"I think you start doing what you already are," Melody said. "Get that flyer up everywhere, concentrating along Eighty-second Avenue and the surrounding neighborhoods. Grocery stores, restaurants, coffee shops, hotels and motels. I'll be doing the same, but I'll focus mostly on the business travel hotels all the way around the city. We've developed decent partnerships with a lot of them, and that's where a lot of the Internet-based prostitution takes place these days. We'll shake down some of our confidential informants, see if anyone has seen or heard of her."

Wilcox said, "I'm going to meet with the FBI field office this morning. We'll get a look at the security videos here. And we'll run this new photo through the NCIS and the National Center for Missing and Exploited Children. The tattoo and—that looks like a cigarette burn scar—are pretty distinctive. Those might help us get a lock on any ads that have been posted of her."

"What do you think the odds are?" I asked.

"If she's being trafficked—and we've got every reason to believe she is—then I think they're pretty good."

I nodded slowly and took a deep breath. "Thank you," I said.

We had a plan.

Twenty-Three

~~~~~~

Brenna. Two Years Ago

"**W**hat I don't understand is why you stay with him. He hurts you all the time and waves that gun around. He's *such* a fucking asshole."

Nialla shrugged, her eyes downcast. We were sitting next to each other on the floor in a sterile two-bedroom corporate apartment in Atlanta. I didn't know exactly where we were, not that it would have mattered if I had, because I had no access to a phone. We'd been here for four weeks, taking incalls only. Rick had made it clear that soon we would begin doing outcalls, a prospect which frightened me. At least here I had the relative security of Nialla's presence, and often Rick was in the apartment. During outcalls I'd be on my own, with even more dangerous men.

This afternoon we had a welcome respite with no appointments lined up. Rick had ordered take-out Chinese then left, leaving the door locked. Neither of us had a key to the deadbolt and the apartment was on the fourth floor, so there was no way out. I sometimes wondered what I would do if there was a fire while he was gone. We'd have to jump forty feet to the ground, a prospect that sometimes seemed pretty appealing.

We'd watched *Pretty Woman* with Richard Gere and Julia Roberts. Crazy. Stupid. How that movie could romanticize the life, I didn't know. At points I found myself getting angry. This was a bunch of fantasy, and it made me ill when I compared it to the violence I'd suffered over the past few weeks.

But both of us cried when Richard Gere climbed the fire escape to go get her. At first it was just a few tears, but then I freaked out because I began sobbing as I leaned on Nialla. I felt her tears splash on my face and I put my arms around her.

I felt ridiculous reacting that way. But how else was I supposed to react? When he talked about rescuing the princess, it hit me that no one would ever call *me* Princess. No one would ever rescue me. No one would even *want* me. I was sixteen years old and I'd already lost count of how many men I'd had sex with. I had long since stopped fighting, because I didn't want to die.

Except that most of the time I did want to die.

It was after the tears finally stopped that I asked Nialla why she stayed with Rick.

She thought about it for a long time while she carefully packed pot into a bowl. Then she lit up, stoking the coal and inhaling deeply, then passed the bowl to me. "What else am I going to do? I don't have anywhere to go. My father's the worship leader at the Calvary Baptist Church in Richmond. He'd die if he knew his daughter was a whore. I'm sure he'd rather I'd be dead. I don't know what else to do. Where would I go?"

I thought about that, and it made my stomach turn a little. I felt the same black tendrils of shame. What would my parents think? And Sam? She practically worshiped me. When I thought about how disappointed Sam would be I wanted to sink through a hole in the ground and disappear.

"How did you wind up with him?"

Nialla sighed. "Not so different from you really. I fell in love with him. I kept it a secret, because Dad would have gone batshit if he'd known I was dating an older guy, or dating *anyone* really. And Rick was so sweet sometimes. He gave me jewelry and stuffed animals, and even though I couldn't take any of it home, he kept it at his place. He talked about how some day we'd go away together."

"Was he your first ... guy?"

She bitterly shook her head. "No. That was my uncle when I was eight."

Oh. She said the words in such a flat, emotionless tone that I wanted to cry for her.

"Rick was the first person who ever really treated me like I was worth something."

I asked the next question very carefully. "Do you still love him?"

For the first time in that conversation, she met my eyes. Just for a second, then she looked away. She nodded. "Sometimes."

Crazy, but I felt sorry for her.

The next day, Rick ordered us to pack our bags. We were leaving. This time, our destination was Dallas, Texas.

***

251

winter flower

A few days after we got to Dallas, I was lying on my side in bed after a john had left, just thinking how awful things were. The year before, in my sophomore year history class, we spent almost a week on World War II and the Holocaust. One of the books we read was called Night. By Elie something. Wiesel? I don't remember for sure. Anyway, the book was about a boy whose family ended up in a concentration camp. The boy related his experiences of horrible brutality, of the gas chambers and ovens, of torture and murder. When I read it, my brain couldn't accept what I was reading. I couldn't grasp it as reality. I couldn't imagine how anyone could continue living under those circumstances, how they wouldn't just curl up and die.

Now, I sort of understood. Because as horrible and pointless and brutal as my life had become, I was still functioning on some level. And I didn't understand why. Because I felt ... not just dirty—that wasn't a strong enough word. I felt *filthy* inside, ashamed and disgusted by what I had become. Ashamed, because I hadn't killed myself. I hadn't overdosed, or slit my wrists open, or jumped from a high window. I thought about such things constantly. I had fantasized about what it would feel like to draw a blade across my wrist and watch the blood bubbling up from the line, dripping and dripping.

I hadn't had the courage to do it. And I hated myself because I was a coward.

You're nothing but a dirty whore.

The words Rick had made me say stuck to me, an invisible coating that somehow I was sure anyone who met me would be able to sense.

The john had been gone for maybe five minutes when I saw it. He had taken his jacket off when he came in and casually laid it on a chair before getting undressed. I had asked him the usual questions. What was his name? What did he do for a living? Was he married? The answers were generic, hardly different from any others I heard. Jack, he said. He was a high school teacher. Married, two kids, but he and his wife were estranged. The phone he left behind, the phone that had fallen down beside the chair, unnoticed ... it was an old flip phone.

I stared at it, stunned. Everywhere I'd been since my abduction, there had been no phones except for Rick's. He removed them from hotel rooms, and when he left he locked us in from the outside if possible.

I could call home. Or 911. Would a phone like that have a GPS? Would 911 be able to find me from it? I didn't know the address here. I was paralyzed. Who should I call? Sam? My mom? What would I tell them?

You're nothing but a dirty whore.

Rick's words were an assault. I simultaneously felt nausea, terror, despair.

For the first time in days I began to cry. *How can I go home now?* I didn't have a home. I wasn't the same person I had been, and the one thing I couldn't bear was to see the disgust my parents would feel about me.

I groaned. I *could* be free. All I had to do was walk across the room, pick up the phone, and dial.

If I was going to do it, it had better be soon. I was running out of time.

Instead, I picked up the pack of Pall Malls from the bedside stand and lit one. The rush of nicotine brought clarity to my thoughts. But I was no closer to an answer. I stared at the phone like it was a poisonous spider.

Are you fucking crazy? Call! Call!

Call who? I couldn't go home. They'd never understand.

You're nothing but a dirty whore.

I was still paralyzed and smoking a cigarette, tears streaming down my face, when the door opened. It was Rick. He looked murderous.

"Where the fuck is it?"

I barely moved, just nodded in the general direction of the phone. He swept it up in his hand and opened it up, looking at it. "Did you fucking call anyone?" He must have been checking through the call history.

I shook my head.

After a minute he looked up from the phone. He looked surprised. Then he smirked. "Guess that's it, then." He started to walk out of the room then looked back in. "You've got another client in twenty minutes. Be ready."

He walked out, shutting the door behind him.

I lit another cigarette and stared. What did it mean? Why hadn't I called? I lay down on my side again and held the cigarette in front of me, watching the smoke slowly twirl up. What it meant was obvious. He owned me now. The things he had said, the things he had made me say, they were true now.

***

Not long after that, Rick made me get my first tattoo, an intricate scrollwork just on the edge of my pubic hair bearing the label, *Rick's moneymaker*. I wasn't a person anymore. I was a product to be bought and sold. In each city, the pattern was the same. We would arrive and spend an hour on the first morning posting ads on Backpage, my face obscured in the ads. The phone calls would pour in within minutes of posting the first ad. Typically we would take a couple of lunchtime appointments, then things would slow down for the early afternoon. Then from five in the afternoon until two or three in the morning I would see one man after another.

By that time I was regularly doing outcalls. For those, Rick would drive me to the location—typically hotels, but sometimes people's houses or apartments—and then pick me up an hour later. We had a system for outcalls, for safety. As soon as we were settled at an outcall and had determined it was safe and that the client had paid, then we would call. Not getting a call within five minutes of going in meant there was trouble.

And trouble happened often enough. Most of the time it was guys who didn't want to pay. These were guys who would call an escort, refuse to pay and rape them, figuring that it would never get reported. They were probably right. After all, what good would it do to call the police?

So the plan was, if I didn't call and check in during the first five minutes of the visit, Rick would return and bust down the door. It happened more than once.

***

We had left Dallas and moved on to Cincinnati before I heard a client tell me, "Merry Christmas." Somehow I had survived three months of terror and the loss of whatever innocence I had.

When he said those words, the guy was putting his tie back on. Like most of them, this one had a wedding ring. Did it mean nothing to these men? Were they all like this? In the last three months I'd had sex with men barely older than I was, men my father's age, even men my grandfather's age. They were teachers and cops and ministers and accountants. And so many of them were husbands and fathers.

Christmas Eve was especially busy, and Rick made us do half-hour appointments at the normal charge. The money made no difference to me one way or the other, I never saw any of it anyway. Rick's warnings of what would happen if I dared to hide any money from him had been effective. Rick picked me up from my final appointment of the night at four a.m. on Christmas morning. The streets were glistening with icy cold grey sleet, and the Mustang slid while we were on our way to pick up Nialla.

When we picked her up, she looked as bitter as I felt. Normally, I got in the back seat as soon as she came to the car, but tonight she waved me to stay where I was and slid into the back. I was silent as we drove back to the hotel, but Rick began to talk in a soft monologue. I tuned him out—sometimes when he was in a talkative mood, he could go along for quite a while without saying anything meaningful.

This time, however, was different. After a couple of minutes of seemingly aimless talking, he said, "Tomorrow should be light for you girls. You've only got a couple of appointments each."

Nialla's voice interrupted from the back seat. "On fucking *Christmas*? You've gotta be kidding me."

Rick's face flushed with rage, and he turned around in his seat groping for her without slowing down the car. When he couldn't reach her, he grabbed me by my shirt and slammed me into the glass window. I cried out in pain.

"Shut the *fuck* up, bitch!"

She did, instantly. Rick never hesitated to hurt either one of us; it didn't matter who had committed the offense. I slumped in my seat rubbing my head. Underneath my hair on the right side of my head, I felt what seemed to be a small lump. I took my fingers away from the lump and looked at them. They were lightly spotted with blood.

"Jesus, Rick, she's bleeding."

Rick sneered. "She'll be fine."

"Either way, you should let us have tomorrow off. It's Christmas."

"Baby, you know I'm trying to save up to get us a big place. You know that. We can't do that if you're not making money."

Nialla muttered, "You and your *bullshit* house."

When I woke up the next morning, the lump had grown larger, but it was only noticeable to the touch. I stared bloodshot in the mirror as smoke curled up from my cigarette, and I wondered what Sam was doing. Had she woken up early that morning like we always used to and gone downstairs to see what presents there were? I leaned against the sink and closed my eyes, trying to envision the scene. Mom and Dad would be in the next room cooking, the smell spreading throughout the house. Mom would be playing classic Christmas carols on an old vinyl record that her mother had given her. She'd said more than once that album was the only reason she still had a record player.

When I looked at myself in the mirror, I didn't recognize who I was. My hair was in messy ringlets from the perm Rick had insisted I get. The ugly neck tattoo of a dragon with Rick's name written through the middle of it marred my neck, making it something that wasn't even mine anymore. My eyes were sunken. I was thinner than before, a lot thinner. Rick constantly called me fat and wouldn't let me eat as much as I wanted. Once when he decided I'd eaten too much, he forced me to take a bunch of laxatives.

I can't make as much money off a fat bitch.

I hated him. It was like he wasn't even human. He had no feelings, he didn't care about anyone or anything. He pretended sometimes, even made *me* believe it sometimes. But at moments like this I had some clarity. He was never going to let me go.

And what about *me*? When I had the chance, I didn't call. All I had to do was press three simple digits—911—and I could have been free. Why hadn't I done it?

The answer was simple enough. I was too damaged. I felt like I was filthy, like I was going to hell, like I might be contagious. How could I ever face Sam again knowing what I'd spent those months doing? It was better to pass out of their lives quietly.

He'd even left his gun out on a couple of occasions. Never far away, never further than arm's reach; once he set it down on the table between the beds in a hotel room. My eyes were instantly drawn to it.

"Grab it, why don't you?" He grinned as he said the words. When I didn't respond, didn't move, he gave a soft laugh. He knew he owned me by then.

My first appointment that morning—Christmas morning—was an electrical engineer, a father of five kids, three of whom were in college. He wore a cross on a gold chain around his neck, and he talked about how much he loved his wife and didn't understand why he couldn't stop seeing escorts.

I wanted to say, *I'm younger than your kids.* I wanted to say, *Help me.* I wanted to say, *Go home to your family.*

I didn't say any of those things. I nodded and listened and pretended I sympathized. I stared up at the ceiling while he fucked me, and in my head, I just left the room. Usually I went somewhere emotionally neutral. I imagined myself comfortable and safe and alone, maybe reading a book while drinking a cup of tea. But that time, my mind turned back to Christmases past. I remembered Mom's stunned surprise when Dad bought them new wedding bands for their tenth Christmas together. She had started crying, and I had asked, "What's wrong, Mommy?"

She had shaken her head, replying, "Nothing's wrong, baby. These are happy tears, because I've got the best husband in the world, and you've got the best daddy."

I remembered one of those rare Christmases in Virginia when we had lots of snow. After presents and breakfast, Sam and I had gone outside sledding. We had saucer-shaped sleds that flew down the hill. Every single time, Sam would shriek with delight all the way down.

I missed Sam, and my mom and dad.

I didn't realize I was crying until the guy finished in a chorus of huffing and blowing. He lay breathing heavily, his sweat-sticky body covering mine, his face buried in my neck, and rolled over heavily. For a second he looked stunned, then he said, "Are you crying? Did I hurt you?"

Did he hurt me?

He actually *sounded* concerned. Normally, I tried to stay numb. Normally, I tried not to feel anything anymore. But when he asked that, I felt as if I'd been stabbed.

Tears running down my face, I shouted, "Don't act like you give a shit! If you did, you'd be at home with your own kids instead of fucking a sixteen-year-old in some crappy hotel! Go! Just *go*! Go home!"

Suddenly he looked desperately afraid. His face red, he began throwing on his clothes. "You're sixteen? You didn't tell me that! I didn't know!"

He stopped getting dressed long enough to realize he still had the condom on. He threw it on the floor, a disgusting exclamation, and continued getting dressed. "You didn't tell me that. Don't you know I could go to jail for that? What kind of bullshit is this?"

I sat up pulling the sheet around me and screamed, "Do you think I like this? Do you think I want to be here? Get out! Go home to your kids! Merry *fucking* Christmas!"

He was out the door before he even had his shoes on or his shirt buttoned. The door slammed shut behind him, and I lay in the bed crying for a long time, trying to blot out the pain and the fear and shame. But the shame was so heavy, it was starting to blot *me* out.

I don't know how much longer it was before I heard the door click and Rick and Nialla came back from the outcall he had taken her to.

Rick muttered, "What the fuck is wrong with her?"

"Leave her alone," Nialla said.

Then I felt her arms around me and I cried even harder.

257

Twenty-Four

~~~~~~~~~~~~~~~~~~~~~

Cole

Even though it was late September, summer still clung on with fierce intensity. The air was thick with humidity, leaving everything with a moist texture reminiscent of my childhood summers. The smell of this time of year was often enough to transport me back to that last summer riding in the truck with Lucas. I remembered hiking at Tallulah Gorge, and a weeklong road trip to Panama City, nights partying with his friends and avoiding Big Bill.

All of it represented a life I had always intended to leave behind. The one thing I *never* expected was to find myself living again in the rural South.

Everything was strangely normal when I got to the restaurant at six o'clock the next morning. Same routine as always. Check the parking lot. Go inside; check the condition of the bathrooms; walk through and look at the floors, the grills, the waffle irons; check temperatures for the hot and cold stored foods.

As I made my way along the area behind the back counter, I realized that things weren't normal at all. The grill filters were gleaming, as were the backs of the egg pans which had been scrubbed to a mirror shine. The floor deep under the dish pit, and even the pipes, had been scrubbed clean. Someone had to have been down on their hands and knees under there. The windows were clean, everything was put away properly. Even the waffle irons, which were a bitch to clean because they maintained a constant temperature of four hundred degrees, had been thoroughly cleaned.

There were no customers in the restaurant yet, and my third shift, Linda and Dakota, were lounging at the counter as they often were when I came in. Dakota was going through her tickets for the night. I looked over at them, then back at the gleaming clean kitchen, then back at them. "Did you guys do this?"

Linda said in a slow drawl, "Second shift did a little too."

I could imagine. Keeping a twenty-four hour a day, seven days a week restaurant clean was a constant battle. Motivating my employees to become engaged in keeping it that way? Insurmountable. I was stunned by what I was seeing.

"It looks great. Good job, guys."

I turned to head to the back room and unlock my office, when Linda called my name. "Cole?"

I turned around.

"We heard you got in trouble for kicking those guys out."

I shrugged. "It's no big deal," I said.

"Is to me," Dakota said. She didn't really look at me when she said it.

I gave them a half smile, but there was little else to say. So I turned and walked into the back room.

They'd been at work back here too. The shelf area where the hourly employees kept their coats and bags and purses had been decluttered and organized, and the floor had been detail-cleaned right down to the grout in the corners. I didn't understand it. I'd had this restaurant for almost three months and had struggled against a long-term trend here of neglect. My predecessor hadn't been that interested in keeping the place clean, which was one of the reasons why our business was so slow. Correcting that trend had been a goal which I hadn't accomplished yet, one of my biggest frustrations about this job. I couldn't understand what had prompted the sudden change. Had Brian offered them all bonuses or something?

I was unlikely to answer that right now. I unlocked the office and began preparing for shift change. I scanned through the notes left behind by Bryan's manager-trainee, who closed out yesterday's first shift, then started counting the drawers.

As I was doing that, the swinging door to the back room opened and Julie entered. She was wearing a sweatshirt and carrying her uniform shirt as she walked by, saying, "Morning, Cole."

"Morning," I said without pausing what I was doing. As I finished my count and began entering the numbers into the computer, out of the corner of my eye I caught Julie peeling her sweatshirt off.

What the hell is she doing? She had her back to me, revealing a well-muscled lean body. She wore a nude strapless bra. Christ. I diverted my eyes, back to the computer and my work. But the whole time, my mind was running in circles. Was she being intentionally provocative? What was she trying to do?

I could still partially see her reflected in the glass one-way mirror between my office and the rest of the restaurant. She was getting her uniform shirt on.

I tried to formulate a rebuke. But I had no idea what to say. I finally decided to let it go then picked up my phone to call Brian and report my numbers for the day. The conversation was short and awkward. Brian didn't mention our argument from yesterday. I wasn't foolish enough, however, to think that he would let it go. I would hear more about it.

When I was finished with that, it was time to head up front. But Julie appeared at the door of my office.

"Hey, Cole. Are you doing okay? After, you know … yesterday?"

As she asked her question, she leaned against the doorframe with her arms crossed under her breasts. The effect pulled at my eyes and was obviously intentional. "Yeah, I'm fine. Thanks for asking."

I stood up from the stool at my desk, with the intention of her getting out of the way so I could go out front. Instead she stayed, blocking the door, which had the effect of putting us two inches away from each other.

She spoke in a breathy voice that disturbingly reminded me of Teagan. "You know, while your wife is out of town, if you need a home-cooked meal or anything…" Her voice trailed off suggestively.

Shit.

Crazy. I remembered the crazy emotional high when Teagan first approached me, when we first had dinner on a business trip, when I kissed her for the first time. I remembered how *alive* I felt, how fucking amazing it was.

I remembered how *stupid* and *entitled* I was, how much I hurt my family, and it was like someone had dumped a bucket of ice on me.

I didn't want a young pretty waitress. I wanted *Erin.* I wanted my family.

I pushed past her. "No, thanks, Julie."

Sam

My text message was simple. **Dad, can I take Mom's van?**

I sent it about eight a.m., but I knew he'd be busy, so I logged into Second Life while I waited. The sim was usually quiet this time of day, and that morning was no exception. For the past few nights, I hadn't played much, just a couple of hours a night. Gunstock was usually on when I was, and we'd been spending more and more time together. I'd kind of hoped he would be now, but no luck. Maybe tonight.

It was weird. Neither of us knew who the other was in real life. And he could *never* know. But in the confines of our little world, I was … falling for him?

No. Not really. This was all fake. But our characters? That's what they were doing. And sometimes it felt almost real.

I wandered around aimlessly online for a while. There were only a couple of people in Erie, and they were players I never actually interacted with. I wasn't in the mood. I felt strangely restless, and very, very nervous.

I was planning to talk with Mrs. Mullins today. About Hayley.

I didn't hear from Hayley at all last night. Which was unusual ... unusual enough that it made my stomach knot up in fear. I tried to tell myself to not be paranoid, but I hadn't heard from her this morning either.

At eight thirty, Dad texted me back: **What for?**

Great. He wanted to ask questions. I responded: **I want to go buy some drugs and bring girls back to the house.**

I could imagine his expression. There was brief pause, then he responded: **All right. Be careful. Don't scratch up your mother's van.**

I laughed. **LOL. Thanks.**

I quickly sobered up though. I dialed the school and asked to speak with Mrs. Mullins. After a few moments, she came on the line.

"Mrs. Mullins, am I allowed at school to meet with you?"

"Officially, no. But what's this about?"

I took a deep breath. Then I said, "I need to talk to you about something really, really important. And it needs to be in person."

She didn't respond right away. But after a few minutes, she said, "This had better be *really* important, Sam. I'll meet you at the Starbucks in fifteen minutes. Will that work?"

Fifteen minutes? I could make it, barely, if I skipped my shower and just got dressed and went. I scrambled, throwing on whatever clothes were handy, then had a panicky moment when I couldn't find Mom's keys. That's because they were hanging on the hook where they were supposed to be.

I drove carefully. I'd only had a driver's license for a few months and hadn't had much practice driving lately. But since Mom was gone, I decided to ask Dad if I could use the van to go to school. It would be nice to stay clear of the school bus for a while.

I made it in exactly fifteen minutes. I looked around: she wasn't there yet. So I took a seat and waited. I didn't have to wait long—she strolled in just a couple of minutes later.

"I'm getting a coffee. Would you like something, Sam?"

"I —"

"Don't worry, I'm buying."

"Coffee, then. Thank you."

After she ordered and got our drinks, I poured a *lot* of cream and sugar in then sat down at the table facing her.

"All right, Sam. So … what's the mystery?"

I took a deep breath. I still had incredibly mixed feelings. What if I was wrong? What if this was only going to cause trouble for Hayley? What if she decided we couldn't be friends anymore?

"Sam…" she said.

"It's Hayley," I blurted. "I'm worried about her." I closed my eyes. I felt like I was betraying Hayley. But I continued. "Her father is the one who gave her the bruises. And when she was late yesterday, my Dad and I dropped her off—I was worried. Her father was real mad."

She nodded. "I see." Her tone was grave. "How many times do you know of that he's hurt her?"

"I'm not sure. Sometimes she has bruises on her arm, like he twists it. And sometimes she … she winces when she moves. Like somebody hit her, but I couldn't see the bruise."

Mrs. Mullins nodded. She leaned close to me and said, "Sam, thank you for coming to me. I'm going to tell you something in confidence now. I shouldn't, but I think you need to know."

I tilted my head, afraid to ask what she was talking about.

"This morning Hayley came to school with a black eye. Mr. Flowers and I had already discussed it, and this was the last straw, so to speak. I called Child Protective Services this morning."

I gasped. "Oh my God. Wh-what … what happens now?"

"Well, a caseworker is meeting with her at the school right now. They'll be calling her father soon. It's really up to the county now."

"God," I said. "Was she badly hurt?"

Mrs. Mullins sighed. "It's hard to say, Sam. But the bruise on her face was bad. Almost like yours. But … a little worse."

I shuddered. Billy had punched me in the face more than once. My face still hurt, and the bruises hadn't even begun to fade. The thought of somebody hitting Hayley like that made me want to scream. My feelings about her confused me. They *really* confused me. I loved her like I'd loved Brenna—I trusted her and looked up to her and cared about her. But there was more, a pink feeling of unexplainable warmth and fear at the same time. She was so pretty. I wanted to *be with her*, and not just as a friend.

It was confusing, because whenever I thought of romantic things, I'd always thought of boys. I used to fantasize about going to my prom. Of being recognized by everybody else as a woman, just as sure as I knew I was one. This made me—what? Gay? Was I a lesbian? I didn't know what I was. All I knew was that aside from my sister, Hayley was the best friend I'd ever had. I … I loved her.

"Where did you go?" Mrs. Mullins brought me right back to reality with her question.

"I worry about her."

Mrs. Mullins nodded. Her face looked serious. "I do too, Sam. Domestic violence is nothing to take lightly."

I opened my mouth to ask another question and froze. I couldn't. I *couldn't*. But I was tired of being so incredibly alone. I was tired of no one knowing anything about me. I was tired of having no one to talk to. I took a deep breath and froze again.

"What is it?"

"A … friend of mine. From Virginia. He told me that he was a girl. Like … inside. What would you do if a friend told you that?"

Mrs. Mullins looked at me over her glasses for just a moment. Then, quietly, she said, "I suppose if a friend of mine told me that I'd have to give her a big hug. Our society is tough on people who are transgender. They probably need love more than just about anyone else."

Hearing that made me want to cry inside. But I kept as firm a grip on my face as I could as I said, "Isn't that against your religion?"

She frowned. "You'd think that from all the yelling and screaming you hear about in the news, wouldn't you?" She pointed a finger at herself. "The Jesus *I* follow told his disciples that whatever they did to the poor and oppressed … what he called *the least of these* … that they did that to Him. I think what he meant by that was that if you were mean to people, or treated them like there was something wrong with them, or especially if you harmed them in their spirits, then it would be as if you were doing that very same wrong thing to God. Jesus told me to love everybody, even my enemies. And that's what I'm gonna do, no matter what a bunch of TV preachers say."

I tried to hide it. I tried to stay stone-faced, emotionless. But I couldn't help it. My eyes watered and tears poured down my face. I was stricken and grabbed at a pile of napkins on the next table, trying to wipe my face.

Mrs. Mullins said in a very quiet voice, "Sam … you're not talking about a friend, are you?"

I couldn't speak. I shook my head.

"It's you?"

A sharp, stabbing anxiety came and then passed. And then I nodded.

She turned slightly in her chair. "Well, it sounds like you need a hug, baby. Come over here."

winter flower

She held out her arms and I fell apart. Because I'd finally told somebody. And it was okay.

Cole

It was a little bit after noon, and I was standing at the grill, completely in the weeds. I had fourteen plates lined up with orders, both grills were covered, and there were people sitting in the waiting area waiting for booths.

Julie called out an order with three different plates then started to run off before I had a chance to even begin marking the order down. She'd been doing that all morning and it was pissing me off.

In a sharp tone, I said, "Julie! Stay until I call the order back!"

She muttered something, I don't know what. A moment later the other two waitresses both called out, "Good morning!"

I echoed the call without looking around. Their greeting meant someone had entered the restaurant. I just kept doing what I was doing. It had taken me several months, but I was finally getting some kind of a rhythm down. I wasn't good at it, but I was slightly better than I had been. I'd have done a lot to be able to have a backup cook at times like this. But staffing levels were determined by corporate, and my store didn't have enough sales to allow me a second cook. And if I kept getting this backed up, then turning out food that wasn't great because I was too rushed, we never would get those kind of sales.

Wanda, my most experienced waitress, came over to me. She stood next to me at the grill and said quietly, "That's the health inspector."

Son of a *bitch!* "Now?"

The question was nonsense of course, just my own sense of sudden helplessness. We weren't even due for inspection for two more months, though I'd been working to prepare my crew for when it happened. This would be my first since taking over the restaurant, and I was fairly confident we would do well. I glanced over my shoulder for just a second, and saw a sour-faced man standing next to one of the booths holding a clipboard and talking with the customers in that booth. That didn't look so bad.

I kept track with occasional looks as the inspector worked his way through the front of the restaurant. He looked under the booths, went back into the bathrooms, then returned. He stood there watching for what seemed like an hour but was probably more like ten minutes, occasionally making notations on his clipboard.

Wanda escorted the health inspector to the grill, and I said to him, "I'm almost finished here and I'll be right with you, sir."

He replied in a thick Alabama accent I could barely understand. "That's all right, son, I can examine some of the equipment and food back here. You keep on doing what you're doing."

I didn't have much choice. As I finished the last orders, I watched him run a thermometer through the dishwasher to check the operating temperature, then he checked the temperatures in the sandwich board beside the grill where all of the cold toppings and meats were stored.

I felt my stress double as he frowned, shook his thermometer, and then muttered, "Tsk, tsk, tsk."

It couldn't be that far off … I checked the temperature not long before the rush and it was well below forty degrees. A few more minutes, and I'd be finished.

Only Julie called another order in, and then Wanda did, and I was still stuck on the grill. I was starting to feel desperate.

Just as I was getting the next meal on the plate, the inspector approached and said, "I'd like to see your food storage in the back."

There were only a couple of orders left. I called over Wanda. "Can you take over on these last couple of orders?"

"Sure thing, boss," she said. I pointed out what I was cooking, and she said, "I got it." She reached for the spatula, and I said, "Wanda. Hands. Wash. Please."

She flushed red. "Yes, sir."

Once she was done and back at the grill, I turned and faced the inspector. He still had a very sour expression on his face. I was increasingly nervous.

"This way," I said.

"So you're the new manager here," he said.

"Yes, sir, since the beginning of summer."

He grunted in a way that made me more nervous than ever. I led him to the back and unlocked the stockroom.

He pointed at the boxes of freeze-dried hash browns stacked next to the shelves. "Those need to be six inches off the floor," he said.

Crap.

He opened the walk-in refrigerator and walked in, stabbing his thermometer into a shrink-wrapped steak that was on top of a stack. I watched as the thermometer dropped down to thirty degrees. He shook his head and said, "Too warm."

What? "The required temperature is forty-one or below, right?"

"That's right. You were forty-five. You need to get this equipment looked at."

265

Motherfucker. This was a setup. This guy was either friends with Mayor Prichard or owed him something. I didn't know which.

"Can you double-check?"

He raised his eyebrows. "I already double-checked. Now if you'll excuse me, I'll go write this up."

He marched back to the front of the restaurant. Holy crap. I needed to be calling Brian right now—that was SOP when the health inspector showed up, to let higher level management know. I looked at my cell phone for a moment, sighed, then dialed.

He answered on the second ring.

"Health inspector is here," I said.

Brian immediately asked, "Is it a young woman? Thirty-ish? Or an old guy?"

"Old guy," I said.

"Son of a *bitch!* I'm in Alexandria, I can't get there any time soon. Call me when you get the score."

"Will do." I hung up, walked back to the front of the restaurant, and washed my hands.

The inspector approached me, tearing off one copy of the inspection.

My eyes immediately landed on the large letter F in the upper right corner. My mouth dropped open.

"Here's your copy, son. You've got some serious issues here. You've got four-teen days to correct them, or we'll close this restaurant down. Understand? In the meantime, you post this where it's visible."

"No way," I muttered.

"Excuse me?" he said, sounding offended.

I scanned down the checklist.

Filth and garbage under the cookline.
Ready-to-eat food incorrect temperature.
Uncooked food incorrect temperature.
Incorrect hand washing.

It went on and on.

"You're friends with the mayor, huh?" I was on the verge of losing my temper, and I *couldn't* do that.

He sneered. "Who I'm friends with, and who I ain't, ain't none of yer business, son. You just get your restaurant up to snuff."

He turned and walked away as I stood there, openmouthed. I couldn't get my mind around what had just happened. I looked at the inspection report again. The score was a *forty-three.* That was impossible. Nobody got a forty-three on a health inspection, even the dirtiest of restaurants. Which this wasn't. This was nothing but retribution.

The more I thought about it, the more I felt the rage threatening to bubble over. They weren't just threatening me. They were threatening my family, my livelihood. I was shaken far beyond my expectations.

"Boss, you okay?" Wanda stood there looking deeply concerned.

"Yeah," I said. I looked around. The lunch rush was over, and the restaurant had mostly emptied out except for the old guys who sat at the counter. They looked pleased with the turn of events … a little bit of drama to liven up their day, I guess. I needed to clean up from the lunch rush and I had a lot to do. But first I needed to make the phone call.

Performance on health inspections was a basic requirement of my job. The company had 1,400 restaurants spread across the Southern states, and when a restaurant failed health inspection everyone in the company heard about it. It had only happened once since I'd started, about three weeks into my training. One of the restaurants in Mississippi had gotten a sixty-nine.

The manager of that restaurant had been yanked from his position and put back as a manager trainee.

I dreaded making the phone call. "I gotta call Brian," I told Wanda. "I'll be back in a few minutes."

I walked right past my office and out the back door of the restaurant, dialing Brian's number as I walked. He answered on the second ring and said, "How did it go?"

"Brian, this was set up." I hated that my voice shook as I spoke.

"I know that. Your inspector—Nick Corcoran is his name—he and Mayor Prichard are poker buddies. How bad was it?"

"We got a forty-three, Brian. It was utter bullshit. He failed us on equipment that was working perfectly. I saw the temperatures. I can't believe—"

Brian's voice went dangerously quiet when he interrupted me. "Did you just say a forty-three?"

I was out of words and explanations. "Yes."

"I'll be there in an hour." He hung up the phone without waiting for a response. I felt shell-shocked. I stumbled back into the restaurant and began cleaning up from the lunch rush, trying not to think about the possibility that I might lose my job by the end of the day.

Sam

I was starting to panic.

I had tried to reach Hayley all morning long, via text message, Instagram, Snapchat. She didn't respond anywhere. It wasn't like her, and I was worried that wherever she was, she didn't have her phone, or something even worse.

I wanted to do something. I thought I could get in the car and go search for her or stop by her house, but I knew she wasn't at home anymore. Where was she?

I sent her one last message on Snapchat. It was a picture of the two of us laughing together that she had taken two weeks ago. For the caption I wrote, "Worried about you."

It was about one in the afternoon when Dad called. "Listen, Sam, my bosses are calling a meeting for four o'clock this afternoon. I don't know when I'll be home, but it's likely to be after six. If you want to order a pizza, or go out and get something, there's a twenty on my bedside stand."

I knew about the twenty. Occasionally he had to work late—sometimes very late—and when it happened it was usually without warning. Since Mom left, he had left the money there for me in case he wasn't home, cautioning me not to use it unless he gave permission.

He sounded really bummed out. "Is everything okay?"

There was a long pause, as if he were trying to decide how to answer. Finally he said, "It's been a really rough day here."

Man. Sometimes Dad seemed really remote—his dispirited tone worried me. I thought for a second about driving up there and keeping him company while he did his afternoon stuff, but I rethought that. If his bosses were coming, and he was in trouble yesterday, he wouldn't thank me for being there.

I didn't know how to approach this. If it were Hayley, I'd tell her I wish she felt better, or that things were going better for her, or I would give her a hug. It felt like a tectonic shift, as if the very structure of my relationship with my dad had suddenly morphed. I finally said, "I hope things go better for you, Dad. I'll save you some pizza, and I'll straighten up the kitchen so you won't have to mess with it when you get home."

Dad responded in a warm tone. "Thanks, Sam."

That meant I had four or five hours to kill. I thought about my box with the too–small dress that Brenna had bought me. I really needed to replace it. For half a second I had the crazy thought of going to Target with the money and buying something new. But I couldn't do that. There wouldn't be any pizza at home when Dad got home and that would be impossible to explain.

The money was in Mom and Dad's room ... and there was a closet full of Mom's clothes.

The thought was stunning. Mom wouldn't be home for days, possibly weeks. I felt emboldened. Somehow the tears I cried with Mrs. Mullins that morning left me feeling both raw but also courageous. I couldn't believe I had actually told someone … *and* that they had accepted me.

I got up, shaking. As I walked toward my parents' room, I thought about it only being two years before I'd be eighteen. Maybe I could get a job now and use that to pay for the hormones.

How could I ever pay to actually transition? Dad's health insurance certainly wouldn't cover it, and I'd read that the procedures could cost tens of thousands of dollars. For a second, despair threatened to well over, but I pushed it away. I opened the door to Mom and Dad's room, and slid open her closet.

I sucked in a deep breath.

I reverently began to slide the hangers. Here was a pale blue sundress she wore in the summer. A formal evening gown that felt like silk, black with lace at the edges. There was a red sleeveless dress with a short skirt that I didn't think I had ever seen her wear. Simple skirts and sweaters. I wanted to try all of them on.

Part of me wanted to start with the gown and the heels, to make myself beautiful. But not today … I wanted to be comfortable. I wanted to feel like I was home on a normal day, in normal clothes, for once being myself. I took down a short-sleeved baby blue button-down shirt and one of her ankle length skirts. I took the clothes out of the closet like they were spun of gold. I knew I was taking a terrible risk—if my dad came home right now, there's no way he would ever understand.

At this point, I couldn't be deterred.

I found a pair of her sandals, flats, that looked like they would fit. I didn't know her shoe size, but my feet were small. I took the clothes back to my own room, undressed, unceremoniously dumping my own clothes to the floor. I began to dress.

The skirt fit okay, despite my lack of hips. The blouse fit, though it was a little tight across the shoulders. But it looked all wrong. I dug into my closet, pulling out the box where I had my own things hidden. I squeezed into the bra that Brenna had bought me, despite the fact that it was painfully tight. I stuffed the bra with socks, wishing with everything I had that I could one day get the hormone treatments that would make it real. With the shirt back on, I looked better.

I carefully brushed my hair, smoothing it out as much as I could. Then ever so carefully, I began to apply my makeup. I didn't care about the risk anymore. I didn't care how long it was going to take, or whether or not Dad came home.

269

winter flower

For once, just *once*, I wanted to feel like *me*. I wanted to feel like a real person, not some shell that satisfied everyone else's expectations but my own.

Foundation and blush, eyeshadow and eyeliner and mascara. Brenna had taught me long ago that less was more when it came to makeup. And I had watched plenty of YouTube tutorials that made the same point.

Finally finished, I slid my feet into the gold strapped sandals and stood in front of the mirror mounted on my door.

Immediately I had to struggle to hold back tears, which would have laid waste to my mascara. But my breath caught as I looked.

What I saw in the mirror wasn't a gangly, nerdy teenage boy. What I saw was what I had always wanted to see... a pretty, self-possessed girl. A *beautiful* girl.

I saw *me*.

Again, I had to fight back tears.

I wanted to see Brenna, and I wanted her to see me.

Maybe it was time to stop keeping secrets. Maybe I could tell Hayley. Or Dad or Mom. I was so sick and tired of pretending to be someone else.

I sat down at my desk, knowing that one of the few places I felt really comfortable as myself was online. I started Second Life and waited for my world to load up on my computer screen. My avatar appeared, and I thought maybe I should go shop and pick clothes similar to what I was actually wearing. As the sim finished loading, a note card popped up, labeled, "A note from Gunstock."

I instantly double-clicked on it and began to read.

Dearest Tamara,

I hope I don't have to tell you just how much I love the time we spend together. Last night was magical, and I hope you will give me the opportunity to take you out again sometime soon.

For a second I closed my eyes in happiness. It really had been wonderful. After Dad had gone to bed last night, I had signed on and immediately been greeted by Gunstock. The Twilight were hosting a rare sim-wide formal ball. To anyone watching, it probably would seem silly ... seventy or more people spread across the globe manipulating electronic avatars who were dancing and talking with each other in an imaginary world. But it was real enough to me. These were people I spent a lot of time with, people I cared about. Of course none of them except Gemini knew about my real-life situation, but that was fine. They knew me as a woman. They knew me as I really was, not as the exterior shell I had to carry around and show to everyone else.

Gunstock and I had danced for a long time, as we chatted about everything under the sun. I had finally collapsed into bed at three a.m., glowing like a coal inside.

Gunstock's note continued, *I would like to propose that we have a date off-sim soon. I know a lovely place where we can dance and voice chat. I would very much like to do that with you. Faithfully yours, Gunstock Valor.*

Voice chat. No. That couldn't happen. Not now, not ever. Not just because I would sound weird. My voice wasn't nearly as deep as most of the other boys in my class—thanks to the puberty-blocking hormones I had taken for a long time—but my voice would also attract attention from my father, late at night, something I didn't need or want. Nothing could ever come of a relationship in real life anyway.

My thoughts were interrupted by the ping of an incoming chat. It was Gemini.

Gemini: **Does Gunstock know that you are a boy? And that you aren't even old enough to be playing in the sim?**

I felt my chest spasm. I typed: **What are you talking about?**

Gemini: **You gave me enough information to go on. I'm sorry about your sister. But you know that you have to be eighteen years old to play in Erie. You're breaking the rules, and you're lying to Gunstock.**

The pain in my chest and throat was so bad, and I was so focused on it, that I didn't even hear the noise at my window. Frantically, I typed: **You don't know what you're talking about.**

Gemini: **Of course I do, Sam Roberts.**

I couldn't stop the tears that suddenly ran down my face. No no no no no no no no no. I typed: **You can't tell anyone. What did I ever do to you?**

Gemini: **You're constantly getting into other people's business, Sam. You think everything revolves around you. Everybody in the sim heard you and Gunstock last night at the ball. Why do guys pretend to be girls online? I don't get it. But you're not going to keep it up. I already sent notes to Gunstock and the GMs.**

I gasped. I was panicking, but there was nothing I could do. If she was telling the truth, and she had notified the GMs, then I would be banned from Erie permanently.

I typed: **Please don't do this.**

As I typed the words, I sobbed. And that was when the noise at the window finally caught my attention. I jerked around and gasped.

Billy Townsend was standing at the window. And he had his phone out. *Oh my God.* Had he taken a picture of me? He turned and ran.

I jumped to my feet and ran to the window. I didn't know what I was going to say or do. In less than one minute everything that was left of my world had just blown up.

winter flower

But it was too late. Billy was gone.

Twenty-Five

~~~~~~

Cole

The restaurant was quiet when my phone rang at two thirty. First shift was over, and my second shift had come in to prepare for the next day. We typically didn't get any business in the afternoon ... that was when I pulled the next day's food and worked on wrapping up my own day. Today, though, was different. Not long after the health inspection results had come in, Brian called me back again. He would be coming later than he originally said, and he wouldn't be alone — he was riding with David Johnson, our area vice president.

Like a lot of the senior management of the company, David was a graduate of Georgia Tech. He'd been fast-tracked—one year as a unit manager, one year as a district manager, two as a division, and now he had an area and reported directly to Jeremiah.

I didn't like David, although there was nothing really wrong with him. He rubbed me the wrong way because he was only in his twenties and he was smug about how fast and high he had risen. He rubbed me the wrong way because he reminded me of *me* and some of my worst traits.

I'd been smug too. I'd risen far and fast in my own career, and because I hadn't finished college, I'd credited it all to my own hard work, smarts, and my superior abilities. It never crossed my mind to consider the fact that I was lucky enough to fall into the right place at the right time with the right skills at the very birth of a brand-new industry. In the mid-1990s in Northern Virginia, we were hiring car mechanics and air-conditioning technicians and training them from scratch because it was so difficult to find skilled systems engineers. Starting salaries for system administrators with no experience at all were getting to seventy thousand dollars a year because the demand had so far outstripped the supply.

On the other hand, it was the same Georgia Tech good-old-boys network that had gotten me this job in the first place. After all, it was my college roommate, a senior vice president, who had gotten me this job.

I had a dull dread forming in my stomach, the kind of anxiety I never experienced when I was young. Not until the affair and the damage it did to my marriage, not until Brenna was lost, not until I'd destroyed my career with a felony conviction.

Was getting a forty-three on a health inspection a firing offense? It might well be. And if I lost this job, I didn't know what I would do. Would I end up as a cook for minimum wage somewhere? We could barely afford what was left of our bills now.

I tried to clear my head and focus on what I needed to get done. I still had to finish pulling supplies for the next day then do my closeout paperwork and head to the bank, and I needed to have it all done by four when Brian and David would arrive.

I checked my list again. There were only a few supply items left: to-go cups, dish soap, and paper towels. I tossed them on the cart and rolled it out front. "I'm leaving this here for you guys to put away," I said to Bubba, my second shift cook. Bubba's real name was Eugene Clarence Reynolds, but he insisted we just call him Bubba.

"Brian and David are going to be here at four and I need to get to the bank before then."

Bubba nodded. "No problem, I got it."

My phone rang as I was headed toward the back room again.

It was Jeremiah.

"I hear you had some problems with the health inspector out there," he said. "Everything okay?"

The second the phone rang I felt an immediate pressure release. "It was a setup," I said. "The guy didn't even look at his thermometers, he just started randomly checking stuff off the list and failing me on it."

"What the hell did you do to piss him off?" Jeremiah asked.

For the second time that day, I went out the back door of the restaurant so I could pace while I talked. I told Jeremiah the story of the mayor and Dakota the other night, Brian's insistence that I apologize to the mayor, and being sent home yesterday.

"Are you serious? He sent you home because you wouldn't apologize? I always knew he was a weasel motherfucker."

"I don't know what's going to happen now. David's coming out here with Brian at four o'clock to meet with me. Be honest with me, Jeremiah—what are the odds I'm going to get fired?"

Jeremiah cleared his throat, then said, "You remember the part in your training where we said the company doesn't tolerate sexual and racial harassment and whatnot? Believe it or not, they take that shit seriously at corporate. If we let that kind of harassment continue, it's a hostile work environment. Believe me: it's not just the right thing to do—it also protects the company from lawsuits. We don't need to be making any million-dollar settlements. You did the right thing, Cole."

I took a deep breath. "So what do you recommend I do when Brian and David get here?"

"Stand your ground, my friend. I'm not sure what we'll do about the inspection and the mayor—I'm going to talk to Jimmy Junior about that and get his thoughts. But frankly, I'm kind of pissed that Brian and David didn't tell me the whole story. They reported the health inspection results but not the background."

Jimmy Junior was the company's CEO and son of the founder. I didn't know if I was reassured or not.

"Okay. Stand my ground. What happens if David tells me I'm fired?"

"Hmmm. It's been a while since I visited any of the restaurants in Alabama. I think it's a good day to go for a drive and drop by and visit."

"Where are you?"

"Carrollton. I was visiting with the new manager here, but we're all finished. I'll see you in about an hour."

I closed my eyes and sagged with relief. One time, twenty years ago, I'd defended Jeremiah from some assholes near the Metroplex in Atlanta. He'd been returning the favor over and over and over and over again ever since. "Thanks," I said.

"Cole—you're welcome, but understand, this isn't special treatment. I'm not going to see any manager under me screwed over for doing the right thing."

I nodded, even though he couldn't see me. "Well, thanks anyway. You don't know what it means to me."

I heard the steel back door screech a little as it opened behind me. Bubba stuck his head out the door. "Cole, you've got a call—it's some girl, she says it's an emergency."

Sam

I don't know why I reacted the way I did, but when I saw Billy running through the yard away from my room, I panicked. I was already crying, almost hysterical. I had to leave—I had to go *now* and run as fast and as far as I could.

A new chat had popped up on my screen. It was Lilya, the leader of the Brigade—and one of the GMs. The message said: **Tamara, are you around? We need to talk about a note card I just received.**

No, no no no. I was freaking out. I dumped out my backpack on the bed, textbooks and notebook scattering everywhere. Then I began to stuff the bag. My makeup case and my journal. The pathetic amount of money I had. I started to put clothes in there, but then I stopped.

Fuck that. I was never going to dress as a boy again. I hoped Mom would forgive me. I went into her room and stole two dresses, a shirt, and her boots. Twenty dollars wasn't going to get me anywhere, but I'd figure out something. Right now I just needed to get out of this house and out of this town.

Maybe it was because of my irrational panic, or because I wasn't paying enough attention to my surroundings, or … maybe it was just fate. I don't know. But when I ran out that door, tears running down my face, I ran right into Cody Hendricks.

He had been standing right behind Mom's van, but that didn't excuse my not seeing him. His truck was parked right there in the driveway. When I bumped into him, he got a stupid grin on his face, and said, "Holy *crap*, Billy, you're right. He really *is* a fag." I started to run, but before I had a chance, he gripped my arm in a vice. "I wouldn't do that, *faggot*."

Jesus Christ. Billy was behind me. And Cody had a knife. "Get in the truck. You behave and I won't hurt you too bad."

Terror had me frozen. A litany of names ran through my head: Brandon Teena, raped and murdered. Paige Clay, shot in the face. Kyra Cordova, executed with a shot to the head. Brandy Martell, shot in the privates before she was shot two more times in the chest and left to die. I knew the names, the statistics. They were people who had been murdered because they were like me.

I was shaking, terrified.

"Get in the fucking truck, *faggot*."

I didn't have any choice. But I needed to run at the first chance I had. I shook, terrified, as I got in the truck. Billy followed me in on the passenger side, and Cody got behind the wheel, leaving me between the two of them.

Cody laughed. He started the engine, commenting, "I thought you were fucking with me when you said he was wearing a dress, Billy. I can't believe it."

Billy was fiddling with his phone and laughing at Cody. Where the hell were they taking me?

Cole

When I got to the front of the restaurant, I reached under the register and picked up the phone. "Waffle House, this is Cole. How can I help you?"

"Mr. Roberts?" It was a girl, and her voice sounded frightened. "This is Hayley."

I had to think for just a second before I put it together. Hayley, Sam's friend who I had met yesterday. What was going on?

"Oh, hey. What can I do for you, Hayley?"

"I'm really scared about Sam, sir. I'm really scared. Have you talked with him?"

A chill ran through me, instantly freezing me in place. "What's wrong, Hayley?"

She started to babble, and I interrupted in a stern voice, saying, "*Hayley!* Calm down and tell me what's wrong."

She took a deep breath, then said, "Cody ... the guy Sam hit with the rock yesterday? He posted on Twitter a little while ago that ... he was going to fuck somebody up. I didn't really think anything of it, but then Billy posted a picture ... of Sam. The picture's going everywhere on Snapchat. They Photoshopped it or something because in the picture Sam's wearing a dress."

As she was speaking, I took out my cell phone and looked up Sam's location. He wasn't home. The map showed him moving west on Hubbard Lane.

As I watched the screen on my phone, she continued. "Mr. Roberts, I tried calling him, but he's not answering. I know he was trying to reach me earlier, and I didn't answer because I was upset, and I'm afraid—"

"Thank you, Hayley. I'm going to call him right now."

She started to say something, but I didn't wait to hear what it was. I disconnected and dialed Sam.

Sam

The phone had rung three times and popped up with messages from Hayley during the five minutes we'd been in the car.

Billy said, "For a really ugly girl, you sure are popular."

Cody thought that was fucking hilarious. He burst out laughing, slapped his knee, and for good measure, slapped mine, really hard. The pain was sharp, bringing tears to my eyes. Then my phone rang again.

"Awww, fuck," Billy said. "It's the faggot's dad."

Cody frowned. "Answer it, and tell him you're going to a friend's house. You say anything else and I will throw you out of the car and then stab you to death. Under-*fucking*-stand?"

My heart beating a thousand beats per minute, I nodded.

Cody took the knife in his right hand and rested it on my thigh. It was a huge knife, at least six inches long, with a serrated back edge. I looked back and forth between him and Billy as the phone rang again.

Billy handed me the phone. "Answer it, *faggot*."

Cole

Sam answered on the fourth ring, and his tone of voice immediately put me on edge. "Hello?" His voice trembled just a little.

"Sam," I said. "I just got a weird call from Hayley. Is everything okay? Where are you going?"

He didn't bother to ask how I knew he was going somewhere. Instead, he answered in an unusually slow voice, "Dad, everything is fine. I'm going over to Brenna's. For her birthday. I'll be home really late, okay?"

I had a visceral reaction. What the fuck did that mean? *Going to Brenna's?* I felt nauseous. *For her birthday?*

In a quiet voice, I asked, "Sam, are you in danger?"

Sam sounded like he was going to cry, even while speaking in a fake cheery voice. "Yes, I am. Everything's fine. A couple of friends picked me up and they're taking me to Brenna's for her birthday party."

My heart was thumping wildly, and I felt rage coursing through my veins. "I understand. Try to keep your phone turned on. I'm coming after you right now. I love you."

"Okay, Dad! Talk to you later, love you!"

Sam clicked off the phone. For three or four seconds I sat there, panicking, then I looked up at Bubba. "Call 911. Tell them to send the police to Hubbard Lane, headed west, they'll see me speeding. Someone's kidnapped my kid."

Bubba gaped. I was already headed to the door, and he hadn't moved yet.

"Do it!" I shouted.

Sam

Cody drove the truck south out of Oxford on Route 21. It wasn't long, maybe ten minutes, before he turned left onto a gravel road and entered the woods. The truck bounced in the deep ruts as we went further back into the woods, finally leaving the gravel behind and driving down nothing but a dirt road.

The road ended abruptly in a tiny clearing. I had to get away—I had to get away, or I was going to die here. I knew just as sure as I knew anything in the world. I was terrified, drenched in sweat. Billy and Cody both opened their doors and Billy got out.

Cody said, "You get out that side."

"Please let me go," I whispered.

In a vicious tone, he responded, "Get the fuck out of the truck."

I slid over and got out on the passenger side.

I scanned the clearing and realized this might be my only chance. Cody was still getting out of the driver's side of the truck, and Billy was at least ten feet away, fiddling with his phone again. I didn't hesitate—I took off at a dead run.

Billy and Cody both shouted, and I assumed they were running after me, but I didn't take even half a second to look. I ran as fast as I could, sucking in painful gasps of air as I sprinted toward the road.

But I was wearing goddamned sandals, and I stubbed my toe once, then twice, and then one of the straps broke. I felt one of their hands grabbing at me, and I lurched ahead, then went flying. I landed flat on my face and cried out.

"Motherfucker," Billy screamed. He kicked me hard in the side, and I cried out and curled into a fetal position, and then Cody kicked me in the back.

I shielded my face with my arms and started to scream.

A second later, I felt Cody's arms grab me, and one hand clamped down over my mouth. I tried to bite, and he hissed, "Stop screaming or I'll fucking cut your throat."

I stopped, and he let go, shoving me roughly to the ground.

Cody said, "If it's a girl, maybe we should fuck it."

Billy said, "I don't think it's no girl. Look at that, its boobs are crooked." He reached out and grabbed my blouse and tore it open. I flinched.

Cody guffawed. "Is that fucking socks?" He doubled over, laughing in hysterics.

But Billy looked at me with utter hatred in his eyes. "Fucking *freak*."

Cody said, "I can't fucking believe it. Get some pictures." He started to yank at the socks, pulling them out of the bra. While he did it, Billy was taking the pictures with this phone and laughing.

"I'm gonna make you pay for hitting me with that rock and getting me and Ashley suspended." Cody brought his knife up, waving it slowly in front of my face.

My eyes tracked it, and I began to tremble.

"That's right, bitch. Watch the knife." Then he flicked the knife out, and I felt it slice at my cheek.

I screamed, and Billy shouted, "Holy *shit*, Cody!"

Cole

I slowed down at the main intersection near the mall, making sure I wasn't going to hit anybody, but I didn't stop for the red light. My phone was leaning against the speedometer with the map on the screen, the little icon representing Sam updating its location every minute. His phone was still on, and he was still in motion, headed south now on Highway 21.

When I ran a second red light, almost immediately a police car pulled out of the intersection behind me, blue lights flashing. I didn't stop or even slow down. The police car kept pace with me, siren blasting, and I just prayed that Bubba had actually called 911, and that this police officer was going to help, rather than hinder.

A moment later I got my answer. As I was approaching the busiest intersection in Oxford, just south of Interstate 20, the police car nosed ahead of me and into the intersection, blocking traffic and letting me by. As soon as I passed, he pulled out again. A moment later we were joined by another police car.

I drove as quickly as I could once I was on Route 21, and the two police cars kept pace with me. In less than five minutes, I was approaching Sam's position. Whoever had him had pulled off onto a side road and I began to slow down as I reached the spot.

There it was. A gravel road that cut into the woods. I took a quick left turn and pulled to a stop at the edge of the gravel road. I got out of the car as quickly as I could, as the first police car pulled up next to me. The officer motioned then reached across and opened the passenger side of the car.

I got in and said, "They're not far ahead. Or his phone is anyway." I showed him the point on the map.

The officer said, "There's a clearing back there. Sometimes the stoners at the high school hang out there. We'll go in quiet." He made a quick call on his radio and pulled forward with the lights and siren off. He didn't drive recklessly, but he didn't drive slowly either. As the police car rattled in the ruts and dips, he said, "Your cook from the restaurant said you thought your son was kidnapped?"

"Yeah."

A second later we drove into a clearing, and my eyes widened, as I tried to make sense of what I was seeing.

A gleaming black pickup truck was in the center of the clearing, both doors standing open. Nearby, two teenagers, one of them huge, were kicking at a prone body. I opened the police car door before it had even stopped and jumped out, running for Sam.

"Freeze, police!" I heard behind me.

That came from one of the police cars; the other officer ran beside me and grabbed my arm. "Stop!"

The two teenage boys heard it and started to run away. But the big one, Cody, was too late—the cop who'd shouted to stop raised his Taser and fired, a loud clicking sound followed by a scream as the guy hit the ground.

I tugged away and ran to Sam. At first I couldn't make sense of what I was seeing. He wore a skirt that looked like one of Erin's and a blue blouse that had been torn open. There was blood everywhere. Sam's cheek had been cut below the eye, a tiny slice but it was bleeding profusely. His chest was a mass of bruises and one of his hands was bright red, swollen. Even with all the blood, it was obvious that Sam was wearing makeup, mascara and I didn't know what all. He looked like a young woman.

Sam groaned, and I knelt beside him. "Sam? Can you hear me?"

One of his eyes was swollen shut and bruised almost black. But the other one opened, and my son looked out at me with such an expression of terror and grief that was worse than anything I'd seen since—ever. "Daddy?" His voice rose in a squeak as he said the word.

"You're gonna be okay, Sam. It's okay." I did my best to put my arms around my son, but I tried not to move him. God only knew if he had broken bones or what. He began to wail tears of pain and grief.

The cop who had given me the ride knelt beside me and said, "Ambulance is on the way. You did good, Dad. That was really quick thinking. I'm Officer Richmond."

"Cole Roberts."

I hadn't done good at all. I got here in time maybe to avert the worst disaster, but how the hell did this happen in the first place?

Thank God I'd made him keep location services on his phone.

Thank God Hayley had called.

Thank God he was smart enough to say the one thing guaranteed to make it absolutely clear what kind of danger he was in.

I looked around for just a second. Cody was being stuffed in the back of a police car. The other kid was nowhere in sight, but it seemed to me that the police would have him soon enough. In the meantime, I held my weeping son.

I heard the wailing of the ambulance as it approached down the dirt road, and a moment later the paramedics boiled out of it and surrounded Sam.

They gently pushed me away and began examining him. They spoke to each other in low professional tones, words like contusions and fractured ribs. Taking their time, they got Sam onto a stretcher and loaded into the ambulance.

"You're the dad?" one of them said.

I nodded. "Yeah."

"You can ride over with us. Hop in back."

I wasn't about to let anything else happen to Sam.

Twenty-Six

~~~~~~

Cole

At the hospital they made me wait outside of the emergency room. It was an old hospital. It looked like it had been built in the 1970s back when Fort McClellan was still open and the economy in Anniston wasn't crap. The waiting room was nearly full with tired people.

I paced for a few minutes then dialed Erin's number.

As I heard the first ring, I felt a layer of panic inside. Would Erin blame me? Would this be all about how I was a lousy dad and neglected the kids? My mind ran through a thousand possibilities of the kinds of conversations we'd had in the past. It happened quicker than thought, and then I stopped.

No.

Forget the past. Worry about *right now.*

She answered on the third ring.

"I don't want you to panic," I opened with. "Sam got beat up pretty bad by some boys at the high school, and we're at the hospital. It's not life-threatening." I tried to get the words out all at once, because I could only imagine the fear they would rise in her when I told her that Sam was in the hospital.

She gasped. "In the hospital? What happened?"

"I don't really know any details yet. They've got him in the emergency room and wouldn't let me back there. So I'm not sure exactly what happened."

She sounded a little impatient when she said, "Well, what *can* you tell me?"

I started telling her what I knew, starting with the rock-throwing incident yesterday afternoon. I told her about meeting with the assistant principal and his counselor, and ice cream with Sam and Hayley. From there, I moved on to this afternoon when I was waiting for Brian and David to show up, when Hayley's phone call came in.

That's when I lost my composure. "Erin, Sam said he was going to see *Brenna*. That a couple of friends had picked him up and were taking him to see Brenna for her birthday party." My voice cracked as I finished the sentence.

She gasped. "You've got to be kidding me."

"No … I'm not. I don't think he could say anything about being in danger, so he said that instead. Because he must have known how I would react. I followed his phone to them. These fuckers had taken him in the woods—I don't know what would have happened if I hadn't gotten there with the cops."

Erin's response was abrupt. "I'm coming back there."

It felt like being punched in the stomach. "No … no, you're not. This is the best chance we've had to find Brenna since she disappeared, Erin. You need to stay right where you are."

She struggled to speak but finally said in a choked voice, "But Sam needs me."

The emotions that ran through me were so incredibly complicated. I closed my eyes and stood stock-still. Of course Sam needed his mother. But he also needed me. That had been our pattern—I went off to work, and she took care of everything with the kids. But she couldn't be everywhere, and I had the feeling that right now what Sam needed more than anything else was for *me* to be right there with him through this.

My voice cracked again as I responded to her. "I know, Erin. Brenna needs you too. I've got Sam, and I promise you, I'd die before losing another one of our kids. I'll take care of Sam."

Shit. I was on the verge of crying. What was wrong with me? She didn't answer, and the silence stretched for a long time. Finally I said, "Erin, I need you to trust me with this."

When she finally replied, it was in a high-pitched voice, near tears. "It's hard to trust you."

I closed my eyes and covered my face, because now tears really were running down my face. I whispered, "I know. I'm sorry."

She responded in a quiet voice, "Me too. You're sure Sam will be okay?"

I exhaled a long breath. "The EMTs said it didn't look like he would suffer any permanent injury. I promise I'll look out for him. You focus on Brenna. How is that going?"

"It's really hard, Cole. I've been putting up flyers everywhere … I have to get more printed. But I found at least two people who say they've seen her in the last month. One was a prostitute. The other was the late shift waitress at a twenty-four-hour diner here. I'm working with a detective with the Portland police, she gets it. She *really* gets it. And Stan Wilcox flew out. He's trying to see if they can get a match for the tattoos Brenna had in her picture."

I swallowed. "So there's hope."

"Yeah," she replied in a breathy voice. "There's hope."

I scanned the waiting room but still no one had called for me. I didn't want to get off the phone. This phone call, as tenuous as it was, seemed like the closest connection Erin and I had made in a long time.

"How's work?" she asked.

I sighed. "I don't even know where to begin."

"Is everything okay?" she asked in a concerned voice.

I collapsed into one of the waiting room chairs. "No. It's a disaster." I told Erin the story, starting with the night before last, when Dakota had walked into the back room crying and ending with Brian telling me to wait at the restaurant to meet with him and David.

"That's when I got the call from Hayley. I don't even know if I have a job right now."

In a hesitant tone, she asked, "What did Jeremiah say about all of this?"

"He said not to worry … that he was going to talk to the CEO about it and that I had done the right thing. I just don't know what happens next. I'm afraid to lose my job, Erin. I don't know what we would do if that happened."

She was silent for a long time. I felt like I was dangling on a rope twisting in the wind. Saying that made me feel naked, exposed in a way that seemed wrong and uncomfortable.

"Try not to worry about it. You did the right thing."

I wondered what it cost her to say that.

The tone of a second call coming in interrupted us. I glanced at my phone … it was Jeremiah. "I gotta go, Erin. Jeremiah's calling."

"Okay. Cole … thanks for telling me how you felt about the work thing. And for watching out for Sam."

I responded, "I love you."

She disconnected. As I switched to answer Jeremiah's call, I tried to remember the last time she had said those three words to me.

All I could do was keep trying.

"Cole? Where are you? Your cook said some crazy shit about something happening to Sam?"

"I'm at the emergency room at the Regional Medical Center. Jeremiah … some guys from Sam's school grabbed him and took him out to the woods. They were kicking the shit out of him when I got there. He's hurt pretty bad."

Jeremiah said in a low tone, "I'll be there in fifteen minutes." Then he disconnected.

I sank into my chair and stared. I didn't feel anything like the confidence that I had expressed to Erin about Sam's prognosis. It was true that the EMTs had reassured me. But the anxiety I felt right now, not knowing what was happening inside the emergency room, was threatening to overwhelm me.

There was nothing I could do ... just wait. In the meantime, I puzzled over some of the details. Why had Sam been dressed in Erin's clothes? There was something strange there. Was it some kind of prank? Had the two boys, Cody and the other one, broken into the house or somehow forced Sam to dress that way before they left? That made no sense at all, nor did it jibe with the fact that Sam was clearly wearing makeup.

I felt like there was something else I was missing here, some piece of the puzzle that, when it appeared, would make everything else fall into place. But I didn't know what it was.

My phone rang, an unfamiliar 256 area code phone number. I answered quickly.

"Mr. Roberts? This is Patricia Mullins. I'm Sam's counselor, we met yesterday? I was calling because I received an urgent phone call from Sam's friend Hayley ... I wanted to find out how Sam was."

I closed my eyes and let out a long breath. "I don't have Hayley's number or I would have called her by now. You can let her know that she probably saved Sam's life."

At the other end of the line she gasped. "Can you tell me what happened?" In a few brief sentences I outlined what little I knew.

I was surprised by her response. "Mr. Roberts, I care about Sam a great deal. Would I be intruding if I came down there and waited with you?"

I don't know why this request suddenly caused me to get all choked up. But it did.

"Of course not," I said. "Please come. Sam's spoken very highly of you."

At that moment, Jeremiah walked through the revolving door. I said, "I've got to go now, but at least for the moment we're in the waiting area outside the emergency room. I'll let you know if anything changes. Is this your cell phone?"

"That's right. I'll be there shortly."

As Jeremiah approached, I stood up. Without a word, he walked up to me and wrapped his arms around me in a bear hug. "Jesus, Cole. I'm so sorry this happened." He let go and stepped back, putting one hand on each shoulder. "How is he doing? How are *you* doing?"

I shook my head. "I haven't heard anything in the last little while. And, I'm hanging in there. Just worried about Sam."

Jeremiah nodded and leaned back. He closed his eyes and seemed to be mouthing something. After a minute he opened them and he said, "I don't want you to worry in the slightest about work, okay? I've got you covered there. Right now I want you to worry about Sam and nothing else."

I froze at that moment. A woman in a blue uniform opened the locked door to the emergency room. "Mr. Roberts?"

I was on my feet headed toward the door instantly, Jeremiah trailing right behind me. When I reached the door, the woman said, "Dr. Sims will see you now. Just family."

I put a hand on Jeremiah's shoulder. "He *is* family."

Without further comment, she led us beyond the door into a bustling ward. I looked around, but I didn't see Sam anywhere. A young-looking doctor approached, in his early thirties with slightly longish black hair and a dark five o'clock shadow.

"I'm Mark Sims," he said.

"How is Sam?"

With a concerned look on his face, Dr. Sims said, "Sam's going to be just fine. I'd like permission to do a CT scan just to be on the safe side, because I'm concerned about a possible concussion. It looks like she had a fairly serious blow to the head. I don't expect the cut to scar at all. It was a very sharp knife, so it was a clean cut and it should heal up nicely. Two cracked ribs. That's the worst of it, the rest are minor cuts and contusions and look a lot worse than they actually are. I'd say she's very lucky. But I do have some questions for you, sir."

My eyebrows pressed together in irritation at the repeated use of the pronoun *she*. Surely the doctor knew the gender of his patient. I looked at Jeremiah, who seemed just as puzzled as I was, then back at the doctor. "What questions?"

"Are you aware Sam has been taking puberty-blocking hormones? At least until recently?"

"What are you talking about?"

The doctor frowned. "To be honest, at first we thought she was twelve. Because of Sam's size and build, it's obvious she hasn't gone through puberty—"

In a much sharper tone than I intended, I said, "Why do you keep calling my son *she*?"

Doctor Sims frowned and said, "It's like that, is it?"

"What?" I cried. "I don't know what you're talking about!"

287

He stared at me with a skeptical expression on his face for a surprisingly long time. Then he said, "You really don't, do you? Here ... have a seat in here, so we can talk for a few minutes." He gestured toward an empty exam room.

I stepped into the room he indicated and sat on the hard metal and plastic chair. The doctor took a seat on a rolling stool across from me. Jeremiah stayed in the doorway.

The doctor sighed. "Mr. Roberts, first you should know that it took me a long time to convince Sam to let me discuss this with you. She's terrified you're going to kick her out or worse. Are you familiar with the term gender dysphoria?"

I shrugged. "No."

He nodded. "It's the medical term for when a person's interior sense of their own gender is in conflict with the gender they are assigned at birth."

I was starting to get a sharp headache. "Like ... transvestites?"

"No, not at all. We're not talking about a sexual kink or something, where people occasionally like to cross-dress. What we're talking about is a deep-seated sense of identity. People with gender dysphoria frequently have a terrible sense of distress about their gender. Inside they think and believe and act as if they are one gender, but it's not the gender consistent with their genitalia at birth."

I rubbed my forehead, struggling with a tempest of emotion—shock and grief and anger, and on some level, a complete lack of surprise.

"And you're saying that Sam is ... is..."

"Transgender." The doctor rubbed his hand on his chin, making a slight scratching sound. "I'll be perfectly honest with you, Mr. Roberts. I wouldn't typically tell a parent about this. But there are two factors which drove me to do so. The first is that, based on the things Sam was saying in the exam room, I believe that she may be suicidal. She's in shock but clearly believes that you're going to reject her after seeing her dressed as a female. The second reason is that it's plainly obvious that Sam has been taking puberty-blocking hormones. She refused to tell me where she got them, which means she probably bought them on the Internet. That's extremely dangerous."

I shook my head. "What are puberty-blocking hormones?"

He responded, "There are pretty specific guidelines from the American Medical Association on how to treat adolescents with gender dysphoria. One option for children Sam's age are puberty blockers, because they are fully reversible, unlike the types of hormone therapies and surgical interventions if someone was to actually transition after the age of eighteen."

I felt myself involuntarily recoil. Medical procedures ... transition ... the doctor was talking about a sex change. For my son. I had to struggle not to get up and march out. Instead, I kept a tight grip on the arms of the chair I sat in as he continued.

"What puberty blockers do, is they buy some time for the patient to make a decision. With women who transition, it's not as difficult for them to pass, because hormone treatments and breast reduction are generally enough, and there are increasingly effective surgical options for a complete transition. It's much more difficult for men who've fully gone through puberty to pass. Sometimes doctors will prescribe puberty-blocking hormones in order to give the child time to determine if this is truly what they want, before permanent physical changes happen."

"And you're saying Sam probably got them off the Internet?" For some reason I wanted to cry.

The doctor nodded. I leaned back in the chair and rubbed my hands on my face, closing my eyes for just a second and trying to get a grip on myself. I couldn't get this wrong. I'd already lost one child.

I felt Jeremiah's hand on my shoulder. That contact gave me strength I needed. I dropped my hands and said, "So ... what's next?"

Dr. Sims took a deep breath and said, "That's largely up to you. But I can lay out some of the options, as well as potential consequences of some of those options.

I nodded. "Please do. I'm lost."

He had a grave expression on his face. "First, I want to make it clear that something like a third of transgender children end up either kicked out of their homes, or they run away after being rejected or mistreated by their families. The statistics are horrible. The kids who experience that have an extremely high suicide rate, as well as an extremely high mortality rate from homicide. If you reject Sam based on this, you will be sending her down that path."

I flinched. "Go on," I said, my voice breaking up.

"Sam may or may not want to live as a female now. She says that she does—she says she's unwilling to ever present as a boy again. That she'll run away if you make her. We don't exactly live in the most progressive part of the country, Mr. Roberts. Sam is going to need a lot of strength and courage to go through with this, and the odds of success are extremely low without some support."

I felt my hands squeeze around the arms of the chair, and I completely lost control of my voice as I said, "How long has he been keeping this a secret?"

Sims frowned and said, "She says she's known her whole life. And that the only person who knew was your daughter Brenna."

I gasped. Sam had been keeping this huge secret for years. And had lost anyone to confide in at all when Brenna disappeared. I wanted to go find him right now and just hold him forever. In a hoarse voice I said, "Brenna's been missing for more than two years. Sam must have felt so alone."

I blinked my eyes as my voice cracked, trying to hold back the emotion threatening to pour out. I put my face in my hands and felt my whole body shudder.

Then I felt Jeremiah's arm on my shoulder. In a voice as emotional as mine, he said, "Sam is going to be just fine. We'll take care of him, okay? All of us. We won't leave him alone."

With that, I fell apart. I wept like I haven't since Brenna disappeared. The doctor said, "I'll give you a few minutes."

Then he stepped away.

It took me almost ten minutes to pull myself together. "I'm sorry, man."

Jeremiah looked at me and just said, "Don't be sorry. Seems to me those tears were a long time coming."

My phone buzzed and I reflexively took it out of my pocket and looked at it. It was Mrs. Mullins, Sam's counselor. I wondered how much she knew about this, if anything. I thought about it for a few seconds, then said, "Sam's counselor from his high school is here. I want to bring her back here and talk with her about this. Sam needs all the help he can get.

"I'll go talk with her," he said. "You go see Sam."

I stood and put my hand on my friend's shoulder. I said, "I won't ever forget what you've done for my family."

Jeremiah grinned. "We *are* family."

Doctor Sims had returned and was standing in the doorway.

I turned to the doctor. "Can I see Sam?"

The doctor looked as if he wanted to say something else. He studied me for a minute, as if trying to determine what kind of a man I was. The look made me self-conscious, uncomfortable, and fully aware of the fact that in this area, in my past, I had never measured up.

I was going to do the best I could now. "Please," I said.

"This way."

Anxiety ripped through me as I followed the doctor across the crowded emergency room. My kids had been hurt enough. Too much. I felt raw and damaged. But wasn't that what my whole family was like? Damaged? For the thousandth time that week, I wished that I could pack Sam in the car and drive west.

The doctor opened the door and poked his head in. "Sam? Your father's here to see you."

I closed my eyes for just a second and took a deep breath into my lungs. I could do this.

The doctor stepped out of the doorway and motioned for me to enter.

I stepped into the room. Sam was half sitting up in a hospital bed. A large bandage covered the cheek that had been cut, but nothing could disguise the swollen eye socket and the black and blue bruises disfiguring the right side of Sam's face. But the hardest part was Sam's eyes. He was afraid. No ... he was terrified. He was terrified of *me*, and the possibility that I would reject him, that I would reject who he was. He was afraid of being rejected and alone.

Images flashed through my mind. Sam as a toddler, stumbling along behind his older sister, giggling and waving his fat little hands in the air. Sam falling asleep in my lap the day he was stung by a bee in our backyard. Three-year-old Sam shrieking with delight as I tossed him in the air.

But other sights went through my mind, harsher ones. I remembered sitting at the table talking about the news with Erin, when a felon had sued the state to pay for a gender reassignment surgery. I'd been caustic in my arguments, hostile. *Why in the hell should the taxpayers pick up the bill for sexually confused freaks? They should be in therapy, not getting surgery.*

For Christ's sake, comments like that must have been like knives to Sam. How could I have been so hideously blind?

"Sam..." I didn't know what to say.

Sam tried to put on a defensive face, jutting his chin out just a little bit. "Do you hate me now?"

I jerked my head in negation. "Of course not. Sam ... you're my son—my child," I corrected myself. "I know you were afraid of how I would react. And I'm sorry that I made you feel like you had to hide this from me."

As I talked, Sam began to sob. I walked over and crouched beside the hospital bed, taking Sam's right hand between both of mine. My voice dropped, and I struggled to get the next words out. "I'm so sorry, Sam. But I promise you, there's nothing you could do to make me stop loving you."

Sam's face seemed to contort as he cried. I stood and leaned over the bed, carefully hugging him. He couldn't speak anymore, he was crying so hard.

I just whispered, "I'll always love you, no matter what. Always."

It was incredibly awkward standing and bending over the side of the bed, so I climbed up in it and let him cry on my shoulder. I kept my arms around him, and stroked his hair, and told myself that there was no way I was going to lose *this* child. I couldn't change the past, but everything I did, now and in five minutes and forevermore, would make up the future. And it was going to be a future where my kid didn't have to be afraid to talk to me.

Twenty-Seven

~~~~~~

Cole

Twenty minutes later, the doctor poked his head in the door, a quizzical look on his face. I raised a finger to my lips, and whispered, "Sam's asleep."

Very carefully, I extricated myself. The left side of my shirt was wet with Sam's tears and some of my own. He stirred just a little bit, but I tucked him in and he fell into a deeper sleep. I stood there for just a second, watching the rise and fall of his breath. Then I turned back to the doctor. We stepped out of the room.

Jeremiah and Mrs. Mullins were in the hallway.

Jeremiah immediately said, "Seems like Sam just told Mrs. Mullins this morning."

My eyes darted to her. She nodded. "I have to say, Mr. Roberts ... Sam was deeply afraid that you were going to reject her."

I took a deep breath. "You can call me Cole, please. And five years ago, or maybe even a year ago, I might have. I don't know. But it seems to me that Sam is hurting more than any kid deserves to bear, and I can't add to that." I turned to the doctor and raised an eyebrow. "In the meantime, we got sidetracked into that discussion, but you didn't say very much about Sam's physical prognosis."

The doctor smiled. "Sorry, I was still doing mental triage—we take care of the most serious injuries first. Physically, Sam is going to be fine. I don't think she is going to have much of a scar from the cut on her face, and while the bruising looks awful, there's no swelling inside her skull or other signs of concussion. She'll have to keep her chest bound for possibly a few weeks, there's two cracked ribs. But with some painkillers, I'm comfortable releasing her tonight."

Thank God. I exhaled, not even realizing that I had been holding my breath. I staggered, and Jeremiah took my arm.

"Hold on there, buddy," Jeremiah said.

"I've got other patients I've got to get to," the doctor said. "We'll check back in with you when Sam is ready to be released."

I looked at Jeremiah and Mrs. Mullins and realized that it was really only just beginning. I didn't know whether this was a permanent condition or a phase or what, but I had to be prepared to support Sam regardless. I was going to need to learn about the subject. But there were other complications. When would Sam go back to school? And, based on what the doctor said, would Sam want to go back dressing as a girl? I couldn't imagine what that would be like for … her? The doctor seemed to use female pronouns. Was that the right thing to do? I didn't even know that much. I asked the two of them to come with me to the hospital cafeteria to talk about this.

Once we were settled in at a table, I said, "Mrs. Mullins—"

"Pat. You can call me Pat."

I took a deep breath—stalling for time I think—then said, "Look … I know next to nothing about gender, uh, problems. I'll learn. I'll learn whatever I need to help Sam. But right at this moment, I'm at a loss."

Pat said, "You should understand that it was only this morning that Sam told me. Although it makes complete sense in retrospect."

"How so?"

"Well, I met Sam on the first day of school. He … well, *she* … was hiding in a stairwell because she skipped gym. I took her back to my office and was prepared to call the assistant principal, but we ended up talking. Sam wouldn't say why she didn't want to go to gym; it was very clear that she was terrified. That's when I learned about her sister. So I made arrangements for Sam to take gym one-on-one with me."

I tried to imagine the scene. I'd never known Sam to skip a class.

"Can you imagine being a girl and being forced to use the boys locker room in high school?" Pat said the words in a slow, sad voice. My mind latched onto one phrase. *Being a girl.* Not *feeling* like a girl. *Being* a girl.

I had never really believed that people who were transgender should be taken seriously. They weren't women, they were *men dressed up* as women. But now, I was faced with dealing with this on a personal level, with someone I cared about, with someone I loved, it forced me to rethink everything. I had always thought of people who were transgender or whatever as mentally ill. They "felt" like they were a different gender. I even remembered that obnoxious debate in college about it, when I said, *I feel like a hippopotamus, but that doesn't make it so.*

293

"That raises an important question. What happens when Sam goes back to school? If he follows through with publicly identifying himself."

Him. Her. Even something so simple as pronouns became complicated.

She said, "I'm not going to try to lie to you, Cole. The other kids will make life very difficult for Sam if she chooses that."

"I figured as much." I let out a deep sigh. "What I really wish I could do is just pack Sam up in the van and drive to Oregon. Let him ... her ... spend some time figuring things out while we help Erin look for Brenna."

Pat nodded. "If it's an option, it would be worth doing. That would also give some time for this afternoon's events to die down a little. Taking a semester to heal might not be a bad thing."

I shook my head. "I was just thinking out loud. That's not an option."

"Hold on a second. Why isn't it an option?" Jeremiah asked.

"Well, the job. You know how difficult it was for me to find work. Not to mention I'm on probation. And while you and Ayanna have been insanely generous, I can't ask for more. I can't."

Jeremiah shook his head. "I'll talk to Jimmy Junior. We'll get you a leave of absence. You'll have to go back on deck when you come back, and wait for a new restaurant, but that might not be a bad idea anyway, given the business with the mayor here. We could potentially move you to the Atlanta area. That way you could get Sam enrolled in a school where he'd be a little more accepted."

I stared at Jeremiah, stunned. "Do you really think that's doable?"

Jeremiah grinned. "I do."

I grimaced. "Where does that leave Dakota?"

"She the waitress they were messing with?"

I nodded yes.

Jeremiah said, "I'll make sure that she is taken care of. I'll happily make an appointment with the mayor myself." He finished that sentence with a grin.

I flashed to the things I would have to do. We'd have to triage our things and figure out what we should bring with us, and I'd have to go see my probation officer to get permission to leave the state. Would she even authorize it? When I thought about it, all I could feel was hope. I didn't know if we'd find Brenna or not, but we'd damn sure try. I nodded.

"If it is doable, then I want to do it."

Jeremiah replied, "I'll make the call."

Cole

An hour later I was back in the exam room with Dr. Sims and with Sam.

"I'm giving you prescriptions for painkillers. One is for high-dosage ibuprofen. Unless it gets really bad, stick with that. But if it gets bad, I'm also giving you two days' worth of OxyContin. Just a reminder that OxyContin is highly addictive. You'll want to limit your usage and only take it if it's really bad. Okay?"

Sam nodded, and I said, "Okay."

The doctor gave Sam a stern look. "I want to be clear that buying mail order drugs from another country is a highly dangerous activity. Taking the puberty blockers without a doctor's prescription … not smart. And you're a pretty smart kid."

Sam nodded then opened his mouth as if to try to explain. The doctor cut him off. "I understand that you felt desperate, but I want you to exercise more caution in the future. I'm giving you a prescription for a sixty-day supply. Not renewable … you'll need to follow up with an endocrinologist at a minimum. I'd also recommend seeing a psychiatric specialist who has worked with gender issues."

Sam shook his head. "There's nothing wrong with me, I don't need—"

The doctor held a hand up, palm toward Sam. "I know that. But I also know you've been through a great deal of trauma, and you're talking about taking on an incredibly stressful transition in your life. It's to help you cope. If the insurance is a problem, there's a sliding-scale clinic in Anniston that you can go to. Besides, if you're really determined to transition completely, almost no doctor in the country will approve it unless you have two years of therapy first."

I didn't know how I felt about the doctor giving a prescription for hormones. I hadn't asked for them, and I wasn't sure they were necessary. On the other hand, if I didn't fill that prescription, would Sam somehow order more? I decided to table it for now until I could learn a little more.

With that, we were finished. It was almost eight p.m. now and Sam was obviously exhausted. When we walked out into the waiting area, Pat stood and walked to Sam and wrapped him in a gentle hug. Jeremiah looked at me and said, "You've been approved for two months' leave. Paid."

Two months? That was far longer than I had expected. I almost physically staggered. Sam stepped back from his counselor and said, "Two months' leave? What's going on?"

I said to Sam, "We're going to go to Portland. To look for your sister."

Sam's eyes widened. "Are you serious?"

295

I nodded.

Sam leaned against me. Then, in the barest of whispers, he said, "Thank you. *Thank you.*"

I thought I had run out of tears, but at that moment, I felt more welling up.

On the way home, Sam asked me, "Before we leave tomorrow, can I go see Hayley for a little while? She texted me. She's in an emergency group home and won't be going to school tomorrow."

"Of course. It'll take some time to get things packed. I still have to get permission from my parole officer, and I don't know how hard that's going to be. Or even if it will be possible."

Sam said, "I understand. And Dad?"

"Yeah?" I scanned the road ahead of us.

"I know we don't have much money. I'd be willing to go to Goodwill or wherever … but can I get some clothes?"

Sam was right. We *didn't* have much money. It was hard for me to classify the money that Jeremiah had deposited into our account as ours. But this was a test, in a way, and one I was determined to pass.

"Yeah, of course. We can't spend a lot, but we'll go and you can pick some things out."

That night, after Sam went to bed, I stayed up late. I spent the night reading about gender identity, about how it manifested, and how people dealt with it. Much of what I read was not encouraging. People who were transgender who didn't "pass" often faced a tremendous number of walls, hostility, and discrimination.

Now that I was looking for it, I found far too much information. People who had been murdered or beaten because of who they were. Housing discrimination, and job discrimination, both of which were perfectly legal because gender identity wasn't a protected status under civil rights laws. Bathrooms were an issue, especially in public places like schools, universities, and employers.

In that context, the hormone-based puberty blockers made a lot more sense. My own preconceptions and prejudices against transgender women were based on the worst kinds of stereotypes. I think the first time I had ever encountered anything of the sort was watching The Rocky Horror Picture Show as a teenager, and I felt ashamed that I had judged an entire class of people based off of that.

With that, I made the decision to support Sam with the hormone blockers. Erin might fight me on it … I didn't know. But if that's what Sam truly needed, then I was going to do everything I could to make sure he … no, *she* … got it.

My confusion about pronouns turned out to be not that uncommon either. Thanks to Google, I learned that it was often a controversial topic among transgender activists. But the bottom line seemed to be that the appropriate pronoun was whatever gender the subject identified as. So I steeled myself to remember that Sam was a girl, and that she needed me to recognize that.

I felt an odd sort of grief. I would do whatever I had to do to take care of Sam. Even if that meant that Sam became a daughter instead of a son. But *I would miss having a son.*

It was after eleven before I called Erin back. I had texted her throughout the afternoon from the hospital, most recently with the update that Sam was definitely going to be released. But I hadn't felt equipped to talk about the rest of it. Now, armed with some knowledge, I felt like I could.

I didn't know how to have this conversation. So I walked outside then sat on the rocker on the front porch. A chilly breeze blew over me, the coldest I had felt this year. Maybe summer was finally going to release its hold.

Erin answered on the third ring.

"How is Sam?"

I took a deep breath. This was going to be difficult. "Sam will be okay. No concussion, just lots and lots of bruising and two cracked ribs. But … there are some things we need to discuss."

Her voice went tense and high-pitched. "What is it?"

I tried to breathe in, the words caught in my throat. I didn't know why I had so much anxiety about this.

"Cole … *what is it?*"

"Erin … Sam is transgender."

"What? What are you talking about?"

I sighed. "It means that … her internal sense of self, her perception of self, is female."

Her response was caustic. "I know what the word means. But *Sam* isn't transgender. What gave you that idea?"

I tried to be as gentle as possible in both my tone and words. Erin had always been highly liberal compared to my own conservative politics. But sometimes things were different when it was your own kid involved. "We talked about it for a long time, Erin. Sam's kept a secret, but she's felt that way for a very long time."

She sounded like she was going to break into tears. "And you just … accepted it without question? You start calling Sam *she*? How much do you know about this stuff anyway? You've always been the one who said that people with gender identity issues were *freaks.*"

I flinched. Because no matter how harsh it sounded, she was right. I *had* always been that person. I sighed. "Erin, I know I've been incredibly judgmental in the past. This is our *kid* we're talking about."

297

Her rejoinder was harsh. "This is our *son* we're talking about."

The pain in her voice made my heart ache. "I know, love. I know."

We were silent for what seemed like a long time. Then she said, "Can I talk with him?"

In as gentle a tone as I could muster, I said, "Sam went right to sleep when we came in. It's been a really traumatic day. We'll call first thing in the morning."

"I feel like I should come home. And be there for Sam."

"No ... it's too early to give up. Plus, things here have changed dramatically."

Hard to believe that in the midst of the news about Sam, that I had left out such important things. There was too much going on. "Jeremiah was at the hospital with me. He talked with the CEO and got me approved for two months of paid leave. He's going to try to find a restaurant in Atlanta for me to take over so Sam isn't stuck going to school here anymore."

"What about school?" Erin asked in a sharp tone.

"I was planning on withdrawing her from school in the morning," I said. "We'll let her have a couple of months to adjust and figure out what's next."

She sighed. "Are you sure that's a good idea?"

"Erin, it's *essential*. Sam really needs some time. I'm going to talk to my probation officer in the morning and get clearance to travel. Then we're going to pack up and head to Portland."

She sniffed, and I could tell that on the other end of the line she was silently crying. In an unsteady voice she asked, "Tell me about your talk with Sam. Tell me everything."

So I told Erin the story. Starting with finding Sam in Erin's clothes, and the initial tense discussion with the doctor.

"And then the doctor started talking about how many kids like Sam get kicked out of their homes, or run away, or end up committing suicide or murdered."

I had to struggle to keep my voice under control as I continued talking. "Erin, I knew right then that no matter what happens we have to let Sam know that we love him, that we accept him *or her* for who she is. I'm *not* going to lose another child, Erin."

At the other end of the line, almost three thousand miles away, Erin sobbed. For what felt like the hundredth time that day, I felt tears going down my face too. What was *happening* to me?

In a choked whisper, she said, "Do you ever wish we could go back? To when they were our babies? To when ... when we loved each other?"

"Yeah," I said in a very quiet voice. "I wish for that all the time."

Twenty-Eight

~~~~~~

Brenna: Four Weeks Ago

When I walked out of the front door of the jail, I saw Rick and Nialla sitting in a gleaming white Mercedes right across the street.

Rick had spent two months scheming to get the car, pushing us to make more and more money. It was the longest time we'd stayed in the same place in a while, almost three months in Las Vegas. But Cinnamon got arrested in Vegas, and word on the street was that she'd talked. I wasn't clear what happened after that, except that we left Vegas without her. For the first time in a year, we were back down to the three of us, Rick and Nialla and me.

I didn't want to go out on the track anyway. I hated working the street. But after buying the fucking car, then relocating us to Portland, Rick was short on cash. On the first night here, he'd said, "I'm raising your quota to fifteen-hundred dollars a night."

The second night, I'd failed to make that quota, coming up short almost two hundred dollars. So at three o'clock in the morning, he dumped me out of the car and said, "I'll be back in an hour. You better have my fucking money then."

Instead, an hour later, I was in jail.

I got in the back of the Mercedes and sank into the leather seat. As usual, Nialla rode in the front passenger seat and Rick drove. He didn't say a word when I got in the car.

"You okay, sweetie?" Nialla asked.

I shrugged. "Tired. It was awful in there." From the moment that cop Mackey had grabbed my breast—*just checking for weapons*, he said, smirking—I knew I was in trouble. Maybe not from the cops: Rick had coached me over and over again, for two years, on how to deal with them. But from *Rick*. Because he was unpredictable and dangerous. And now, sitting in the back seat of the car, I felt a cold, sinking sense of dread, because he wasn't saying anything, not anything at all.

Nialla asked me something, but it took me a minute to even realize she was talking, because every nerve ending was tuned toward Rick. The muscles in his hands were twitching on the steering wheel, the veins on his forearms prominent. He was furious about something.

Nialla gave me a warning glance, a look I recognized. When Rick was like this, we kept our mouths shut. We only spoke when spoken to. We jumped when he said jump.

When he was like this, he was terrifying. The one time I'd been in the hospital in my life was when Rick thought I had disobeyed him. He hit me twice with a baseball bat, then when I collapsed he carried me to the emergency room and told them I'd been mugged. I verified the story, of course. What else was I going to do with him sitting right there in the waiting room?

"Did you fucking snitch?" This question was in a deceptively calm tone. I was in deadly danger if I responded the wrong way now.

"No. Of course I didn't."

His shoulders tensed at my response. "Then how the hell did you get out so quickly?"

"I don't know, Rick. They said I had to come back for an arraignment a week from Tuesday. They took my fingerprints and asked a bunch of questions and let me go."

Rick was driving in circles in the darkness, up Eighty-second Avenue, across and back down. In a couple of minutes we were going to pass the police station all over again. "What kind of questions?"

"My name and age and where I was from. I gave them the story you always told me to, that I'm from Maryland, that I'm nineteen. They wanted to know if I had a pimp and I told them no."

I had a flash of memory, of me and Sam with Mom at the fire station, being fingerprinted. I was maybe ten. Was it for a missing kids' program of some kind? Did they still have those fingerprints on file? No one had said anything while I was in the jail, but would they figure out who I was?

On our right, we passed the church parking lot where I'd been arrested just a few hours earlier. A moment later, the police station on our left. A block beyond there, a girl who looked maybe thirteen stood on the corner. Just before we passed her, a car pulled up and she leaned forward to talk to the driver. She nodded once, then opened the car door and got in, taking one quick look around for cops. A moment later Rick pulled into the parking lot at the diner. He drove to the back of the lot and parked next to the dumpster.

Rick casually turned around in his seat and pointed his pistol at my face. I froze, all of my attention narrowed down to the circle of the barrel, inky black steel in the darkness.

"Are you telling me the truth?"

A jumble of words poured out of me. "Yes, Rick, I'm telling the truth, please don't hurt—"

"Shut up. You stupid fucking whore. Worthless. Why did you let yourself get arrested? I can't fucking believe it. I ought to shoot you right here and now and then drop you in the dumpster."

"Rick…" Nialla said his name in a pleading tone.

He never looked at her, just kept his cold eyes on me. "Should I do it, Strawberry? Should I pull the trigger now?"

I shook my head. "No. Please, no. I didn't say anything. I didn't give them my real name. I didn't mention you at all. Please…"

He stared at me for a second more then shook his head. "If I find out you're lying to me, you are dead. Understand?"

I didn't let my sudden relief show. Instead I just said, "I understand."

He put the pistol away. "Let's get some breakfast then." He said it in such a casual tone, the last ten minutes might not have ever happened.

***

Two nights later, Nialla said to me, "I can't do this anymore."

I was a little hazy at that point—I'd had three drinks in little more than an hour — but that statement caught my attention. I sat up and looked at her. "What?"

She looked at me. Her expression looked dead. "I hate this. I've always hated it. Maybe sometimes I thought he was telling the truth, or that he'd change or something … I don't know, but one of these days he's going to kill you or me or both of us."

I swallowed. The idea of Nialla leaving me alone with Rick was inconceivable. "Where would you go?"

She shrugged. "I don't know. Just somewhere Rick can't find me. Maybe put up my own ads and go independent."

Rick would find the ads. She was deluding herself. She said, "Come with me."

I shivered. "I'm afraid."

She whispered her response. "I know. Me too."

winter flower

I got up and fumbled through the drawer beside the hotel room bed then packed a pipe with weed. Once I had a good lungful, I passed it to Nialla.

Talk of running away reminded me of Rose. Rose had been about my age when Rick picked her up at the bus station in El Paso. She had run away from home, right into the arms of a nightmare. She was only with us for a few weeks—she tried to run away in Tampa. But she didn't have any money or anybody to call, and she quickly went rogue, working the track.

We'd already stayed in Tampa longer than we normally did in any one place. Not long after that, about two weeks, Rick showed up at the apartment as agitated as I'd ever seen him. "Pack up, we're leaving," he said.

Both of us had gaped at him … he'd lined up a dozen appointments between the two of us. Leaving now meant abandoning a lot of money. Rick didn't walk away from money unless there was a really good reason.

The next night, in Miami, I saw on the news that Rose's body had turned up. She'd been murdered.

"We'll have to be careful," I said. Even though Rick wasn't around, I found myself whispering. "I don't want to end up like Rose."

Nialla shuddered.

"Where is he, anyway?" I asked.

She sneered. "He's got a new girl he's trying to recruit. Eighth grader he met the other day."

"Jesus Christ."

Nialla shook her head. "I know."

"What's her story?"

Nialla shrugged. "He said she's a foster kid. I don't know what else."

I shook my head. This girl wouldn't be the first. Rick's pattern was to watch for girls who were a mess. The girls who were in trouble, or from broken homes, or into drugs. He'd fascinate them, then reel them in like fish; they were about to be thrown out on the deck of a boat, wriggling and flopping, unable to breathe. Sometimes he'd only keep them for a week or two and then move on. He had sold two girls, one nineteen years old and the other fifteen years old. I had watched helplessly from a locked apartment as the younger one was taken away, tossed into the back of the van and taken who knows where. He threatened more than once to do the same to me if I ever tried to contact anyone from home or make trouble for him. But his darkest threats were for girls who ran away, and Rose was proof he meant it.

Whatever else Nialla was thinking about leaving had to be tabled—we had appointments scheduled.

That week we were doing incalls; typically, the first week in a new city that's all we'd do. It was safer that way. Once Rick had a feel for the tempo of a given location, we would start doing limited numbers of outcalls. He could charge more for those, but they were far more dangerous. Not from police arrest, but from the customers. Twice, once in San Francisco and once in Atlanta, customers had pulled guns on me. Several other times I'd been raped when I refused to have unprotected sex or to do certain acts which were uncomfortable or painful. At least with incalls, usually either Nialla or Rick was nearby if I needed to call for help.

The next few days were uneventful. I skipped my arraignment hearing—at Rick's orders, of course—and on our tenth day in Portland we started taking outcalls.

A few days after that I met Kaylee, the girl Rick was trying to recruit. We were at a tiny dive bar on Eighty-second Avenue, sitting in the back. I sat beside Rick and kept my mouth shut. He faked listening sympathetically as she talked about her foster father (who hit her) and her stepfather (who had raped her). He showered her with compliments, telling her how beautiful she was and how sorry he was that she had to live like that. I almost rolled my eyes, but I knew if I did he would likely kill me.

Kaylee was thirteen. She had chestnut hair that hung well below her shoulders and wore a too-small tank top which revealed just budding breasts, a flat tummy, and a tiny waist. She was falling for his bullshit.

All he could see was dollar signs.

He didn't take her back to the hotel that night. Rick would keep working her for a while, with soft words and gifts, until she was so confused about who she was that she'd believe anything he told her.

I put her out of my mind. Nialla didn't bring up running away again, at least not in the next couple of weeks. Not until the night of my eighteenth birthday.

The fourteenth of September arrived like any other day. I crawled out of bed a little after eleven in the morning, drank a Jolt Cola, then sat smoking until I felt alive enough to move around. A few days earlier, Rick had moved us from a pretty swanky upscale hotel to a dump on Eighty-second Avenue. He didn't explain why—Rick never explained *anything*.

We had two adjoining rooms. One that we worked out of, and one where we slept. As I was smoking my fourth cigarette, Rick opened the door from the adjoining room and said, "Your first appointment is at noon."

I waved my hands at him, a non-verbal *whatever*. Then I got up and walked into the bathroom, cigarette still dangling from my lips. There I stood, staring at myself.

Objectively—not that I could be objective—I looked like shit. The circles under my eyes had become permanent, wrinkled like someone twenty years older. I was pale and looked sick. Rick's tattoos marred my body, along with the cigarette burn some asshole managed to give me before Rick busted down the door one night about a year ago.

I was pretty sure I didn't have HIV, though it had been a couple of months since I'd been tested. I had, however, contracted other STDs. I'd gotten treatment of course, at local clinics, but the infections weren't enough to cause Rick to let me stop working, not even for a night.

By the end of my self-assessment, I felt nothing but hopeless. I had nowhere to go. No one to turn to. *I should just kill myself.* At least then Mom and Dad might find out and get some closure. And poor Sam ... it broke my heart that I would never see her again.

Half an hour after my lunch appointments were over, Nialla came into the room followed by Rick. At the time I was sitting on the edge of the bed staring into space.

Nialla held up a box in green wrapping paper.

"Happy Birthday, Strawberry."

I gave Nialla a look of gratitude. I didn't really care what was in the box, but I was thrilled that she had remembered and gotten something. Anything.

"You have to open it right away," she said.

I nodded and looked to Rick for permission. He nodded, and I began tearing the wrapping off. Inside was a white box. It felt cold to the touch. I lifted the lid and saw inside.

It was an ice cream cake. I swallowed. I had once mentioned to Nialla that my favorite flavor had always been cookies and cream. She'd remembered.

"Oh, that's so sweet!"

Rick's voice immediately jolted me back to reality. In a harsh tone he said to Nialla, "I told you to get her a gift. Not to fatten her up."

Nialla and I met each other's eyes. His tone had a very sharp edge to it. I jumped to her defense. "It's okay ... I don't have to eat it. It was the thought that matters. Thank you, Nialla. And Rick, since you sent her out for a gift for me. Thank you."

His shout made me jump. "DID I FUCKING ASK YOU?"

Rick was working himself up to a rage now. He looked back to Nialla and said, "You're so fucking stupid. I ask you to do *one* thing, just one fucking thing, and you can't even do that right."

Nialla's eyes watered. "But, Rick—"

Whatever she was about to say, she never finished. He lashed out with a fist and punched her in the side of the face, knocking her head back with a jerk. She stumbled backward, hitting the television and then falling down.

He turned to me, rage on his face. "You want to eat the fucking cake? Is that what you want?"

"Rick, please…" I pleaded. I set the cake on the bedside table between the two beds.

He shouted, "Eat it! All of it."

With shocking violence, he grabbed the back of my hair and slammed my face into the cake once, twice, three times. Cake and icing were smashed across my face, in my nostrils and eyes, in my mouth. The third time, my face hit the stand so hard that my vision went white. He kicked me in the side then turned and kicked Nialla even as she scrambled away.

He glared at both of us. "Clean up this *goddamned* mess."

Later that night, when Rick was outside talking with someone on the phone and smoking, Nialla whispered to me, "I'm so sorry. I'm making a plan. I promise. We're leaving him."

Brenna

Our rooms were silent and sullen the first two days after my birthday, with few words passing between the three of us other than the practical in nature. Where's the next appointment? What hotel? What time? As it always happened, on the third day, Rick came to me.

"You know I only reacted that way because I love you. Nialla's jealous, that's why she's always trying to get you to eat crap and do more drugs."

I didn't answer, just looked away. We were sitting in the hotel room side by side on the bed. He reached over and touched my chin with his finger and thumb, gently pulling my face toward him. "Come on, Strawberry. You know I'd never hurt you for real."

I avoided his eyes. I didn't want to hear anything he had to say.

"Come on, baby. It's not going to be much longer that we have to do this … you know I've been saving up. Pretty soon I'm getting us a place. I've already scoped it out, it's a beach house near San Francisco. You'll love it. You can lay by the beach and read your books and we'll be happy, just the two of us."

I finally looked at him. "What about Nialla? You going to throw her in the garbage?"

winter flower

Inside, I froze. It was stupid, foolhardy, for me to say something like that to Rick. At any minute he could explode into violence, any provocation.

He gave a mock hurt face. I didn't think he was capable of a real one. "You don't believe that, do you? Not really. I know you've seen the way she looks at us. I think she's planning to leave. She doesn't think I know it, but she cut out one of the seams of her purse and she's been stashing money inside where she thinks I won't find it. You know how I feel about you girls holding out on me."

I shook my head. "She wouldn't do that, she wouldn't."

Rick went completely still, his pale eyes fixed on me. "I bet she's talked to you about it, hasn't she? Did she tell you she was leaving? That she'd take you with her? Are you going to believe that lying whore over me?"

I had to answer quick and without any hesitation. "No, no, of course not." This was bad. If she was really stashing money and he knew about it, then any minute things could get very ugly. I had to calm him down, distract him. "Rick, you know I wouldn't leave you. Nialla wouldn't either. We couldn't live without you."

He shook his head. "You girls think you have it bad. You don't even know what bad is. I'll tell you something. When I was six, I lived with my stepdad. He used to fuck me all the time. I hated it. It went on for years."

I wanted to vomit.

He pointed at me. "One day—I was sixteen by then—I knifed him. I was done getting fucked by that old bastard. So you know what? They charged me as an adult, sent me to prison. I did four years, and you know what happens to a sixteen-year-old in fucking adult prison? Same old thing. There I am, with some asshole's dick up my ass. Don't you *ever* act like you've got it bad. You get paid, you get drugs and pretty jewelry and all that bullshit. Everybody gets fucked in the end. Everybody."

Rough, he shoved me back on the bed and pawed at my jeans. Then he pulled off his own clothes and without bothering with any of the niceties of foreplay he mounted me and began to fuck. As always, I looked at the ceiling and imagined myself someplace else, someplace happy. I imagined myself sitting on the porch of the big house next to Sam, laughing and giggling. I tried to shut out his words, shut them out forever, because for just a second, they made me feel something ... compassion? No, not that. Not for him.

Rick didn't take long. Spent, he rolled off of me and got up and began to get dressed without words. I lay there staring off into space. Finally he said, "I got you something for your birthday."

He dropped a small jewelry box next to me. I sat up and opened the box. It was a pair of diamond earrings.

I felt nothing but anger. He hadn't bought the earrings. *I had.* I paid for them with countless men using my body. I wanted to flush them down the toilet. Instead, I looked up at him and met his eyes. "I love them. Thank you so much."

Brenna

It rained heavily for the next several days. Rick was grumpy because business was slow, so I did my best to stay out of his way.

The day after Rick had said it, I whispered to Nialla that Rick believed she'd been stashing money in the lining of her purse. She nodded wordlessly and no more was said about it. I hoped that meant she was going to get rid of it.

One early morning Rick and Nialla picked me up from an outcall. I climbed into the back seat and he began to drive back toward the motel where we were staying.

"I'm starving," Nialla said.

Rick said, "Let's get some breakfast."

Nobody consulted me, of course. I just went wherever Rick took me. Even after two years, Rick treated me more like a piece of baggage than a person.

Rick parked the car in the side lot next to Dave's Diner, a crappy little place. We'd eaten there a couple of times before. I hated it. Early morning hours, the place was usually full of pimps trying to show off their girls. Sometimes they'd buy and sell girls in those booths.

When we walked in, Rick went for one of the booths in the back.

"I've got to go to the bathroom," I said.

Rick looked around, assessing the layout of the place, looking at the exits, the people, the locations of windows. He already knew there were no phone booths where the bathrooms were—the first time we came here, he'd walked me to the bathroom.

He nodded permission. "Go ahead."

I turned and headed to the back as he and Nialla sat in the booth. As I walked down the short hallway to the bathroom, I passed the bulletin board and kept walking—then I froze. And turned back to the bulletin board. My heart started to pound, the pulse rushing through my face.

A flyer was stuck on the bulletin board. A flyer with my face on it.

I looked back toward the restaurant. Rick and Nialla were around the corner and couldn't see me. I quickly tore the flyer down and ducked into the bathroom and locked the door.

I gasped as I looked at it.

307

winter flower

The top of the poster said in all caps: "HAVE YOU SEEN THIS GIRL?"

Underneath, in smaller letters, it said, "Our daughter Brenna was kidnapped in Virginia. She was last seen in Portland three weeks ago. Reward for information leading to her recovery. Brenna, we love you. Mom and Dad. Call 571-555-1572."

On the left, a mug shot from three weeks ago, me staring dead-eyed at the camera. On the right, me two years ago. I didn't even remember that picture being taken. I was wearing the same clothes I'd had on the day I was kidnapped, and behind me was the VW Beetle Mom and Dad bought me for my birthday. On my face in that picture, I had an innocent, happy smile.

The girl in that picture still had her mom and dad. She still had Sam. She still had her life, and innocence, and happiness. She was me ... but not ruined.

I began to weep. Most of the time I could contain the pain. Most of the time I could just keep going. But this was *too much*. This meant that they were still out there looking. They were still out there wondering where I was. They hadn't moved on, they were grieving, they *wanted me*. All of Rick's fucking *lies* were just that, they were lies meant to confuse and destroy me and keep me in his power.

How close were they? My mom and dad might be right down the street? Had my mother touched this very flyer? *Sam* might be nearby. For a second, the old shame almost overpowered me. They had the mug shot, which meant they *knew* what I'd been doing when I was arrested. The shame was so overpowering I wanted to die.

But then I realized *that* was lies, too. That was one of *his* lies, meant to keep me from them, meant to keep me leaning on *him*, listening to *him*. They knew what I'd been doing, and they'd still come all this way, they'd still come looking for me. They still wanted me.

I clutched the flyer against my chest and struggled not to wail. Every part of me ached with longing and pain, emptiness and hurt, and loneliness so powerful I felt it like a yawning chasm in my soul.

I wanted to go home.

Twenty-Nine

Erin

"Hi, Mom."

Sam's voice was hesitant. Breathy. It was eight o'clock in the morning, and the dirty motel room seemed particularly oppressive. I could hear the rain beating on the metal gutters, a loud clatter that portended floods. I'd opened the slightly mildewed curtains so I could see outside and maybe get a little light in, but it was pointless. It was a deluge outside.

"Hey, Sam. Your dad told me ... well, a lot. How are you? Are you in pain?"

"I'm okay. My ribs hurt, and my face. But it could be worse. They gave me meds."

I swallowed. Despite the drenched world outside, my throat was dust. "I wonder if you can talk to me about ... your dad ... he said that you ... that you were..." I trailed off. I seemed to have lost my ability to articulate anything.

"A girl?"

Sam's statement was bold, challenging, firm.

"Yes," I said. "Can you tell me about that?"

Sam took an audible breath, then said, "I-I'm not sure what to say, Mom. I've been this way my whole life."

I swallowed. "Your whole life?" I asked. "Really?" I didn't mean to sound skeptical. But I'd *known* Sam his whole life. This seemed like a shot out of the dark.

"Yes, Mom." Sam went quiet for a moment, then said, "Do you remember throwing away Brenna's old princess dresses? When she grew out of them, and I kept wearing them and you got mad? I'm not even sure how old I was, but it's one of my earliest memories."

Jesus fucking Christ. I had to cover my mouth with my hand to keep from gasping audibly. Of *course* I remembered that. Sam had been inconsolable, he'd cried all afternoon. He was four when that happened.

I didn't take it seriously at all.

Brenna had begged me not to throw them away, too. I remembered that. I had said, "But they don't fit you, sweetie."

Six-year-old Brenna had looked me in the eye and said, "No, but Sam likes to wear them. Why would you take them away?"

I had responded, "Sam is a *boy,* Brenna, and boys don't wear dresses."

"Yes. I remember," I whispered. "Brenna knew, didn't she?"

"Yes," Sam said.

A wash of memories flooded over me. Sending Sam back to the *boy* aisle in the toy store because he wanted to get the same Barbie dolls as Brenna. Christmas mornings, when Sam would turn up his nose at G.I. Joe gifts from Cole's father, or those ugly alien toys that he never even took out of the box. He would politely say thank you but displayed no enthusiasm for such gifts.

I remembered Brenna buying a purple leather-bound locking diary for Sam for his twelfth birthday. It had silver flowery detailing along the edges. Brenna had saved her allowance for several weeks to buy the gift. Sam had bounced out of his seat and spontaneously hugged Brenna.

How could I have been so blind?

"Tell me more," I whispered.

"Do you hate me?" Sam whispered back.

I sucked in a breath. "*No.* I'd never hate you. Never. I just … I wish you could have told me. I wish you hadn't had to keep such a lonely secret. I'm—" Oh Christ. I was starting to cry. I sniffled then wiped my eyes. "I'm so sorry, Sam. I'm sorry you didn't feel like you could tell me. I'm sorry I didn't *know.*"

"It's okay, Mom," Sam said.

But it wasn't. It was *my job* to know. The only thing I had to do with my life was protect my kids. And I'd obviously failed both of them.

Sam said, "Please don't cry because of me."

"I'm not crying because of who you are. I'm crying because I wasn't there for you. I'll try to do better. I promise. Just … do me a favor?"

"Yeah?" Sam asked.

"Just talk to me, okay? I promise I'll listen and won't judge and … I miss you so much, you know."

"I miss you too, Mom."

I felt like I'd been holding my breath, and I'd just let it out. That was okay. I could do this. "So … can I talk to your dad for a minute?"

"He went to see his parole officer. I don't know how long that's going to take."

Probably all day, I thought. "What are your plans?"

"Packing. I'm going to see Hayley in a little while. She's ... in an emergency shelter. Her dad beat her up."

"Oh," I said. I hadn't met Hayley, but Cole had told me he thought she was being abused.

"After that, we're planning to get going. We'll take turns driving so we can get there quicker."

"I'll see you in a few days, then," I said.

"And then we'll find Brenna," Sam said.

I didn't answer. Because I didn't want to say I was beginning to lose hope. But I was. I'd been putting up flyers for days. Talking to people up and down the track. I'd ridden along with Melody as she questioned informants and visited what seemed like every business hotel in the city.

Stan told me he thought they'd left Portland and moved on to another city.

"We'll try," I said. "Just ... Sam—it's still a long shot, okay? I don't want you to be heartbroken if we can't find her."

"Mom, I've been heartbroken since the day she disappeared. This won't change that."

Of course that was true. But I'd been too selfish to see it. I'd let Sam wander off into his own little world on the Internet while I drank and mourned Brenna. I couldn't do that anymore. My kids needed me.

"I know," I finally said. "I'm sorry."

We hung up, and I got up to take a shower. That morning, I was planning to canvas the side streets a little further south of here, then in the evening, I would be visiting the strip clubs along Powell Boulevard. *That* was a long shot, but both Stan and Melody told me that sometimes trafficked girls ended up working in strip clubs at least some of the time. I'd take the flyers and show them to the dancers.

I turned on the water, which never got really hot enough here, and stepped into the shower. As I washed my hair, I couldn't help but step through so many memories. Sam and Brenna playing in the backyard, four and six years old, all of their stuffed animals lined up around them as they had a tea party.

We'd been happy then. Not just the kids, but me and Cole.

We could be happy again. After we found Brenna, and brought her home. She'd need therapy. Lots of it, I'm sure. I couldn't imagine how traumatized she was. But we had *hope*. Jeremiah's offer to transfer Cole to Atlanta, to a new restaurant—it was stunning. In Atlanta, the odds of me finding a decent job—

311

maybe one with decent health insurance—were much better. We could build our family again.

I missed Cole.

I'd not thought about it in a long time, but I still remembered waking up on Christmas morning in 1994, just a few months before I was to graduate from Georgetown. I'd been sulking for days because Cole couldn't come back to North Carolina with me for Christmas that year, *and* he'd been mysterious about his plans for Christmas. I'd wandered downstairs to find Lori already rummaging through her stocking and Mom and Dad making breakfast.

"Hey, sweetie," Dad had said, his eyes bloodshot. He looked and smelled like he'd already been hitting the pipe, no matter how early it was. "Got something for you." It had been a card.

I opened it, puzzled. The card was handwritten, in Cole's handwriting. The message didn't say Merry Christmas, or anything normal like that. It read: *Go to the place where you keep your shoes.*

Weird. I had gone out to the front hall, where Mom and Dad had a plastic tray we kept shoes in. There was an envelope in there. It led to the shed out back. Another card led to the living room.

"Do you know what this is about?" I'd asked Lori as I passed. She just giggled.

I huffed and followed the next clue to the upstairs bathroom. This one said, "Close the door and count out loud to ten."

I shook my head. Bizarre. I did as the note instructed me.

When I opened the door Cole was on the other side, down on one knee. I screamed a little, startled. But then he had smiled and held out a ring, and said, "My love. Will you give me the best Christmas present ever, and agree to marry me?"

I'd told Brenna and Sam that story a hundred times when they were growing up. We'd gotten married in Raleigh, terrified that Cole's dad—unrepentant racist—would collide with my godfather, James Redford, an African American sociology professor.

Both of us had stared, fascinated, during the reception. The one thing the two men had in common was Vietnam service in the Marine Corps. They'd started a conversation about places I'd never heard of—Da Nang and the Mekong Delta and I don't know where—and ended up talking the entire night over drinks. A *lot* of drinks.

It was crazy, but the two men became friends. Seventeen years later, I'd woken up on the most desolate Christmas morning ever. My daughter had been missing and my husband was in prison. Sam was all alone, and I hadn't decorated the house, or even gotten dressed, in days.

I had no idea that James and Cole's dad had hatched a plan. I'd told everyone to stay home, that we weren't coming to visit anyone, that we needed quiet time, that we needed to be alone.

They ignored me.

Jeremiah and Ayanna had been the first to show up with the twins. Without warning, they'd driven up overnight to Virginia.

I'd stared, dumbfounded, as they just came in the house and put up a tree. Sam cried, and the kids had decorated the tree together. Not long after, Cole's parents arrived with James. My parents were next, then Lori.

I'd cried in my sister's arms, and she'd said, "You'll never be alone, sis. We're always there for you."

But I was too far gone. I'd forgotten what my life was like. I'd forgotten the love in Cole's eyes when the two of us danced at our wedding. I'd forgotten watching him roll around on the ground wrestling with our kids as they giggled and laughed. I'd forgotten everything that mattered. By the time Brenna disappeared, all I could remember was the hurt and betrayal that he'd had an affair with that woman.

I sifted through those memories that morning in the shower and I began to weep. I wept for my daughter who was missing, and for my son who might be a daughter. I wept for Cole, and the bitterness and loneliness I'd seen in his eyes for far too long. I wept for all of us.

I wanted my family back. And I didn't know if it was possible.

Sam

"I'm not allowed to give out the address at the shelter," Hayley said. "That's why I asked to meet here."

We were sitting in a booth at the Waffle House in Anniston. Dad had spent some of his time in training here back in the spring, but I'd never been in this one.

"We make quite a pair," I said. Her right eye was black and blue, though not quite as bad as mine. The waitress had stared at us both for an uncomfortably long time before she came over and took our orders.

I hadn't told Hayley yet.

"So ... what happened?" I asked.

"Well, after you and your Dad dropped me off, my father, he…" She looked away. "He hit me. A bunch. I would have contacted you that night, or in the morning, but he took my phone. At school the next morning, Mrs. Mullins called me in. She said she had to call Child Protective Services."

"I'm so sorry," I said. I didn't want to say the next part, but I had to. Because even though it was already too late, I'd betrayed Hayley's confidence.

"You should know—I hope you can forgive me—but I told Mrs. Mullins. It was too late, she'd already called. But I couldn't keep it a secret. I'm sorry."

Hayley took my hand and said, "It's okay. I-I needed to get out of there. I'm sorry I made you promise not to. Now … tell me about you."

"You probably saved my life," I whispered. "Dad found me in time. But Cody cut my face with a knife." I patted the oversized Band-Aid on my cheek.

Hayley's eyes widened. "Is it bad?"

I shook my head. "I hurt everywhere, but the doctor says there shouldn't be much scarring."

"I heard things are crazy at school today. The cops have been calling people in and they're searching phones. They're trying to figure out who all shared that picture that Billy posted."

I felt myself cringe. "How many people saw it? Do you know?"

Hayley shrugged. Then she said, "It was on Twitter."

That meant *everybody* saw it. I whispered, "I don't know if I can go back to school here."

Hayley tilted her head slightly to the left and studied me for a minute. Then she said, "Did Cody and Billy make you dress up that way?"

I looked down at the table. I couldn't meet my best friend's eyes. But I shook my head and whispered, "I was already dressed that way when they showed up."

"That's what I thought," she said.

Confused, I asked, "How come?"

"Your makeup. They might make someone dress up like a girl to humiliate them, but they wouldn't have any idea how to put on makeup. In the picture you looked scared, but you looked pretty."

The heat spread across my face instantly. I couldn't look at her. But she reached out and grabbed my hand in hers.

"Is it like being gay?"

I shook my head. "No. It's … Hayley…" I finally looked up at her. Her pale blue eyes were fixed on my face. "It's not that I dress up as a girl sometimes. I *am* a girl. And I hate hiding all of the time. I hate pretending to be someone I'm not."

Hayley smiled at me and took my hand in both of hers. She leaned forward and said, "You don't have to hide with me."

I closed my eyes. This wasn't possible. I was confused, but relief coursed through me.

I knew that not everyone would react like Hayley. There were people out there like Cody and Billy, people who would hate me for who I was, or be disgusted, or even hurt me. But for the first time in more than two years, I didn't feel alone anymore. I still couldn't believe that my parents hadn't freaked out—especially *Dad*. Every time I thought about his reaction I wanted to cry with relief. I felt ... *free.*

But it wasn't just about me.

"What about you? What happens to you?"

She shook her head. "I don't know how it works. There are social workers and cops and ... I don't know what. They arrested my dad ... so I just don't know what happens next."

"It really bothers me that I'm leaving," I said. "I don't know how long I'll be in Oregon, but I want to be here for you."

"I want you to go. Find your sister. Just—can we talk? I'll text you? Every day."

I nodded. Then I felt myself tear up as I said, "You're the best friend I've ever had."

"Me too," Hayley whispered.

Cole

Erin's text message was a surprise. **What are you doing now?**

I typed a reply: **I'm sitting in the waiting room at the parole office. What about you?**

I had called and left a message with the parole officer first thing this morning. In my message, I told her it was an emergency and I needed to see her today, and that I would be in the waiting room until she had a moment. I'd been here for an hour waiting.

I didn't even know if she would see me today, but all I could do was wait and try.

Erin's response said: **Having breakfast soon then canvassing a different part of town. This evening I'm visiting strip clubs.**

I closed my eyes, trying to shut out my surroundings for just a second. The reality of the places Erin was searching made my stomach ache. After I took a few breaths, I responded: **If we find her—WHEN we find her—she's going to need a lot of help. Therapy. Hugs. Just lots. Everything we can give**.

A few seconds passed before I saw the little dots appear, which indicated she was typing something. Then her message appeared: **I know. She's going to be really damaged. You saw the picture of her. That was a hard-looking woman in that mug shot. But our baby is underneath.**

Jesus. My eyes watered uncontrollably.

"Cole Roberts." The voice was loud, impersonal. The door to the back was open, and Sergeant Friendly looked out at me.

I typed: **They're calling me.**

I stood up and strode to the door.

"Your voicemail, you said it was urgent?"

"Yes, ma'am."

"Come on back, then," she replied.

She turned and headed into the back office. I followed her into the crowded cube and sat across from her at her desk.

"What can I do for you, Cole?"

I took a deep breath. *Please,* I thought. Then I spoke. "The FBI called a few days ago. My daughter turned up in Portland, Oregon. She was arrested for solicitation then released before they realized who she was."

Understanding flashed across Friendly's face. "You want to go out there?"

I nodded. "Erin's already in Portland, she has been for several days. My son—we're going to withdraw him from school for the remainder of the semester anyway. He was severely assaulted yesterday and is going to need some time away from the school here. My boss approved a leave of absence."

She nodded. "I see. How much time did they give you?"

"Two months."

"Can you get me the name and number of your boss and the FBI agent who called? So I can verify everything?"

"Sure," I said. I took out my phone and pulled up the contacts. "Got a sheet of paper?"

She slid one across to me with a pencil. I wrote Jeremiah's name and number first, then Stan Wilcox.

"Agent Wilcox works with the Child Abduction Response Team in Washington, but Erin said he's in Portland right now."

She nodded. "Okay. I'm only allowed to authorize thirty days at a time. Which means if you're still there in 25 days, I want you to call me and we'll talk about next steps."

316

As she spoke, it took a moment for it to sink in. She was going to authorize it! I could go.

"Okay," I said, nodding. "Whatever you need."

"I'm going to make arrangements for you to meet with one of my counterparts in Portland. We'll say in two weeks."

"All right."

"Give me a moment then."

She turned to her computer and began to rapidly type. I waited patiently—nothing else I could do, of course. A couple of minutes later, her printer began to warm up and spit out pages.

She took the papers out—one looked like a letter, the other was a dense form. There were multiple copies of each. She signed and stamped them, then said, "I'll be right back. I need to get my supervisor's signature on the travel authorization."

She stood and walked away. I typed a message to Erin: **They're giving me permission to go.**

She responded: **I'm so relieved.**

Was she really? Was she saying that because she felt like she had to? What did Erin even want anymore? More to the point, was there any hope that she could ever forgive me or trust me again? It seemed, from our talks and messages over the last couple of days … that there just might be some hope.

What if the shoe were on the other foot? What if Erin had an affair, and I had been the one to find the careless evidence of a profound lie?

I don't know what I would have done a year ago or five years ago. I knew I didn't have any right to expect it—I had no right to even ask for forgiveness—but I would crawl on my knees from Alabama to Portland if that's what it took to convince her to take me back into her heart.

I looked up from my phone when Sergeant Friendly reappeared. As always, she had a brisk expression on her face. She rapidly shuffled through a set of papers, dividing three copies of the documents into three separate folders. The first, she labeled and stuck in her own file cabinet. The second, she stuffed in a manila envelope, tied it off, then wrote a name on it. I didn't think anyone used those anymore. The third folder, she handed to me. I flipped it open.

On the left side was a letter from her to *"To whom it may concern."* The letter stated that I was a felon, and I was authorized to travel from Alabama to Oregon, and gave her office and cell numbers in the event contact was needed. The second was an Alabama state form, which was the official travel pass.

I closed the folder and looked at her. "Thank you for this."

"Just stay out of trouble, Cole."

317

"Yes, ma'am."

She smiled, and said, "God go with you searching for your daughter."

Once I was outside of the building, I texted Erin to let her know I had the travel pass, and then I sent a message to Sam: **I'm all finished at the parole office. How are things with Hayley?**

Sam replied immediately: **We just said goodbye. I'm walking back to the van now. Meet you at home?**

I responded: **See you there. I have to stop at the restaurant on the way so I may be a little later than you.**

Forty-five minutes later I drove up to the house. On the passenger seat were the very few personal things I'd kept in my office at the restaurant. Brian had already installed a relief manager there, and I didn't expect to be back.

The goodbyes at the restaurant had been surprisingly tough. Susan had cried, telling me that she hadn't had a manager she liked in years. I'd asked her to talk with Dakota and the other second and third shift staff, to tell them I was sorry I had to leave so suddenly.

I scanned the inside of the house doing a mental triage. I would pack clothing for myself and some of the things Erin had forgotten. I'd take some of my tools in the event we had a problem on the road, and would stash some emergency cash under the spare tire.

I called out, "Sam, you here?"

Sam called from the bathroom, "In here!"

I started in the kitchen, packing a few things in the cooler like the peanut butter and jelly, but tossing perishables that I couldn't bring with us. Once that was complete, I carried the garbage out, then went back to our room to begin packing.

I was zipping up the suitcase when I heard the bathroom door in the hallway open up.

"Dad?"

"Yeah?" I said, as I turned to look. Then I stopped and stared.

Sam was wearing his— no, *her*—own clothes, a white Oxford cloth shirt and a pair of black pants. She wore a pair of black loafers I never really noticed before and a pair of blue crystal earrings that matched her eyes, or would have if she hadn't been wearing a pair of Erin's oversized sunglasses. The black eye was noticeable, but not so much under the sunglasses as it might have been. She had very carefully applied makeup, disguising the rest of the bruising on her face, though the fine red C-shaped cut was clear. Her already long hair had been carefully styled into a feminine look.

If I hadn't known Sam his—*her*—entire life, I would have simply taken her as a youngish teen girl.

"Are you going to say anything?"

Sam looked anxious, and my stunned silence surely hadn't helped that. It was a shock though, seeing Sam like this. For a second I doubted my ability to follow through, and a stab of grief for my *son* swept through me.

But it wasn't about me, it was about Sam.

"You look pretty, Sam."

The sunglasses masked her expression. But with a lopsided smile, she said, "Thanks, Dad. I'm going to go finish packing."

Sam walked away, and I continued with what I was doing, even as I asked myself if I was making a mistake. Should I have pushed harder? Or insisted that Sam do some amount of therapy before ... no. If Sam decided she was going to grow out of this, she had a couple of years before any permanent changes were even possible. I had to leave it to her to explore. No matter how strange it might seem to me.

Forty minutes later, it was clear just how right that decision was, at least for now. I took Sam to Goodwill and gave her a fifty-dollar budget. For the next hour I was treated to the sight of Sam smiling for the first time in years, as she tried on outfit after outfit, twirling in front of the mirrors, trying on shoes and dresses and skirts, and each step of the way asking me how she looked.

How could it be that I hadn't realized how profoundly sad Sam was? We all were, of course, but Sam had carried extra burdens, including two parents who had simply failed to be there when she needed them.

When I finally paid for the clothes, she asked the grey-haired woman at the register if she could put on her new clothes in the changing room before we left. The woman smiled and nodded, and Sam ran to the changing rooms practically giggling.

"Your daughter's beautiful," she told me.

"It's her smile," I said.

Thirty

Sam

During our first stop headed west on I–20, Dad mapped out our route. The total driving time from Oxford to Portland was about thirty-eight hours. We were leaving at noon, so the plan was to drive eight to ten hours the first day, then twelve each on the second and third days. If all went well, we would arrive in Portland by Saturday evening.

The first day we were mostly quiet, sometimes listening to my music and sometimes Dad's. We stopped for dinner not long after crossing the Mississippi in Memphis—it was the first time I had ever seen the great river—and then got back on the road.

During the drive, I felt surreal. After years of hiding and pretending, I was out, feeling like myself, and Mom and Dad were okay with it. I kept feeling like it was a dream, that I would wake up and find myself back in Oxford, in my room, door locked. Hiding. But here I was.

Neither of us were ready to stop when we had our eighth hour on the road, so we decided to keep going, finally dragging into a cheap motel in Rock Port, Missouri at two o'clock in the morning.

"Six a.m. okay?" Dad had asked, setting the alarm.

"Yeah." I wanted to get where we were going as quickly as possible, and we still had a long way to go.

My dreams that night were confusing and muddled. Images of Cody going after Brenna with a knife. In the dream I got between them just in time and felt Cody's knife sinking into my shoulder. In the dream it happened over and over again. The dream transitioned in the psychedelic way that dreams do, and I found myself in a long hallway with doors stretching into the distance. The

320

doors were mug shots, Brenna's face in the picture that Mom had sent. Somewhere in the maze of doorways and halls I could hear her crying, a broken wail that made my heart ache.

"I'm coming!" I cried out in the dream. But I kept opening doors and not finding her. An alarm went off somewhere, and I was running out of time, running out of time to find her, and I began to run down the hall, throwing open doors and barely looking inside before I ran to the next. The alarm was getting louder and louder and so were her cries, and then I jerked up to a sitting position, wide awake, my heart thumping wildly.

The cheap plastic alarm between the two beds was blaring. Dad was slapping at the alarm, finally hitting it with a loud bang, and the silence descended on the room. He sat up, his face bleary.

Both of us stumbled around, foggy, as we got ready to get back on the road. While Dad was in the shower, I took a long and careful look at the kaleidoscope of yellow, purple, and black bruises spread across my face. It was actually worse today than it had been the day before—a good look at my face would give little kids nightmares. I covered it up as best I could—not very well—and by six thirty we headed next door to the stone-faced building labeled RESTAURANT in foot-high capital letters on the roof. Inside it turned out to be half country-store, half diner.

It was weird. We'd talked so little, for so long, that in some ways I wasn't sure what to talk about with Dad. We stumbled around different topics then went mostly quiet.

We'd been there about ten minutes before two police officers approached.

"Sorry to bother you both, but could we speak with you for just a moment?"

"Sure," Dad said. "What can I help you with?"

What was going on? Did this have something to do with Dad's probation? Was there some other issue?

One of the officers motioned to me. "If you could come with me, Miss?"

I looked at Dad, alarmed. He nodded to comply, so I got up from the table. The officer led me to the opposite side of the restaurant then stood so that my back was to Dad.

The officer studied me impassively for a moment, then said, "That's a pretty good shiner you got there, kid. And ... is that a cut on your cheek?"

"Yes, sir," I said. "I got beat up pretty bad. Day before yesterday."

"Someone here called it in. Suggested maybe that your father did it. Is that your father?"

Comprehension suddenly swept through me. "Oh! No! He *is* my father, and *no,* he didn't hit me. It was a bully at school. Really bad scene."

321

"You're absolutely sure?" The officer looked concerned. "We can protect you if your father did. You don't have to be afraid to tell us the truth."

I was starting to get anxious. What if they didn't believe me? Dad had a criminal record for assault. Would they arrest him? Would he go back to jail? What would happen to me? Or Mom or Brenna?

I shook my head. "No ... he *didn't*. If you want to call the cops where we live, they'll tell you. It happened in Oxford, Alabama. Or you can check with my school. My dad's never even spanked me."

"Oxford, Alabama? What brings you to Missouri?"

"We're on our way to Oregon. My sister was kidnapped two years ago. She just turned up there a few weeks ago and we're going to see if we can find her."

The officer tilted his head. "Kidnapped?"

I nodded. "It was in the news and everything then."

"And school?"

"Dad withdrew me for the rest of the semester."

"I see. Can you wait here for a moment?"

I grimaced. "I'd really like to finish my breakfast."

The officer smiled. "Okay. Have a seat, eat your breakfast, and I'm sure we'll be able to move on in a moment."

"Thanks," I said. Then I walked back to the table.

Dad was still talking with the other officer, clear on the other side of the restaurant, but after a minute he, too, returned to the table.

I said, "I'm nervous."

"Don't be," Dad said. "You told them what happened?"

I nodded.

"Okay," he said. "I did the same. And gave them the number for your counselor at school."

I swallowed. "Dad ... do you think we'll be able to find her?"

He looked stricken. It took several seconds before he finally took a breath and started to answer. "I ... I hope so. I don't know. It's still a long shot."

"But we'll do everything we can," I said.

"That's right."

I didn't find his answers that satisfying. Of course we would try our best. But it was bigger than just finding Brenna. The last couple of days I felt like a veil had been lifted. After all, what had hiding gotten me? Beaten up. That's what it got me. If Dad hadn't showed up when he had, if Hayley hadn't called, if I hadn't had location services on my phone ... *if, if, IF*... Cody might have murdered me.

I felt encouraged by Mom and Dad's response. It was hard to tell with Mom, of course—we only talked on the phone for a little while—but Dad was present and engaged in a way I hadn't seen in a long time. I knew he worked really hard, that he struggled to be able to make ends meet so we could eat. But when he wasn't working, he was often at one end of the house and Mom at the other. And that wasn't any good, because Mom needed him. And if we found Brenna, she would need both of them.

I was trying to figure out how to say some of what I was thinking, how to put some of this into words.

The thing was, at least for the last couple of years, neither of my parents had been there for me. Not just the big stuff, like being a girl or losing Brenna, but the small stuff too. They just checked out.

What if we found Brenna? What if we brought her home and Mom and Dad still hated each other? What if we brought her home and all they could do was fight in front of her? I sighed.

Well, if they couldn't get it together then at the very least I would be there for my sister, no matter what happened.

"What is it?" Dad asked.

Could I even say what I was thinking? How could I?

"Sam. You can talk with me."

"I'm afraid…" I felt my chin began to tremble and I stopped. I closed my eyes and said to myself, *say it*. I opened my eyes and looked at Dad. "I'm afraid we'll find her and bring her home and nothing will be any different, because you two will be fighting or hiding from each other all the time and Brenna won't be able to … be able to…"

I closed my eyes, struggling to hold back tears.

Dad said in a quiet voice, "You are afraid that Brenna won't heal if me and your mom are still at odds."

I nodded. But I whispered, "Yeah."

Dad exhaled, his shoulders visibly sinking. "I'm afraid of the same thing, Sam. But I promise I'll do my best."

There wasn't much more I could ask than that.

The waitress dropped our check off at the table, but for the moment we were stuck until the police let us go. So we waited and finished our coffee. A couple of minutes later both officers came back into the restaurant and approached the table.

The older officer said, "Y'all are free to go. Sorry about the trouble."

Dad shook his head. "No problem. I'm glad you're looking out for folks."

Five minutes later we were on the road again headed northwest.

323

winter flower

Brenna

Nialla said, "We've got to talk, Strawberry."

I looked at her wordlessly. The room was heavy with the pungent smell of marijuana smoke from my pipe. I took a deep drag as I listened to her.

"Baby, if we're going to get away, you're going to have to lay off of that stuff for a while."

If we were going to get away. That was never going to happen. Rick would come right after us and that would be the end.

For three days the flyer had been burning in my mind. I'd memorized every word. I'd thought about it constantly.

But I couldn't call. It wouldn't just be *me* that Rick killed. I wasn't going to put Mom or Dad or Sam in that kind of danger. He *would* come after me, and he *would* hurt them.

I took another deep drag. I was still in a considerable amount of pain from a client who had gotten too rough the night before.

At least the bleeding had stopped.

Nialla looked distressed. "Strawberry, come on. Please? Just listen?"

I shrugged. She leaned close. "We can do this. I figured it out. When we run, we can head south, to San Francisco. I figure if we work a week or two we can raise enough money to fly to Hawaii. Rick won't have a clue. He'll never come after us that far away. Besides, he'll be happy here with Kaylee."

The thought of Kaylee made me shudder. Was she less of a fool than I had been or more? I had, at least, been older. Thirteen was too young.

"It's a fantasy. Don't waste your time." I felt immense weight on me as I said the words. I just wanted to curl up and be left alone.

Nialla shook her head. "We can do this. We can." Tears were running down her face as she said it. "I want out."

Bitterness was all I could taste. "What's your name? Not the name *he* gave you. What's your real name?"

She whispered, "You know my name."

"You don't want to say it? You can't? Because I can't remember. All I know is the name he gave us. All I know is to fuck who he says to fuck and to go to the bathroom when he says to go to the bathroom and to sleep when he says sleep and eat when he says to eat. I don't know anything else." My voice raised higher and higher as the words spilled out of me.

Her face was bleak. "Laura," she whispered. "My name is Laura."

I desperately wanted to hear my own name spoken. But it was too late. I heard a loud click, the hotel room lock, and the door opened.

It was Rick. He leered at us as he came in. Was he drunk? He looked at both of us with an amused expression. "Turn out, hoes."

I felt a chill even through the weed haze. "Turn out" meant to turn out our pockets, our purses. It meant to give him any money we had—which most of the time was nothing—and it was often a precursor to violence if he believed we were hiding something.

Nialla rolled her eyes, but I wasn't taking any chances with him. I grabbed my purse and dumped it out on the bed. The contents made a pathetic little pile. I had a pack and a half of cigarettes. A bag of weed, and another bag of assorted pills—Xanax, Valium, and Oxy. A box of condoms. A fake ID from Maryland identifying me as Miranda Harrison. I had a prepaid cell phone designed for children, which allowed me to dial two numbers only—Rick's and Nialla's. Hair ties, makeup, lipstick, lubricant.

The contents of my purse were a reflection of my entire life—they were the things he allowed me to have, when he allowed me to have them. I had toyed the other day with keeping the flyer; after all, it was rare that Rick searched our things. But in the end, I had decided it was best to tear it up and throw it in the garbage. Safest.

Rick made a show of going through our things. He picked up Nialla's bag and made a point of sticking his fingers through the seam into the body of the purse and feeling around. He raised an eyebrow at her when he discovered nothing then shrugged and dropped the purse.

His heart didn't seem to be in the search. He looked at me. "You won't believe who I just met, Strawberry."

I stared at him and didn't answer. Was he expecting me to guess? Had he run into some celebrity pimp that only he would care about?

"Not even curious?" He raised an eyebrow. He slipped a hand into his back pocket and took out a sheet of paper and began to unfold it. I forced myself to keep my expression impassive, because I recognized the paper he was unfolding. It was another copy of the flyer I had seen.

"It looks to me like they finally put together who you were after you got yourself arrested, you dumb bitch. Look here ... it's you! Kind of a before and after. Which one do you like better?"

I began to shake with loathing.

Nialla muttered, "*Asshole.*"

"You seen this flyer before, Strawberry?"

I shook my head.

He grinned. "Too bad you weren't with me. I was at The Knights Club getting a blowjob from one of the strippers. When I came out, I met your mom. She's kind of a senior citizen, so she wouldn't make any money at this business, but she might be fun to fuck for novelty. You're not thinking of calling her, are you? Because things would get pretty ugly for her, if you know what I mean."

I shuddered. "I'm not calling anybody, Rick."

His smile was cold. "You sure? We know Nialla is planning on running, what about you?"

Nialla said, "Rick, I'm not—"

"Shut up! Stupid bitch. Did I ask you to open your fucking mouth?"

My mind was still focused on his words. He'd seen my mother? She was here, in Portland, looking for me. I whispered, "How did she look?"

He shrugged. "Fuckable."

"I hate you," I whispered.

He half snorted, an amused look on his face. He walked over and pinched my chin between his thumb and index finger. "Hate me all you want. But don't even think about calling her or anyone. You know how bad things can get, don't you? Or you think you do. You've got it pretty good really. Did you know there are people out there on the Internet with rape fetishes? I could make pretty good money from a video of your mom being gangbanged by a dozen or so guys."

I tried to look away, as my stomach started to turn. But he forced my face toward his. His voice took on a rough tone as he said, "Can you just imagine her cries of pain? The jiz running down her face? I bet she's never had it up the ass, she'd probably bleed—"

I screamed as loud as I could, "*Stop it! Shut up!* Leave her alone! I'll do anything, don't hurt her!"

The horror was that I could see everything he described. I couldn't block it out of my mind. I jerked away from him and put my face in my hands and tried to block it out, but the images wouldn't stop. When I couldn't clear the vision I slammed my fist against my head, over and over, screaming, "*Stop it!*"

He chuckled. "Don't think I won't do it. You don't want to do that to your mother. Make sure you behave. We're leaving town in a couple of days. Hold it together until then."

He stepped back and I sank down to the floor. A moment later he said, "Get yourselves together. You've got clients."

Erin

A pattering sound broke the silence as tiny raindrops began to sprinkle the windshield of the car. I sat, eyes unfocused as I stared into the distance.

I was exhausted.

For almost a week I'd been wandering Portland at all hours of the day and night. I'd been to massage parlors and viewing booths, lingerie modeling businesses and strip clubs. I'd wandered along the track in the middle of the night, searching for my daughter, and instead, I found a wasteland full of pimps and their women and girls; a no man's land between the police and the ignorant public who had no idea—or didn't care—that literal slavery was happening in their midst.

Since that first morning, I'd found no traces of her.

The girls I'd spoken to on the track had seen nothing, and the waitress at the diner hadn't seen her either. I'd been to half a dozen strip clubs, where I was met with hostility and anger, and from one heavily tattooed redneck, little more than a smirk as he took the paper.

"Pretty girl," he'd said. But he didn't mean it in a complimentary way. He meant it as lust.

It was too early to give up. *Anytime* would be too early to give up. But how long could I go on doing this? It was so much harder than I'd imagined. It wasn't like canvassing a neighborhood. I felt like I was canvassing a swamp.

I couldn't even get up the energy to get out of the car and walk across the parking lot to my hotel room. My plan had been to nap then get up late and revisit the clubs. Just at the moment, I felt like that was going to be impossible.

Okay. I could do this. I needed to fight the depression, fight the blackness that threatened to overwhelm me; above all, I needed to fight the urge to drown myself in a bottle of wine that would dull the ache.

I opened the car door. Just as I stood up, the phone rang. My eyes dropped to it.

It was Stan, who I'd barely heard from in the past two days.

"Hello?"

"Erin. Where are you?"

"I just got back to my hotel." I felt my eyebrows push together and my back tense.

"Meet me at Detective Michelson's office. I'll be there in fifteen minutes."

"What is it?"

winter flower

"I'll get you the details when we meet. But we've got a lead, an important one."

"Stan!" I blurted. "You can't—"

"Erin, we got a match on the tattoo to an ad. That led us to phone numbers, more ads, more phone numbers, a street name. She's here, somewhere in Portland. Right now."

I began to hyperventilate. I closed my eyes, trying to force calm. "I'm on my way."

Part Three

Thirty-One

~~~~~~

Erin

I was shaking by the time I parked and walked into the police station, alternately expectant and terrified of what I might learn. The building itself was no more pleasant than it had been during my last visit. The walls were dingy, and the lobby area smelled faintly of ammonia.

Once I identified myself, I was whisked into the back of the building and a small conference room. The same officer who greeted me the first day I came here offered me a cup of coffee and informed me that Agent Wilcox and Detective Michelson would arrive at any moment.

The officer brought me the coffee a couple of minutes later. It was unpleasant tasting, slightly burnt and exactly what I needed at that point. I sat down at the heavily scratched table and waited.

Agent Wilcox came into the room first. "Good morning, Erin." He busied himself connecting his laptop to a small projector. By the time he finished and turned the projector on, Melody arrived. She sat down across from me and said, "Stan, it's your show."

He opened his mouth to speak but stopped when the door opened. It was the precinct captain, Ed Ramos. He said, "Go ahead, I'm just going to observe."

Wilcox didn't look precisely annoyed, but he clearly wasn't thrilled about the new arrival.

"I want to be up front, Erin, so we have clear expectations. I don't know if you have read much about the technology we use, but the magnitude of this task is incredible. Something like one million prostitution ads are posted every single day. Most of them on Backpage, but also on a variety of other sites. We work with the National Center for Missing and Exploited Children and several

331

technology companies to archive those ads, get them into databases, and search for faces."

I nodded. "I'm familiar with the program."

"We've been obstructed by the fact that as far as we could tell, no ads were ever posted that showed a clear view of Brenna's face. Without that, it was near impossible to imagine we'd be able to get a hit on a photo in one of the ads. But the mug shot changed things. It's a very unusual and distinctive tattoo on her neck, and she has what appears to be a scar from a cigarette burn on her collarbone. The center fed those into the computer and we finally got a match."

I swiveled my head to look at Melody then back to Stan. He pulled up a series of images on the computer. I put my hand over my heart, as if that could somehow contain the sharp pain I felt. The first ad was clearly Brenna. She stood in profile to the camera with her face mostly turned away. The dragon tattoo was clear on her neck. She wore almost no clothes.

The headline said: **Strawberry, 5'5" young fantasy. $200.**

Stan gave me the compassionate look, but it did nothing to ease the severe pain I felt in my chest as the panic attack began to overwhelm me. I tried to breathe, as slowly and deeply as I could, to combat the feeling that I was suffocating.

"I'm not going to show you any more pictures of her. But that's her. Almost certainly."

I nodded and squeaked out the word, "Yes."

He said, "That particular ad was posted in San Diego about five months after Brenna went missing. Between the picture, the phone number, and the street name, we have a lot more to go on. She goes by Strawberry—we've known that since her arrest—and she's often with another woman using the name Nialla. They've been all over the country, usually for a month or two at a time at any given spot."

I nodded and listened, struggling to stay calm.

"You okay?" Melody asked.

I nodded fervently but said nothing.

Stan said, "We're certain that both girls are controlled by a pimp. He's dangerous. After correlating the phone numbers and the locations over the past two years, we believe it's possible he murdered two girls: one in Orlando about a year ago, the other in Las Vegas last month. It's possible that a john committed the murders in both cases, or someone else, but unlikely."

Melody leaned forward. "Why do you think it was the same killer?"

"Both girls were shot in the back of the head with a large caliber pistol. They were executed. I'm waiting for ballistics results, but we should know in another day or so if these two women were killed by the same weapon."

I was intentionally breathing as slowly as I could, trying not to hyperventilate. "What else do we know now?"

"We've been able to plot out their movements over the past couple of years. They've switched up their phones a couple of times but have generally used the same photos in different cities." He paused for a moment, as if reconsidering whether or not he wanted to say what he was about to say. "We know that the scar that appears to be a cigarette burn first appeared in her pictures about nine months ago. She's been in at least fourteen different cities, possibly more, but that's all we were able to identify from the ads."

I shook my head. "Is that why it's been so difficult to find her?"

He shrugged. "Among other things. It's not unusual for pimps to move trafficked women around from place to place. They'll do everything they can to keep the women isolated, friendless, rootless."

"Okay. What else?" I was getting my breathing under control and was able to get the words out with some semblance of normality.

Stan said, "Going back through the ads from the same phone numbers, there are matches for ads for the other girl, Nialla." He typed on his computer for a couple of moments and two more ads appeared on the screen. The face was blurry but somewhat visible. "The first time this ad appeared for her was a little bit less than two years before Brenna disappeared. That timeframe matches up with the disappearance of *this* girl."

He pulled up another picture, this one a yearbook photo of a young woman with light brown hair. She had a warm smile and looked directly at the camera. A gold chain with a tiny cross hung around her neck. "This is Laura Felker. She went to meet some friends at the mall one day about four years ago and was never seen again. The last photo we have of her was taken at the mall by a security camera."

He talked again and pulled up a photo I recognized. I felt a chill; I remembered seeing this photo on the news. I looked at it for a moment and felt my chest tighten and my breathing grew shallow again.

In the photo, the girl was dressed in a miniskirt and tank top. She was walking with a taller man, lean and muscular with tattoos all over his arms. No. It couldn't be. *It couldn't be.*

"I've seen him." My voice came out in a squeak.

Stan and Melody simultaneously said, "What?"

"He was at The Knights Club this afternoon. I spoke with him. I gave him a flyer and asked if he'd seen her." As I spoke, the pitch of my voice rose higher and higher. I was nauseous. He must have known who I was. He was laughing at me.

The detective and the FBI agent looked at each other, both of them shocked. Then Melody said, "You're certain?"

I nodded.

She turned to the captain, who had been standing silently against the wall. "What are the odds we can get a warrant to dust the place?"

The captain said, "Probably not that good, at least not to do a broad search. But we might be able to get a warrant limited to checking the security cameras and finding out where he sat and moved and dust just those places. It's worth a try. We'll have to move quick though, that place starts getting busy in the late afternoon. Once a couple hundred guys have been in there, there'll be no chance of getting usable prints."

Melody nodded. "Okay. We'll try to get an ID on the pimp that way."

Wilcox said, "This is the final piece of information we have. It's from the security cameras at Dave's Diner here in Portland—where we had breakfast the other day."

He pulled up another photo.

I let out a long sigh. In a corner booth was that man. He had tattoos all over his arms. Muscular arms and legs. His expression was hard. On either side of him were Brenna and the other girl, Laura.

I wanted to cry. I took a sip of the hideous coffee in hopes of wetting my throat. "What do we do now? Since we know they're *here.*"

"*You* are not going to do anything," Stan said. "Neither of your kids will be helped if you end up getting killed. We're going to collect a small joint task force and set up an appointment with her. It'll be tomorrow night, and—"

I interrupted. "Why tomorrow? Why not tonight?"

He shook his head. "We tried to set one up for tonight, but they're booked up. And we can't afford to rattle this guy … first, because he might leave town suddenly, and second, because we can't take any chance that he's going to hurt the girls. Do you understand? We *will* want you close by, so you can come immediately once we have her."

I nodded. "Okay. But I want to be really close. Put me in the same hotel a few doors down? Or another floor?"

Wilcox nodded at me then looked at the captain. "How many officers do you think you can detail for this?"

The captain said, "If necessary I'll get you the SWAT team."

334

Wilcox shook his head. "Once we have Brenna, we'll get the address from her for where they are staying. We'll need the SWAT team on standby for that. But for the initial operation, can you detail four officers? I should be able to get some assets from the field office too."

Stan turned to me. "I want you to stop canvassing with the flyers now. We're getting close, and we don't want to spook them and have them rush out of town before tomorrow night. Understood?"

"Yes." I said. But then I spoke the words I'd been afraid of. "What if it's too late? If they're running now because I talked to him?"

"We know their phone numbers and street names and photos now. Worst case, if they leave Portland, we should be able to identify where they go pretty quickly. I don't want you to panic about that. I've got a couple of agents who are calling every once in a while from different numbers to see if they can get an earlier appointment. Just in case somebody cancels or doesn't show. Different voices each time so they won't suspect."

I closed my eyes. I wanted to call that number. But I couldn't.

"Okay. Just tell me where to be and I'll be there. I'll do whatever it takes. And Stan ... one favor? Are you in touch with the parents? Of Laura Felker?"

He nodded. "We have someone from the response unit visiting them this evening to let them know what's happening and that we believe we've found her."

"Would it be possible ... I mean ... I'd like to talk with her mother."

Wilcox gave me a long, compassionate look. Then he said, "I'll find out if we can give you her number. But I don't know that it will do you any good."

Sam

Dad and I took turns driving from seven in the morning until eleven that night, when we finally gave in to exhaustion and stopped in Burley, Idaho. We stayed in an even grosser hotel than the night before—a tiny one floor brick building with half a dozen rooms. The word MOTEL in three-foot high block letters was mounted on the roof, and between the doors were plastic chairs.

Dad turned up his nose when we got there. "Maybe we should try some place else?"

"This looks cheap," I said. "And we're only going to be here for a few more hours."

"Point," he said. "We've only got about nine hours left ... I'm figuring if we leave early enough, we can be there mid-afternoon."

He went and checked in while I fumbled with getting our things together. After two long days in the van, it was starting to look like a real mess. A few minutes later he came out.

"Well, we're in room three," he said.

Once inside, we both had second thoughts. The walls looked mildewed and the two beds looked saggy.

"It's just for a few hours," he said.

So we got ready for bed. I was both wired and exhausted. The news that the police were going to try to make contact with Brenna tomorrow night had me jittery. But I needed to rest.

First, I sent a Snapchat to Hayley. It showed half my face on one side of the picture, with our crappy hotel room in the background. I added the caption "5 Stars" to the photo.

She messaged back: **Where are u?**

Me: **Idaho.**

Hayley: **Basically nowhere.**

Me: **We'll get to Portland tomorrow. My mom called. The cops think they've identified Brenna and they're going to try to arrange a meetup. Like … an appointment. Then snatch her away from whoever has her.**

Hayley: **That's exciting. Scary even.**

Me: **What's happening with you?**

Hayley: **They can't find Mom. She's off doing meth somewhere.**

Me: **Will they send you back to ur dad?**

Hayley: **Foster home. Probably. Or stay in the emergency shelter for a while. I hope not it's scary here**

Me: **I wish u could stay with me**

Hayley: **Me 2**

Me: **Good night. Let me know what happens tomorrow? Text me? I'll be on the road all day.**

Hayley: **Good night**

There was a thirty-second delay, maybe even a minute, as I got situated under the covers. Then my phone beeped again.

"Can you turn that thing off? Or silence it?" Dad sounded groggy.

"Okay," I answered. Then I looked at Hayley's message.

It said: **I love you**

I answered back right away: **ily2**

I didn't know if she meant it as a friend … or what? Right now it didn't matter. What mattered was that she was my best friend. That I *had* a best friend.

"Dad?" I said once the lights were out.

"Mmm-hmm?"

"Do you think Mom … how will … how will she react? To me?"

Dad was silent for a long time. Long enough that I started to think he'd fallen asleep. But it turned out he was just thinking about the question, giving it real consideration. He finally responded.

"Your mom loves you. I think that's more powerful than any questions or concerns she may have. We both love you."

With that, we both drifted off to sleep.

Brenna

The door closed with a loud clang when Rick stepped outside. He'd be out there smoking and talking on the phone for a while. Then he'd come in and fuck one of us and pass out snoring.

We didn't dare try to sneak out while he was sleeping. Rick kept his gun under his pillow when he slept.

"Strawberry," Nialla whispered. "I've got a plan."

"What is it?"

"Tomorrow night, once we get on the road. I want you to pretend you're sick. Really sick. Start complaining in the morning about an upset stomach. We'll make him stop at the first rest stop out of town. He'll send us in together—once we're in there, we'll ask someone to call the police. We stay in the women's room. You be loud, sick."

"Are you crazy?" I asked. "He'll kill us."

"No way. Not if he's got that eighth grader in the car. He'll put the car in drive and just go. Or even better, they'll arrest him."

"What about when he gets out? He'll come for us, Nialla."

"We'll be long gone. I mean it. I've been stashing money. I've got fifteen hundred dollars."

"Holy shit! I thought he looked in your purse! He'd kill you for sure if he knew you had that much."

"*Fuck* him. It's under the sole of my sneakers. I cut out a square in there."

"Jesus," I said. My heart was thumping. Could we really get away? For just a second the idea flashed through my mind: if I told Rick about the money he'd be grateful. Maybe he'd finally trust me. Maybe he wouldn't hurt me anymore.

But this was *Nialla*.

"You just … be sick, okay? Can you do that?"

"Yeah," I whispered. "I can do it."

winter flower

"This time tomorrow we'll be free," Nialla said.

I closed my eyes and prayed she was right. But I didn't think she was. Rick was too smart and too dangerous for that kind of trick. He'd kill us.

That was fine. I didn't want to live any longer. Better I die now, rather than let him hurt my family any more.

Thirty-Two

~~~~~~

Erin

"Hello? Hello?" A woman answered the phone. "Mrs. Felker? My name is Erin Roberts."

I heard an intake of breath at the other end of the line. Then she said, "The man from the FBI asked me if you could call. He explained everything yesterday afternoon." She had a rich Southern Virginia accent, subtly different than what I'd grown up around in North Carolina. But there was something different about it. The same thing that was different about me. A part of her was missing. A part of her had died, and I could hear it in her voice.

I closed my eyes. A long silence stretched out between us. Finally she said, "What can I do for you, Mrs. Roberts?"

I didn't know. I didn't know why I'd wanted to call her. I didn't know what to say. Finally I whispered, "I just … I-I thought maybe we should talk. There's a chance we'll get our daughters back tomorrow. And … I don't know, I guess…"

I trailed off. I had no idea what to say. But her response made me sit up straight.

"Mrs. Roberts, my Laura is dead."

"What? I don't understand. The police think she's with—"

"I don't care what the police think. They tell me she's been selling herself all over the Internet, all over the country. That she's been whoring. That's not my daughter. Not anymore."

I found myself standing up as I listened to her hateful words. "How can you say that?" I asked. "She was abducted. Both of our daughters were abducted."

In a dead, sad tone, the woman said, "She'd be better dead. She *should* have died instead of allowing herself to be used as a harlot. Now she'll burn in hell."

winter flower

I wanted to puke. Surely she didn't mean this … was this woman mentally ill? Brainwashed? How could she say this about *her child?*

"How dare you?" I spoke in a savage tone. "How *dare* you judge her like that? Hell is where she's *been!*"

I hung up the phone. I couldn't bear to talk with that woman any more. Not even for a second.

I looked at the clock. I'd been pacing in my room for hours. It was eleven in the morning, and it would still be hours and hours before the police operation mounted.

I should sleep, I thought, but I couldn't. Instead, I paced more.

Brenna

I bent over the sink in the hotel bathroom, halfway through doing my makeup. "Oh, God," I said.

Nialla spoke, her words coming out too quickly. "You okay, baby? Something wrong?"

Rick gave her an annoyed look, then said to me, "The fuck is wrong with you?"

I shook my head. "Stomach hurts."

He snorted. "Well, get all the shit out of your system now. Because you're working tonight. You got a full lineup of appointments."

Nialla said, "Do you ever get tired of acting like an asshole?"

Rick slapped her but not as hard as he could have. "Shut up. You've been gettin' out of pocket lately. Don't think I don't notice. Don't start thinking you're anything more than a whore."

She cringed back from him. He walked away, lighting a cigarette. "You bitches get ready." He let the door slam behind him.

She gave the door a look of naked hate.

Cole

The approach into Portland on I-84, driving alongside the impossibly blue Columbia River, was beautiful. Driving with Sam beside me as she smiled and chattered and took a thousand selfies felt impossibly *normal.* The pines, swaying in the breeze, whisked past us as the miles disappeared behind us.

Then, almost without transition, we crossed a bridge into Portland. Before the bridge, there was little more than trees, but after, the scene shifted immediately to a suburb that could have been anywhere in America. Large developments, big box stores, chain gas stations. As soon as we crossed into the city, Sam tensed up. She started tapping her fingers on the doorframe, then pulled down the visor to look at herself in the mirror.

She started to fidget with her makeup—which she'd insisted on spending twenty minutes on before we could leave the hotel this morning. Powdering herself. Fixing her eyeshadow. The bruises were still visible on her face, but the swelling had gone away completely by now, and makeup covered the worst of it.

"Nervous?" I asked.

"Wouldn't you be?"

I smiled. "I would. But you know what? It's going to be okay. Mom is going to see exactly the same thing I do."

"What's that?"

I took a deep breath. "She's going to see you smile. That's all it will take." I got choked up before I could finish my statement.

Sam blushed. "Have I been smiling a lot?"

I looked almost skeptically at my son. *Daughter.* "Sam, you've smiled more in the past two days than you have in the last four years. It breaks my heart that you were so unhappy … because I'd do anything to make you and Brenna and your mom happy."

Now it was Sam's turn to look skeptical. "Even Mom?"

"*Especially* her," I replied. "Whatever else happens … I want her back. I've loved her since the minute I laid eyes on her twenty years ago. We grew distant. I screwed up and betrayed her in the worst possible way. But I swear to God, I'm going to do everything I can to bring our family back together."

Sam stared at me, her blue eyes watering. A tear ran down her cheek, and another. "I love you, Dad," she whispered.

"I love you, Sam."

We merged onto I-84 as traffic became heavier. Trees on both sides of the road, pines and firs and I didn't know what all.

Sam took another selfie and started typing. She must be sending a Snapchat to Hayley.

There it was. Exit 19, Division Street and Powell Boulevard. "This is our exit," I said.

Sam went silent. I felt anxious too. I'd thought about reuniting with Erin for days. Things had been *awful* between us. She'd been drinking, distant. We hadn't slept in the same bed in weeks—truthfully, except a few times, in months.

Would she turn me away? I couldn't blame her if she did. Our marriage had been on the rocks for four years, since well before Brenna's disappearance, and that was mostly my fault.

As I turned on to Eighty-second Avenue, my phone announced, "In one thousand feet, you will reach your destination."

I swallowed. We stopped at a red light and I tapped my fingers on the steering wheel. And then something crazy happened.

"Dad?"

I looked over at Sam. "Yeah?"

"She loves you too, you know."

"Who?"

"Mom. She's always loved you. You can do it. You can win her back."

My eyes watered uncontrollably. I wiped at them furiously and muttered, "Jesus Christ."

The light turned green. I began to drive forward and said, "Thanks, Sam."

She shrugged and went back to looking out the window.

One more red light, and then I was turning right into the parking lot of an awful-looking motel.

It was dirty and old. It had bare metal poles supporting the second floor walk, and a window to one of the guest rooms was boarded up.

I parked the car and took a deep breath.

"At least it looks better than the place we stayed last night," Sam said.

"That's … optimistic," I replied. I got out of the van at the same time Sam did and we walked across the small parking lot.

The door to her room opened. She must have seen us coming across the parking lot.

I stopped for just a second and caught my breath as Erin stepped out of the darkness into the bright sunshine. The rays caught her hair, highlighted red glints. Her blue eyes were flooded with tears.

Sam approached her slowly. She'd dressed carefully that morning in a flowered sleeveless dress. She really did look like a girl. It was hard to watch—but good at the same time. It was so confusing.

Erin didn't seem confused at all. She looked at Sam with wide eyes and said, "Oh, baby, you're beautiful."

Then the two of them were embracing. Erin had her arms wrapped protectively around Sam, one hand on the back of her head. Sam winced—her ribs were still very painful—and Erin eased the pressure.

I approached slowly. I didn't want Erin to jerk away. Then ... I wrapped them both with my arms. The three of us stood there, arms around each other, for a long time.

Thirty-Three

~~~~~~

Sam

I bore the hug as long as I could, because, despite the pain in my ribs, I knew that this was an essential moment. I couldn't remember the last time my parents had embraced like this, and held me like this. And even though Dad said he was determined to win back Mom's trust, I knew it wasn't that simple. I knew that this might be the *last* time they embraced like this, and I wanted to memorize this moment. I wanted to memorize the love I felt, the sunshine and the cool air.

But then I had to break it off, because it hurt too much.

Mom and Dad were looking at each other with expressions I couldn't read. Mom said, "Come on in, you can see where I've been staying. It's not much … I told them this morning I'm checking out so we can move to a place big enough for all of us."

Mom's room was gross. Unidentifiable stains marred the carpet, and there was mold on the ceiling. The room smelled vaguely of cigarette smoke and sweat.

Mom was jabbering on about random stuff … the room, how much she had paid, where we were going to be staying. I barely heard her, because my eyes fixed on a stack of paper sitting on the small desk next to the television.

I swallowed looking at the flyer. It was titled, *Have you seen this girl?* Two photos of Brenna were displayed side by side on the flyer. One of the pictures was from before she disappeared, and the other was the mug shot which had been taken when she was arrested.

I stared at the mug shot, trying to see through the surface of the paper into my sister's soul. I was frightened by what I saw. There was anger there, but little else. She looked as if someone had squeezed all the life out of her, leaving an empty shell staring at the camera.

I looked in my sister's eyes. *What have you been through? How can I help?* We'd have to find her first.

I was concentrating so hard on the flyer that I didn't realize both of my parents had fallen silent.

Mom said, "Are you okay?"

"Yeah." I looked back and forth between them and said, "But can we grab some lunch? I'm starving."

Erin

I couldn't keep my eyes off of Sam. And it was more than just the makeup and clothes that he—she—Sam—wore. Yes, that was astonishing. Sam wore a lovely dress, sleeveless and calf-length, displaying obviously shaved legs. Sam's makeup was inexpertly done, but it wasn't bad, nor was it overdone.

Sam moved carefully, protecting his broken ribs. Underneath the makeup, the black eye and bruising was visible, as was the very thinly visible scab in the shape of a letter U on his cheek.

Those were surface differences, however. There was more happening here. For most of his life, Sam shuffled around life looking down at the ground. He shrank back at social events and stood off to the side at school dances. But something had changed. When Cole and Sam had walked across the parking lot to me, Sam had looked directly at me, making eye contact and smiling. Sam moved with an easy confidence, which was a dramatic change from normal.

In response to Sam's question, I said, "Let me check out, and we'll go eat." It didn't take long for me to pack my remaining belongings and check out. I won't pretend that I wasn't relieved to be out of this motel—aside from the dirt, I feared for my safety the entire time I was here.

Sam rode with me the couple of blocks to the diner. I felt awkward … I didn't know what to say, what to ask. I didn't know how to begin the conversation with my son who transformed into a young lady seemingly overnight.

The diner was nearly empty when we went in, the only customers an elderly couple sitting in one of the booths. We selected a booth, and for the next forty-five minutes we talked and caught up. Cole told us about work, about Oxford's mayor making the racist comments, the conflict with Cole's boss, and the disastrous health inspection.

I watched Cole as he spoke, and halfway through his story I realized that something had changed with him. It wasn't just that he talked about work, something which he normally didn't do. It was that he talked about how he felt about it … his fears that defending his waitress would cost him his job. I found the experience confusing and a little upsetting. I didn't know why it upset me. Was it that I felt like it was too little, too late? I had wanted him to talk with me four years ago before the affair started. I had wanted him to talk to me before he chose to commit a felony.

Why was I upset? And how much of a role had I played in his inability or unwillingness to talk about his fears? What did it cost him now to tell me he'd been afraid?

Sam told us some of what had been happening in school. With a lot of prompting and questioning, Sam talked about the bullying, the photos that had been distributed, his conflict with Cody and Ashley and defense of Hayley.

Her. I needed to remind myself … Sam seemed to have no hesitations or doubts. And Cole was right about one thing—for the first time I could remember, Sam seemed happy. As disturbing and difficult as it was for me to see my son sitting there with blush and mascara and eyeshadow and a sleeveless dress, it wasn't nearly as disturbing as seeing my son shuffling around looking dead inside.

"You seem pretty serious about the gender … switch."

Sam's eyes widened a little. "Mom, it's not a switch. It's me finally telling the truth about who I am. You've always told me to be honest and true to myself. But this is the one area where I couldn't. I was too ashamed. I can't hide anymore. I'm not going back. You can't make me—"

As Sam spoke, he—she—became more and more visibly upset with each word. I finally held up a hand as if to say, *stop*. "Sam—I wouldn't dream of trying to stop you." I took a deep breath, trying to contain my emotion. "The only thing I want for you in this world is for you to be happy. If this is what you need, I'll back you up."

She seemed to deflate, relaxing a little.

Cole said, "Just understand, Sam. It's difficult for us both. Not because we don't love you or don't accept you. We absolutely love you and accept you. It's just a big change—and it's going to mean you're going to have a lot of very difficult challenges ahead. I'd spare you from those if I could, but I can't. But I'll be there for you through it all, no matter what."

I did something then that startled Cole just as much as it did me. I reached across the table and took his hand, wrapping mine around it. "We both will."

Cole gripped my hand back.

346

Cole

After lunch, I drove behind Erin as she led the way to the new hotel she had selected. Sam rode with her, and I was almost ashamed to feel relief for a few minutes alone to collect my thoughts about the dizzying changes of the past few days.

The frisson of her touch on my hand seemed to throb with the intensity of a flame. I drove with both hands on the wheel, and I could see the spot where her hand had gripped mine. We hadn't held hands in years. I was drunk with questions. What did it mean? Was she signaling me? Was she taking a step closer to me, or even a step closer to forgiving me? Was it a signal to Sam that regardless of what happened to our marriage, that we were united in supporting her?

And then there was Sam. Her counselor, Mrs. Mullins, had been quite pointed in her questioning about Sam's need for therapy. She'd been through incredible trauma — the loss of her sister, and if I was honest, the loss of her parents. I couldn't help but wonder if that had somehow led to Sam's gender difficulties.

No. Maybe it had accelerated it. But in retrospect, I felt like an idiot for not realizing it years ago. As early as kindergarten, Sam had expressed preferences for shows and toys marketed toward girls, to sparkly clothes and nail polish. When we bought the kids a Nintendo Wii, Sam had mostly ignored Lego Star Wars in favor of Dance Party Three.

While I couldn't prevent the stab of regret and missed opportunities I felt, I had to set that aside. I couldn't fix what I had failed to do in the past, but maybe I could make some amends now.

That feeling was only underscored when I stood in line to check in at the Holiday Inn several miles from where Erin had been staying. The hotel was a decided step up, and while we couldn't afford to stay here for long, this was where Stan Wilcox had told Erin to be. From the check-in line, I looked back at Erin and Sam, who were standing next to our bags near the front door. They stood side by side, Erin's arm around Sam's waist. Sam leaned her head on Erin's shoulder, with her eyes closed, and was listening as Erin spoke quietly. I couldn't tell what Erin was saying, but her eyes were glassy with tears. Sam had a contented smile on her face.

I would have done anything to see Erin smile like that.

Finally, we got upstairs into the room and began to unpack. Sam threw herself on one of the beds, bouncing slightly, and grabbed the remote control.

She looked at us and said, "You guys need to talk. I'll hang out here and watch TV, so you can go."

I looked at Sam and shook my head slowly, then at Erin. She gave me a wry smile and shrugged. "She's right."

We left Sam there watching a show about ... *werewolves ... in high school?* Erin and I were silent as we walked to the elevator, rode down, and exited the front of the hotel. A restaurant was attached to the hotel, so we walked over. The whole time I felt anxious.

We made inconsequential small talk as the hostess led us to a table. I ordered a bourbon and Coke; Erin a cosmopolitan.

Once our drinks arrived we didn't really have any excuse to put it off.

I swallowed and said, "Erin—" just as she looked at me and said, "Cole?"

"Go ahead," I said. "Sorry."

She said, "No. You."

I took a deep breath. "Listen ... I know I've fucked our lives up in so many ways. I ... wasn't honest with you. I wasn't there for you. I cheated. I got thrown in jail and lost my job, and—"

"No—" she started to say.

"Let me finish, okay?"

She nodded.

"I need you to know I accept responsibility for the areas where I screwed up. And I want to do better. I want ... Erin..."

She stared at me, rapt.

"Erin, I love you. I've always loved you. I know we grew apart, and that was mostly my fault. But, I want a second chance. I want our family back. I want ... I want *us* back. I'd do anything in the world for your forgiveness..."

Ahhhhh, shit. I was getting choked up, my eyes watering. Tears were running down her face too, and she had her hands somehow clasped around each other, as if she was forcing herself to hold back. I wiped a hand across my face and said, "Erin. Can you give us a chance to be husband and wife again? Will you forgive me?"

She nodded, rapidly, then said, "Yes. I forgive you. Can you forgive me? I ... I left a long time ago. Not physically, but I was ... I was so angry, way back when you told me you didn't want me to work for Win Without War. I just got more and more angry and resentful. I—"

"I'm so sorry," I said. "I'd give anything to change that."

She shook her head. "I mean it. I forgive you. Just ... please forgive me too. Can we try again? Can we start over? We have to for the kids, but ... I mean ... for us? Can we do it for me and you?"

I reached across the table and took her hands. Both of us were crying. But the touch of her hands across that table reminded me that Erin meant everything to me, that she was the love of my life.

I stood up, and she slid out of the booth. I pulled her to me and buried my face in the hair at her neck.

"I'm so sorry," I whispered. "I love you."

Then she finally said the words I hadn't heard in I didn't know how many years. "And I love you, Cole."

It was several minutes before we separated and awkwardly sat back down in the booth. Probably everybody in the restaurant was staring but I didn't care. All I cared about right now was my kids and the woman who sat across from me.

The spell was broken a moment later by the ringing of her phone. She ignored it for a moment, but then said, "It might be—"

"Go ahead."

She pulled out her phone and said, "It's Stan Wilcox."

"Hello?" she said, putting the phone to her ear. She turned it slightly so I could hear it.

"Erin? Are you at the Holiday Inn yet? If not, we need you there as soon as you can. We reached them. We've got an appointment set."

Erin started to slide out of the booth as I waved at our waitress. I pulled out my debit card and handed it to the waitress as she approached. "I need to pay right away," I said. "We've got to go. It's urgent."

In three minutes, we were half walking, half running back to the hotel.

Thirty-Four

Cole

An Asian American woman in her early thirties met us at the entrance to the hotel. She wore blue jeans and a sweatshirt bearing the logo Portland International Beer Fest. Sam had already responded to my text and was in the lobby, pacing nervously.

"Cole, this is Melody Michelson, she's with the human trafficking task force in Portland. Melody, this is my husband Cole, and s—*daughter*, Sam."

Even that small sentence seemed like a test. And from Sam's expression, Erin had passed.

Detective Michelson didn't waste any time on small talk. She led us through the lobby to the elevators and up to the second floor to a small conference room.

The conference room was dominated by a large table. Around it, several men and women were seated—four of them uniformed police officers, the others in civilian clothes ranging from very casual to suits and ties. I recognized one man, Stan Wilcox.

Wilcox stood and approached as soon as we entered the room, holding his hand out. "Cole, it's good to see you."

"You too. You remember our daughter, Sam."

Wilcox didn't even blink at the introduction of Sam as our daughter. I hadn't expected it to be an issue ... except that maybe I continuously expected it to be an issue. He shook Sam's hand and smiled at her, then said, "Let's get this show rolling."

Wilcox introduced the police and FBI agents in the room. Then he said, "Most of you are familiar with some of the basics of this case. The girl we're trying to recover was kidnapped two years ago in Northern Virginia. Her name is Brenna Roberts. She's been trafficked in multiple cities over the past two years, and is currently in Portland. Our objective is in two stages—free her, then when we know where her pimp is staying, we're going to go after him, as well as another woman who has been trafficked."

Nods around the table. Wilcox continued. "This is her family," he continued, pointing in our direction. "We've asked them to be present in the command center so that we can reunite them with the girl immediately once she is free. Here is how this is going to go down. Detective Yeltsin will pose as the buyer and will be in the room to meet Brenna when she arrives."

Wilcox nodded at a fortyish man who wore a suit with a blue shirt and an open collar.

"Detective Michelson, you and officers Linley and Morris will be in the adjoining room. Officer Auburn will be in the room directly across the hall. You all will be waiting for my signal to enter the room. Once she's in custody, we'll immediately send Mrs. Roberts upstairs to the room."

I interrupted. "Why not all three of us?"

Wilcox said, "We should be able to do that almost right away. But it's important we make sure everything is secure before we get a crowd in there. Okay?"

It wasn't okay but I would have to live with it. I nodded.

"I would like the three of you," Wilcox said, pointing to three of the FBI agents, "to be watching the entrances to the hotel for her arrival." Wilcox handed out copies of the mug shot.

Wilcox walked the team through several different possibilities, such as if the pimp came into the hotel with her or if she ran. As he spoke, I watched a technician setting up three large-screen laptops on the desk at the end of the conference room. He was pulling up software I didn't recognize, but its function became clear enough. One showed a camera view of a hotel room, facing the door from across the room. Another was a hallway, presumably the one leading up to the room. Another was trained on the front entrance of the hotel.

As the meeting broke up, Wilcox gave more detailed instructions to the officers who would be in the adjoining room. Then he sent them on. Turning to us, he said, "From here on out I want the three of you to stay here. There's a restroom off the conference room right over there, and we'll order in pizza. But the pimp has seen Erin—we can't take a chance of him spotting you."

Sam whispered to me, "I'm scared."

I put my hand on her shoulder. "Me too," I said. "I'm scared something will go wrong. Or that she won't come at all. Or … I don't know what all I'm scared of."

Erin said, "Whatever it is, we'll meet it together this time." Sam's eyes watered, and Erin continued. "I know we fell apart the past couple of years. We blew it. But I promise we'll try to do better."

Brenna

The gas station bathroom was disgusting. A single bulb barely illuminated the room with its filthy walls with obscenities scrawled everywhere. The floor was wet.

I took a drag off my cigarette as my eyes scanned the writing on the walls, most of it obscene. My hand shook as I held the cigarette.

Banging on the door. "Strawberry! What the fuck is taking so long?"

"I'll be out in a minute," I said, trying my best to sound sick. Finally, I tossed the cigarette in the toilet and flushed. A moment later I stepped outside.

Rick glared at me as I walked out into the parking lot. The sky overhead was clouding over, darkness gathering.

"Sorry," I said. I kept a hand clutched over my stomach. There was no way Rick was buying this act. He didn't seem even remotely concerned.

"Get in the car. We're late."

He reached for my arm but I pulled away. There was only so much defiance he would put up with before hurting me, but sometimes I pushed those limits. "Leave me alone. I'm coming."

I got in the backseat of the Mercedes and curled my legs up, leaning against the door. Rick slammed the front door when he got in, as Nialla said, "You okay, baby?"

She sounded so fake I didn't see how Rick could miss it. He just said, "She's fine."

She gave him a withering look. "She might have food poisoning."

He muttered, "If she doesn't hit her quota for the day she might get fist poisoning."

I stared at him with a dull hate that burned, leaving a twisted and tortured thing that was all that was left of me. I'd gladly die if I could somehow take him with me, erase his petty abuse and violence from the face of the earth.

"Put your seatbelt on, Strawberry."

I did, quickly. Rick didn't say that out of concern … he said it because we were approaching a police car. We stopped at the red light beside the blue and white car with the words Portland Police emblazoned on the side. One of the cops looked over at us, eyes bouncing from Nialla in the front seat to me and back.

I once thought that if I could just get to a police officer, I'd be safe. I'd been kidnapped after all. All I had to do was find a police officer and ask for help.

The first cop I met after Rick took me quickly disabused me of that notion.

Some cops were good, I was sure. That's what my mom and dad had told me growing up, anyway. But in several different cities, Rick had used me to pay for protection from the cops. Nothing like a sixteen-year-old girl to get a corrupt cop to look the other way. After all, I was just a whore as far as they were concerned.

The light turned green and we moved on. It was fully dark now, the headlights on the other cars glaring in the darkness. Rick began to talk.

"Make this guy happy, Strawberry. When he found out you had an appointment already he doubled the rate. Maybe you can get him to give you an extra tip."

I shrugged, indifferent.

He saw it in the rearview mirror. "Both of you are getting out of pocket lately. Fucking burnouts. I should sell you to the Mexicans and get a new stable."

Nialla said, "I don't give a shit what you do anymore."

The crack of his hand slapping the side of her face was loud enough that I flinched. He didn't say anything else.

Ten minutes later we approached the hotel, one of the thousands of midgrade anonymous hotels where horny businessmen traveled away from their wives for meetings and conferences. Mostly middle-aged, mostly overweight, they left their wives and kids at home and traveled across the country, ordering up girls like pizza.

Rick turned into the parking lot just before the hotel. Asshole had been doing that ever since he got the Mercedes. He didn't give a shit what happened to us, but he didn't want the police impounding his car.

I got out as he called, "Be right here at 8:15."

I waved a hand at him, acknowledging his order, and pulled my skirt down around my hips. There was no fucking sidewalk, so I had to tiptoe across the damp grass in my heels. Then I walked across the hotel parking lot and into the lobby.

I had learned long since that the best policy was to march straight to the elevators without acknowledging the front desk staff. As always, the front desk clerk eyed me suspiciously. But he let me pass without comment.

I clutched my bag close to me, pressed the up button, and waited for the elevator. A man with salt and pepper hair approached and stood next to me, waiting for the elevator. In the reflection of the polished doors I saw his eyes trace the curves of my body. I ought to be used to it by now, but it made my skin crawl anyway.

The warning bell dinged and the elevator doors opened. I stepped on and moved to the side, expecting him to stand opposite me. But no ... this guy was a charmer. He stood no more than an inch from me, both of us bunched on one side of the elevator.

I exhaled gratefully when the elevator stopped at my floor and I squeezed past him. As I stepped off the elevator, I felt his hand touch my ass and I spun around. "Keep your fucking hands to yourself, *asshole*."

I didn't wait for an answer. I turned away and looked for the numbers on the walls that would indicate which direction to go. These hotels were mostly laid out the same everywhere, so I found my way almost instantly and began walking down the hall.

I passed room 506, then 508. I could hear a television blaring in one of the rooms. On Saturday evening, there would be few people as always, but if I did see people they might be wives or kids—business hotels like this had a much higher frequency of families traveling on weekends.

I kept walking quickly, finally coming to room 522.

Every time I did this, no matter how many times, I felt a twisting in my gut at this moment. Twice in the past, I'd walked through doors like this and found men with guns on the other side. I'd been raped too many times to count, and it was just a matter of time before one of them killed me.

Maybe it would be tonight.

I lifted my left hand and knocked on the door.

Erin

Sam was eating her fourth slice of pizza. Putting on women's clothing hadn't reduced her appetite at all. Cole was pacing at the other end of the room. Every few minutes he would come and sit down next to me and we would hold hands and talk. Then, the inability to do anything would set in, and he would have to get up and pace again.

Sam's phone buzzed again, for what seemed like the thousandth time in the past hour. She tapped on her phone with her thumbs, hair dangling down over it. It was surprising really that she didn't get stuck that way.

Abruptly, Stan Wilcox sat up straight and muttered a curse. Then he spoke into his radio. "Subject is in the hall, everybody in positions! How the *hell* did she get past the front door without anyone seeing her?"

Sam let out a plaintive moan, and all three of us moved to stand behind Wilcox. I leaned close over Wilcox's shoulder. Suddenly I was second-guessing myself. Should I have allowed Sam to be here? What if something went wrong? Would she be further traumatized? What was I thinking? But I kept coming back to the discussion we'd had earlier. Trauma or not, Sam would never forgive us if we didn't let her stay.

My eyes were drawn back to the monitor. To the figure moving down the hall.

She was walking down the hallway away from the camera. She wore a too-short form-fitting black miniskirt and a sleeveless blue shirt. She walked in high heels, but expertly.

When Brenna was fifteen, she'd refused to wear heels under any circumstances.

As she walked down the long hallway, Sam began to let out a high-pitched moan and waved her hands. Cole pulled her to him and said, "It's okay. It's okay."

Brenna reached the door and stopped, facing it, maddeningly far from the camera. I couldn't even make out her face. She lifted her right hand and knocked on the door.

Thirty-Five

Erin

The next few seconds happened so fast I barely saw what happened. In the camera showing the room, Detective Yeltsin walked to the door and opened it. At that moment, two of the police officers opened the door across the hall, charged across and shoved into the room. Seconds later, she was standing back against the wall as Melody Michelson came in from the room next door.

Sam let out a cry, and Cole yelled, *"Fuck!"*

The girl in the room wasn't Brenna. Now that we could see her face, it was utterly clear. This was the other girl. Laura Felker.

As the realization came over me, it was like I'd fallen off a cliff, my stomach twisting with nausea, terror sinking over me. *Where was Brenna?*

Over the radio, we heard Melody's voice. "Get Erin down here *now*."

Wilcox said, *"Go.* Cole, you and Sam stay here."

I ran down the hall with one of the police officers, going as fast as I could.

Then we waited for the elevator. One minute. Two. *For fuck's sake!* Finally the door opened, and we rode upstairs. The officer escorted me down the hall, where two more were guarding the door.

I walked in the door of the room, struggling not to cry.

The girl who stood against the wall sucked in a breath when she saw me. "You look like Strawberry. You her mom?"

I staggered, and Melody took my arm. Forcing my voice through tears, I said, "Yes. I am. Do you know where she is?"

She looked like a caged animal. "Yeah," she said. "I'll help. I need to call though, or Rick will know something's wrong."

I looked at Melody, frantic, wondering if this was a trick.

Melody nodded. "You have a safe word or something?"

"No, just I'm supposed to call within five minutes. And it's almost been that long."

Melody said to the uniformed officers, "All of you step out except Linley—you can stay by the door." She stepped back, away from Laura, and waved a hand toward the bed, where a small handbag lay.

Laura took a small phone out of the bag. It looked weird, with only five brightly colored buttons on it. She pressed one and held the phone to her face.

"Hey. I'm clear ... yeah, everything's fine. I got hassled at the front desk, but I'm in the room now. Yeah ... yeah ... okay."

She hung up the phone and sat down. Then she closed her eyes and exhaled a long, slow breath.

I sat down on the bed across from her. Hesitantly, I said, "My name's Erin. Erin Roberts. Brenna's my daughter."

"I'm Nialla..." She looked at me and blinked and her eyes watered. "No. My name's Laura." Her face worked, and I realized that she had a nasty bruise forming on the left side of her face. She closed her eyes, and a tear started to fall, and then another. She wrapped her arms around herself and tucked her face down, then sucked in snot.

"Sorry," she said, demonstrating a degree of self-control and repression I didn't think I'd ever seen before.

"It's okay," Melody said. "Listen—I'm with the Human Trafficking Task Force in Portland. We're here to help."

"Cops help? Yeah, right."

I leaned forward, reaching out for her hands. "Please. Please. I just want Brenna back. I want her free."

Laura closed her eyes. "Okay," she said. She fished in her bag and brought out a pack of cigarettes and lit one. She inhaled the smoke deeply. "Tell me more."

"We thought Brenna was coming—but really the plan stays the same," Melody said. "You give us the address where you were staying. We have a SWAT team standing by. They'll move in and take down your trafficker and free Brenna."

"Rick," Laura said. "His name's Rick. He's dangerous. Brenna *was* coming to this appointment, but some guy called and really wanted her. He said he'd pay double, and all Rick gives a shit about is money."

My stomach turned. He'd pay double. For my daughter. I knew, of course, I already knew, but the rage was overwhelming.

357

"She misses you, you know. She told me the other day she found one of your flyers. It really broke her up. But she's ... I don't know..." Laura shook her head. "She's given up."

Given up? "What do you mean?"

"Lately, she just seems ... at the end of her rope. At the end of her strength. I've been afraid she's going to kill herself, so I made a plan. An escape plan." She stared at me then shook her head.

"Your idea won't work."

My stomach sank.

Melody said, "Why not?"

"Rick checked us out of the hotel earlier. After we finish our appointments, he's planning on leaving Portland. He's got a girl he's picking up, her name's Kaylee. She's thirteen. He was planning on getting her, picking us up, and leaving town."

Melody asked in an urgent voice, "Where are you going?"

Laura shook her head. "I don't know. I really don't, Rick never tells us."

My mind was racing. If we couldn't get the SWAT team, and this Rick guy left town with Brenna and another girl—*thirteen?*—where would they go? We had no idea. She'd be lost again.

"We can't let them go," I said.

Melody looked at me then at Laura. In a gentle tone, she said, "Laura, can I bring in the FBI agent who has been searching for you and Brenna? He's right upstairs, with Brenna's father and sister. I think we need to get him in on this."

"Sure. Bring whoever you want." She looked around for an ashtray. This was a nonsmoking room, but I wasn't going to tell her that. Instead, I got up and filled a plastic cup with water and brought it to her.

"Thanks," she said.

Five minutes later, Agent Wilcox entered the room without Cole and Sam. I wondered if they had to arrest Cole to keep him from coming down here.

"Miss Felker, I'm Agent Stan Wilcox. I'm with the Child Abduction Response Unit of the FBI. I've been looking for you for a long time. Brenna, too."

"Hi," she said. She looked frightened. How old was she? Twenty? I wanted to hug her, for as long as she needed. I thought for a second about the witch of a mother she had, who would say *she'll burn in hell with all the other whores.* This poor, poor girl.

Melody said, "Stan, we've got a problem. They've already checked out of their hotel. She's getting picked up from here and they're leaving town."

Wilcox frowned. "All right ... we'll get them when they come to pick her up."

"*No!*" Laura said in horror. "Rick will fight … he'll shoot. You'll get Brenna killed! You can't!"

Jesus Christ. I felt confused and frustrated.

"Laura," Melody said.

"No. I'll go back. And I'll find a way to call you. Brenna's supposed to be faking sick. She's been doing a good job of it, all day. Our plan was to make Rick stop at a rest stop. We'll go in the bathroom and borrow someone's phone."

Wilcox shook his head. "Too dangerous. I don't have any tracking equipment and we don't have time to get any."

"I don't care," she said. "You can't shoot it out with Rick. He's fucking crazy. He'd kill Brenna for the fun of it."

I squeezed my eyes closed. This girl—this woman—was offering to go back into hell in order to protect Brenna. I had to fight back tears. I opened my eyes and said, "Let her take my phone. We'll silence it, but leave location tracking on."

"Erin…" Wilcox said. "I don't see how—"

"We can track my phone. That's how Cole found Sam when she got attacked."

Laura nodded. "I can do that. Just make sure it can't go off or buzz or anything. If Rick finds it…" She shuddered.

I took out my phone and silenced it. Then to be sure, I went to the settings and turned off vibrate mode too. "Call me," I said.

Wilcox sighed. "All right…" He dialed.

My phone lit up but didn't make a sound.

"Can you make the screen all the way dark?" he asked.

"Close," I said, dialing the brightness down all the way.

I looked up at Wilcox. "Can you call Cole down here? So we can make sure he can track the location?"

Wilcox nodded, but he looked dubious.

Laura took the phone from me. Reaching into her purse, she slid the phone in between the seam and the outside. She shook the bag.

"Can't see it," she said. "But it's hard. If he touches my purse, he'll know."

Melody asked, "How often does he do that?"

She shook her head. "Not often. And he'll be distracted tonight. With this girl Kaylee, I bet he won't even look at me. He's always like that with the new ones, and especially the young ones."

The young ones. I wanted to vomit. I wondered how many women's lives this man had destroyed. I could hear Stan saying, *Both girls were shot in the back of the head with a large caliber pistol. They were executed.*

"Are you sure you want to do this?" I asked, trying not to start crying. "You're putting yourself in danger."

She shrugged. "I'm always in danger. But I want you to get Strawberry out. She's…" Laura closed her eyes. "I love her. And I'm afraid of what will happen."

I don't know why, but impulsively I said, "Can I give you a hug?"

She sniffed hard and nodded. I carefully moved over to the other bed beside her and put an arm around her. She took a deep shuddering breath, and then sniffed again, while tears began to roll down her face. "I'll try to help her. I will. I'm sorry I couldn't stop him back then, back when he picked her up." Her voice was a light almost extinguished. Sad and quiet and understated. But she shook as she said the words.

I looked over at Melody. Her eyes were glassy.

When Cole and Sam came in the room, Melody walked over to them and began speaking in a low tone. Explaining what was happening, I guess. I couldn't really hear over Laura's sob's. I slowly stroked my fingers through her hair and whispered, "It's okay. It's all going to be okay."

Brenna

It was still early for me when I left the hotel, but the exhaustion and stress of pretending to be sick was wearing on me. I was pretty sure this was my last appointment though. Rick was in a hurry to get out of town.

I felt sick. The client I'd just come from had hurt me, twisting my nipples so hard I cried out in pain. I barely cared what happened to me anymore, but at least Nialla's plan was worth a try. Maybe we could run for a while before he found us and killed us.

A drop of rain hit my face, then another, as I walked across the parking lot and back to the sidewalk. I dialed Rick. He answered right away.

"I'm coming out now."

"Go down to the gas station and wait for me. I'll be there in five minutes."

Fine. Fucking walking in the mud with no sidewalk in heels. Why didn't they put sidewalks in neighborhoods like this? The gas station looked like it was a hundred yards away. I walked that way, finally giving up and taking my shoes off.

I finally got to the gas station and waited near the ice machine. A couple minutes later Rick drove up in the Mercedes.

The eighth grader, Kaylee, was in the front seat next to Rick. Jesus. She had no idea the hell she was in for. None. I walked over and climbed into the back seat, behind Kaylee. I didn't want to be close to Rick.

Before he could even tell me to, I got the money out of my purse and passed it to him. Three hundred and fifty dollars.

"Oh nice. He was feeling generous, huh?"

"He was a fucker," I said.

"Shut up," he said. I turned and looked out the window. "We're gonna pick up Nialla and blow this town. Fucking hate it here. Maybe we'll go to San Francisco again, pick up some high rollers."

I didn't give a fuck what we did, so I didn't answer. It was really starting to rain now.

Rick's phone rang. He answered it. "Yeah. All right. Meet me where I dropped you, then." He gunned the engine to race through a yellow light then turned onto another road, this one with fewer lights. I could see a Holiday Inn ahead.

A couple of minutes later, Rick turned into the parking lot of a chain restaurant next to the hotel and drove the car around back. Nialla stepped out of the shelter of an awning.

"Get in the back, Kaylee."

"What?"

"Nialla rides up front. At least while she's still my bottom girl. Though she's a fucking burnout—might not last much longer."

Kaylee looked put out but got in the back with me. Rain was coming down harder now, and Nialla was dripping wet when she got in the car.

But I could see her face well enough ... she'd been crying. Her mascara had run and been wiped away.

"You look like shit," Rick said. "Why don't you clean your face."

Nialla shook her head and opened up her purse, handing over money. It looked like a couple hundred dollars. Then she set the purse down on the floor, next to her right foot.

That was weird. In a strained voice, Nialla said, "Strawberry, you doing any better?"

I shook my head. "Stomach hurts like hell," I said. Something was wrong. She spoke in a wooden tone, like she was freaking out about something.

"What the fuck is wrong with you?" Rick asked.

Nialla swallowed, glanced back at me, then at Rick. "Asshole was rough. My throat's scratched."

Rick chuckled. Because he thought shit like that was funny. He turned right, headed down a busy divided highway with businesses on both sides. "Seriously, though. What the fuck is wrong, Nialla?"

"Nothing," she replied.

"Are you fucking holding out on me?"

"No, Rick. I just don't feel well. Maybe I'm coming down with what Strawberry has. I don't know."

He pulled to a stop at a red light. Then he said, "You're holding out on me, aren't you. How much? You gonna fucking betray me? Run away?"

"Rick, I'm not. Really, I'm not."

His eyes fell on me in the rearview mirror. "Are you in on this bullshit, Strawberry? I didn't fucking smell anything when you came out of the bathroom."

"Gross, Rick!" Nialla shouted.

He stepped on the gas when the light turned green and drove with his left hand. He held his right out. "Give me your purse."

"There's nothing in there!" Nialla said. Now she sounded genuinely afraid. What the hell was going on?

To my left, behind Rick, Kaylee had shrunk down into her seat, eyes wide, as if she was just now realizing what kind of trouble she might have gotten herself into.

Rick shouted. "Give me the goddamned purse!"

Lightning outside illuminated everything. Traffic was lightening up, but rain was starting to really come down.

The next words out of Rick's mouth were quieter, but deadlier in tone. "Don't make me say it again, you fucking bitch."

Then I realized Rick was pointing the gun at Nialla.

She shook harder than I'd ever seen her before. I didn't know what was wrong. But it was serious, whatever it was. She picked the purse up and turned it upside down, dumping everything out.

"There, do you see?" she shouted. Condoms and her phone and cigarettes and other stuff fell out all over her lap.

"Pass it to me," he said, his voice cold.

She closed her eyes. I didn't know what was happening here, but it wasn't good. She passed the bag over.

Rick took a right turn onto a highway ramp. As he did so, he said in a low, dangerous voice, "What the *fuck* is this?"

He held up an iPhone.

"Rick..." she said. "I—"

"*Whose is this?*" he shouted. "Did you fucking steal it?"

"It's ... I—"

He pressed the power button. The face of the phone lit up.

Impossibly, the picture on the phone lock screen—it was a picture of me and Sam. *No. No. No.* This couldn't be. What the hell was happening? I sank my head into my hands. Was I going crazy?

Rick opened his window. I glanced up to see him throwing the phone, hard, away from the car. He was silent now, brooding, as he drove, fast, *way too fast*, down the highway, weaving in and out of traffic, around the other cars. Horns honked at us, but then he braked suddenly and got off the highway.

At the bottom of the ramp he jerked the car to the left, drove under the bridge, then got back on the highway going in the opposite direction.

He kept a few miles over the speed limit and said in a low, dangerous voice, "Everybody shut up."

None of us had spoken in minutes. And I wasn't going to start now.

Where did the phone come from? How could it have that picture? I didn't understand it, and the implications were scaring the crap out of me.

Had Nialla somehow encountered my *parents?*

Not possible.

Cole

"Okay," Wilcox said, standing near the conference table. He sipped a cup of coffee. "We got a charger for Cole's phone, right? We don't need it running out of battery now." He took a deep breath. The entire team was gathering in the conference room.

I put my arms around Erin. "I'm proud of you. That was tough."

"She was so lost," Erin whispered. "But she still went back for Brenna."

Sam stayed close. She hadn't moved from my side in a long time now.

I turned toward Wilcox and kept an arm around each of them.

"All right. James, did you get the make and model of the car?"

"White car ... I *think* it was a Mercedes. Not sure what year. They were mostly blocked by the building next door."

Melody said, "We've got two unmarked cars headed that way. Linley's giving them directions. Right now they're headed down Sandy Boulevard, I think they're going to get on I-84."

Wilcox nodded. "Soon as we can, we need to get trail cars in sight of them, in case the battery on that phone fails. Melody?"

"Working on it."

"All right." Wilcox took out his own cell phone and dialed a number and began to speak with someone.

I said to Sam, "You hanging in there?"

Sam nodded. "I'm just ... I-I wish it had been Brenna."

"Me too," Erin said. "But that girl ... she cares about Brenna a lot. She's going to look out for her."

"I hate waiting," Sam said. Then she leaned back in her chair and took out her phone.

"Well," Erin said to me. "That was a lot of words all at once for a teenager."

"Yeah. Yeah it was."

"I meant to ask you, have you talked with Jeremiah?"

"Not since last night. I'll text him— oh, I can't, can I?" My phone was sitting with the three computers, as Officer Linley watched the map as it updated and relayed instructions over the radio.

I watched, puzzled. Linley was looking at the phone, consternation on his face. "Detective Michelson?"

"What is it?" she asked.

"The position hasn't moved in like three or four minutes. It's just sitting on the on-ramp to 84."

Everybody in the room froze except Wilcox, who strode across the room. "What did you say?" he asked.

"The position hasn't updated at all. They're not moving."

"*Shit!* Get all the units you can and move in on that spot. Tell them there are potentially three captives in the car! Melody, get that SWAT team moving! And get the highway patrol. They were headed onto 84 West, maybe they ditched the phone."

Around us, the police and FBI agents boiled into action.

Thirty-Six

Brenna

The silence in the car was suffocating. At least an hour had passed since Rick had last spoken, and as that time stretched by I became more and more afraid.

After Rick had turned around on the highway, he drove three exits, then got off again. I quickly lost track of where we were, as he took seemingly random turns onto more and more isolated roads.

I was barely conscious of my surroundings anyway. All I could see was the picture on that phone. Me and Sam.

Where had the picture come from? Where had the *phone* come from? It wasn't possible, unless somehow Nialla had encountered my mother. She must have, but why did she have Mom's phone? Was she planning on using it to call from the rest stop later? Why take that kind of risk?

Then it hit me. The phone had a GPS. Somehow after two years my mom or dad or both had found where I was, and had called to make an appointment to try to rescue me. That's the only thing it could be. And because that *other* asshole had offered more money for me, Nialla was sent instead.

But why in God's name did she come back? She was already planning on trying to escape.

Unless it was to come back for me.

Oh, Nialla.

We were deep in the woods in the middle of nowhere when Rick finally came to a stop. He parked the car next to a boarded-up convenience store on an isolated stretch of a two-lane highway. Knee-high grass grew up through some of the cracks in the parking lot, and the pavement was so broken up it looked like gravel in some places.

Rick turned off the engine. I heard no sound but ticking from the engine.

365

He kept his hands on the wheel and spoke in a deceptively mild tone. I knew the tone was a lie—the veins on his forearms had popped out, prominent against his skin from rage.

"Where did that phone come from?"

"Rick, I—"

"Answer me. How did you get a *fucking* iPhone, why was it *hidden* in your purse, and why the *fuck* did it have a picture of Strawberry?"

In a pleading tone, Nialla said, "Please … I didn't … I just—"

"You just what?"

Nialla sobbed and struggled to put together a coherent sentence. "Rick, I didn't mean to lie to you. It was Strawberry's mom … at my last appointment. She begged me to bring the phone. Just so she could talk to her. That was all. I swear to God. She just wanted to know that she was alive."

I gasped. I didn't mean to, I couldn't help it.

"What about the cops? How many of them were there?" His voice was urgent.

"I swear, there were no cops. It was just her. Rick, you gotta believe me. I didn't—"

"Get out of the car."

Rick's command was spoken in a low, deadly tone. My stomach began to twist. What was he going to do to her? In the past two years I'd seen him commit unspeakable cruelties against me, against Nialla, against others. But I'd almost never heard this deliberate tone. My heart was beating rapidly in my chest.

"Rick, please…"

Without a word he opened the driver's side door and stepped out into the darkness. He strode around to the passenger side of the car, so confident in his evil that he left the keys in the ignition and knew that we would do nothing. He yanked open the passenger side door and stuck the gun in Nialla's face. With his left hand he grabbed her hair and started to tug her out of the car.

Terror gripped me. *He was going to kill her.* I screamed right along with Nialla as she fought with all of her strength to stay in the car. He hit her across the face with the butt of the pistol, cutting her scream short. And then he threw her onto the ground.

I didn't think before I acted. I opened the door of the car and ran out at him screaming. There were no words, no meaning outside the visceral cry for him to *stop*, to stop before he took away the only thing I had left in my world, before he—

He spun around and hit me in the face with the pistol. The heavy metal knocked me back and he followed that with a kick to my stomach, knocking me to the ground.

"No!" I screamed as he grabbed her by the hair and slammed her face into the ground.

Incredibly, his face was actually twisted in tears as he shouted at Nialla. "You betrayed me? *You?*"

I struggled to my feet and ran for him again, screaming, "Stop!"

My scream merged with the sound of the gunshot. My momentum carried me into his back and knocked him forward across her body.

I grabbed for his hand and the pistol, and all rational thought had left me as I screamed, "Please kill me! Do it! *Kill me! Kill me now!*" My words morphed into agonized howls.

He hit me in the face. Then again. I fell back but didn't stop screaming. I scrambled toward him again and he kicked me.

My eyes fell on Kaylee, sitting open-mouthed in the backseat, staring in horror, as she realized the hell she had walked into. Then I jumped up and ran at Rick again. "*Kill me! Do it!*"

He knocked me to the ground and wrapped his left arm around my neck and began to drag me toward the car. I fought, but then he squeezed harder and I couldn't breathe. I struggled against his arm but couldn't move. My vision began to go hazy and black, everything going dark, but I could see, through the darkness, Nialla's body on the ground, not moving, blood soaking the concrete. I felt myself lifted into the air and thrown into the trunk of the car. I screamed again but it was too late—as I lurched for the opening he slammed it shut, leaving me in the darkness.

Brenna

Something I remember: On my seventeenth birthday, I fell apart.

See, by that time I thought I'd gotten used to it. I thought I was hard, that it didn't matter anymore. We were in Cleveland at the time, and for a full year I'd seen an average of six clients a day, every single day. One time I tried to do the math, but the numbers I came up with were so horrible that I had to stop. Rick hadn't allowed me to take days off, even when I was sick, even when I was so badly hurt that I could barely move.

That night, after our last appointments, I was lying on my side on the bed, with my head in Nialla's lap.

winter flower

Out of nowhere, a special report came on the news, and there was *my* face. A special report. Missing for one year. They interviewed Mom and Dad, who were utterly devastated as they looked into the camera and pleaded for anyone who knew anything to come forward.

Then Sam came on the screen. That's when I started to cry, because Sam looked as lonely as anyone as I had ever seen. I wanted to reach out and pull her to me. I wanted to go home.

I wanted my mother.

Rick came in to the room in the middle of the show. He stared at it in disbelief then shouted, "Turn that shit off."

I couldn't move, I was crying so hard. But Nialla launched off the bed and started to shove him out of the room. "Leave her alone, goddammit!" she screamed.

For once, Rick actually listened.

That's when I knew I loved Nialla, and that I would do anything for her.

Because she had risked a brutal beating just so I could cry in peace.

But now … now she'd risked her life for me … now she'd *lost* her life for me, and there was nothing I could do to ever pay her back.

Thirty-Seven

Sam

I sat in a chair, eyes half closed, drifting. Across the room from me, Dad lay on one of the two couches in the room. Mom sprawled on the same couch as him, her hand and head resting on his chest.

Twice, Agent Wilcox had pushed Mom and Dad for all of us to go back to our room and sleep. Dad insisted on staying and listening for updates. But then he turned around and wanted to send *me* out. I made it clear that there was no way in hell I was going back to the room by myself.

And so we waited. Wilcox and Michelson stayed next to the radios, talking with their teams who were spread out around Portland searching for Brenna.

I drifted in and out of sleep, and finally moved to the other couch. I was half awake when Detective Michelson took a call shortly after sunrise, the sky still a deep blue.

"Yeah? Christ, are you sure? Where?"

Her voice dropped, quieter, and she murmured something else. Then clearly she said, "Okay."

I watched through half-lidded eyes as she stood up and stretched. She walked over to my parents and touched my dad on the shoulder. I sat up.

Dad moved first, groggy, then Mom did. Finally, both of them were sitting up.

"Is there news?" Mom asked.

Detective Michelson nodded but then glanced toward me and said, "Maybe Sam should—"

"No way," I said. "You're not sending me away like a baby. Do you think there's anything you can say that's worse than my fears?"

I was wide awake and angry.

Still groggy, Dad said, "Let her stay."

Michelson said, "Around two a.m., a retiree living in Lewisville, Washington, called the police after hearing a gunshot. This is about an hour north of Portland. By the time police got there, the retiree who reported it had found a young woman shot next to an abandoned gas station. It was Laura Felker. She was shot in the chest."

I thought about the young woman who I'd seen weeping on Mom's shoulder. She knew Brenna and cared about her. I didn't know what their relationship was, but I knew she'd gone back to help my sister. That's all I ever needed to know.

"Is she dead?" I asked.

Michelson shook her head. "No … she was flown into the Legacy Emanuel Medical Center here in Portland. She's in critical condition. Right now they don't know if she's going to make it. But we've lost the trail."

Mom shook her head, dazed. "What do you mean?"

"I'm sorry, Erin. We don't know where they went from there."

We don't know where they went from there. They'd lost her. They could be in Washington or Idaho or even Canada by now. We'd been so close, so incredibly close to finding her. I fought to keep my breathing under control as I watched the news sink in on Mom and Dad's faces.

"You lost her." Dad's voice was bitter.

Detective Michelson said, "I'm sorry."

Mom's voice was hoarse and broken as she asked, "So what happens next?"

"We have an APB out searching for a white Mercedes, and we distributed pictures of Brenna and her trafficker in all the surrounding states. We're going to shut down here, we're all finished at the hotel obviously. Agent Wilcox will coordinate the response out of the FBI field office. We have a detective at the hospital in the event Laura regains consciousness."

Mom replied, "We're going to the hospital then."

Michelson shook her head. "That's probably not the best idea, Erin. They're not going to tell you anything or let you see her, only immediate family—"

Mom's face twisted in anger. "I spoke with her so-called *mother. She* says that Laura is going to hell because she's a *whore.* She doesn't have any immediate family, except maybe Brenna. We're it." Mom's eyes watered and her voice rose in pitch. "That girl risked her life for my daughter and got shot because of it. You find somebody to tell the doctors that. Because we *are* going to the hospital."

Detective Michelson nodded slowly. "I'll see what I can do."

Mom said, "Thank you."

I got up and moved over to the couch where Mom and Dad were.

Detective Michelson said, "I'll give you all some privacy. The technician will be back shortly to pick up all the gear."

"We'll find her. We'll keep looking, and we won't stop until we find her," Dad said.

His voice broke on the final words, and Mom sobbed. Dad pulled us both close to him.

Our tears could have drowned the world.

Thirty-Eight

Brenna

I don't know how long it was before I stopped screaming. I don't know how long I was locked in the trunk of the car, or how many hours passed before the driving pattern changed from continuous driving to stop-and-go. But eventually it happened. I felt my body shifting position as Rick braked and accelerated, each time shooting pain across my body.

We were in a city or town somewhere now.

Nialla was dead. No—*Laura* was dead. Never again was I going to think of her with the name that *he* gave her. Maybe I would never know how it had come about, what sequence of events had led her to have that particular phone. But it was clear that she had sacrificed her life for me. She'd risked everything and lost.

Even from the beginning, she had tried to warn me away from Rick. She'd told me to run. And then when I was too confused and ignorant to run, she took care of me through the depths of hell.

Sometime during the hours I was locked in that trunk, I realized that I had to live. I owed it to Laura to fight, to survive as long as I could. To stop Rick from making any more broken lives.

So I lay in the trunk quietly, trying to assess how badly I was injured. In a way I was lucky—the trunk was full of Rick's suitcases and the two bags that contained all of Nialla's and my belongings.

Laura.

I had to remember. I had to use her real name. Because her name mattered. Rick giving us *street names* gave him a sort of power over us. It gave him the power not just to physically intimidate us, or to throw us around or make us do things—it gave him power over our identity. And he didn't deserve her identity. He couldn't have it. I wouldn't let him.

I arranged myself as securely as I could, praying that we didn't get in an accident. With my right hand, I explored the swelling and bruising on my face. I had a nasty cut on my right cheek and my eye was swollen shut, not that I could see anything in the darkness anyway. My head was throbbing and I was in a lot of pain, but there was nothing I could do about it. My pills were in my bag, in the backseat. They might as well have been a thousand miles away.

In some ways this wasn't that different from the ordeal I'd gone through in the closet two years ago. Then I had only a tiny sliver of light as my sensory input. Now, there was no light, but there was the noise of traffic, the vibration of the tires against the road, the occasional horn honking.

Traffic.

Where there was traffic, there were police. I couldn't trust them to protect me; past experience had taught me that. Cops didn't care about people like me. They didn't care about *whores.*

But would they care about the fact that he just killed somebody?

It was worth a try. I struggled to reposition myself so that I was facing the rear of the car, and then carefully I felt along the back wall. Would it be possible to disconnect the taillights? Would that be enough to get us pulled over? There had to be a way to get at the brake or taillights from in here.

I felt all around and found carpet and metal. No wires, nothing I could find that turned or twisted or disconnected. I kept searching, pulling at the carpet, trying to find a corner or something that bent down or shoved out of the way. Did they replace them from the outside? I'd never seen it done, I didn't really know.

Nothing!

I hit my fist against the back wall in frustration, but it did no good.

For just a second I considered setting a fire in the trunk. If the car was on fire it would surely attract the attention of the police, and there was no way he'd be able to explain my presence. Even if I died back here, unable to get out, even if I burned to death, at least he might end up in prison.

But what if he didn't? Would I be throwing my life away for nothing?

I sighed. It didn't really matter. I didn't have matches or a lighter or anything else with which to set a fire.

The car came to a stop. I didn't know if it was at a red light or a parking lot or the edge of a cliff. I had no way of knowing. But just as he stopped the car, Rick turned on the stereo loud. *Metallica.*

He was trying to cover the sound if I screamed.

The car rocked with the slamming of the door. I waited what seemed like an eternity, two or three minutes. Then I started to scream and kick.

"There's nobody," I heard her shout over the music. Kaylee, the little girl. I stopped screaming and listened. "There's nobody around. We're in a dark parking lot next to a motel."

"Is he gone?" My throat felt raw.

"He went inside. I think he must be checking in."

"You should run," I said. "You should run while you still can. Get as far away as you can."

She didn't respond at first, but then I heard a noise that I recognized. Crying. "I can't," she said. "He tied my wrists to the steering wheel with plastic ties. I want to go home…" Her words devolved into a plaintive moan.

Fuck.

I tried to calm my breathing down. There was nothing I could do. I had no way out of the trunk, and she was stuck too. Soon, Rick would come back, and it would all start again. I didn't even have to see to know the kind of motel this was. Half occupied, with owners who probably didn't speak English, and the staff willing to not ask questions. It would be dirty, with sheets that hadn't been washed, showers that were dark with mildew and mold, and draperies that reeked of cigarette smoke. I knew the place, even though I'd never been there, even though I hadn't even seen it yet. I'd been in a hundred others like it. That was how Rick liked to travel, because nobody asked questions and they took cash.

Once we arrived in the city, things would change. We'd switch to higher-end hotels, or stay in one of many corporate apartments that were scattered across the country. I didn't know if they were places that he rented or shared with other people. But like the dismal hotels, I'd seen enough of them to recognize them.

The mystery would be cleared up soon enough. A moment later I felt, more than heard, one of the doors open, then slam shut. Rick was back. He started the car and drove for less than a minute … undoubtedly moving to the darkest back parking lot. The car shut off, followed by the music, leaving my ears ringing.

I heard Rick murmur something, quietly at first and then in a sharper tone.

"My wrists hurt," Kaylee said.

"You'll be fine. Let's go in the room." His voice rose to a shout. "Strawberry? I'll be right back for you."

Jesus. He wasn't taking any chances.

I waited. Probably no more than two or three minutes passed, but it felt like an eternity. Then I heard the click of the trunk unlocking and light flooded in. I shaded my eyes but uncovered them almost immediately.

It wasn't actually bright … it was dawn. The sky was clouded, dark thunderheads moving quickly across the sky. After hours in total darkness, the light hurt my eyes.

"You look like shit," he said. *Asshole.* "Get out of the trunk."

I struggled up, but my limbs weren't cooperating; I had no sensation in my legs. As I moved they began to tingle with circulation returning.

"I said get the fuck out," he said. He grabbed me by the arm and yanked me out of the trunk. I screamed and fell to the ground, scraping my arm and hands on the concrete.

"Broken down old whore." His words dripped with contempt. I struggled to my feet and glared at him.

"You gonna give me any more trouble? Or do I have to stuff you back in there and send you where I sent Nialla?"

"I won't be any more trouble," I whispered.

"Then get inside," he said.

I tried to gauge the odds of being able to run away from here. But there was no chance. We were in the back parking lot away from everything. The only other cars were flashy, expensive vehicles: Mustangs and Lexuses and Mercedes. People driving those types of cars didn't stay in this kind of hotel unless they were pimps. I was trapped.

I limped toward the hotel room.

Inside the room, I quickly confirmed everything I had already known about the place. The carpet looked ancient, and Kaylee was sitting in a rickety wooden chair looking anxious.

I walked past her, straight to the filthy bathroom. The faucet had left a rust stain down the back of the porcelain sink. The tiles in the floor, possibly once decently installed, were now a mess. I used the toilet then faced myself in the mirror.

My face was a ruin. The cut on the right side of my face was much worse than I had thought, and the bruise spreading under my eye was so dark that I wondered if I'd been permanently marked. I had an awful headache.

When I stepped out of the bathroom, Rick dropped my bag on one of the beds. "Why don't you smoke a joint, Strawberry? Maybe that'll make you happy again."

I searched through my bag. *Maybe that'll make you happy again.* Because getting high will make me not feel hate *after you murdered her.* Rage was building up in me, rage and fear and an overwhelming need to vomit. My head was splitting, and I needed something a lot stronger than a joint. In the bottom I found two pill bottles. One was Oxy. I took one and dry-swallowed it then lit a cigarette.

The smoke flooding my lungs brought instant relief, my muscles relaxing even as I felt clearer-headed. I winced, though, at my headache, and wondered if I had a concussion.

It wouldn't be the first time.

Rick stepped out of the bathroom. He had taken off his T-shirt, balled it up and threw it across the room, revealing his muscular torso covered in tattoos. As always, his pistol was in his waistband, the deadly metal drawing all the life out of the room.

I looked away from him, my eyes falling on Kaylee. She stared at him, terrified. If he had been planning a slow seduction of her like he'd done to Nialla—Laura—then he'd blown that with Laura's murder last night. She might obey him out of terror, like I had, but never out of love.

Either way, she had a narrow window of time before her life was going to change irrevocably. If I had to guess, he would rape her within the hour.

"It looks like you might have to work the track for a few days, Strawberry," Rick said. "With you looking like that, ain't no way you're gonna make any indoor dates."

I took a drag off my cigarette and ignored him. He sat down on the other bed, set his pistol on the end table, and patted the bed. "Kaylee, come sit over here."

Her eyes widened and she started to shake.

"You heard me. Come sit over here."

She just looked more frightened.

"Rick, leave her alone. She's scared," I said.

"Did I ask you? Christ, you look like a fucking bag lady. And you used to be so pretty."

He turned his attention back to her. "Get *over* here. I'm not going to ask you again." The shift in tone caused the skin of my neck to tense. I knew that shift in tone, because it was often followed by a fist or some other cruelty.

She didn't know that yet.

Hell, did it even matter? She came from such a completely fucked up background that running off with some random dangerous guy had actually seemed like a good idea.

Running to him had seemed like a good idea to me after Chase dumped me. For an idle second, I wondered where Chase was, what he was doing with his life. I knew that Dad had gone to jail for assaulting him. But nothing since. Was he alive? Had he forgotten about me? The truth was, I'd mostly forgotten about him. I couldn't imagine feeling the sixteen-year-old crush I'd had ever again. Would I ever love anyone? Or be loved?

It didn't matter. All I could hope for was an end to this.

Kaylee moved to the bed and sat down next to Rick. She cringed away from him. In a second, he was going to rape her right here in front of me and I wasn't going to do anything to stop him. Because that's the way it worked. That's the way it had always worked. Laura hadn't intervened when he raped me the first time, or the fiftieth. Of course not, how could she? He might have killed her then and spared her two more years of pain. Neither of us had done anything when he picked up Rose—and later murdered her when she dared to run away.

I was so tired.

Rick said to Kaylee, "Trust me, you're going to love it."

"I'm not ready," she whispered. "I told you that."

"You are."

She shook her head violently.

He reached out and grabbed her shirt and yanked at it. "Get undressed. I want to see those titties."

I flinched. She cried out as he suddenly shook her hard, a rag doll, a thirteen-year-old eighth-grade rag doll who deserved something better than this. He pulled at her shirt, finally tearing it off of her. She screamed now, and he muttered, "Shut *up*, bitch," then clamped a hand on her mouth as he started to pull on her jeans.

I sat there on the other bed, trying not to look, tears running down my face because I couldn't stop him. He had her bra off now, and her pants, and she was struggling and crying. He slapped her—hard—once, twice across the face. She stopped struggling, then he unbuttoned his jeans and began to pull them down.

He got them down around his knees before I moved.

With a gasp, I reached over to the end table between the beds and grabbed the pistol and jumped back, away from the bed, standing up now and holding it in both hands.

Rick snarled and yelled, "Strawberry!" He turned, Kaylee forgotten as he struggled to pull his pants back up.

She wriggled away from him, her voice a low keening cry.

"Put it down, Strawberry! If you don't, I will fucking *kill you*. Or I'll sell you to some fucking fishing boat from Japan and let them fuck you to death and throw you overboard. No one will ever even care that you lived. *Put it down!*"

"My name is Brenna," I said, almost a whisper.

As I said my name, tears poured down my face again.

winter flower

"Come on, baby. You want to go by Brenna? I'll call you that. I'll call you whatever you want. You *know* things are going to get better—"

"Shut up."

"Come on, Strawberry—"

I pulled the trigger. The bullet hit him square in the chest, a dark red spot suddenly appearing over his sternum. Blood spattered Kaylee and the wall behind him. Kaylee shrieked.

He lurched toward me, and I pulled the trigger again. This time he went down, on his back on the bed, his pants still around his knees, his still-hard dick waving like another limb, and I shot that too, obliterating it in a mess of blood and tissue.

I walked around the bed, closer to him, still terrified he was going to get up and run at me. I was crying, no, *weeping,* the tears coming in a flood as I approached the man who had tormented me, who had tortured me, who had murdered Laura and Rose and God only knew how many others, the man who had started to rape an eighth grade girl right before my eyes, and I pulled the trigger *again.*

This bullet went through his left eye and blasted the back of his head across the bed.

I dropped the gun on the floor with a loud thump. The room was full of smoke. Kaylee's shrieking had subsided to loud sobs.

I stared at Rick. He looked … like nothing. Like there was nothing left, that whatever evil had animated him was gone out of his body and out of the room and out of the world. Now he was just a bag of flesh and bones spread across the bed in a nasty hooker hotel somewhere in the Pacific Northwest.

Fuck him.

I sobbed. I searched the room, now flooded with acrid smoke, and my eyes fell on his phone, sitting on the dresser by the television. As I searched, I could hear cars starting outside, the squeal of tires as the pimps and their prisoners fled the building. They'd heard the gunshots.

I picked up the phone. I'd seen him unlock it a thousand times, his code was seven-one-nine-four. I unlocked it and from memory I dialed a number that represented love and safety and *home.*

I closed my eyes and put the phone to my ear. It rang twice, then a deep voice answered. "Cole Roberts."

Out of my control, my voice rose to an uncontrollable shriek. *"Daddy?"*

Thirty-Nine

Erin

All three of us were exhausted and needed a refresher, so we moved down to the hotel room we had barely used to change clothes and get showers before searching out Laura at the hospital.

It was difficult to comprehend my emotional state. It felt almost as if I had lost Brenna all over again. We were *so* close to finding her. All three of us had wept in the conference room, and even though my common sense told me I should have shielded Sam from the additional trauma, in the end I knew it was the right thing to have her there, and for the three of us to grieve together. We *hadn't* grieved Brenna's loss when she originally disappeared two years ago, not together. Instead, we'd gone our separate ways and fallen apart separately. Maybe Sam, more than any of us, needed that.

Sam showered first then sat down in front of a mirror to put on makeup while Cole showered. I sat on the bed, fascinated as I watched this half-stranger child carefully apply mascara.

I had a million questions. I wanted to know where Sam had bought makeup and how she picked it out. I wanted to know when was the first time she dressed in women's clothes, and if there was a precipitating event that made her realize for sure how she felt. I wanted to know why she trusted Brenna and not us, and I wanted to be worthy of that trust now that we had it.

Cole had been right when he said that we weren't going to lose another child. Not if we could help it. I desperately wanted Brenna back. I wanted to bring her home and hold her in my arms and do whatever it took to help her heal from the hell she'd been in. But even if we never saw her again, even if she were dead, it was time for me to be there for my youngest child, the daughter I didn't know I had, the child who had in some ways borne the weight of our entire family.

I had tremendous doubts about the idea of Sam being transgender. It's one thing to advocate for people's rights in the abstract, but it's something else entirely when it's your own child. Had he *really* been this way secretly his entire life? Or was this some kind of reaction to being so alone? To losing his sister? By supporting this change, was I making life harder for my child? What if we supported him now, in this, then years from now he realized it was a terrible mistake and it was too late to go back?

But whatever doubts I might have inside, whatever fears I might have, for now I would keep them to myself. My only job right now was to be there for *her*.

I didn't know where to start.

Sam said, "Why are you staring?"

I took a deep breath. "I was just thinking how much catching up I have to do. How much getting to know you I have to do. I like watching you do that."

Sam flushed red all the way down to her neck. "I barely know what I'm doing. I watched some YouTube videos, but I can never seem to make it look right."

It took me a second to realize just how vulnerable a statement that was. It was all tied up in the fact that Sam had no one to teach her, no one to talk about it with. I remembered sitting with my mother close, her scent in the air around me, as she braided my hair. Learning about things like makeup and hair—it was often a ritual for mothers and daughters, a way they bonded, that Sam had missed out on.

Tentatively, I asked, "May I help? I could teach you some things."

Sam nodded. She didn't say anything else, but I had a sudden flashback to having a similar conversation with Brenna when she was about twelve years old. I took a deep breath. "Let's start by tying your hair back, get that out of the way. I think we should take a trip to the hair stylist together soon, don't you?"

Sam nodded again. I felt like I was holding my breath as I began to talk with her about picking the right colors and how to apply foundation.

As we were talking, Cole came out of the shower wrapped in a towel, his hair dripping wet. He gave me a brilliant smile, a courageous smile, because I knew he was hurting just as bad as I was, then he ducked back into the bathroom. I heard him turn on the faucet—he must be getting ready to shave—when his phone rang.

It was barely eight o'clock in the morning. "Who is that?" I asked.

"Don't know," he said.

Then he answered it. "Cole Roberts."

380

Even fifteen feet away I heard the cry over the phone, the frantic high-pitched voice that cried out, *"Daddy?"*

"Brenna?" he replied, stunned.

Sam and I both jumped to our feet as Cole burst out of the bathroom, towel still wrapped around his waist. His eyes were already turning red, wet with tears.

He said, "Honey, slow down, I can't understand you. Where are you?"

As he listened he grabbed the notepad off the stand next to the television then scribbled with the hotel pen, *"Call Stan Wilcox. 911."*

Cole's face looked panicked, almost terrified. I started dialing as he said, "Okay—" He started writing an address on the notepad.

Azalea Motel, 33250 Pacific Highway South, Seattle.

Underneath, in large block letters, he wrote:

SHE SHOT AND KILLED THE PIMP.

Oh my God. Sam handed me her phone and I dialed Stan's number.

I almost hung up in frustration when Stan's phone rang for the fifth and then sixth time. But finally, he answered.

"Erin, I'm sorry we didn't have any—"

"Stan, *shut up and listen, please.* Cole has Brenna on the phone. She just called, she's in a motel in Seattle. She shot and killed her abductor."

Stan was immediately all business. "How long ago? Are the police there?"

"I don't know!"

"It's fine. I'm going to call the Seattle Police Department right now. You stay right where you are. Don't do *anything* until you hear back from me, okay?"

Bullshit. We were leaving for Seattle right now. "Sure, but call me back immediately. You got the number? This is Sam's phone."

I gave Stan the address for the motel.

Cole was saying, "Brenna, I'm going to put you on speaker. Your mom and Sam are right here. I need to throw some clothes on and then we're on our way to you. We're not far, we're in Portland."

And just like that, I heard my daughter's voice for the first time in two years. "Mom? Sam?" She sounded frantic, her voice harsh and scratchy. It sounded like someone else was crying in the background.

"Baby, I'm right here. Sam's right here. Sam, get your shoes on, we're leaving. Baby, I promise you you're going to be okay. We're on our way to you." As I was pulling my boots on, Cole threw on jeans and a T-shirt and his shoes.

"Leave the rest of it," Cole said. "We'll deal with it later."

We ran for the door and down the hall to the elevator. Cole said, "Brenna, we're getting in the elevator now. If we lose you, call back right away."

Brenna's voice still sounded raw, but she was no longer crying. "Okay. I don't know the number for this phone, do you see it?"

"Yeah, I got it on my caller ID," Cole said.

We clambered onto the elevator together, as the crying in the background grew louder and more hysterical. Then, a second later, I heard thumping over the phone. Then a muffled voice, barely understandable. *"Police."*

Shit! The door to the elevator had already closed, it was too late to stop. Brenna's voice began to break up as she said, "What do I do? What do I do?" The panic and fear in her voice chilled me to the bone.

As the elevator door opened, Cole said, "Can you hear me? Listen—stay calm. We've already called the FBI investigator who was helping us. If the local police don't know who you are yet, they will very soon. Just make sure you're not holding the gun, and stay calm, and let them in. Okay? Just don't give them any reason to think you're dangerous. Okay? Stay calm. Move slowly. Hands where they can see you."

We walked out into the lobby of the hotel, rushing toward the front door. A wall of water was pouring out of the sky. Even deep under the shelter of the porte-cochere, I felt rain hitting me.

Cole said, "Stay here and talk her through this, I'll get the van." He shoved the phone at me then ran into the storm.

Over the phone, I could hear the thumping again. "Police, come to the door with your hands up."

In a thin voice, Brenna responded, "I'm not armed. I'm gonna open the door."

Sam grabbed my left hand, and I squeezed hers back.

Brenna

I was so afraid. I was so afraid of what might happen when I opened that door. If the police came in and saw Rick lying there dead, would they shoot me? And say that I had threatened them? Did they know him?

Some of the places we'd stayed in the past, Rick had been well acquainted with the local police.

I put the phone on speaker and laid it on the table next to the television and walked to the hotel room door. Kaylee had moved to the corner of the room furthest away from Rick's body, where she sat with her arms around her as she sobbed.

I called out, "I'm opening the door now."

I turned the knob and pulled the door open.

There were four police cars, lights flashing in the rain, with officers crouched down behind the vehicles. As I opened the door, from my left and right police officers rushed at me. Two of them grabbed my arms, while another kicked the door all the way open.

Everybody was shouting, as the two officers who had grabbed my arms rushed me away from the door. From the doorway, I could hear my mom shouting on the speakerphone. "Brenna, what's happening?"

I shouted back, "Mom, I'm okay."

Sam

The drive to Seattle seemed like the longest ride of my life. I sat in the middle seat of the van, messaging with Hayley, as Dad drove through a downpour, the windshield wipers on high, making a *thump-thump-thump-thump* sound that punctuated the loud clattering of the heavy rain against the roof of the van.

We'd been driving about twenty minutes when my phone rang, a Washington, DC number. I handed it to Mom.

"Hello?"

She hunched over, plugging her left ear with a finger while holding the phone to her right. The rain was so loud, she must be having a hard time hearing.

"Uh–uh ... yes ... okay. Let me know as soon as you hear anything more, please? Okay."

Mom put a hand to her chest and took a deep breath.

"What is it?" I asked. "How is she?"

Mom looked at Dad then back at me. She began to speak in short, clipped sentences. "Agent Wilcox said they're taking her to the hospital. Apparently she was beat up pretty bad. He said there was nothing life-threatening. The guy ... her trafficker ... was dead from multiple gunshot wounds. She told the police she shot him. He said there was another girl there, a thirteen-year-old from Portland. The important thing is, she's ... we found her. She's free." As she said the last words, Mom broke down and began to weep. "She's free."

Dad reached over the space between them and held her hand.

winter flower

Brenna

The questions seemed to take forever. What was my name? Where had I come from? How did I get the gun from Rick? Was I really abducted or had I run away? All the while, I sat on a plastic chair sheltered from the rain fifty feet from the hotel room door where Rick lay dead.

But nobody hurt me. Nobody groped me or did anything awful. A few minutes after the police had arrived, a female police officer walked over and sat down in the plastic chair next to me. "Hi, Brenna. I'm Officer Lopez. An ambulance will be here in a minute, and we're going to take you to the hospital and get you checked out, okay?"

I nodded.

"The FBI called. They said you were abducted two years ago."

I nodded. Then I said, "On my sixteenth birthday."

She gently laid a hand on my shoulder. "You've had a tough time, haven't you?"

I nodded.

"But you can go home now."

I nodded, swallowed, and didn't say anything. Could I go home? Really? I didn't know. I was filthy inside. *Filthy.* I had to hold back tears. I'd done all the crying I could take. "Is Kaylee okay?"

Officer Lopez said, "She was pretty shaken up. But not physically hurt other than some bruising. She told the other officers that the guy you were with was attempting to rape her when you shot him?"

I nodded. "Yeah," I whispered.

She leaned close. "I'm sorry you had to do that, Brenna. But you did good."

I nodded. I couldn't answer that. "Can you ... were you ... did anyone find out anything about Laura? My friend. He shot her last night because she tried to help me..." I sucked in a breath.

"I'll see what I can find out. Let's head to the ambulance now."

"Okay." I stood up and walked with her. The ambulance had pulled up next to the hotel, lights flashing. The door stood open, and Kaylee was scrambling in. At the edge of the covered walk, I turned to Lopez. "Officer Lopez ... thanks. Thanks for being so kind. I didn't—I've not had very good experiences with police."

She closed her eyes and said, "It's our job, Brenna. I'm sorry you've had bad experiences before. Maybe later you could tell me about that?"

I nodded. "Okay."

We ran through the rain and she helped me up into the ambulance. I sat down next to Kaylee and put an arm around her. "You okay?" I whispered.

She leaned against me and closed her eyes.

Forty

~~~~~~~~~~~~~~~~~~~~~~~~~~~~~~~~~~

Cole

Seattle Children's Hospital was a huge building, six or seven stories, glass and stone. Despite the heavy rain over the area, a break in the clouds let the sun shine through, reflecting off the building. As I pulled up to the emergency entrance, I said, "See if you can find out anything. I'm going to go park."

As I said the words, a police officer approached. He had ruddy skin and dark almost-black hair and a surprisingly thick five-o'clock shadow for nine o'clock in the morning. I rolled down the window.

"Excuse me, are you Mr. Roberts?"

"Yeah," I said.

"You can park right over here," he said, pointing to a spot near the entrance. "The captain's asked me to take you up to your daughter's room."

I turned and looked at Erin then back at the officer. "Thanks," I said. Wilcox must have called, or maybe Detective Michaelson. I parked the van, and the three of us ran through the rain to the cover of the awning. As we approached the officer, I realized he was young, maybe in his early twenties. His name tag bore the name Lahoud.

That's when I saw the reporters. A tall man in a suit, followed by a cameraman. He approached rapidly, saying, "Mrs. Roberts, can you comment on the rescue of your daughter?"

"No comment!" I shouted. The officer stepped between the reporter and us and we ran for the entrance. A news van was pulling into the parking lot as we entered the building.

A moment later the young officer stepped into the building. "They can't come inside," he said. "But there was some chatter earlier, the reporters probably heard over the scanner. I'm afraid you may be dealing with the media."

"It's fine, if you could just take us to her," Erin said.

"Of course."

We followed him through the emergency entrance, down a long hall, and stopped at a bank of elevators. And waited.

Sam said something I think we probably all felt. "I'm afraid."

"Oh, baby," Erin said. She wrapped her arms around her. "It's okay. It's going to be hard. She's going to be a long time healing. But we'll take care of her."

The elevator dinged and we stepped in and rode to the fifth floor.

Down another hall, and then we were in a small waiting room. A bulky man in a police uniform stood by one of the inner doors. The officer who had escorted us said to him, "This is the Roberts' family."

I was startled when he demanded that we show identification. But then he explained that Brenna had been assigned a protective detail until they knew more about what had happened—out of concern that someone associated with her pimp might show up to harm her.

A moment later, a nurse led us down another hall. She knocked on the door and opened it slightly, and said the words, "Brenna—your family's here."

She pulled the door open all the way and I stopped breathing.

Some things in my daughter's life I recall with precision.

Especially, I remember the moments I first held her in my arms, the moment I first fell in love with the tiniest little baby just seconds after she was born. She had huge blue eyes and tiny little hands, and one of them wrapped around my finger as I held her.

Seeing her now was like that. When the nurse opened the door, Brenna was sitting in a wooden chair next to an exam table. Her right eye widened and flooded with tears. The left was swollen shut, bruised and purple. She stood and stumbled toward us, her face twisted in an expression of indescribable grief.

I stepped forward as she staggered, catching her as she fell to her knees, and I dropped to my own knees and wrapped my arms around her. Brenna buried her face in my neck and began to wail. Then I felt Sam on one side and Erin on the other as all three of us held her, arms and hearts intertwined.

I didn't know what horrors Brenna had endured in the past two years. I didn't know if I could ever really understand. Her voice seemed to carry all the pain of the world as she gagged and wept.

We stayed there for a long time, all four of us weeping until it seemed there were no more tears. We would calm down, and then as soon as one of us tried to talk, we broke down into tears again. My knees were starting to hurt, but I didn't want to get up. I didn't want to move or leave this place, where for the first time in I didn't know how long, I had my family right there in my arms.

Eventually, we got up off the floor. Sam and Brenna sat together on the exam table, Brenna leaning her head on Sam's shoulder, their arms around each other. In halting words, tentative and unsure, we began to talk about what the past couple of years had been like. We didn't dig deep—it was way too early for that—and I wondered how much Brenna would ever talk about what she experienced.

When a doctor came in, a woman in her late thirties, I caught a glimpse, maybe just a small one, of what she was going to have to overcome. The doctor said, "If you all will excuse us for just a few minutes, I'd like to have a moment with Brenna?"

Brenna grabbed Sam like she was clutching a life preserver. "No! Please, I want them to stay." The panic in her eyes was unmistakable.

Erin said, "It's okay, baby. We're not going anywhere."

The doctor had come with news, which with Brenna's permission, she shared with all of us.

The good news was that the injuries she sustained weren't life-threatening.

But they *were serious.*

The fragile bottom of the orbital bone of her left eye had been fractured. That, the doctor informed us, might take several surgeries to correct, if it could be corrected at all.

"Does that mean I'll be blind?" Brenna asked.

The doctor shook her head. "No, but you may not have the same range of motion in your left eye. You'll need to see a specialist to determine what the next steps are."

As the doctor spoke I took a long look at my daughter. The tattoo, which I noticed earlier, seemed to come into focus for the first time. The script in the center of it, which read, *Property of Rick,* shook me and twisted at my stomach. Someone had permanently labeled my daughter as their *property.*

I wished she hadn't had to be the one to do it, but I was glad the son of a bitch was dead.

The doctor turned toward us and looked over her glasses at Erin and me. "You aren't from the area, are you? Is your plan to take her back home?"

I nodded. "To Atlanta."

"I'll get you some referrals then, both for ocular surgeons, and especially, therapists. You've been through a lot, young lady. I want you to promise that you'll spend some time in therapy. Not because there's anything wrong with you, but because you've been through a horrible trauma."

Brenna asked in a rough voice, "Will they let me go? The police?"

"I'm fairly certain they won't press any kind of charges against you," Erin said.

Then Brenna asked something that nearly broke my heart all over again. "You'll let me come home? After everything that happened?"

I leaned forward and laid both of my hands on her knees. "Brenna, we love you. You can always have a home with us, no matter what. Always."

She gave a tiny nod and whispered, "I want to go home with you."

Sam

The doctors decided that Brenna would have to stay overnight, so they moved her to a semi-private room on the third floor. There was a lot of waiting around, and the nurses insisted that she be moved in a wheelchair, something Brenna looked acutely uncomfortable with.

Not long after that, we had an awkward discussion about lunch, finally settled when Brenna said to Mom and Dad, "Go! Sam can stay here with me, and when you get back she'll go. Or you can bring something back for her. I'm okay."

Brenna's hospital bed was positioned with the back up high so she could sit up. As soon as our parents left the room, she turned to me. "Tell me everything. How long have Mom and Dad known about you?"

I felt a strange anxiety about talking about it. Why? Was it because for so long Brenna had been the holder of my secrets? For some reason I was reluctant to tell her about Hayley and how important my friendship with her had become. In slow, hesitant sentences, I began to tell her the story of Dad's imprisonment, our move to Alabama, and the last few weeks of school.

"What does Hayley look like?" Brenna asked.

I took out my phone and switched it on. The lock screen had a picture of me and Hayley together, just a few days before everything blew up.

"I'm glad you made a good friend like that. Does she ... does she know you're a girl?"

I nodded. "I told her right before we left town to drive here. She's okay with it."

Brenna looked at me with an expression of heartbreaking loneliness. "I'm sorry I wasn't there for you, Sam. I'm sorry I was so stupid."

I shook my head. "Brenna, you don't have anything to apologize for … I mean, it wasn't your fault—"

"But it was," she interrupted. "I was—I snuck out. I went to my boyfriend's and when he told me I was a stupid kid—like I was—I put myself in danger out of … I don't know … spite."

"It must have been terrible," I whispered.

She closed her eyes. "I can't talk about it. Not that stuff."

"The girl who was shot—Laura—did she help?"

Brenna nodded slowly. "She helped me stay alive."

"Maybe we can go check on her, if they let you out of here tomorrow. She's at the hospital in Portland."

Brenna blinked at me in disbelief. "She's alive?"

I nodded. "She was this morning. We were getting ready to go to the hospital to see her, if they would let us, when you called. Mom said—Mom said that she'd risked her life to help you."

Brenna sucked in a breath. "Yeah," she whispered. She closed her eyes. "I'm so tired. Do you think … can you ask the nurse to come by?"

"You okay?" I asked, suddenly frightened.

"I'm in some pain. And I don't even know when I've slept. I just need to rest."

I nodded and jumped to my feet. "Be right back," I said.

By the time Mom and Dad got back, the nurse had brought Brenna two pills and Brenna had slipped away into a restless sleep. I sat watching her as she tossed and turned, occasionally muttering.

Once, she clearly said the words, "Stop, Rick. Please, stop."

Cole

While Brenna slept, Erin and I divided up the necessary phone calls. She would talk to her parents and her sister. I would call Jeremiah and my parents. We both called from my phone—hers would have to be replaced.

Jeremiah declared Brenna's recovery a miracle. And he was right. It was nothing short of miraculous. But I also knew that in the near future, we were going to have to pull off more miracles. In the immediate term, I had to find a place to rent in Atlanta and get my parole switched there, *if* a judge would approve it. Most importantly, we had to figure out treatment options for Brenna. I had kept Brenna on my health insurance, and the hospitalization and ocular surgeries would be covered at least to some extent. But my health plan didn't cover mental health, and she was going to need a lot of help. Both kids were.

In truth, all of us needed a shitload of therapy.

"You know, Jeremiah—this wouldn't have happened if it hadn't been for you. I can't even begin to explain how much it means—"

"You don't have to. Listen, Cole, we paid off the house fifteen years ago. We don't have any debt. We've been letting money accumulate and giving away as much as we felt like. We've been blessed and I'd never consider not passing it on."

"I don't know when or how I can pay you—"

"You don't. You take care of those kids of yours, and when you have the chance to help someone else, you do it. Understand? That's all the thanks I want."

I remembered all those years ago, treating this incredible friend with considerable condescension. Instead of a flashy job, he was going to work in the restaurant business. Instead of moving up to bigger and better houses, they bought a small three-bedroom ranch and stayed in it. He had somehow found real wisdom and stability that I wanted.

Daddy answered the phone on the third ring. That was unusual—most likely it meant that Mama was out.

My guess was confirmed when he told me she was at a bridge game.

He gasped in stunned shock when I told him we had found Brenna and told the story of how it happened. Things had happened so fast in the past few days that I hadn't called my parents to tell them we were going to Portland.

"It sounds like she's had a terrible time of it," he said. "Will you bring her back to Alabama?"

"Daddy…" I stumbled a little, not wanting to tell him I'd fucked up at work. You would think at this age I wouldn't have that fear anymore. I told him the story of what had happened in Oxford with the mayor, ending with the news that we were going to move to Atlanta as soon as I got clearance from the courts.

His voice sounded rough when he spoke again. "Well, I reckon y'all should come stay with us. While you get your feet back under you."

The suggestion stunned me. I don't know if I would have been more shocked if my father had leapt through the phone lines to materialize directly in front of me.

"How will Mama feel about that?"

"Didn't ask her. You let me deal with your mama. I want you to bring your family here, son."

For some reason, I couldn't breathe. I stood up from the plastic chair and paced for a second trying to get ahold of myself. Erin gave me a quizzical look. I swallowed, took another breath, then somehow choked out, "Daddy, there's something you need to know before you make that offer."

The thing was, I had no idea how my parents would react to Sam. I couldn't imagine how my mother would react to any of us, but especially Sam. I wasn't going to take her somewhere only to be made to feel unwelcome. But I had no idea how to say any of that. Daddy was an old conservative Marine from the Deep South. It wasn't until the past twenty years that he'd begun acknowledging black people as human beings. How would he react to Sam?

"Well, spit it out, son."

I closed my eyes and did just that. "Daddy, Sam is transgender."

Across the room from me, Erin's eyes widened. Daddy said, "What does that mean exactly?"

Expecting an explosion any second, I said, "It means that Sam isn't a boy. On the inside, where it counts. She'd reached a point where she couldn't pretend anymore, and the thing is, we're not going to make her. And ... I can't put her in a situation where she's going to get hurt any more. Things got pretty bad."

In a low, slow tone, Daddy replied, "Son, I don't care if he turned into a *tarantula*. You just bring those kids home so we can love them. You hear? I won't lie and say I know anything about this transgender business. But I'm not too old to learn something new. You tell me what to read or whatever. I'll talk to Virginia; she won't say a word against Sam while I live and breathe."

I found that difficult to believe. Daddy might have gone through some shifts in his retirement, but my mother still had a stiletto tongue. I let out a long sigh. "Thank you, Daddy. I'll discuss it with Erin."

"Well, that's all I can ask. And listen, I know you have to do what's best for your family. Just let me know. Because just about the only thing that matters to me in the world is you and Erin and those kids."

I didn't know how to respond to this. I felt like I was putting together a thousand-piece puzzle in a darkened room, and half the pieces were missing. My father had done a lot of changing in the past few years, but it was hard for me to wrap my mind around the idea of Daddy as someone who would defend a transgender kid, even one who was family.

Did Sam and Erin have the same doubts about me?

Who was I kidding? *Of course* they did.

"Thanks, Daddy..." I trailed off.

We said our goodbyes, and I slumped down into the seat near Erin.

"How did it go?" she asked.

I began to tell her the story of my call with my dad. We were only a few inches apart, but out of long-standing habit, we weren't touching. But as I told her about my father's offer, I consciously reached out and took her hand and held it. The touch brought on an immediate shock of recognition, the comfort of familiarity combined with tension and fear that she would pull away.

She didn't pull away. For just a fraction of a second, she tensed. Then she relaxed and squeezed my hand back.

"I think we should do it," I said. "I don't know what's come over the old bastard, but I believe him. They've got plenty of room, and it'll give us a little time to get our feet underneath us."

Erin gave a faint smile. "Jim came from a different era ... but part of what I've always liked about him is that when confronted with evidence, he's willing to revise his opinions. It's your mom that worries me. But I think you're right. And honestly, I think it would be good for the kids." She sniffed, her eyes watering a little.

She continued. "I just want to ... I don't know ... build a wall around them ... around us ... *all* of us. And hunker down behind it and just keep them as safe as we possibly can." As she finished her sentence, she started to cry.

I put an arm around her shoulder, but in these metal armchairs that was awkward as hell. As her shoulders began to shake more, I slid out of my seat, stood in front of her, and pulled her up to me. As I wrapped my arms around her, she seemed to stagger, as if letting go of a massive weight.

Her voice was nearly incoherent as she continued speaking. "She's so badly hurt, Cole. Not just the physical stuff but ... inside. Can you even imagine what she's been through?" With that, she broke down completely, sobbing against my shoulder. I squeezed her to me, as tears ran down my own face.

Through clenched teeth I said, "We'll help her. We'll be there for her, and love her, and help her heal. Together. We'll be there together. Okay?"

She sobbed harder, and whispered, "Okay."

And that was when I fell apart. "Baby, I'm so sorry. I'm sorry I wasn't there for you." My arms around her, I sank to my knees, burying my face against her stomach.

She slid down to the floor next to me and whispered in my ear, "We start over today. Me and you. Our family."

And so we did.

Part Four

Forty-One

Sam

And they all lived happily ever after.

That's how we're supposed to end the story, right? Mom and Dad stayed together, won a million dollars and bought a new, appropriately-sized house. I magically transformed into the girl I always wanted to be, and Brenna was healed from her trauma, went back to school and on to college, and became an interior designer. Or something.

But real life isn't like that. I do believe eventually we'll all live happily ever after, but there's a long way to go to get to that point.

The day they released Brenna from the hospital, we drove to Portland so she could visit her friend Laura. I only met her for a few brief minutes. Mom told me she was twenty, but I would have guessed closer to thirty. Like Brenna, she had a hard look about her, with tiny lines around her eyes and world of hurt behind them. Brenna stayed with her for a couple of hours, talking about I don't know what. The whole time, we were downstairs in the cafeteria—me texting with Hayley and Mom and Dad talking quietly.

They were holding hands.

Every once in a while I'd look up and try to hear some of what they were saying to each other. I didn't catch a lot of it, but that wasn't what was important. The important thing was, they were looking at each other, *really* looking at each other.

Brenna eventually came down and met us. She didn't say much—she'd barely spoken since we'd been reunited. But she came and sat beside me and leaned on me. I put an arm around her. She was smaller than I remembered, skinnier, and not in a healthy way. I knew she was eighteen and all, but I made a promise then that I was going to take care of her and help her get back to health.

I didn't know, then, how difficult that promise would be to keep.

The next morning we left Portland. Our trip back across the country was slow. Slow because we stopped a lot. We got out of the car and walked in the mountains and played mini-golf and visited weird tourist spots. It felt almost like a family vacation along the way, as we tentatively worked to get to know each other. Because that's what it was like—four strangers who had once been close, slowly trying to pick up the pieces.

We were just outside Pendleton, Oregon, maybe four hours after we left Portland, when I realized something was wrong with Brenna. She'd been sleeping a lot, and yawning a lot when she was awake, but this time when she woke up she kept sniffing until I finally dug around in the back of the car and found some tissues for her. I handed her the tissues—and saw that her face was beginning to sheen with sweat.

"What's wrong?" I asked.

She just shook her head. "It's okay," she said.

Mom, sitting in the front passenger seat, turned around. "Everything okay back there?"

"It's fine," Brenna said, just as I replied, "I think something's wrong with Brenna."

"Nothing's wrong," she snapped.

"Brenna?" Mom asked, as if to somehow confirm that's who had spoken the sharp words.

"Sorry," Brenna said, pushing the words out between clenched teeth. Then, she almost-whispered, "I've been taking a lot of pills."

That was months ago, of course, and the memory of that day, and the days that followed, feels like it's in a haze. We drove across the country while Brenna went through opiate withdrawals. Before you think my parents were completely negligent, we did stop at urgent care centers twice on the way back, though I'm not sure the doctors did much. They gave her some meds.

Mostly Brenna slept, lying on the bench in the back, often running a high fever. Other times we had to stop so she could puke, or more often just sit on the ground, arms across her stomach, moaning with terrible stomach cramps.

She smoked constantly, and Mom and Dad finally gave in on that, even to the point of putting the windows down on the highway and letting her smoke in the very back of the van. I didn't mind. We didn't have a lot of choice. There was a lot of talk about insurance, and phone calls, but the bottom line was clear: Mom and Dad's insurance wasn't paying for any inpatient treatment.

***

We didn't even stop in Alabama, but went straight to Atlanta, pulling up to Grandma and Grandpa's house on a late afternoon in early October.

I had felt myself tensing up hours before we reached Atlanta, the anxiety settling into my bones and gut, my stomach twisting itself up into knots. For days, I'd been comfortable in my own skin. I'd worn clothes that felt right. I'd been *me*.

But I was about to see Grandma and Grandpa again. And I didn't know what that was going to be like. I didn't know what *they* were going to be like. Grandpa especially—he was a Marine, basically a throwback. He'd fought in Vietnam and killed people, and even though I'd never heard him say anything bad about anyone (except Yankees) it was almost intuitive that he probably hated people who were gay or transgender or anything else that fit outside his boxes.

But as it turned out, Grandpa wasn't the one I needed to worry about.

The day we got there, it was beautiful outside—the sky clear, temperature warm. Brenna was curled up asleep on the back bench, as she'd been much of the previous few days. When I realized we were getting close, I texted Hayley one last time: Almost there.

Hayley: lemme know what happens. ily

Sam: ily2

I felt a spasm in my stomach when Grandpa and Grandma's brick house came into view. I knew the house well: we had visited often when I was younger, though this was the first time since Brenna's disappearance. For half a second I wondered why that was, but then the answer hit me. *Stupid*. Dad had to get permission to travel, I knew that.

Then I saw Grandpa. He was in the front yard, kneeling next to a bed of flowers, a look of intense concentration on his face. He looked the same as always, not even slightly older than the last time we'd seen each other. His hair was a shock of white, buzzed close to his scalp, his face the weathered, deeply creased look of a man more comfortable outdoors than anywhere else.

He was going to hate me.

The tension in my stomach shifted from anxiety to terror at the sight of him. My heart began to thump in my chest as my breathing constricted. I couldn't breathe. I put a hand to my chest and struggled to get a breath.

"Sam, what's wrong?" Mom asked in an urgent tone.

I fought to answer her question. I struggled to say anything, but I couldn't breathe, and she looked increasingly alarmed as she twisted around in her seat and stared at me. Then I croaked out one word: "Scared."

"Oh, baby," Mom said.

I felt Brenna's hand on my arm as she leaned forward. "You'll be okay, Sam."

Mom reached back and took my hand as Dad parked the van. She met my eyes and said, "Breathe deep. Slow. Breathe with me, Sam. One—two—three…"

On three, she took a deep breath. I matched it, keeping my eyes locked with hers. We did it again, and again. Then I said, "I'm sorry. I'm all right."

And I was, just barely. I reminded myself that there would be worse things than having Grandma and Grandpa reject me. Living a lie was one of them. I wasn't going to do that anymore. I closed my eyes, counted to ten, then reached for the handle to open the door.

By this time, Grandpa was approaching the van. Brenna had gotten out on the passenger side, her expression unreadable as she stretched, and approached our grandfather.

"Oh, my soul." Grandpa's face worked, the lines around his eyes deepening as his eyes watered. "Can your grandpa give you a hug?"

What a weird question, I thought. Why would he ask her that way? But Brenna gave a faint nod, and he wrapped his arms around her. Then I realized—he was asking permission. He knew that people—men—had been touching her without her permission. It was crazy that he thought of that. Crazy and respectful and kind.

"I missed you so much, kiddo," he said.

"I missed you, Grandpa."

Not letting go of her, Grandpa looked up at me. I was acutely aware of my knee-length skirt, my makeup, and the purple clips in my hair. What must he be thinking? Did he see my eyeliner and blush and feel contempt? It felt he was looking right through me. I felt another stab of terror.

I almost broke when he reached out his right hand and said, "You too, Sam, come hug your grandpa." The terror dissipated, and I stepped forward. Wrapping his arms around us both, he said, "You kids are my life. You know I can't promise you nobody will ever hurt you again, but I can damn sure try my best. I'm glad you're home."

I didn't answer. I couldn't. There were no words to respond to this, no way to say what it meant. I just asked one question. "You don't hate me?"

He shook his head, stepping back, a hand on my shoulder. "Hate you? Nah, I could never hate you. I can't say I understand, but I want to. Is that okay?"

I nodded, silently.

"Where's Mama?" Dad asked.

Grandpa sniffed and answered in a dismissive tone. "She ain't feeling well. She'll be down later."

Erin

Getting settled in at Cole's parents' took a little while, but I was thankful they had the room for us. Cole and I shared one of the upstairs bedrooms, and Brenna was in the room next to us, with Sam in the guest bedroom downstairs at the front of the house. As soon as we got our things inside and gathered back downstairs in the kitchen, Brenna asked if she could go outside to smoke a cigarette.

Jim looked startled but let that pass quickly. "Come out here on the back patio, I'll find you an ashtray."

As soon as they were out of the room, I said, "I really wish she'd quit."

Cole frowned. "It's too soon, I think. After what she's going through with the drugs, I wouldn't press her on it. Not now, maybe not ever. We've got to talk with her about getting her hooked up with a program of some kind."

"What kind of program?" Sam asked, looking suspicious.

"Like, a detox or drug addiction program." Cole's face looked serious as he said the words. "You've seen what she's like, Sam. Addiction isn't something to mess around with. She's going to need a lot of support. Honestly, if we had a way to get her into an inpatient program I would."

I glanced out the back window. On the brick patio out back, Brenna was sitting in one of the white painted rockers. Jim had taken a seat next to her. It didn't look like they were talking. Just sitting next to each other.

Sam started to rummage through the refrigerator and wandered off a moment later.

"Your mother," I said.

"Yeah." Cole's mouth compressed in a flat line. "I don't know what to make of that."

"She didn't come down and see her grandkids," I hissed.

He nodded. "I know. God only knows what's going on there. We'll have to take it as it comes."

"But Jim is okay. Look at him, sitting with her."

Outside, Brenna looked sleepy, her eyes drooping, but Jim made some comment that caused her to laugh.

Cole gave a wry smile. "It's nice to see her laugh."

"Tell me it's going to be okay," I said.

He wrapped his arms around me. "It's going to be okay, love."

Two hours later, Cole's mother made her appearance.

The last time I had seen Virginia Grady Roberts was the Christmas Cole spent in jail. As always, she had been elegant, appearing at our door from a twelve-hour drive with her makeup in place and wearing pearls. Virginia was one of those ladies for whom appearances mattered more than anything.

That's why I was more than a little bit shocked at her appearance when she came down the stairs that evening. Jim had completely sidestepped the issue of the non-appearance of his wife, and Cole didn't want to talk about it at all. There was no bustling about the kitchen preparing for the meal—Jim simply ordered Chinese.

She appeared without warning a few minutes after the food arrived. Her hair, dyed a reddish bronze, had been loosely tied up, eschewing the elaborate French braids she normally preferred. Her clothes looked perfectly normal, a green blouse with matching pants, but she was barefoot. I didn't think I had ever seen her feet before. But most shocking was the fact that she was visibly drunk.

"Cole, my baby." She slurred the words as he stood and kissed her on the cheek. His expression was carefully blank, and I knew he was hiding his own surprise and shock.

Virginia's eyes skimmed past Sam as if she didn't see him and landed on Brenna. "Come here, child." As she said the words, tears ran down her face. "We're all so grateful you are home."

Brenna stood and let Virginia embrace her. Once they broke up the embrace, Virginia said a perfunctory hello to me, then said, "Well, then, let's have dinner."

We all went silent. Her exclusion of Sam, to the extent of not even looking at him (*her, damn it*) was painfully obvious. I wanted to speak up, and I wanted Cole to speak up, but I had no idea how to say it and it was obvious he didn't either.

"Mama." Cole's voice suppressed fury. "Don't you dare treat my children that way—"

He was interrupted, by Jim of all people. "Virginia, say hello to Sam." His voice was low and firm and had a threatening edge to it.

"Hello, Sam," she replied.

Sam looked desolate. "Hi, Grandma," she whispered, then she turned away, hunching over her phone as her thumbs began to move furiously. She must be texting Hayley.

Jim stood, his expression furious. "Excuse us," he said to us, before grabbing Virginia by the arm. "We need to have a moment."

She pulled her arm away from him. "We need no such thing. We'll eat now, thank you. Pour me a glass of wine, please."

"You've had plenty." Jim sounded like the Marine he'd once been.

She straightened, wiping unconsciously at her sleeve where he had grabbed it, then walked around him, eyes straight ahead. At the counter, she pulled the cork from an already open bottle of Chianti, poured a very heavy portion into a wine glass, then walked out of the room.

Jim spoke to Sam in a sad, remote voice. "Sam, please accept my apologies for her behavior."

Sam looked up at her grandfather, tears brimming in her eyes. "It's not your fault, Grandpa. It's okay." But I could see it wasn't okay. She looked heartbroken. "I'm gonna go lie down for a while, okay?"

"Don't you want to eat?" Cole asked. "We got you General Tso's chicken."

I didn't think dangling Sam's favorite food was going to help here. Sam stood. "I'll eat later, I'm tired." She left the room, barely looking up from her phone.

I took a deep breath. "I'll go talk to her."

"Are you sure that's a good idea?" Cole asked.

I looked at him, helpless. How was I supposed to know if it was a good idea, or the right thing to do? I was lost. "I don't know. But I have to try."

I found Sam in his new room, lying on the bed, holding the phone up in front of his face. *Her* face. Damn it, it was a struggle to remember. But every time I got it wrong out loud, it hurt her. And I didn't even know if it was the right way to deal with all of this.

I sat down on the edge of the bed.

"You okay?"

She didn't answer verbally, just gave a barely noticeable shrug.

"Sam, I need you to know that you are loved. But I think you already know—some people aren't going to know how to deal with this. Some people will be terrible. But I promise you, we'll be there through it all the way with you. We love you."

The only acknowledgement I received was Sam's eyes tearing up. She rolled to her side, away from me. In a muffled voice, she asked, "Can I borrow the van to go see Hayley on Saturday?"

A thousand objections immediately formed in my mind. Was it safe for Sam to go to Alabama? It was a three-hour drive. The guys who beat her up were there. Anything could happen. We didn't have money for gas.

But all I could see was her lying there on her side feeling rejected by her grandmother. "Yes, that should be fine. Can we talk?"

403

In a tiny, tortured voice, she said, "Please leave me alone."

Cole

Brenna wasn't out of the woods yet.

The first week of her withdrawals were the worst—sweating and pain. She'd slept much of the time, and when she wasn't asleep she twitched and moaned. On the third day of driving home we'd taken her to the emergency room when she started vomiting. The doctors there gave her buprenorphine to help with the withdrawals, and it did seem to take the edge off, at least enough that we were able to continue the drive.

Almost every night she woke up screaming from nightmares. One of us would go lie down with her and she'd cry herself to sleep, sometimes mumbling things that sent chills down my spine.

She needed more help than we were qualified to give.

Erin and I worked together to help find her the resources she needed. We found two inpatient treatment centers, one with a thirty-day program and one with a twenty-one-day, both of which would take her for free, but she begged to stay home with us. So we found other resources. A sliding-scale therapist in Sandy Springs agreed to meet with her twice a week. A low-cost addiction treatment center with daily outpatient visits and group therapy. And the day after we arrived in Atlanta, Sam drove her to her first Narcotics Anonymous meeting.

One of us was always with Brenna unless she specifically asked to be alone. She took to spending a lot of time outside with Daddy in the garden. He'd point out what he wanted done—weeding or trimming or various other tasks—and they'd work side by side, neither talking much. When she was out there with him in the garden, Brenna sometimes even looked content.

A week after we arrived, I drove back to Alabama to meet with my parole officer. The whole drive back to Alabama I had a pit in my stomach. They didn't have to let me move to Atlanta. They didn't have to let me take the job there. In fact, they didn't have to let me leave Alabama at all, ever. I still had several years left on my sentence, and my life was entirely under the control of Joyce Friendly and—if she gave the go-ahead—a judge who would make the final decision.

Everything was so fragile. I had both of my children at home, and Erin back in my life, and it could all be swept away in a moment.

The drive to Anniston that day was cold and grey, with stop-and-go traffic much of the way until I was well outside of the Atlanta area. As I drove, I did my best to marshal my arguments. I had a letter from Jeremiah, which indicated the company wanted to transfer me to the Atlanta area, and Stan Wilcox was sending another describing the circumstances of Brenna's disappearance and her rescue. Maybe Brenna's new therapist could write one before I went to court, but she'd only met with her once.

When I finally got there—and waited nearly an hour in the lobby—Officer Friendly ushered me to her cube, sat down and said, "Tell me what happened."

So I told the story. She didn't comment as I narrated what had happened, except to gasp when I described the shooting of Laura Felker.

When I finally reached the end of the story—including the fact that we were in Atlanta and I had a job starting the next week—she sat for a long time, thinking. The silence made my stomach twist. Nervously, I took out the letter from Jeremiah and handed it to her. "This is from my boss—it's about the job transfer. I know that asking to move out of state is unusual, but the kids—they need it. You're also going to get a letter from Stan Wilcox with the FBI—"

She waved a hand to interrupt me. "I got the letter from Agent Wilcox already. Cole, you don't have to convince me. It's plain that you'd be best off with your probation transfer being approved. I'm just thinking through the best approach for Judge Riley—it's not me you have to convince."

I exhaled. "Okay. Okay. Sorry—I—" I closed my eyes and took a breath. Calm *down*. This wasn't me, getting this wound up with anxiety.

But I finally had my family back. And I was terrified of losing them again. I opened my eyes. "Sorry. I can't even begin to tell you how important this is. How fragile things are, and I'm just trying to get my family back in one piece again."

She leaned forward. "You're doing just fine, Cole. Here's what we're going to do. I'll approve a travel pass for you to Georgia for six weeks. You go do your job, then come back and see me then. We'll get you set up for a court date, and I'll recommend that you be transferred to Georgia's Department of Corrections. And we'll move forward. Call me in two weeks, and I'll let you know what I've found out. Okay?"

I nodded. "Okay. Okay. Thank you."

I drove from her office to the tiny little house we'd rented in Oxford. Erin had given me a list of things to bring back to Atlanta, and so had Sam (*Dad, I need my computer*). In a couple of weeks we would come back out and pack everything to actually move. Most of what we owned—which wasn't a lot—would go into storage for the time being.

Finished, I headed back home. Barring any unforeseen problems, I would be home in time for dinner.

winter flower
Brenna

"What's this one?" I asked, pointing to a section of richly colored red blooms that seemed to grow vertically.

"Snapdragon," Grandpa said. "That's a good one. If you take good care of it, and cut it back a little in the heat of the summer, it'll bloom year-round. Doesn't like the heat, but around here it'll flower all the way through winter if we don't get too bad a frost. And winter flowers are beautiful."

I touched one of the delicate blossoms. Not so delicate, if it could survive and bloom through winter. Rubbing the blossom between my thumb and index finger, it felt like silk. I breathed in the smell of the flowers, a complex floral smell that reminded me vaguely of childhood. It seemed strange to me, foreign, to sit in a garden and look at flowers and smell them and care for them.

I told Laura about the gardening the other day. She laughed but then told me she thought it was great. She got accepted to a program in New York for girls like us—girls who were trying to leave the life. She said they're tough, but it's good. She said she might come visit, but I don't think she will.

Grandpa went on. "By spring there will be a bunch of dead stuff to cut back—flowers and stems. Lot of people think they're dead, and take them out, but all you gotta do is cut it back. They're hardy. One of my favorite flowers."

I wiped sweat off my forehead. I was in a T-shirt and jeans, sweating like a pig. Grandpa wore a sweater.

"You okay, sweet pea?"

"I'm all right," I said. "I think I might have a case of the shakes coming on."

He nodded. "It'll get better soon. The physical stuff. When I came home after my second tour in 'Nam, they had me on morphine for a long time. Terrible stuff. But after about four weeks, the physical craving died down."

I sat back, legs splayed out on the ground, leaning on my hands behind me. I hadn't known that. I'd vaguely been aware Grandpa was in Vietnam, but wounded? I swallowed, then said, "You were addicted? How long before you stopped craving it in your head?"

"Well, that's different," he said. "I don't know that I was an *addict*, but I sure as shit went through withdrawals. It was tough. And—well, that's been forty years ago, and I *still* occasionally feel it. Like a nagging sort of itch in the back of my mind. Might be different for you. It's been longer, and different circumstances."

That was true. I lit a cigarette. I could feel and hear my pulse in my ears. "Everybody looks at me like I'm broken. Like I'm one of these flowers, and if you just breathe near me I might fall apart. The thing is ... Grandpa ... there were times when I could have called. When I-I could have gotten to a phone. But by then, I believed his lies."

He nodded and stripped off his gloves. "You'll grow back. Just like these flowers. You'll have to trim some dead stuff—especially the lies that son of a bitch told you. But you'll grow back. And I'll be right here with your mom and dad and Sam."

He didn't mention Grandma. That's because *she* thought I was a whore. And deep down in my heart, where I was like one of these crushed flowers that lay curled on the ground, cut off from the main branch, I believed it too. But I knew those were lies. Lies he told me. Lies I told myself.

I didn't have to live those lies anymore.

Forty-Two

~~~~~~

Erin

The day after Cole got back from Alabama and the meeting with his parole officer, I started looking for work. We had talked a lot about it during the drive back from Oregon. Waffle House had insurance, but it didn't cover mental health, and we *needed* mental health coverage. And with a felony conviction, Cole was lucky to have the job he had—he wouldn't be going back into the corporate world, not for a long time—if ever.

For the first time in a long time, I'd stopped resenting him for that. I understood what had driven him to hurt Chase the way he had—I'd always understood that. More importantly, during that long, slow drive back from Oregon, we'd gotten to know each other again. For the first time in years—hell, for the first time *ever*—Cole actually talked with me about how he was feeling. We spent long periods of time on that drive in silence. But we also talked—about his job, about our fears, even about a possible future.

Sometimes, during the drive home, I would ride in back, holding Brenna or sometimes Sam. Brenna slept much of the time, when she wasn't puking. One the second day, Cole stopped the van at an overlook somewhere in the mountains. The sky was clear and we could see for miles, the land laid out below us in sweeping hills of green and blue. The air was cold, just enough to hurt when I inhaled, and I thought we were only going to stop for a few minutes.

But Brenna got out and looked around. "I can't remember the last time I saw something so beautiful," she said. And then she started to cry.

We all cried a lot in those days. And that was another change for Cole. Before Oregon, I couldn't remember ever seeing him weep. But something had broken the dam. Something.

It wasn't *something*, it was *Sam*.

408

When faced with the realization that he was at risk of losing her too, everything had broken through. Now sometimes it seemed like he couldn't stop crying. At the mention of Brenna's return, or Sam's struggle, or how badly he wanted us back together, his eyes would water and he'd get an embarrassed look on his face as he wiped tears away.

"You don't have to hide that," I said.

"I couldn't if I tried."

Cole went back to work a few days after we arrived in Atlanta. At first they set him up as a relief manager—working a few days in one restaurant, then a few at a different one. He worked a lot of different hours and through weekends, but somehow it was different. In the meantime, I began poring through the job websites and circulating my resume.

I'd been through this in Alabama, of course. Day after day of filling out job applications, and even two interviews. But looking back now, it was hard to get my mind around how serious a depression I'd been stuck in. Cole too. All of us. I'd barely been functional, and it wasn't surprising at all that I hadn't been able to find a job. But now? Now I was determined. And in a city the size of Atlanta, there were a lot more opportunities.

I started with signing up with several different temp agencies. I went through two weeks of interviews followed by mostly electronic based tests—typing speed and Word and Excel and other office products. It had been a while since I'd used any of them, but they came back quickly.

At the same time, for the first time since years before Brenna's disappearance, I began to reach out to my own network. I graduated from Georgetown, after all, and had friends all over the country in different industries. I dug through my alumni directory and looked people up online.

Every time I picked up the phone I felt a pit of anxiety. Would my old friends and acquaintances blow me off? Was I wasting my time? I listened for tones of contempt or pity; after all, most of my acquaintances from college had moved forward with careers instead of taking a decade and a half off for child rearing.

I used to be defensive about that. And resentful. But after Brenna disappeared, I was grateful for every second I'd had with her. So what if I was starting from scratch now? I had my daughter home. Nothing else mattered anymore, except putting my family back together.

Cole was gone from five until four, but usually I would have lunch with Jim, Brenna, and Sam in the kitchen. Jim would crack jokes and tell dirty stories about the Marine Corps, a regular running patter of words that helped smooth out the gaps and silence.

Because that silence existed. The silence was not knowing how to ask Brenna all the questions I needed to ask. How had she survived? What kind of trauma had she endured? How could I help her when I didn't even understand really what she'd been through? Some days she seemed fine—playing games with Sam, laughing and joking. Other days she would retreat to a remote place I couldn't touch. She would sit on the back porch, smoking cigarette after cigarette, staring into space. Those days I was terrified for her. And I knew I made her nervous, hovering and asking her ten times a day how she was doing, but I couldn't seem to stop myself.

One afternoon in late October I was looking for Brenna and found her on the porch smoking again, sitting in a rocking chair. Jim sat in the other rocker. They were quiet.

"What do you guys want for dinner tonight?" I asked.

"Whatever," Brenna said. She shrugged and looked away.

"You okay, baby?"

She barely grunted a response, and then that was followed by a coughing fit.

I sighed. "Brenna, I know you don't want to think about it, but maybe it's time to think about quitting smoking—"

"*Just leave me alone!*" Her shout was unexpected and loud. "I don't want to quit smoking, and I wish you'd just stop nagging me about it!"

I didn't physically stagger back, but it felt like it. It was unjust. I hadn't said anything to her about the smoking in weeks. But she was obviously feeling something. She stood up and stamped out her cigarette.

"There. Are you *happy?*" She stomped off, slamming the door behind her.

I sighed, eyes falling on Jim, who hadn't moved during the exchange. He gave me a sympathetic look and said, "She'll be all right. Just having a rough day."

"Withdrawals?" I asked. I sank into the rocker Brenna had just vacated.

"She had nightmares last night and couldn't go back to sleep."

"Oh, I didn't realize. Did she tell you—?" I trailed off.

"I don't sleep so well these days, Erin, so I heard her crying out. No way you could have known."

"Did she say what it was about?"

He closed his eyes. "Yes. She talks to me sometimes. But you don't really want to know."

"Of course I want to know. She's my daughter."

He leaned close and touched my hand. "Listen, Erin. She went through some stuff that I can barely comprehend, and I've seen people chewed up by artillery in war. You *don't want to know*. And more important, *she* doesn't want

410

you to know. She already feels like you think she's broken forever, like you are ashamed of her."

"Of course I'm not ashamed of her!"

"It isn't about you. For Christ's sake, did you know she found a cop and asked for help at one point? And was raped by him! She was locked in a closet for days. She was tortured. She may *never* heal from that. You *don't have a right* to demand that she tell you *anything.*"

I sagged back into my seat, involuntary tears running down my face. What kind of secrets did she have? My poor girl. "She told you that? I just want to help," I whispered.

"Yeah, she told me. A little. The biggest thing you can do to help her right now is just give her the space she needs. Love her. Be there for her. But don't demand anything. She's going to therapy and her meetings and right now that's going to have to be enough."

I looked out at the garden that Jim had so meticulously cultivated over the years, with Brenna increasingly helping him. "I don't know how to help her."

"You help her every day by letting her know that she's loved. By letting her know that ... that she's going to be okay. That she's not dirty, that it didn't change the way you love her. Deep inside she feels like she's ... like she's ruined. She doesn't feel like it happened to her, she feels like it ... like it soiled her. And that may never get better."

I looked over at him. Cole's father was in his late sixties now, and after five years of retirement he looked happier than I'd ever seen him. At peace. I found it perplexing that the man who had so confounded me when we met twenty years ago had somehow become the pillar of our healing family.

"You know, I don't understand you. When we met I thought you were—please don't be upset—well, I thought you were kind of a small-minded bigot. But you've been the first to reach out and be open to Sam and ... I just don't get it. What changed? Or was I just wrong?"

He shook his head. "You weren't wrong. You weren't wrong at all. I *was* a bigot. But look—I spent most of my life driven by rage. My daddy died early from a heart attack. My brother-in-law murdered my sister. In some ways you were instrumental in some change in perspective for me. I liked that you challenged me. But the biggest difference happened not too long after you and I met. I got a call that one of my old sergeants was dying. Lymphoma. Might have been Agent Orange. Might have been something else entirely. Who knows? But he was a good man, and he lost his leg beneath the knee saving my life. So I had to go, you know? I spent a week in Mississippi, in this piss-poor town in the middle of nowhere. He'd stopped doing chemo and radiation because it was too late, there was nothing to be done. But, the thing was, I'd known plenty of black men in the Corps. Good ones and bad ones. But I'd only known them in the military. I didn't know their families or their lives. And here—I got to know him. I got to know his family and the things they'd been through. Sergeant Groves—he told me about when his father got home from World War II. Nothing those Mississippi white boys hated more than seeing a black man in a uniform. They grabbed his daddy off the train the day he came home from war, and beat him, and took his uniform. And here Sergeant Groves came home from Vietnam in 1969, missing part of one leg, and the first word someone says to him as he's getting off the bus is *nigger*."

Jim paused, then said, "I promised him I'd never use that word again."

I felt my forehead wrinkle between my eyes as he told the story. He was getting worked up, his face red, by the time he talked about Groves coming home from Vietnam.

"I ended up staying out there three weeks. Virginia was fit to be tied, I'll tell you what. But I'd come to realize that—I'd been lied to, and I'd done my own share of lying. So I decided it was time to branch out, learn some more. Jeremiah pointed me to some books to read—"

"Wait, what?" The idea of James calling up Jeremiah seemed preposterous.

"Well, I told him. That I wanted to know more. He asked me to read some people. James Baldwin and Malcolm X and some others. Let me tell you, there's a real eye-opener. Now, with Sam—when Cole told me about this transgender business—I just knew y'all needed help, the kids needed help, and I told him to come and told him Virginia would keep her mouth shut about it, which isn't a promise I've been able to keep, unfortunately. But I got online and did some reading. Because I thought it was all—I don't know what I thought. Crossdressers and perverts or something. I didn't know. I just didn't know. I didn't *want* to know. But—ahhh, crap..."

He wiped his eyes, which had gone red with tears. "Sam's world is going to be so hard. And the only thing we can do is try to protect him. Her. As much as she'll let us."

I shook my head in wonder. "What about Virginia?"

He shrugged. "I had to threaten her. I know it's not how you're supposed to do things in a marriage. But I couldn't get her to listen no other way. She kept saying ... well, you don't want to know the actual words she used, they were terrible—wailing and crying—and I finally told her that if she used that kind of language around the girls I'd pack her up and move her out. Because otherwise, she'll push and push and twist and turn and I won't have it. I won't have her digging her claws into Sam and Brenna."

We sat silently for a long time, watching a lone robin as it poked in the recently disturbed soil, searching for worms. It was brilliantly colored, its red breast contrasting with nearly black back and wings. It chirped, and Jim's face jerked a little.

He swallowed, then said in a faraway voice, "You know, when Sam was little and you sent the girls to visit—one time he was out back here playing with some of Virginia's old dolls. She, I mean. I think she found the dolls in the attic. She was—she was having a tea party, just all by herself out here. And I come out, and she said, 'Grandpa, come have tea with me and the girls?'"

He blinked his eyes quickly as he told the story, not looking at me, or at anything but the past. He cleared his throat and continued.

"Anyway, she said … she said, 'Will you come have tea with us?' And I told Sam … I said, 'Boys don't have tea parties. Boys don't play with dolls.'"

The old man's chin shook as he spoke the next words. "Sam said to me, 'I'm not a boy.' And she looked at me and meant it. So I … I took the dolls away. I told her to go play ball, and leave them for her sister. And I could see it, Erin. I could see it hurt her, that it damaged her spirit. I don't know if I'll ever be able to forgive myself for that. It didn't really surprise me, when Cole called and told me."

He shook his head and swallowed. "I wish I knew how to tell her … how sorry I am."

I took his hand. "You already did, Jim."

The next morning I dropped Brenna off at a Narcotics Anonymous meeting in Sandy Springs—some days she went to as many as two or three meetings a day. Watching my daughter walk away from me always gave me a twinge of fear. But as she approached the door, she saw a woman she recognized from her meetings. They embraced, and Brenna's face lit up with a smile. I started the car but didn't move for a few agonizing seconds. Brenna lit up a cigarette and the two women sat on a bench at the entrance to the building. The other woman began to tell a story, her hands waving around, her smile infectious, and I knew Brenna was in good hands.

Unexpectedly, I felt my eyes water. I put the car in gear and headed out.

That afternoon I finally locked down a full-time job.

Cole

The cards were stacked between us in sets—we were playing gin—but neither Erin nor I were paying close attention to the game. We'd made a point since getting back from Atlanta to do two things without fail. At least one night a week, we sat down, just the two of us, and played a game. And another night, we went out on a date, regardless of whether we had the money.

We'd barely touched the cash that Jeremiah and Ayanna had given us since our return, considering that to be emergency funds. That meant spending less than my meager paycheck of twelve bucks an hour.

But things were looking up. Erin was flushed as she talked about the new position. "I know it's not a lot of money," she said, "but the health benefits are great."

"The money's not bad either," I said. "More than I'm making." Her salary as deputy communications director at the art museum would pay forty thousand dollars.

"Well, once you get your own restaurant again, you'll be making more."

"We'll be able to afford to get an apartment somewhere," I said.

She tilted her head. "I wonder..." she trailed off.

I raised an eyebrow. When she didn't continue, I said, "What is it?"

She smiled. "I wonder if we should stay here for a while longer. If it's okay with your parents, of course. But Brenna's spending so much time with Jim, I feel like it's really good for her."

I nodded. "It's true. She hardly talks with us, but when I got home from work this afternoon and I looked out back, the two of them were talking away. Brenna was going a mile a minute. I couldn't tell what about, but ... I wouldn't want her to lose that."

"What do you think they talk about?" she asked.

I shrugged. "God only knows. I know he's been encouraging her to wait before getting a job. She's talked about it a little, but Daddy told her to wait a year, and just go to her meetings and focus on her recovery."

"And she listens to him," Erin said.

"Wonders never cease." I smiled slightly as I said the words.

She set her cards down—I'd lost track of whose turn it was—and reached across the table. I took her hand in mine. Then I said, "I'm proud of you, you know. And excited for you, with this job. You'll be great at it."

She squeezed my hand. "I love you, Cole."

The words sent a warm wave through me. For I don't know how many years, we'd stopped saying it. We'd stopped believing it. I looked in her eyes. "I love you too."

Sam

In January, I started school again.

I'd missed an entire semester, but with a couple of extra classes in summer school I'd likely be able to graduate on time. The bigger issue was what it would be like dealing with the other kids. I was presenting as a girl now, and I refused to go back.

Dad, in his typically awkward way, asked me if I wanted to consider other options. Georgia had a virtual high school where you could take all of your classes online. Private school wasn't an option, but there were others. I could get a GED and go straight into college maybe next fall. With the level of AP classes I'd taken freshman and sophomore year, it was likely I'd pass.

But I didn't want that. I wanted to go back to school.

It seemed crazy. I *hated* school. Or more accurately, I hated being harassed. I hated dealing with bullies. I hated dealing with hiding myself. But I wasn't hiding anymore. I had a best friend now. I wanted to try. So Mom and Dad helped set it up, and I started school in January.

I won't lie and say it was easy and that everyone accepted me. But it wasn't terrible either. I actually made some friends. And ... I bought tickets to prom. Hayley had to get special permission from Children's Services in Alabama, but she got permission to come to Atlanta that weekend and come to prom with me. She's my best friend ... and maybe a little more.

Brenna has been talking about maybe going to community college in the fall. In the meantime, she's been in a lot of therapy and addiction treatment. She's nothing like I remember. She's scared all the time and sometimes angry. But every once in a while she smiles, and in that smile, I see the sister I lost, and I know that slowly, ever so slowly, I seem to be getting her back.

It won't happen in a hurry. It can't. She'll be broken some ways her entire life. We all will. I don't know how she'll ever trust again, except that in small increments, she does it every day.

She goes outside and sits in the sunshine with Grandpa, and she goes to her meetings, and every day she adjusts a little more to being back in our lives.

On my birthday, Grandpa gave me a hundred-dollar bill. Brenna and I went to the mall, and then we went and got a very early dinner at a nice restaurant. Even though I'd been presenting as a girl for months, I still felt a small shiver of a thrill inside when the waiter asked, "What can I get you ladies?"

"I don't have much to give you for your birthday since I don't have a job yet," Brenna said. "But I did make you something small."

winter flower

She handed me a tiny box, wrapped in bright gold gift wrap. I thought I recognized it, maybe from Christmas? Maybe Grandpa helped her wrap it.

I tore open the paper, because why screw around when it's your seventeenth birthday?

Inside was an old jewelry box. I opened it and stared. It was a bracelet, made of small smooth stones, mostly grey, but some tiny white and pink polished quartz crystals.

"You don't have much to give me?" I squeaked. "How much did this *cost?*"

She blushed. "It didn't cost anything except some digging and work. I found all the stones and polished them, and Grandpa helped me drill the holes."

Unexpectedly, I felt tears run down my face. She must have spent weeks working on this. "You did this for me?" I whispered.

She didn't answer.

After a long few seconds I said, "All I ever wanted was to get you back, you know. I missed you like crazy. I was so scared without you."

She smiled, a sad smile, but a real one. She took the bracelet and fastened it around my wrist. "You did okay though. Not just okay. You ... grew up. You blossomed. When I left, you were a terrified little mouse, and when you found me you'd become a beautiful woman. I'm so ... I'm so proud of you."

It was too much emotion to handle. I wiped my face and she wiped hers and we ordered our dinner. We laughed and joked. After dinner we went for a walk, mostly just people-watching in the mall. It was crowded, and there were all kinds of people around us.

It was all terribly boring and normal. And I was with my sister.

###

Author's Note

The Roberts family's story was fiction, but the experiences of Brenna and Sam were not unique.

Transgender youth in America are far more likely than their peers to end up homeless, drug addicted, sex trafficked and to be victims of homicide and suicide. This is significantly aggravated by the fact that they are often rejected by the people they need the most—their families, churches and friends. It was only until late in the Obama administration that any federal protections existed for transgender people against discrimination in housing, health care and other services. Those new protections have been almost entirely rolled back by the Trump administration in the last two years.

In other words, if you are transgender, you can be denied access to bathrooms. You can be fired from your job. You can be denied housing, kicked out the military or be ejected from a homeless shelter, all based on who you are.

Brenna's experience as described in this novel is also not all that unusual. Traffickers and pimps often prey on kids who are troubled, already abused, isolated or otherwise don't have strong support systems. They manipulate and abuse young women and children, and too often law enforcement treats the victims as criminals themselves, locking them up or worse.

The scale of the problem is staggering. Estimates vary wildly depending on which organization and what research you look at, but it's clear that anywhere from 35,000 to hundreds of thousands of children and teens are trafficked in the United States every year.

To learn more, including how you can help, here are three organizations which provide services, information and advocacy in these areas.

My Life, My Choice
https://fightingexploitation.org

Based in Boston, Massachusetts, My Life, My Choice provides community, stability and hope to exploited children. The average age their clients entered the sex trade is 14 years old. They provide survivor empowerment, prevention, training and advocacy.

The Polaris Project
https://polarisproject.org

Polaris works with a wide variety of organizations to help stop human trafficking.

The Transgender Youth Equality Foundation
http://www.transyouthequality.org

Transgender Youth Equality Foundation provides education, advocacy and support for transgender children, youth and their families.

www.ingramcontent.com/pod-product-compliance
Lightning Source LLC
Chambersburg PA
CBHW072255020726
47501CB00002B/274